S. Falconer

Dying On Principle

Dying On Principle

Judith Cutler

For Jonathan

First published in Great Britain in 1996 by
Judy Piatkus (Publishers) Ltd of
5 Windmill Street, London W1

A catalogue record for this book is available from the British Library

ISBN 0-7499-0362-7

Set in 11/12pt Times by
Action Typesetting Ltd, Gloucester
Printed and bound in Great Britain by
Biddles Ltd, Guildford & King's Lynn

Acknowledgements

I would like to thank the following: David Williams and Nic Landmark for their invaluable help with the electronics; Dr Peter Acland for telling me the effects of the electronics; Geoff Snelling for information about George Muntz; Paul Mackney of NATFHE for help and advice; Edwina Van Boolen and David Stephenson for their constant encouragement; West Midlands Police for their time and expertise; the Further Education Funding Council's Reports of Enquiries into the Governance and Management of St Philip's Roman Catholic Sixth Form College (Sir John Caines) and the Governance and Management of Derby College, Wilmorton (Michael Shattock).

1

If you're going to steal a car, it really would be more sensible to pick one that hasn't been carefully protected by its owner. Not that the kid inside the Montego estate could have guessed that it belonged to a double-bass player who played with electronics in his spare time.

It was Sunday evening, and we were drinking in the Duke of Clarence after a Midshires Symphony Orchestra concert. The Duke is one of Birmingham's smallest pubs, and, despite the ornate jukebox that sits near my usual table, Luigi, the landlord, has a violent allergy to canned music. And a flexible attitude to drinking hours. This suits the musicians – who can't start drinking until after their concerts finish at ten – down to the ground. I sing with the choir they work with, so the place suits me too. A number of choir members had come in that night after a not very exciting performance of a not very exciting work – Elgar's *The Music Makers* – including a quiet black woman whose name I didn't know. She was fairly new to the ranks, and since no one else seemed to be making any effort to talk to her, I resolved to have a word when I'd pushed my way over to the bar.

I caught Luigi's eye. But then he looked over my head and smiled in the way he reserves for his most special clients. I glanced back and saw the other drinkers were making way for someone like courtiers for a queen. As well they might. This was Aberlene van der Poele, all five foot eleven of her. Tonight the way she had sculpted her hair made her look like a black Nefertiti. And they didn't make space simply because she was the MSO's leader, but because they liked and respected her – even the heavy brass, some of whose ideas were antediluvian in their sexism.

I flapped a hand. 'What'll you have, Aberlene? Some of Luigi's Lambrusco?'

And then this appalling electronic screaming cut across the babble.

Simon peeled himself from the silent jukebox. Upright, he was probably six foot three and had the broad shoulders you'd associate with a fast bowler.

'They're playing my tune,' he said, pushing his way out.

We all poured out after him, peering into the ill-lit street.

There was Simon's Montego, its headlights flashing SOS in Morse code. An electronic message pulsed across the screen: 'Stolen car. Stolen car.'

From somewhere came another dreadful scream. And then there was a moment's merciful silence. Only a moment's. Into the silence spoke an electronic voice: 'This car has been stolen. Please call the police. This car has been stolen. Please call the police.'

The car was shaking. At least this was as a result of human activity. A youth inside was desperately trying to open the door.

If he succeeded, he'd fall straight into the arms of Simon and a couple of other bass players. From the approaching baying, it sounded as if Luigi was bringing Jasper to join in the fun. If I'd been the kid, I'd have wanted to lock myself in.

At this point the law arrived in the form of two young men in a Panda. Simultaneously the car returned to normality. The lights stopped. The noise stopped. And the door released the kid into the officers' arms.

'All very coincidental,' I muttered.

Simon patted a rectangular shape in his pocket, grinned, and turned to the two men.

And then the kid broke free.

Simon and I were the ones who caught him first. Simon brought him down in a rugby tackle. The only way I could think of helping – being five foot one is not ideal in these circumstances – was to sit on him. Something wet on my neck told me that Jasper was keen to assist, and when the boy struggled and swore, Jasper offered up some truly Baskervillian howls. His rear end was probably going nineteen to the dozen.

And at this point I was dragged to my feet and hurled against a car.

'You'll be on an assault charge if you're not careful, young lady!'

Winded, I nonetheless scrabbled for my dignity. And when I saw Simon in an armlock, I found it. 'Officer, please deal with the boy and leave Mr Webster alone. If there are any problems with his behaviour or mine, they can be dealt with later.'

There was a little ripple of applause from our audience of musicians.

The two PCs scowled. But they found a scapegoat: Jasper was discovered to be a dangerous dog, and Luigi warned to control him or else. I thought Luigi would have an apoplexy on the spot.

'I reckon we all need a drink, Luigi,' I said quietly

Luigi nodded. 'Come on, Jasper – beer!'

Encouraged by a sharp spatter of May rain, we trailed back into the bar. If Simon could deal with the attempted theft in a low-key way, it would be better. And he knew where to find support if he couldn't.

For a few minutes the conversation predictably circled round the theme of car-thefts-I-have-known, and what ought to be done to the young offenders responsible. Most people were liberal when it came to theft in general, attributing it to everything the *Guardian* would approve, but rather less so when it came to their particular incident. Indeed, the mildest of the viola players was audibly lamenting the passing of a far-flung empire to which miscreants could be shipped, at least those who had removed his cherished Volvo from his garage. As it happened, it was the car he'd been trying to sell to me, so I saw it as an act of a God with a more sporty taste in cars.

I bought a bottle of Lambrusco, sparkling with grapes from Luigi's family's vineyard, and waved to Aberlene. She joined me, and poured.

'Who are you looking for, Sophie?' she asked.

'There's this new kid in the choir,' I said, 'a black girl, and I thought—'

'Stop, Sophie. Stop before you say any more. You thought because she is black and I am black we might have something in common. Well, we might, but not because of that.'

I blushed. I couldn't embarrass us both further by saying that Aberlene is such a remarkable woman I tend to see her as a role model to all women, not just black ones. She is, after all, the leader of one of the best of the provincial orchestras – we in Birmingham are quite sure it is in fact the best – and has been approached by a couple of agents to take up a career as a soloist.

'No matter.' She touched my hand lightly and smiled. 'There are worse things to worry about.'

'Such as?' I asked.

'There's talk of Rollinson resigning,' she said abruptly.

Peter Rollinson is the Midshires Symphony Orchestra's principal conductor and its hero. He's young, he's exciting, he's loyal to the orchestra, and he's been tipped by those in the know to be knighted in the next New Year's Honours List.

'You're joking!' I said.

'They've cut the funding,' she said. 'But perhaps – it's still confidential, really.'

I poured her another glass. 'Silent as the grave, you know me,' I prompted.

'It'll hit the headlines soon enough anyway, I suppose. But all this mess about saving all the London orchestras means they've cut the money to the provincial ones like us. Means reducing the number of players – ending the doubling-up of woodwind, and so on. Means we wouldn't be able to take on extras for pieces demanding more than the standard number of players and instruments.'

'You mean, no *Rite of Spring*, just endless eighteeenth- and nineteenth-century repertoire?' And the orchestra had a name for being innovative and ambitious. I sucked my teeth sympathetically and topped up her glass.

'He says he'll resign rather than let standards drop,' she said. 'And that's not all. They say they'll have to freeze the instrument fund.'

'Instrument fund?' This was a new one to me.

'Good instruments make a better sound. Many of the kids coming through music school now have huge loans around their necks and though they need professional standard instruments they can't afford them. So the orchestra buys them for them—'

'To keep?'

'Not quite. But as long as they're members of the orchestra.' She rapped her glass down but gestured away my offer of a refill. 'Still, enough of our troubles. How are you?'

I poured the wine into my glass and watched the bubbles fizz up. 'I've started a new college, on secondment. George Muntz, just down the road from me. And,' I added, 'I think, for once, I may have fallen on my feet.'

And then it was Monday, and college.

If you live near your work, you can do all sorts of extravagant things like reading the paper with your breakfast, and pegging out a line of washing. You can stroll out at eight forty and still arrive well before the official starting time of nine.

I stood at my front gate relishing the scene. The trees lining Balden Road were green enough to send poets into a flurry of synonym hunting, and the grass verges needed the attention of municipal mowers. One or two prouder householders, those who'd planted daffodils round public trees, had trimmed the grass outside their houses twice already. In the bright morning sun, everything looked good.

'Morning, Sophie.'

I turned. Aggie, my next-door neighbour, had already been to the shops and was returning with her *Mirror*. An early walk was her recipe for keeping fit. She was well into her seventies; her family had been in her house ever since it had been built, and she and her husband had simply stayed on when her parents died. Now she too was a widow, but with an active and attentive family of children and grandchildren.

'Hope you haven't left your washing out,' she said. 'Too bright too early, if you ask me.'

Like her, I scanned the sky. She was right, of course. Clouds were already bubbling up to the west. If I admitted to having a line of towels, she'd send me back to get them in. She might even do it herself – she kept my spare key. But I was always concerned at the amount she did for me without letting me be helpful back. I kept mum. I'd just have to hope that whatever got wet would eventually get dry. I set off down Balden Road.

Muntz College was a low-rise building originally intended

as a teacher-training college. But now teacher training is done by universities – and who'd want to train as a teacher these days anyway? The building, considerably more couth than your average educational cheapo, had been acquired by the local education authority. Of course, I missed my William Murdock colleagues, and to be honest I missed the students as well. The William Murdock authorities had not been entirely sorry to see the back of me, however. I'd been involved in a couple of unsavoury incidents which had brought unwelcome publicity to the college, and though he was the first to admit that my activities had been praiseworthy rather than otherwise, the marketing manager winced visibly whenever he saw me.

Muntz College is next to what is now called the Martineau Centre. This is a wonderful meeting place for teachers, with excellent facilities, including a swimming bath. Needless to say, it wasn't built with the intention of making teachers' lives easier. It was what used to be called an approved school, then a community school. In other words, it housed persistent young offenders in the days when short, sharp shocks were fashionable. But another penal policy had made the school redundant, and since the previous teachers' centre had been on a particularly prime site near the city centre, it was natural that teachers would find themselves relocated out in Harborne.

There was obviously a conference on there this morning: the car park was full of cars with alien parking stickers from many of Birmingham's main colleges – Cadbury, Josiah Mason, Matthew Boulton. I would spend occasional moments wondering how Birmingham would have named its establishments had it not had so many worthy sons and adoptive sons. Pity history hadn't found more daughters to commemorate.

My path then took me into George Muntz's car park, agreeably laid out with flower beds between the parking lots. Horace, despite the arthritis which had stiffened him into a permanent question mark, was polishing the bevelled glass of the heavy front doors. He'd obviously just finished the brass finger plates, but spared me the embarrassment of having to dab my hands on them by opening the door with a flourish. He held the handle with his polishing cloth. George Muntz would look good if it killed him.

The foyer was somewhat spoiled by the regulation dust-catching carpets, but beyond them was polished parquet and the receptionist's desk. Peggy was just watering her greenery arrangement, which responded to her sensitive snipping and feeding by growing in carefully graduated heights. She smiled at me. Hector, the security guard, dusted a speck from his immaculate blazer and also smiled at me.

It was at this point the day started to sour.

Peggy abandoned her little brass watering can and burrowed under her desk. 'Sophie,' she said, 'I know I can rely on you. Would you care to buy a raffle ticket for Oxfam? Thanks! Just put your name and address on the counterfoils. And you, Hector: don't think you can get away from me this week.'

Hector fished in his blazer for his wallet. 'Where will the money go, Peggy?'

'Wherever it's needed, I should think.' She tore off my tickets and handed them over.

''Cause I'd like mine to go to Africa. My cousin, he lives in Sierra Leone. The groin of Africa, he calls it. Sorry, Peggy,' he interrupted himself, presumably out of respect for her forty-year-old's feminine sensibilities. 'The poorest country in the world,' he amended, flourishing a fiver.

'I can't guarantee it'll go there,' said Peggy, eyeing the money with innocent avarice.

'Well, so long as it don't go to buy no arms,' he said, writing his name on the counterfoils and tearing off his tickets. 'What about you, sir?' he added, straightening as a handsome man in his thirties appeared, blue-eyed, blond and extremely sleek. 'Will you buy some tickets to help those starving kids?'

'Mr Curtis, the bursar,' whispered Peggy to me.

Mr Curtis slipped his car keys into his pocket and turned ostentatiously away.

'Raffle ticket to help Oxfam, Mr Curtis?' pursued Peggy. 'Only fifty pee.'

'No,' he said, and was gone.

He left behind a faint smell of leather and Calvin Klein. And a bad taste in three mouths.

'To think that guy earn forty grand a year,' Hector muttered. He stalked off to insist some students show their IDs.

'He may get that much but it doesn't mean he earns it,' said Peggy. 'Jumped-up office boy.'

'Really?' I asked.

'You'd think to hold down his job you'd have to have proper qualifications,' she said. 'Everyone else does, after all. No qualifications, no jobs, that's what I've always dinned into my boys. Oh, I think he got an ONC or something. But nothing special. And then there's this strange rumour about him running over squirrels - Good morning, Mr Blake,' she said, smiling at the principal.

'Good morning, Peggy - and Sophie,' he said.

I was impressed: he'd only met me at the most perfunctory of interviews when the project was set up.

'There goes a proper gentleman,' Peggy said, as he passed into his office. Indeed, he looked it - rosy-cheeked, silver-haired, everyone's favourite uncle. But she did not ask him to buy a ticket.

2

I knew I was doing all the right things, but the computer wouldn't believe me. Or, more accurately, the printer wouldn't. The printer wouldn't do anything. It wouldn't even go on line so I could talk to it properly.

On the grounds that when computers go wrong it's usually not their fault but that of the person using them, I went through my routine again. Yes, everything was connected properly. There was no reason for it not to be, since everything had been working on Friday when I left for the weekend. Yes, there was enough paper in the feed, and yes, the computer was set up for this particular printer. And no, nothing happened when I told the computer to print.

Since I needed to print the set of material for a meeting in half an hour, I did the obvious thing: saved it on to a floppy and toddled off in search of someone else's equipment.

I was still a new girl on the premises: this project had started only a couple of weeks before Easter, and had been interrupted by the two-week break. Since this was only the second week back – and we'd lost Monday for May Day – I didn't feel I knew anyone well enough to go and invade their private offices without permission.

I slipped down from my room on the second floor to the common room on the ground. If there was anyone there, I could ask them for help or, at least, advice. It was empty, but I was tempted to linger: the daily papers were spread invitingly over the coffee tables in the middle, and someone had left open one of the French windows, letting in the sunlight and the sound of the fountain splashing in the small courtyard.

The pond and fountain were no grander than many of my neighbours', but imparted a sense of civilisation quite refreshing after the penury of William Murdock College.

But I had work to do. I would try what ought to have been the obvious place: the computer centre. This occupied a whole new wing. One floor was given over to purpose-built rooms where a whole class could be taught at once. There were also a couple of electronics workshops, a big drop-in centre where students would work on individual projects, and a smaller room at present unoccupied but also full of computer equipment.

Although the pressing need was to print out the stuff on my disk, it would also be sensible to report the fault on my set-up, so I looked round for a technician. There was none to be seen. Scratching at their office door, I pushed it open, half expecting to find a little coven working out their pools over morning coffee, early though it still was; but it was deserted. I scribbled a note asking for help, and then, because I had only fifteen minutes, let myself into the empy room and sat down at the nearest computer.

I had got no further than loading my disk and waiting for the file to be formatted for the new default printer when the door was flung open and a woman's voice yelled at me: 'What in hell d'you think you're doing?'

Fighting down the temptation to ask her what the hell it looked as if I were doing, I got up, smiling politely.

'I'm Sophie Rivers,' I said. 'Part of the team working on computer-based teaching materials. My machine's gone down, and I needed to print this urgently.'

She seemed too angry to speak. She was probably about my age – mid-thirties – but her skin was quite deeply lined, especially around the eyes, as if she'd spent years glaring meanly through a haze of cigarette smoke. Her fingers were certainly stained. Her suit – women wore suits at Muntz, unless they were Sophie Rivers and allergic to them – was this season's, and her shoes looked Italian. But it was her hair that interested me most. Some women – French ones, for instance – adopt a style so short and angular that the chicness is overridden by the fact that it's viciously unflattering. She sported this sort of cut, no doubt quite fiendishly expensive in its asymmetry.

So why was this fashion plate working at George Muntz College and why was she white with anger?

I dabbed a finger on the keyboard – no point in hanging around doing nothing, after all – and my document oozed slowly from a laser printer. I picked up the neat pile of papers, extracted my disk, switched everything off, and then lifted an enquiring eyebrow.

She didn't quite throw me from the room.

As she ostentatiously closed the door behind us, she called out: 'Melina? Melina!'

I prepared to walk away – I had no more business there, and I wasn't prepared for a public rebuke – but then I hesitated. The person who approached, shoulders hunched, eyes placatingly down, was the black woman from the choir.

I caught Suit Woman's eye; I didn't want her to take out her bad temper on someone much more vulnerable than I.

She pinched her lips, acknowledging me reluctantly.

'Melina, this—'

'Sophie Rivers,' I supplied, smiling at Melina.

'Ms Rivers complains that her computer has failed.'

'Printer,' I said. 'I can't get it to go on line.'

'Printer. Fix it. Or get her a new one out of the stockroom.'

'Yes, Ms—'

'Dr.'

'Dr Trevelyan. Shall I do it now or later, Dr Trevelyan?'

'Not now,' I said. 'I'm due in a meeting. I'd rather it were later. Eleven thirty. See you then, Melina.'

I turned and strode off before Dr Trevelyan could point out that Melina did not need my presence to repair or replace my printer.

In fact, I spent the start of the meeting wondering why I'd made such a point of it, and my concentration was so poor I found myself landed with writing up the minutes, a job I'd been intending to avoid.

Melina thought there was probably dirt in one of the switches; it would only take five minutes to repair if it was, but in the meantime she'd leave me with another printer.

She stood clutching the printer flat against her chest, with her back to the door, almost as if awaiting my permission to withdraw. Or was she looking for some excuse to stay?

'How did you think the concert went on Sunday?' I asked, pushing a chair at her.

She sat on the extreme edge. 'OK,' she said. And then she smiled. 'If you like *The Music Makers*, that is. And if you like Blount as a conductor.'

I grinned.

'I mean, it's not very good Elgar, is it?' she continued. 'Not really his best? Oh, dear, I mean—' You could see her confidence ebb and flow.

I shook my head to encourage her. 'Lousy Elgar.'

'And that Claude Blount. *Sir* Claude Blount. Why is he a Sir and Peter Rollinson not?'

'I fancy it's a hereditary title, not one he earned.'

I thought for a minute she was going to relax into a proper natter, but she suddenly looked at her watch and sprang to her feet in one rather graceless movement.

'She'll be expecting me back. Dr Trevelyan.'

I got up too. 'Why don't we have some lunch together?' I added, to give her a chance to be kind to me, 'I'm such a new girl, you see – it's so nice to talk to someone I know. I'm free at one.'

'The technicians have their own canteen,' she said.

'Well, we could nip out to the Court Oak.'

'I don't drink. Thank you, Ms Rivers. I'll report back to you later.'

Why should she be so keen to avoid me? Was it me, or didn't she like people? Just then I didn't have time to worry. I had a class to go to, and teaching T. S. Eliot to A-level students requires all my concentration.

And I didn't have time for any lunch, either. As I came out of class it started to rain, and I literally ran home to rescue my washing. I was just in time to see Aggie locking my front door on her way out. Rather than embarrass her by thanking her, I simply turned on my heel and ran back. What I might do, perhaps, was get too many bedding plants and, by claiming I hadn't room for them, persuade her to do me another favour by accepting them.

Meanwhile, I had another class to teach.

After an exhausting session with GCSE students and the

apostrophe s during which I wondered if even a computer would have patience enough to deal with the little cypher, I staggered back to my office for a drink.

Although there was a perfectly good staff canteen, I was so overwhelmed by the luxury of having a room to myself - even one only about eight feet by eight - after the mêlée in which I had passed my time at William Murdock College, that occasionally I would dive in just to savour it. It struck me that the recent prohibition on making tea or coffee there was unnecessary, but I could easily circumvent it by drinking packet fruit juice, which was probably healthier anyway. I could even look out of the window without being assailed by vertigo, whereas my William Murdock office was on the fifteenth floor.

There was a quiet tap at the door: Melina, clutching a printer.

'Until I can repair yours,' she said, immediately busying herself with cables and plugs.

'Don't worry: I'll sort that out,' I said. 'Fancy an orange juice?' I broke another from the polythene wrapper and tossed it to her.

She caught it, put it down awkwardly, then picked it up and pulled off the straw. 'Thanks.' But she finished the connections before she drank.

To my surprise, I didn't have to choose the next topic of conversation. Perhaps she thought asking me questions would be the best way of fending off mine.

'How long are you going to be working here, Ms Rivers?'

'Sophie.'

'We're supposed to call you academic staff by your name and title.'

'Titles like Dr and names like Trevelyan?'

'She's quite new here too.'

I couldn't quite work that one out. 'How long have you worked here, then?'

'Couple of months, that's all. Dr Trevelyan started at Christmas. But—' She stopped.

I waited. Nothing.

'I should have come in January,' I said at last. 'But there was a big administrative cock-up—' Melina winced. 'Administrative hitch,' I corrected myself, 'so we had to wait till now. And we go back to our own places as soon as we've finished. Not that I for one am in any hurry. I live just up the road, and this place is luxury compared with what I'm used to at William Murdock.'

She stared at me and seemed about to speak when the phone rang: Dr Trevelyan, wanting to know if Melina had finished.

'Just doing a test print now,' I said, grateful that ink jets are so silent as to be undetectable over the phone.

Melina, however, asked the computer for a test print-out. It obliged.

'What did you do before you came here?' I asked, accompanying her to the door.

'Same thing. A small firm in the Jewellery Quarter. We serviced computers for big firms.'

'Who?' I asked, interested that she should have chosen to take a job in education.

'Lots,' she said. And was gone.

3

Synchronicity or coincidence? My evening with Aberlene seemed to pivot round the question, thought I don't recall either of us proposing to debate it.

It started with my chopping fresh coriander to add to a curry for supper. It's my favourite herb. It's not just the taste, the smell, though those are exquisite in themselves. It's because it always brings back my friend George. And the pleasure of being with George, loving him as a dear friend, rather than the agony of his death last year.

The edge had gone off my pain by now. Some of it went when the van he'd left me was destroyed in a fire. But his bassoon still sat on the wardrobe in my spare room.

Apart from singing, I can only play the piano, so the bassoon was never used. It might even be bad for it: some instruments suffer if they're allowed to lie fallow. But then, I could never sell it – how could I make money out of George's death? I couldn't give away anything he'd given to me, either.

With the coriander juice still green and pungent on my hands, I phoned Aberlene.

Which is where the synchronicity came in: Aberlene greeted me with a laugh and told me she'd been in the process of looking up my number. She had something she wanted to discuss, she said, and had been going to invite me out for a quiet drink. But when I established that she had not yet eaten, I invited her round to share my curry; she could bring a bottle if she liked. She liked, and would be round about eight.

This gave me time to tidy my kitchen, and I laid the table in there, rather than attempt to clear my papers off the dining table. We left her wine – a New Zealand Chardonnay – to chill. Neither of us felt it would enjoy the company of my Malaysian chicken curry, creamy with coconut and sharp with coriander. But it helped the cheese and the conversation, chiefly orchestral gossip. I sensed, however, that Aberlene was holding something back, but to ensure an easier time later I decided not to press her.

We took the rest of the bottle into my living room. For a while she prowled, commenting on a watercolour I'd just bought. And then she settled on the sofa, folding her long legs under her, and I took an armchair.

When it came to it, neither of us was particularly keen to broach our propositions. In the end, laughing like teenagers, we flipped a coin.

'All right,' I began, losing graciously, 'I want to say something which may sound – I don't know, quixotic if you like.' I told her about George's bassoon. 'What I want to do is lend it to someone – like that lad who joined in the spring – so it gets played. It doesn't even have to be anyone in the MSO, really. I'm sure you've got contacts all over. So long as it's played and cared for – in both senses, I suppose.'

Aberlene touched my hand gently and poured some more wine. 'But George wanted *you* to benefit from his death if anyone did.'

I shrugged.

'And you've never even bought yourself a car to replace his camper van. I've heard all your excuses – cars in cities, public transport, vandalism at your college, the risk of it being stolen, too little, too big, too fast, too slow. I've heard them all, Sophie. Come on, don't you owe it to George to – to oblige him?'

I spread my hands.

'Tell you what,' she continued, 'I'll mention your offer to someone I know on one condition – that you find some way of letting George enrich your life. It was what he wanted. And I tell you, Sophie, he really did worry that you didn't have safer transport than that bike of yours.'

'But I don't need even a bike at the moment.' I actually felt uneasy having more than enough money to buy a car. George had believed in giving away what you didn't need, and I hadn't even got round to giving the interest on the van's insurance payout to Oxfam as he'd have wanted.

'But you'll be back at William Murdock – when? September? Promise me that you'll have done something about getting a car by then. Or,' she smiled sweetly, 'no deal on the bassoon. And don't say you'll bloody well sell it to spite me because I know you and you couldn't.'

She was right, of course, so I didn't say anything.

'Now,' she said, looking embarrassed. She shifted her legs to the floor and straightened her back, looking magisterial. 'What I needed to talk to you about. And I want you to remember that it is not a response to what you've just been saying. I was about to phone you, remember, quite independently.'

I nodded.

'It's not gratitude, though in a way I suppose it is. But not for that. I'm sorry – I'm making a real hash of this, and don't tell me I'm not.' She paused, took a swig, and settled her hands on her lap as if trying to relax. 'As you know, the orchestra has its own friendly society. We all pay in so much a month, and can call on it for help with health problems – you know, when we need physio before the Health Service can get round to it.'

I nodded.

'After the Maxwell affair,' she continued, 'the role of a trustee is even more important. And with the pressures on everyone's money at the moment we want to make sure our society's money is well managed. These days the orchestra can't afford to make *ex gratia* emergency payments as it might once have done. That's why – now Thomas Kelly and Henry Gibson have retired – that's why the players want to nominate you as an independent trustee. You've been a loyal friend to the orchestra—' She overrode my protests. 'A loyal friend to the band as a whole as well as to some of us individually. If you're happy, we'll be writing to you formally.'

When I demurred it was to make the obvious comment: 'I don't know anything about money – accounts, investments, anything.'

'Doesn't matter. All the other trustees know about money. The other new trustee's sharp enough to cut himself. But these guys don't necessarily know how we feel – you know, about ethical investments and so on. The other thing is that now that there are two more women than men in the orchestra, we'd like a woman trustee. At least one. You're the token woman, Sophie,' she cackled.

'Gee, thanks.' But I was touched, really touched. I got up and filled our glasses again to cover it.

'Welcome and good luck. And the first meeting's on Thursday evening, by the way,' she said. And then, in a change of mood that disconcerted me, she lifted her glass to a photo of George on the piano. 'Absent friends.'

'Absent friends!'

At this point one of them phoned.

'Sophie?'

'Chris!'

Aberlene got up at once, ostentatiously touching her watch and tiptoeing to the door.

'Can I call you back in two minutes, Chris? Home or work?'

'Home.'

'Two minutes, then.'

Aberlene was smiling when I put down the phone. 'Your Chris is still around, I gather?'

'He's not my Chris. He's a friend. I'm very fond of him, but he's just a friend.'

'Not the worst of starts for a rclationship,' she said. 'And he's very good-looking. And a nice body.'

I hesitated. I'd never found him at all attractive, not sexually, but I didn't want to argue.

Grinning in apparent defeat, I saw Aberlene to the door, wondering only as I opened it what she was doing for transport. But a car was parking opposite, and I recognised the features of the principal cello, Tobias Friedman. So Aberlene had got herself a handsome bloke, had she? She grinned, touched her lips, and ran off like a joyous child.

It was never easy to phone Chris, not because I didn't like him but because I did. I liked him too much to enjoy the knowledge that he was in love with me.

But we spoke easily enough when I got through. He'd been

engaged first try, so I stacked the dishwasher – an extravagance to celebrate my temporary upgrading for this new job – and made a coffee before returning to the living room. He started by asking about the job, quite detailed questions, in fact. But he didn't follow up any of the things I touched on. Then I asked about his life: he offered me news of his car and garden. But he was clearly holding something back.

'You might as well spit it out, Chris. I can almost hear you purring. Hey, you've got a conviction in that rape case – yes?'

'Hole in one! I was wondering if you might care to have dinner with me one night. To celebrate,' he added, as if he had to justify the invitation. Which in a sense he did. Although we saw each other regularly, I always tried to ensure that it was in ways that didn't demand either the expression or the rejection of great emotion. We'd been up to the Hawthorns several weekends to cheer West Bromwich Albion up the ignominious Second Division, and if he needed a woman for some police do, I'd sometimes go along. I'd bagged him as an honorary member of our college's indoor cricket team. But the inequality in our feelings always lurked, sometimes rising quite painfully.

'Of course!' I said, without, I hoped, any obvious hesitation. 'My treat.'

'Bugger that! Mine. Not every day we nail a bastard like that.'

'I'll buy the booze then – champagne!'

'We'll argue about that tomorrow.'

'We won't argue at all.'

'I'll pick you up. Eightish?'

'Eightish. How smart? And don't tell me I always look nice, or I'll wear my gardening jeans.'

'You do always look nice – but how about smartish? Suit for me, if that helps. Hell! There's another call waiting to come through.'

'How on earth d'you—?'

'Got one of those clever BT thingies. Look, it could be important. See you tomorrow.'

'See you, Chris; take care.'

I went to bed considering the adjective 'smartish'. Not a girlie dress, of course; he knew better than to expect that.

How about silk shirt and trousers? I could drop them into Harris's at eight tomorrow morning and collect them before they closed. I set the alarm and picked up *Pride and Prejudice*.

There are some cyclists who are accidents waiting to happen. They carry too much, often children perched on little plastic seats, or wobble from lane to lane, or fail to use lights when they're needed. I do none of these. I'm psychotically virtuous when it comes to cycling – helmet, fluorescent jacket, lights, everything. And I've battled in and out of town in rush-hour traffic for at least ten years. I've had lots of near misses, true, with apparently blind motorists, but this morning's little dice with death unnerved me more than it should have done.

I'd made it to the High Street by eight fifteen, and, armed with a cheerful promise that everything would be ready by four, had set off back. I chose as usual a back-street route, and had just turned right past the local junior school – yes, I'd stopped for the lollipop lady, I remember that now – when I found myself knocked to the edge of the pavement, landing on a dustbin liner. Fortunately for me, it was full of rubbish and gave when I landed on it. Less fortunate, perhaps, was the fact this it contained fishbones, and I had to whiz home as fast as my wobbly legs would take me to change and shove all my clothes in the machine.

No witnesses, of course. Though there was a dash of red paint on my mirror, when I came to peer at it later.

I arrived in the common room rather later than usual, but still in time to grab a cup of coffee.

'Enjoy it while you can,' said a couple of people whose names I still didn't know.

Polly, the union rep, came over, flourishing a clipboard. 'Here, you're in NATFHE, aren't you, Sophie? Would you like to sign this?' She waved a petition and produced a biro from her pocket.

'Better read it first,' I said.

'Better read this first,' she said, and passed me a sheet of paper.

*

George Muntz College of Further Education

FROM: Mr D. M. Blake, Principal and Chief Executive

TO: All staff

RE: USAGE OF STAFF ROOM

In the current post incorporation economic climate it is incumbent on us all to make sacrifices to ensure the financial viability of the Corporation. It has therefore been agreed that the usage of the staff room will now be limited. Staff will be able to obtain coffee from the machine in the Student Canteen, which will hereafter be known as the Canteen. The staff room will be known as the Conference Room, and will be bookable only through the Chief Executive's Secretary, Mrs I. M. Cavendish. Staff are further reminded that to make liquid refreshments in individual study rooms is a violation of the Corporation's Code of Conduct and will result in disciplinary action under the Corporation's Disciplinary Code, copies of which are available for inspection.

'What's all this about a corporation?' I asked at last, holding the document ostentatiously between my fingertips.

'That's what the colleges are, technically, since April,' said Polly. 'Come on, Sophie, your old place has been incorporated too. Didn't you get a wonderful glossy folder inviting you to sign up for a new contract? We got them on 1 April – honestly! And a load of people signed, too. Fools.'

'I take it you didn't.'

'NATFHE have tried to black it. It's a killer. I can't believe they've not tried it on you people at William Murdock. Tell you what, I'll show you a copy when I have a moment. But just now I'm more interested in this business.' She flourished the petition.

'Can they really act unilaterally? There wasn't any consultation, I gather?'

'Apparently. And look at this.' She pointed to Blake's title. '"Chief Executive", indeed.'

'I gather his secretary doesn't correct his English,' I said.

'Cavendish? She might be into the other sort of correction!' snorted a tall, thin man. Ben, that was it; he was head of engineering.

I signed the petition, of course, and padded off to teach. *The Waste Land*, indeed.

The way Dr Trevelyan eyed me when I met her on the stairs of the Computer Wing I might have been the original Burglar Bill, complete with mask, a hooped shirt and a bag marked SWAG. As it was, I was merely pursuing my lawful avocation and arriving promptly to teach my dead-end class of the week, elementary word processing. Why they should have landed me with that I wasn't quite sure – to stop me missing Meat Three and Beauty Two, perhaps. Certainly there are few less enjoyable things in the world than facing a group of thick middle-class sixteen-year-old girls. Never mind, if anyone was going to be reduced to tears, a fate which according to rumour regularly befell the visiting teacher I replaced, it was not going to be me. I knew that and, better still, the students knew that. Today we sorted out how to employ the spell-checker and thesaurus, not an easy task when the girls concerned couldn't even work out which of the alternative spellings to choose.

When I returned to civilisation an hour later, it was to find workmen fitting a new touchbutton lock to the room I'd used illicitly yesterday. Melina was Blu-Tacking large notices forbidding unauthorised access. And a couple of WPCs who worked at Chris's station were bowing themselves away from Dr Trevelyan. I fell into step with them.

'Anything interesting?' I asked.

'Hi, Sophie. You heard we got a conviction in the Bridges case?'

'Yes, last night. I'm getting Chris drunk tonight,' I said.

'You know what drink does,' said the second woman – Helen, I think.

'Quite,' I said.

'Poor bugger! When are you two going to—'

'We're friends,' I said firmly. 'You can buy a friend a drink. Any road up,' I pursued, turning Black Country to emphasise the change of subject, 'to what does George Muntz owe the pleasure of your company?'

'Couple of computers nicked, that's all. Fourth or fifth time this year. Happens all the time in places like this.' Helen's radio crackled. 'Better be off,' she said.

'And next time we see you, make sure you've let poor Chris get his leg over!' yelled – was it Sharon? Karen? – as they left.

It was a very surly bunch of men and women who forgathered in what was now officially the canteen for their lunch and machine-made coffee or tea. It was not, however, as surly as the group of students whose regular tables we'd appropriated. The young man who had the doubtful pleasure of being student liaison officer managed to stop one or two youths jostling us, but we were jeered and catcalled as we left. Many students waved brightly coloured pamphlets at us as we went: one made a dart out of his, which I retrieved. The George Muntz Students Charter. No apostrophe – perhaps it was Blake's handiwork. The contents certainly made it clear that the students were entitled to their rights, with the clear implication that if anything went wrong it was the fault of the idle and unintelligent staff. Outside the canteen were blackboards announcing 'Emergancy S U Meating's'. Perhaps the booklet was not to be laid at Blake's door.

I spent the afternoon at the word processor, attacking the minutes I'd been volunteered into. The printer behaved immaculately. Melina must have brought it back. Very efficient of her, of course, and I should have been grateful, but now I came to think of it I'd rather she'd waited till I was in the room. Perhaps it was the morning's attack of management possessiveness, not to mention the students' tantrum, that made me want to guard my territory, no matter how temporary my ownership.

I toyed with the idea of phoning up Dr Trevelyan and moaning. Or dashing off a stiff memo, since these were apparently in vogue. But on the whole I thought I'd speak to Melina herself, and hope for an apologetic explanation.

Suddenly I'd had enough of Muntz for the day. It was nearly five and I had to get into Harborne for the evening's outfit.

Despite the heavy traffic, my journey was entirely incident-free. Until I got into Safeway, that is. They have a convenient trolley shelter with cycle provision, too. All I needed from Safeway itself was some bread, which of course I could have got in a corner shop. But it always seems a bity iffy to take advantage of a store's generosity to my bike without paying backhandedly. With only a few minutes before the cleaner's closed, I sprinted in and ran straight into Melina as I hurtled past the biscuits.

'Thanks for bringing my printer back,' I said.

'That's OK,' she said. She looked around, almost furtively. 'Sophie, I need – can I talk to you?'

''Course,' I said. 'Pop up to my room tomorrow. I can always say I've got another computer fault.'

'I really meant now.'

I glanced at my watch. 'I'm sorry. I really have to dash. Tomorrow, OK?'

'But—'

'See you – any time tomorrow morning,' I said over my shoulder.

I made it to the cleaner's with one minute to spare.

4

Chris collected me by taxi: he obviously intended to accomplish some serious drinking. He was not the sort of policeman to enforce the law while not bothering to uphold it.

When he tried to get out and escort me, I waved him back again. A spring shower was hurling rain almost horizontally, and there was no point in two of us spending the evening in soggy trousers.

The driver chose the Harborne High Street route into town, which meant passing George Muntz again. Perhaps living so close to the shop wasn't such a good idea after all. As we turned along Court Oak Road, the driver pulled over sharply. An ambulance was coming the other way, lights flashing, making a great deal of noise.

Putting the engine into gear, the driver sighed heavily. 'In the midst of life there is death,' he observed.

Nothing we could say to that, really.

Chris had booked us into the Mondiale for dinner. He probably thought he was choosing a sophisticated city-centre hotel with a fine restaurant which collected crossed forks, rosettes and stars as other places collect closure notices from the Environmental Health Inspectorate. I, however, knew it less for its fine cuisine than for a couple of profound personal humiliations I hoped Chris knew absolutely nothing about. Certainly I wasn't going to spoil his enjoyment of this evening by any allusions to the past, and I hoped he'd not destroy mine by any allusions to future use of the hotel's bedrooms.

While we strolled through the white marble foyer, past the elegant little fountain and into the white and gold restaurant, I inspected him. He looked very spruce in a lightweight suit which I'd not seen before, and he nodded his approval of my silk outfit. I'd managed to wash my hair, which always gets rid of the irritations of the day. If I were to mention them later, I'd regale Chris with the funnier side. He didn't deserve any more stress than his job already inflicted on him. His face was more deeply drawn than his age merited - he was thirty-nine now - and he'd acquired a slight, scholarly stoop. When he put his half-moon glasses on to read the menu, he looked like an academic suddenly come into an inheritance. His fingers fidgeted a thread from the tablecloth.

He caught me looking at him, and grinned. 'Worry cotton - I left my beads at home. And you may think I'm crazy, and for goodness' sake don't tell anyone, and I mean anyone, but I'm going to try Alexander Technique lessons. Well,' he continued, as if he needed to justify himself, 'my back gives notice from time to time, and I've started to get indigestion. So I thought, why not give it a try?'

'You'll end up even taller!'

'Yes, I was reading about this guy who started off all hunched and ended up over six foot. You might try it yourself - grow a little bit. Can't be much fun being as little as you.' His eyes disappeared in crow's feet.

'They don't make diamonds the size of pieces of coal,' I said tartly.

'Logs of wood,' he corrected me.

'Pieces of coal in the Black Country!' I was ready to bristle. Then I softened: 'OK. Maybe I'll try it. Give me a report.'

What my offhand comment concealed was a huge desire to sing and dance on the table. When I met him, Chris epitomised conventionality, and I suspected that one of the reasons he found himself attracted to me was what he perceived as my anarchic streak. It was good to see someone as rigid as he unbending, and if I helped in the change, I saw no reason to be ashamed.

Another change I positively claimed to have wrought in Chris was his attitude to food. He used to refer to me derisively as a foodie, but could now tell a sugar-snap from a mange tout with his eyes closed. Accordingly he now gave the menu his full attention, and left me to do the same.

Hors d'oeuvres for both of us, and by chance we both chose guinea fowl. Although the waiter passed him the wine list, we shared the decision and the responsibility: was red too strong for the guinea fowl? No? Valdepenas, then. And champagne, of course, while we waited.

'Right,' I said, settling my arms on the table, 'tell me how it feels to have nailed that bastard Bridges.'

'Good,' he said simply. 'A very sick man, that. Jesus – no, I'm not going to give you all the details, Sophie. But I hope he'll be somewhere nice and secure for a good long time, and yes, I wish they *could* actually cure him. You're making me too bloody liberal,' he added grinning.

'Will this help with your promotion?' Since the Sheehy Report had threatened the future of chief-inspector rank, Chris had been anxious.

He spread his hands. 'The trouble is, that means leaving Rose Road – all the team there. And taking on whatever I'm offered.'

'Better than being abolished?'

He nodded. 'Demoted, at least. Oh, there are some jobs I wouldn't mind doing as an inspector – though how they'd feel about me still getting chief inspector's pay, I don't know! But some ...' He tailed off, as if embarrassed he was giving too much away.

On the other hand, I wanted to probe further: all too often Chris clammed up if I asked him about his work, and particularly his feelings about it. I decided to risk it, maybe for his sake as much as mine. 'What's your worst-case scenario? Back in uniform?'

'Not necessarily. Working with your team all the time – being on the same shift with your mates each time – you can get very close. You can get a great sense of camaraderie. But I'll tell you what – my God, I feel sick at the thought of it, Sophie – the worst case is being the inspector in charge of the lock-up at Steelhouse Lane. All those no-bail prisoners. Druggies, drunks, people who should be in mental hospitals but who are now the lucky recipients of care in the community. The smell. Never seeing the light of day. Awful! I was there for a month when I started. Nearly left the force altogether. Worse than being a troglodyte. And it ought to be done by trained prison officers, come to think of it: waste of police manpower. Whoops! What, not biting?' He replaced his grim expression with a charming smile: he'd said enough about himself.

'"Manpower", you mean? No point. Not when Muntz College talks about "manpower planning", "manning the reception desk" and so on, with far less excuse. I'm surprised they didn't have a man room, not a staff room. Not that we've got one of those either, now.'

I couldn't quite read his expression, but there was an alertness that suggested he was more than casually interested in something I'd said. Or maybe it was just the arrival of the first course.

The Mondiale had done everything it could to make an evening there enjoyable. The table linen was good quality and the right shade of dusky pink to go with the steely blue of the carpet. The cutlery lay well in the hand. The china picked up the silver and gold of the walls and ceiling.

Or maybe the whole lot was kitsch and I'd had too much champagne to notice. The hors d'oeuvres were carefully chosen and beautifully prepared, I'd go on oath about that. Then I did something that surprised me: I found myself telling the worldly Chris about my plans for George's bassoon.

To my surprise, he agreed, and thought it not quixotic but wise. With one proviso: the same one as Aberlene's, that I spend the proceeds of the insurance claim on a car for myself.

'Tell you what,' he said, leaning back to allow the waiter to remove his plate, 'I'm free on Saturday. You decide how much you want to pay and what insurance group you can afford, perhaps read the odd *Which?*, and then I'll take you on a tour round the most promising dealerships. You could phone them first to book some test drives. I'll be your chauffeur and poke my head under any second-hand bonnets you're attracted to.'

'Well . . .'

'Why not?'

'I don't need—'

'What's behind this self-denying ordinance of yours? No holidays abroad, a house that's nice, sure, but less than you could afford. OK, it's only recently you could afford to let yourself go, but sure as God made little apples, you haven't.'

'But it's not like that.'

'Tell me, where did you spend your last summer holidays? The Gambia? New York? That's what George's money should have let you do. And where did you go? Sandwell. Well, good for you. Holiday at home to help the British economy. Saint Sophie.'

'Hang on! This is supposed to be a pleasant evening with a friend.'

'OK. Sorry. I overshot. And I'll tell you this, it was a bloody good job you were there. Now, I'll shut up. Provided you think about what I've said and promise to drive something wild on Saturday. No,' he said to the wine waiter hovering to pour a test glass. 'Let my friend try it, she's got a better palate than mine.'

I knew better than to do a Jilly Goolden spoof; and it was fortunate I didn't. The wine was far too cold – it might almost have been chilled to disguise its age and general nastiness. I shook my head. 'I don't think so, but you try it,' I said, passing him my glass.

I laughed at his face.

Grovelling with apology, the sommelier scuttled away.

To lighten the moment, I told him about the death of our staff room.

'Can the management do that? I thought you lecturers were a stroppy lot.'

'Thank you. I'll take that as a compliment.'

'Thought you would. But surely you've got conditions of service? And in any case, health and safety regulations must apply to colleges like everywhere else.'

'We've got something called a Silver Book,' I said. 'That lays down virtually everything about our contracts. I'd better read it.'

'You mean you haven't!'

'Birmingham's always had conditions much better than the Silver Book ones. But of course, we don't work for Birmingham any more. Since April we work for individual colleges, which call themselves, if George Muntz is anything to go by, corporations. Complete with chief executives and things. Tell you what, there's talk of a new contract.'

'Can I bully you just once more this evening, Sophie?' He sat forward urgently and took my hands. 'Promise me you'll read it cover to cover before you sign it. And ask an expert if you're in any doubt.'

The arrival of the sommelier with a bottle of far more expensive wine – a vintage Rioja, no less – allowed me to move my hands without ostentation.

The tasting ritual revealed a superb wine that we were to have for the price of the Valdepenas. It went very well indeed with the guinea fowl.

Arguing about the bill always gives me indigestion, so I flipped the waiter my credit card while Chris was in the loo getting rid of some of the booze. Fortunately enough remained for him to forget completely until his taxi was driving him away down Balden Road. It put me in a sufficiently good mood to blow him a kiss. Maybe I'd live to regret it.

5

The next morning I felt bad, of course, about Melina. I should have explained about the cleaner's, and then gone back to her. Or suggested I phone her – anything except that brusque dismissal. I wasn't the most obvious confidante, I hardly knew her, but perhaps she had no one else. Certainly her manner had suggested it wasn't my broken printer she wanted to discuss.

I intended to do no more than collect my machine coffee from *the* canteen – and a union handbill inviting all staff to an eat-in in the former staff room at lunchtime – and log on to my e-mail before phoning her. As it was, I found another little gem in my pigeonhole.

> **George Muntz College of Further Education**
> FROM: Mr W. J. Curtis, Deputy Chief Executive
> TO: All staff
> RE: MISUSAGE OF STAFF FACILITIES
> It has come to my notice that some staff persist in making liquid refreshments in their individual rooms. Personnel are reminded that this is an unwarranted misuse of the Corporations electrical power supplies and must cease forthwith. Failure to comply will result in immediate action under the Corporations Disciplinary Code, copies of which are available from the Deputy's Chief Executives Personnel Assistant, Miss S. Blake.

Perhaps I should offer senior staff some English lessons. If it was management training, it should pay well. I screwed it up and slung it into the bin. It landed with a satisfying clunk, the result of hours of practice under my father's gaze. He'd been a cricket pro, and his main regret was that I'd turned out to be a girl. Nonetheless, he'd seen no reason why a girl shouldn't be able to throw, and targeting bins had long been one of my party tricks.

On further reflection I retrieved it to stick it to the office wall with a blob of Blu-Tack. 'Deputy Chief Executive', eh? At William Murdock we had advertisements and interviews for such promotions. And was it simply a curious coincidence that the name Blake appeared twice in key college positions?

It struck me that phoning Melina would give the wrong impression. I ought to seek her out. But what if she came up to see me, despite my snub? I left a Post-It note on my office door promising her and anyone else who might be interested I'd be back in ten minutes. Then I went off to the computer wing, to see if she was there.

The technicians' restroom was in a wonderful state of uproar, which barely subsided enough for me to ask if Melina was in yet.

'Not yet,' said Phil, the chief technician, drawing me to one side so we could hear each other speak. 'But she doesn't have to be. You know we all have to work an evening and have a morning or afternoon off instead?'

I nodded: the teaching staff worked the same system.

'Well, it's her morning off. D'you want to leave a message on her e-mail?'

I shook my head. 'I'm better with paper ones.'

He passed me a sheet and a pencil, and then, after giving the matter some thought, an envelope.

'You've heard the news, have you?' he asked, as I wrote. 'About Trevelyan?'

'News?'

'It's what's set this lot off,' he said, sitting astride a chair and gesturing me to another. 'No point in standing if you can sit. My veins, you know,' he added, confidentially, 'going varicose. Got to watch them. Yours OK?' He peered at my legs dispassionately.

'Fine. What's this about Dr Trevelyan?'

'I was just telling you. Ill. Now, to look at her you'd think she was as fit as a flea. Eats all the right stuff. Mad on this exercise.'

Yes, those expensive clothes had fitted, now I came to think of it, an expensive body.

'Always reminds me of that woman, the tennis player. Navratiwotsit.'

I nodded.

'Tough as old boots, you'd have thought. But it only goes to show, doesn't it? See how the mighty are fallen.'

'What's she got then?'

'Give me a moment, love. A breakdown, they reckon. Seems she thought she saw something last night and called every last one of the emergency services - ambulance—'

'What sort of something?'

'I was coming to that.' He drew a single strand of hair across an otherwise bald pate. 'A body, they reckon. Falling. A young woman.'

'Who?'

'Keep your wool on: there wasn't a body, see. They reckon she had a hallucination. Overwork. Stress. They've taken her off to the Queen Elizabeth for treatment. Sedation. EEC.'

'ECT!'

'Like I was telling you. Poor lass! Never could stand her, but I had this cousin. Only a young chap. Lost his marbles, like her. These electrodes to his brain. Right as ninepence, now. But it's his memory, see. Can remember before he was ill, and he knows about now. But d'you know what? Can't remember anything about when he was ill. He's lost a whole year - memory loss. Nothing about the carving knife or the dog or anything. Nor being in the bin. All Saints, he was in.'

I muttered appropriately.

'So there's no knowing when she'll be back. If ever.' He rearranged the strand by half an inch.

'If ever?' I must have sounded as stunned as I felt. 'She's as bad as that?'

'I was telling you. She signed up for this new contract they want you teachers to be on. I told her, you want to keep off that. Buying a pig in a poke, I told her. And what happens?' He paused but I dared not interrupt. 'She signs. And things like sick leave, they're not like in the old contract. Eight weeks is all she'll get. Two more unpaid. Then out. I did warn her.'

I hadn't liked the woman but I'm not one to bear a grudge. 'Will there be a collection - for flowers and things?'

'I was saying to the lads, there's no one here'll want to put a penny in the hat for her. Made life miserable for us all, she did. Young Darren, now - she had her knife into him something shocking.'

A stout young man looked up and nodded. 'Bloody right.'

I stood up casually, as if to leave. 'Where shall I leave this note for Melina?'

Darren pointed. 'Best place is her bench in the workroom.'

I smiled helplessly at Phil.

'I'm on my way. Follow me.'

He dismounted his chair, and held the door gravely. As we walked down the corridor, I wondered if I dared risk it. 'Tell me ...'

'And young Melina - don't ask me about Melina.'

'I gathered she and Dr Trevelyan—'

'I was saying, cat and mouse. Nice kid, Melina. Dressed smart. Timekeeping a model to them kids. And work - could she shift that work! But whatever she did, it wasn't right for Her Majesty.'

He unlocked the workroom door but stepped in first to tap in a code to a security system. Then he gestured me in. The room was immaculately clean, already humming with soldering irons and oscilloscopes. Melina's bench area was in the far corner, covered with bits of computer.

I tucked my note under her soldering iron and looked round.

'Good bit of equipment you've got here,' I said. And then the sort of impulse Aberlene and Chris would have applauded washed over me. 'Tell me, if I wanted a little laptop, what sort would you recommend?'

He settled down on Melina's stool; I pulled up another. This could take some time.

We talked memory and capacity and size and possible use for ten minutes. Then he made an offer I couldn't refuse.

'Tell you what, young Sophie, I'll get the names of our suppliers. Might be able to get you a good price if you can decide what you want. Go and have a look at those Toshibas, and see if you can find that Zenith, and then we'll phone up for you. Cash, probably, mind. Come on back to our room and you can jot them down off the screen.'

'Access denied.'

However many times Phil tapped in the password – and he took care not to let me see it – the same message came up on the screen.

He swore under his breath and then turned to me. 'Looks as if there's something wrong with the system, love. Could take a while to sort it, too. Tell you what, I'll give you a bell or leave a note on your e-mail. OK? And in the meantime, you go and test-drive a few – right?'

Polly, the union rep, had had the foresight to book the staff room, now conference room, via the chief executive's secretary, Mrs I. M. Cavendish. No doubt she had booked it in the name of some solemn meeting, and indeed we did pass, both as union members and as staff, a couple of solemn resolutions. The union officers were authorised to meet the management on our behalf, and the secretary of the Staff Association, in which I was quickly enrolled, was to book the room for a variety of evening functions. I had not been in a staff association before – social life at William Murdock was nonexistent, for reasons I never knew – but the thought of quiz evenings for the Acorns Children's Hospice, the geography teacher's anecdotes of his life as a professional footballer and a wine-tasting organised by a woman who lived with a wine importer was reasonably enticing.

Yes, I was looking forward to the rest of my time at George Muntz.

I was just dashing off to class when my phone rang. Expecting either Melina or Phil, I took a moment to place the voice as that of Simon, the bass player. There were some complimentary tickets available for that night's concert – would I like one?

'Lutaslawski and Bartók,' he added.

'Which particular bits of Lutaslawski and Bartók?' I asked cautiously.

'*Concerto for Orchestra*, twice.'

The Bartók is one of my favourites, and the Lutaslawski is no more than a challenge, so I accepted gladly.

'There is a catch, though,' he added. 'We're holding a raffle to raise money for Tim, Howard's son. The lad with the blood problem. Needs to go to the States. And the Friendly Society isn't authorised to pay up, even if it could afford it. The draw will be at the charity concert on 11 June, but we'll be trying to sell tickets at every gig we do until then. What we were wondering was whether some of the trustees might help us sell them, and since I've seen you in action with an Oxfam tin—'

'Half an hour separating people from their money seems a small price to pay for two hours' music. See you by the box office?'

'Can you make it really early? Six thirty?'

'What about my tea?'

'Curry afterwards,' he said.

And so it was agreed.

I was just in time for my class: somehow, under this new regime, I didn't think lateness was a good idea.

It was a two-and-a-half-hour session revising set books someone else had taught – another visiting teacher my arrival had thrown out of a job. The kids resented being deprived of someone they trusted so close to the exam, and didn't want to work on *Hamlet*. It wasn't until I asked them what they would do if someone they loved got bumped off by someone they knew that they came alive. One or two Muslims were inclined to think revenge was a duty, but the rest, to my relief, preferred to trust British justice.

I prayed silently that their faith would never be put to the test.

6

I've always liked Simon's greetings. I love being swirled off my feet and soundly bussed. When he was wearing uniform – the white tie and tails of the orchestral musician – the effect was dramatic, particularly when I wore, as I did tonight, a lightweight pleated skirt which flared *à la* Monroe. And in the glossy setting of Birmingham's Music Centre, it reached perfection. We celebrated with a quick Fred and Ginger routine, which drew a smattering of applause from people queuing for coffee.

My excuse was that there is a performer *manqué* in every teacher. Perhaps Simon didn't need an excuse, lurking, as he did, behind possibly the most sober instrument of the orchestra, the double bass. He was also justifiably proud of his physique, though to the best of my limited knowledge the only sport he participated in was crown green bowls.

'Come on, Simon: to business. These 'ere raffle tickets. Point me to them.'

He did better, throwing me across his shoulder and transporting me fireman's lift to the stall the Friendly Society had set up just outside the auditorium. After that, people knew my face – and perhaps other parts of my anatomy – when I approached them with tickets and a predatory expression disguised by a friendly smile.

Most people responded generously enough, despite the occasional comment, which I could scarcely dispute, that Tim's treatment ought to be available on the NHS. The only person who really drew me up short was a man in late middle age. There was a general sleekness about his clothes and shoes that argued a bank balance above the average for even the Music Centre's affluent clients. But I wouldn't have wanted to carry the bags under his eyes.

'Have you bought your raffle ticket to support Tim Stamford yet?' I beamed; surely a tenner at least from a hand with such a ring, such a diamond.

'When is the draw?' he asked.

'11 June,' I said. 'At the Friendly Society charity concert.'

'June? And this is still May. I'll keep the money till then. I'd rather it did some work than sat in some low-interest bank account.'

I gaped.

He walked away.

'And may all your toenails grow in!' I said to his departing back.

The curry was expensive, the taxi fare home expensive, and Simon in private was not nearly as demonstrative as Simon in public. This was a relationship that would need either thought or work. And I wasn't sure that I wanted to spare either just at the moment.

Thursday morning found me at a loose end. I should have been in a meeting with the rest of the team, but two of them were off sick, so Sarah, an ESOL expert, and I, lamenting men's lack of stamina, adjourned the meeting and went our various ways.

Spring was definitely springing at last, and I felt a sudden reluctance to return to my eight-by-eight cell. Ten minutes by the little fountain would have worked wonders, but the only access was via the principal's study - correction, the chief executive's office - or the staff or conference room, which was currently occupied by people in conference: there was a notice on the door telling the world not to disturb the meeting.

The temptation simply to walk out of the building and work in my garden was almost overwhelming, but even I don't do things like that, so I decided to explore parts of the building I'd not yet had reason to visit; the drama studios, for instance, and the music rooms. Since poor William Murdock had neither, I was impressed by the plurals and by the fact they were housed in the performing arts wing.

This lay, soundproofing notwithstanding, at the furthest edge of the complex, where the building was also at its tallest – five storeys. There were practical classes in the dance studios and in the smaller drama studio, but the main drama studio was empty. The door responded to my push, and I found myself in a small theatre. Not so small either – not much smaller than Brum Studio at the Rep. It seemed very well-equipped too. Resisting a sudden urge to play with the computerised lights and sound effects, I took centre stage and made ready to soliloquise – purely, of course, to test the acoustics. Pity a class started to trickle in.

I pushed my way against the tide of people and set off up to the music area. This part seemed less well funded. The piano was badly out of tune, and the electronic keyboards years out of date. The last notice on the board was for aural exams in 1989.

The shoes I fell over on the way out, however, were almost new. I put them neatly to the side of the stairs, more interested in the fact that the door to the roof was open. I'm not, to be honest, a woman for heights, but since I was exploring I might as well do it properly. I'd celebrated the tenth anniversary of my sojourn at William Murdock with a walk on its roof, and hadn't known whether to be relieved or irritated to find I was too short to see over the parapet. Perhaps because the Muntz building was five storeys high, not fifteen, this parapet was the height you could comfortably lean your elbows on. I oriented myself and headed for the corner nearest my house, its roof strangely small and unfamiliar and – now I looked more closely – missing a ridge tile. To celebrate being in the open on such a promising day and to prove I had my vertigo under control, I decided to complete a circuit. Someone had drawn expansive yellow chalk circles around suspect-looking roof felt, and a bucket of tar steamed ready. I dodged round it, and looked over each of the corners. One had an excellent view of the playing fields – fields in the plural when poor William Murdock hadn't so much as a bit of tarmac for kicking a ball on. The last corner was the one nearest the area occupied by the maintenance staff. I looked down at a little shed with a motor mower half out, the canteen bins and a rubbish skip.

On top of the skip were some tar drums, some broken chairs, and a discarded life-size model from the art room. The thoughts came painfully slowly. How enlightened to use a black model. They had posed it clothed. A black young woman. And I knew, as I ran down the stairs two and three at a time, that it wasn't a model.

I could simply have dialled 999. I supposed I should have told someone in authority and let them do it for me: hierarchies clearly operated at George Muntz. But logic deserted me, and I ran all the way to my own office to make the call. Chris, of course. DCI Chris Groom.

His voice was calm and efficient. 'You're sure it's her?'

'Without going closer and having a look—'

'No, don't do that. No point in upsetting yourself, Sophie. And you might just - you know - disturb something. Have you told anyone?'

'No. And I've an idea I should have. But Chris, I couldn't just invite you over here to look at the view, could I?'

'Hardly. Go and tell someone, and tell them you panicked. If it really is Melina, surely they'll have more important things to do than worry about protocol!' He waited for me to say something. 'Come on, Sophie, you're not usually so shy and retiring.'

'It's being new here, Chris. And - look, shouldn't you be putting your underpants outside your trousers and leaping into action? We can talk about my hang-ups later.'

'OK. But I shall need to talk to you officially, mind, so don't worry if you find yourself getting sent for. Take care.'

There was another word, which he choked off. Poor Chris.

And come to think of it, poor Sophie. Now I had time to look, something radical had happened to my room: the arrival of another chair and several boxes of someone else's papers. And an ashtray, heavily used.

First things first, however: whom ought I to tell? The principal, I suppose, or, failing him the less than charming Mr Curtis. On the whole, since Peggy had described him as a gentleman and he'd been charm personified at the meeting that brought me here, I'd try Mr Blake.

When I reached the foyer it was in chaos: piles of the sort of timber I associate with other people's home extensions, and raucous young men in overalls milling round, much to Peggy's tight-lipped irritation. I smiled wanly at her and headed down the short corridor leading to the principal's study. A desk impeded my progress, occupied, according to the gold-printed wooden block, by Mrs I. M. Cavendish, Secretary to the Chief Executive.

She was speaking into the phone when I arrived and chose to continue without acknowledging me: 'I hear what you are saying, Mrs Jeffreys. Yes. I do hear. But I cannot imagine that—' At this point she rolled her eyes heavenwards; I too was invited to condemn her unheard interlocutor. 'Mrs Jeffreys: you are taking antibiotics. You are teaching only a floor from the ladies' lavatory. Surely it isn't too much for Mr Blake to expect you to fulfil your teaching commitment.'

There was an impassioned murmur from the other end, causing Mrs Cavendish to hold the receiver at an elegant angle from her head.

'Mr Blake will expect to see you in the classroom as usual tomorrow, Mrs Jeffreys. He does not regard cystitis as a cause for hysteria.' She replaced the receiver. Now she no longer saw me as an ally against a mischievous world, her eyes hardened.

'Yes?' she said, uninvitingly.

'I have to see Mr Blake, on a matter of the most extreme urgency.'

She picked languidly at a diary. 'Staff, aren't you? Mr Blake sees staff on Mondays.'

'I have to see Mr Blake now.'

'Monday at eleven. Miss – er—'

'Now.'

'Mr Blake is in a meeting.'

'He would want to be interrupted.' I expected her to get to her feet and head for the conference room, but if anything her smile was more languid.

'A meeting at the Mondiale. The College without Walls Conference. Senior staff.'

'Mr Curtis?'

'All senior staff,' she said firmly. There was a distinct stress on 'senior'.

'All right, if you're holding the fort, I'll tell you. Though I expect you'll want to contact them and tell them the police are here.'

To describe Mrs Cavendish's reaction as extreme would be to indulge in understatement. I thought for a moment she was about to pass out, she went so grey so quickly. But she resumed her bored expression with commendable rapidity, touching her fingertips together in an irritating arch.

'In what connection?'

'With Melina. The computer technician. I don't know her surname. Perhaps you should find it and all her other details. I'm sure the police would be grateful for anything that'll save them time.'

'They would indeed,' came Chris's voice from over my shoulder, 'be very grateful.'

He introduced himself, ID and all, to Mrs Cavendish, and prepared to be charmed. Middle-aged ladies often seemed to find Chris desirable, a fact he was rarely slow to play on.

'And of course,' he was saying, 'if Ms Rivers has discovered something untoward, there need be no suggestion of foul play.'

Somehow he contrived to bow himself out without permitting her to accompany him, and somehow he contrived to bow me out with him.

'Ian,' he said, raising his voice, 'could you get a few details about the college from—'

'Mrs Cavendish,' I supplied. And winked at Ian, who responded with a flicker of a smile. Last time I'd seen Ian he'd been winning a case of amontillado in a wine tasting.

'I'll have to show you what I saw, first,' I said, leading the way to the music and drama block, and up the stairs. 'Because I'm not entirely sure how to get to the place from the ground.'

By this time the door to the roof was locked.

'What's up?'

'I'm sure I didn't lock it. I'm sure I just legged it downstairs to phone you.'

'You're sure?'

'I'm nearly sure.'

He looked at me hard, but then smiled. 'Could be important. But we'll worry about it later. Meanwhile ...' He produced an interesting little bunch of keys and coughed gently. No, I wouldn't tell.

The door opened easily. The roof was still deserted but the patches had been tarred over and the buckets had gone. Presumably the workmen had locked the door when they left. Reluctantly I led Chris to the corner overlooking the skip, and pointed.

'I'm afraid you could be right,' he said quietly. He gave my shoulder the nearest he could manage to a merely friendly hug, but released me far too quickly and spoke into his phone. 'No evidence yet to suggest foul play, of course,' he said, more bracingly.

'Trying to fly, was she?' I asked tartly.

'Might have topped herself. Or just fallen. No need to jump to – sorry – you know, no hasty conclusions. Come on, plenty to do, Sophie. But maybe you ought to take a sickie. Go and get Aggie to fuss you a bit.'

We started back down the stairs.

'No. Not until you've—' I gestured. I didn't want to mention Melina yet. 'I'll hang about here until you've got some idea of what happened to her. I've got a room on the second floor. Third on your left as you come upstairs.'

'All to yourself?' he asked. 'Rather a luxury after that maelstrom you called your office at William Murdock.'

'May not be all to myself any longer. But I'll be there. Until you or Ian comes and gets me. I suppose you'll want a statement in any case. I suppose I must be one of the last people to see her alive. Me and Dr Trevelyan. But I don't think she'll be able to talk at the moment.'

The room was still unoccupied, apart from the boxes and the ashtray, so there was no one to take my mind off my part in Melina's death. Fact: she'd wanted to talk to me. Fact: I'd been in too much of a hurry. Fact: she'd begged me to listen. Fact: I'd refused. Fact: she was dead.

Whether it was by her own hand or by someone else's, maybe I could have prevented her death.

The knowledge pounded round my head like a hamster on a wheel. It changed rhythm soon enough – I could have prevented her death; I should have prevented her death.

If I could have a hot coffee to wrap my hand round, perhaps I could have stopped shivering. But getting a coffee meant risking the canteen, and Chris would be coming for me here. I couldn't cry, I couldn't pace, I couldn't do anything until he or Ian came. Nothing except listen to the voice in my head: 'I should have prevented her death. Could have. Should have.'

There was a sharp tap at the door, and Chris was suddenly beside me. 'Sophie?'

The words came out loud now: 'I could have stopped her.'

His voice was very cold and official: 'Do you have any reason to believe she killed herself?'

I told him, haltingly, about our encounter in Safeway.

'If she killed herself, she made her own decision. People who kill themselves do so, as I understand it, because they think their life has become intolerable. One conversation more or less wouldn't change that underlying belief. And if she didn't kill herself, then someone else did. And if she'd given you information this person didn't want passed on, you'd have been at risk too. Now, what about a coffee?'

I pointed to the memo from Curtis about staff refreshments.

'Jesus, we are into abrasive management styles, aren't we? Well, in that case, Ms Rivers, I'll have to ask you to accompany me to Rose Road Police Station to make your statement, aided and abetted by a cup of my coffee.'

I smiled, if wanly: Chris prided himself on the excellence of his coffee.

I set the button in the middle of the door handle and ushered him out, checking, as I always did, that the door had locked – not that it would keep out the owner of the ashtray of course.

'Snib,' said Chris suddenly, as we joined the staff and students milling up and down the stairs.

'I beg your pardon?'

'That thing in the doorknob. Last conference I went to—'

'Hawaii?' I asked dryly. Chris was given to conferring in exotic places.

'Newcastle. There was a notice in the room telling the occupant to set the snib before he left. Took three DCIs and two supers to work out what the hell it meant.'

He said nothing else until we reached his car, which was surrounded by other police vehicles. A uniformed officer was sitting in the driver's seat. Chris would have to hang on here, wouldn't he? The constable started to get out, however, and spoke in an undertone to Chris.

'Yes, perhaps,' Chris replied. 'No, ask Sergeant Dale to take Ms Rivers to Rose Road, will you? You'll find him entrapped by a terrifying blue-rinse female called Cavendish. Tell him you're the fifth cavalry.'

'OK, Gaffer.'

The young man gave a casual salute and loped off.

Chris waited till he was out of earshot. 'That's another worst-case scenario: being trapped behind a desk. Can't bear leaving things to other people.'

'You never could,' I said, thinking of searches he'd led, of other jobs he might easily have delegated.

'If you finish your statement before I get back, Ian'll take you home. No, listen: I want to talk to you, just in case—'

I took a deep breath. 'Do you think it was, Chris? Suicide?'

He shook his head. 'Until the pathologist's had a look, and we've talked to other people, I really am keeping an open mind. According to young Dr Patel, the surgeon, her initial impression is that the injuries are consistent with a fall from a considerable height. The question is ...' he paused.

I finished his question for him: 'Did she fall or was she pushed?'

7

Flapping a hand in vague greeting at a couple of Rose Road's WPCs I'd met last year, I took my seat in a newly decorated interview room and waited for the promised coffee. Ian took my statement without comment, breaking off only when I started to yawn.

'Stress,' he said tersely. 'Hang on a bit.'

He left me to contemplate the grim state of my nails, but was soon back bearing coffee in Chris's china cups. He fished a couple of Kit-Kats from his pocket. I looked on temptation and succumbed.

He was surprised when I insisted on going back to work after lunch, but accepted my explanation that I had a class with an exam in less than six weeks' time. Chris would have to wait until I'd done my duty.

As it happened, he had to wait a little longer. I was leaving my classroom, without any conviction on my part that I had helped the students at all, when I ran into Phil. I locked the door and fell into step with him. He looked nearer sixty than forty and his hair drooped disconsolately behind one ear.

'Bad business,' I said quietly.

'Yes, we could do with a cuppa,' he said. 'Such a nice kid! One of the best I've come across. In here,' he said, opening the door to the technicians' restroom, 'and bugger this.' He flipped a finger at the Curtis memo, which he too had stuck on the wall. He filled a kettle and shook a packet of decaffeinated teabags at me. 'Better for you, except they say there's something in the paper that makes you senile.

But at least if you're mad, then you don't know anything about it.'

'Unless you're Dr Trevelyan,' I risked.

'Like I was saying, she must actually have seen Melina. It wasn't just a figment, was it? She really did.'

'I hope someone's told her. And the hospital,' I said.

'Not my job. D'you want to give something towards her flowers?' He shook a chinking foolscap envelope at me. 'Don't feel you have to: you didn't know her, not properly. None of us did, come to think of it. Not much in here. Won't get her more than a bunch of daffs, and goodness knows who I'll be able to get to take them to her.'

I fumbled some change out of my purse into the envelope, and initialled the front. No, not much of a collection.

'What about flowers for Melina's family?' I asked.

'Hang on, I was just getting – where's that envelope? But it won't be flowers. In some funny sect, she was. They spend a lot of time talking to God, but not on Sundays. We're to give the money to her church to do good with. Ta.'

'I suppose, when you go round with it, I couldn't come too, could I? She was one of the few people at Muntz who I got to know at all,' I fibbed.

Phil nodded absently. 'Wonder why she did it.'

'Any idea?'

'Well.' He made the tea straight into mugs, and sloshed in milk. 'The police were asking and I said no, of course, because I didn't then. But . . .'

I was desperate to prompt him.

'There's something – look, I don't know about this at all. Bring your tea through here.'

Obediently, though he had drowned it in milk and I was hoping quietly to abandon it, I picked up my mug and followed him to Dr Trevelyan's room.

'It's this "Access denied" thing, see,' he said, unlocking the door, and then locking it behind us. 'Worried me, like I was saying. And now she's off for the duration, I had to find my way into the stuff – well, it's my job, Sophie, I need to use the info. Not just being nosy, you'll understand that.'

I nodded: he'd need to know all about suppliers for simple day-to-day matters like ordering paper and ink cartridges.

'So I thought I'd giver her files a scan, see if there was anywhere she might have left her passwords, see.'

I saw.

He switched on her computer. Her printer gave an engaging little set of pings, quite tuneful. The screen prepared for action.

'I thought, while I was at it, I ought to check her e-mail. Just in case.'

'You knew Dr Trevelyan's password?' I couldn't keep the surprise out of my voice.

'You may well ask! Well, to be honest, I watched her type it in once. Same as my bank PIN, as it happens, so I'd be obliged if you'd turn away. Thanks.'

I looked at the room: bare to the point of anonymity. I've seen hotel rooms that were more welcoming. I thought of the posters I'd already stuck up in my new room, and of the plants I was persuading to grow on the windowsill. Dr Trevelyan had been *in situ* longer than I had, but might never have been there at all. And yet she didn't strike me as the self-effacing type.

The tapping at the keyboard stopped.

'OK. Now look at this.'

I peered over his shoulder. He started to read aloud, not well.

I can't go on like this. You know what I feel, but you don't do anything. May God forgive you.

I can't.

M.

'Best show this to the police,' I said.

'You OK? Didn't mean to upset you like this, love. Here, sit yourself down.'

'I'm all right.'

'My Aunt Fanny you are! And I think you're right. It's a suicide note all right.'

Was it? If it was, it was the last thing I wanted to see. Maybe I could have helped. I should have tried. The hamster wheel started turning again.

'And you know what?' Phil continued. 'I think Dr T did see her doing herself in, and that's why she was so upset. And you're right about little Melina – my reading of this is, she was a lezzie, see. A dyke. I wonder if Dr T is? You're right, Sophie: makes you think, doesn't it?'

Wondering silently why he should choose to impute all these conclusions to me, I passed him the phone.

'No, you get on with it,' he said. 'You know that policeman, after all. Nice-looking lad, I thought. And of course, the police get good pensions. I'll have another dig at this password business.'

And he tapped away again while I rang Chris's number. No Chris, but a voice I didn't recognise promised to pass on the message.

The house was terribly quiet. Normally I find Radio Three or Classic FM as soon as I get in, though I switch over to Radio Four for *PM*. But the radio had been giving notice for some time, and it chose this afternoon to expire.

Wanting a voice to keep me company, I checked the answering machine. A little bonus – two messages. One was from Chris, grave and hesitant, thanking me for the news and telling me I should be resting; the other from a buoyant Aberlene, reminding me of the evening meeting and telling me the address: a road in Selly Oak.

I felt too low to cook a proper meal. In the fridge, there were a couple of tomatoes, a tired lettuce that ought to be eaten, an onion no longer young and some furry cheese. All the ingredients for a miserable sandwich. But it dawned on me, as I sat down and sank my teeth into it, that George would have been furious with me for sitting round lamenting my lot. Something bold, that's what he'd have demanded. I could hear his voice, urging me off my bum and on to the bus. Because I was going to Selly Oak, that's why, and the bus would drop me by a big Comet store where I could get myself not just a simple radio, but one of these all-singing, all-dancing affairs. Damn it, I'd been waiting long enough to get a CD player! OK, I'd have to carry a cumbersome ghetto blaster in a huge cardboard box to the meeting, but I could get a taxi back home. And I dived into my bookcase for the relevant *Which?*

The trouble started at the checkout. There were a couple of whispers, and the kids behind the counter started to eye me.

Then a sleek young man appeared and drew me to one side.

They were bouncing my Barclaycard.

'I've only got about £90 on it,' I expostulated. Dinner for Chris.

'I'm sorry. Is there any other way you'd wish to pay?'

I wanted to storm out, but a dramatic exit wouldn't secure me my radio. Neither, of course, would my cheque-guarantee card – £50 limit. And though there were large signs everywhere promising me interest-free credit, I didn't think they'd regard my application with particular enthusiasm in view of my Barclaycard problem. So, having established that they'd keep the radio for me till I returned on Saturday, I left quietly, keeping my temper under control.

I couldn't vent it at Aberlene's, either: a couple of other people had already arrived and were sitting at the dining table in her back room. Hers was a big Edwardian house, and every time I walked down her hall I wanted to peel up the floor and take it home. But peeling up Minton tiles isn't easy, even if she'd let me. Occasionally she tantalised me further by reminding me that her garage floor was even better – it had once been the kitchen.

I knew the two musicians who sat to my left: Simon and Adrian, a tutti viola and very handsome with it. Simon slipped a sealed envelope across to me – my invitation, formal if belated, to become a trustee. Then came Frank Laker, a middle-aged and nondescript solicitor. He sat almost opposite me. We were three short: two apologies, and the other new trustee was late. We dithered about whether we could start the meeting without him. I buttoned my lip: I wasn't going to express an opinion about anything until I'd seen the others in action. Aberlene, on my right, raised a quizzical eyebrow at my continued silence; this was a Sophie she didn't know. Eventually, after what appeared to be a whispered prompt from Adrian, Simon, as chair, decided we should start.

We were about halfway through the second agenda item when we heard a car door slam, and the front-door chimes started on 'Colonel Bogey'. Why Aberlene hadn't got round to changing it I didn't know; but each time it sounded she would wince apologetically.

The man who took the empty seat opposite mine, the other

new trustee, was none other than the man who'd refused to buy a raffle ticket the previous night. How was it Aberlene had described him? 'Sharp enough to cut himself'? Well, his suit was sharp, all right. That clean sort of sharp which speaks of very little change from £1,000. The shirt was silk, as of course was the tie, and he emitted faint but tantalising odours which showed just how excessive everyone else's aftershave was. This, Aberlene told us, was Richard Fairfax.

We all smiled, and he nodded back, hard-mouthed, as if smiles were irrelevant to a serious meeting. Simon restarted the meeting, and the agenda moved along briskly. Then we started on investments.

My only flirtation with the stock market was a few Abbey National shares. I didn't even know where to look up share prices in the business pages, so I thought I had more to learn than to contribute. But I did remember Aberlene saying that the orchestra wanted ethical investments, and here was Richard Fairfax talking about firms everyone knew had connections with the arms trade. When Simon made a gentle protest, Fairfax looked at him coolly. 'Are we discussing what the orchestra want or what would be best for the orchestra?'

'Even if that goes against the wishes of the orchestra?' I asked.

'As a committee, and in particular as trustees, our task is to make money for the society. We have no other brief.'

Frank, I feared, was about to agree with Fairfax, perhaps out of male solidarity. I caught Simon's eye, willing him to call for a vote before Frank could succumb. The problem was, I had no idea of the constitution. Did committee members' votes count as high as the trustees'? Perhaps a vote wasn't the best manoeuvre after all. I coughed gently. 'I'm sure some compromise must be available. Perhaps Mr Fairfax's expertise would enable him to suggest alternative investments with an equally high yield?'

I must have sounded convincing. Aberlene beamed at me, and Frank sighed with what sounded like relief. Simon seemed about to argue, but Adrian touched his hand lightly and smiled at him. Simon flushed with an embarrassment out of all proportion to any implied rebuke. I looked from one to the other.

'How soon would you want such suggestions?' asked Fairfax.

'Would a week be too soon?' Simon asked tentatively.

Fairfax produced a gold-inlaid fountain pen and a slim diary.

Simon looked hesitantly round the table. 'Should we - if it's convenient - decide on a date for our next meeting? We usually rotate venues, Sophie and ... Richard,' he said, with growing confidence, 'so no one member gets lumbered with us all the time. And we like to ask members who don't live too far out to let us use their homes - getting us all out to Redditch or somewhere is a bit of a pain. Sorry, Adrian: Alvechurch is too far.' He smiled apologeticaly at Adrian. 'But at least we won't disturb your cats.'

Adrian held the smile a moment longer than was socially necessary. No one else seemed to notice. I didn't want to.

'How about Harborne?' I asked to end the silence. 'My place.'

'Next Thursday we're in Bristol,' said Aberlene. 'And then the following one it's Newcastle. So it looks like—'

'I would say this coming Monday,' said Fairfax. 'Unless that too is inconvenient?' His voice challenged us to object.

No one did.

The musicians greeted Aberlene's offer of coffee with delight, and settled down for what was obviously going to be a long gossip. But my biorhythms, centred on nine-o'-clock classes, had started to object to late nights, and I declined any refreshment. I considered calling a taxi, but the Outer Circle bus stop was only half a mile or so away down a well-lit road. Then there'd be a similar walk at the other end. On a May evening, walking would be a pleasure.

But when I was only halfway to the bus stop, a red BMW stopped a couple of yards ahead of me. Clearly someone didn't realise that the red-light district of Balsall Heath was two or three miles further into the city. Instead of leaning across to his passenger door, however, the driver opened his own. He winced so badly as he got out I thought for a moment he was ill and needed help, but he soon straightened and applied a social smile. Richard Fairfax.

'I believe you were heading for Harborne, Ms Rivers. May I offer you a lift?' He walked round now to the passenger door, and the smile edged closer to his eyes. 'You can write down my number first if you like. It's what my daughters did.'

Laughing, I did just that, and accepted his invitation.

The price was answering a series of questions which provided him with information about me: it felt more like a preliminary job interview than anything, particularly as he was disinclined to answer any of my questions. I did learn that he had had his family when he was young, and that both daughters were completely independent now; living in the USA. A Mrs Fairfax, if one existed, did not merit a mention. Oh, and he travelled a lot.

'Just got in from Saudi Arabia,' he said casually. 'Arrived about eleven yesterday morning. I know I ought to delegate, but I like to make sure the job's well done. I slept through a lot of that concert, I'm afraid.'

Could he possibly be making an oblique reference to and apology for his odd behaviour over the raffle tickets? I couldn't tell.

From me he extracted a brief CV, which did not excite him. He did ask a couple of questions about George Muntz College, to which I felt it politic to reply with reasonable enthusiasm. And then we established I was to return to William Murdock as soon as our computer project was complete.

That took us to Harborne Baths. To get us to Balden Road I mentioned the inconvenience of my bouncing Barclaycard. He offered computer error as a possible cause. I agreed.

His courtesy extended to opening my door from the outside and escorting me to my door. We bowed, like occidental Japanese, and that was that.

8

Friday might as well have been in February as May. I don't think it got properly light all day, and rain sluiced down, soaking me in the couple of hundred yards or so between home and George Muntz. Four uniformed constables looked self-conscious and cold on the steps. Inside, the foyer was now in absolute chaos, with the whine of drills and a couple of radios on competing wavelengths.

I lounged over to Peggy, who was all too delighted to tell me what was going on. The police were finding out who'd been in the building on Tuesday evening and were interviewing them. Moreover – it was clear where her priorities lay – the deputy chief executive had decreed that only administrative staff were to be admitted to what was to be called the Executive Suite. Or was it Management Suite? That was Hector's theory. Whatever it was, it was not for the hoi polloi: students and academic staff were equally unwelcome.

'And do you know what he called you lecturers?' demanded Peggy, wide-eyed. 'He called you a shower. "The blue-collar shower", that was what he called you.'

'Was it indeed? I thanked providence – which watches, of course, even sparrows – that I was soon to return to the Spartan but familiar William Murdock. But not as quickly as the new inhabitant of my room apparently believed.

All my belongings now sat in a heap on my chair. He had logged into my computer and was tapping determinedly away. He was so busy that he didn't notice when I came up behind him. Little bursts of asterisks, eh? And repeated 'Access denied' messages on the screen.

'Hunting for my password, are you? Try "piss off",' I said.

And he did!

'Never heard of irony?' I asked, reaching across and switching off. 'What are you after, sunshine?'

'Don't sunshine me!' He struggled to his feet, all six foot plus and beer belly of him.

'What else should I call you? I don't believe we've been formally introduced. I presume you know who I am, since my name is on the door, but I sure as hell don't know you. And –' I took the ashtray and ostentatiously put it outside the door – 'I'm not at all sure I want to.'

I removed my gear from my seat and sat down, arms folded and one trousered leg aggressively crossing the other.

It struck me at this point that I wasn't on very good ground. I was a mere visitor here, and could easily be thought to have violated the code of polite behaviour. Perhaps Sunshine thought so too. Getting truculently to his feet, he leaned over me with a particularly thick forefinger inches from my nose. It was too close for me to focus on, but I could smell the nicotine.

There was a tap on the door, and in, uninvited, walked Ian Dale. However casually he might try to dress, everything about him announced that he was a policeman. I'd have loved him to rock backwards and forwards on those large, wide feet and say 'Hello-ello-ello, what 'ave we here?' But he didn't need to.

'I was wondering if I might have a word, Ms Rivers,' he said. 'In private,' he added, holding the door ostentatiously for Sunshine to pass through. 'Hmph. Still, I suppose you can't expect more than a grunt from a pig,' he said reflectively. 'In a spot of bother, were you, Sophie, love?' he said closing the door firmly behind him, and pushing in the snib for good measure. 'Overreached yourself a bit? Like a chihuahua taking on a bloody great pit-bull. You ought to watch yourself, Sophie. One of these days it'll be you we find in a skip.' His smile was affectionate.

'Take a pew, Ian. And tell me what I can do for you.'

'You can tell me what you think of that suicide note. Tell me, would a kid about to kill herself really use a computer to tell the world?'

'To me it smells. But these computer wizards do take them remarkably seriously. There are all sorts of computer notice-boards, people communicating with other users and forming relationships with people they've never seen. The information super-highway, that sort of thing.' And then I looked hard at him. 'Come on, Ian, I bet you've got a lot more information than I have. All those uniform people crawling around looking for forensic evidence. All those statements. I'm looking to you to update me.'

Or Chris: where was Chris if Ian was here?

Ian smiled. 'Let's start with that Trevelyan lady. Doped up to the eyeballs she is, but the medics say they'll reduce her medication as quickly as they safely can. Then we can maybe get a bit of sense out of her.'

'She must really have seen Melina fall, you know.'

'I wonder which window she was looking out of,' said Ian, idly getting up and looking out of mine.

'Surely your forensic people could tell you that? The angle she landed would tell them that.'

Ian narrowed his eyes. 'Why?'

'Because – you're taking the mickey, Ian! You and Chris know all this. Why—'

'Actually the pathologist reckons the injuries are more consistent with her landing on something flat than on that skip.'

'Like paving stones? Jesus, you mean someone moved her? Was she still alive when they – when they ...'

'Don't know,' he said flatly. 'Pathologist will have some ideas, no doubt. But Chris would like to find some evidence. That's why—' He shut up abruptly.

'Ian,' I said amicably enough, 'I have this terrible feeling that you've been sent here to baby-sit me. Chris doesn't want me to leave my room for a bit, right? What's going on outside?'

Ian blushed.

'Are they out there now, looking for bits of her skin and bone?' I said, brutal for my sake, not his. 'And Chris didn't think I ought to have my sensibilities disturbed? Well, tell him something from me – he was bloody right!'

It took Ian a moment to work that one out; then he looked

sheepish. For such a stolid man he could look remarkably sheepish. I grinned. It was good to be friends with him.

'But it's rained a hell of a lot since, Ian. And I reckon they've been doing something with moss killer – weren't there some tins of Patioclean or something in that skip?' Yes, I could see them with my mind's eye. And yet I'd never consciously registered them. I wondered what else lurked in my memory waiting for something to poke it to the surface.

'You're probably right.'

He was going to say something else when the phone rang. I took it: Aberlene.

Ian got up to go; as he did so, he mimed a drink and tapped his watch.

I nodded.

'The Court Oak. One,' he mouthed.

I shook my head. 'Twelve. Teaching at one fifteen. Hi, Aberlene. Sorry about that. How're you?'

She seemed to be hedging. This was obviously my day for people to consider my feelings, Sunshine apart. On those rare occasions when Aberlene is tactful, it usually concerns male–female relationships. Or was it, in this case, male–male ones?

I found I didn't want to talk about Simon and Adrian yet. Not until I'd talked to Simon. So I offered her Richard Fairfax instead. 'I had a lift home last night,' I said brightly. 'From the nabob himself. Mr Big in his BMW.'

'Oh.' This was obviously not the confidence she'd been expecting. But she gathered her wits quickly enough. 'I hadn't got the impression you'd liked each other all that much.'

'Who worries about liking when there's a Seven Series BMW involved?'

'Sophie! You're not like that!'

'We're talking lifts, not relationships, Aberlene. You know me: fall in love with poor impoverished poets.' This was in fact a terrible lie. The last man I fancied myself in love with was a BMW man, but only Five Series. And before that—

'You certainly can't accuse him of being impoverished,' she said. 'Not when I have in my little hot hand a postdated cheque from him for a great deal of dosh for the Friendly Society raffle. And he says he wants just one ticket. Terribly good-looking when he was young, perhaps, but there's something ... unwholesome about him. I don't know. Perhaps he's just not recovered from his operation.'

'What sort of operation?'

'Don't know. He was jetting off to the Middle East within five minutes, so it can't have been anything serious. Doesn't look healthy, though – the opposite of your Chris, if you see what I mean.'

'Chris is not mine. We're—'

'– friends. But he is yours, for all that. The way he looks at you.'

'The way Tobias looks at you?' I like bowling yorkers.

And so I fended her off.

But then it occurred to me that Aberlene might be able to tell me something that would help me understand Melina better, though it might be embarrassing to ask.

'Tell me,' I began, 'though it's none of my business, are you – are you a Christian?'

'I suppose so. If provoked I might write C of E. Why? You're not doing a Billy Graham on me, are you?'

'Do you know anyone who is sort of right of centre in their religion?'

'You mean speaking in tongues and all that? You need a Pentecostalist, surely. Come on, Sophie, you know I'm a coconut: I may be black outside, but I'm as white as you inside. You must know a proper black woman or two!'

'As opposed,' I said, laughing, 'to an improper one. OK, Aberlene. See you – hey, will you lot be at the pub tonight?'

'No. Nottingham. But don't let that stop you drinking, eh? See you Monday – and don't tell anyone else about Toby and me, not just yet, eh?'

'Lips sealed, Ab. See you.'

So no chance of seeing Simon casually tonight. I'd better gird myself up to phone him and suggest a friendly coffee. But first – and why hadn't I done it already? – I'd better get on the phone to Barclaycard and breathe fire.

In the event, my flames were quickly extinguished. What the young woman at the end of the line wanted to know was whether I was still in Birmingham.

''Fraid so.' I gave her my college number and suggested

she call back. But what she wanted was my mother's maiden name. By now I was bemused.

'And you've been in Birmingham all this week? Well, I'm sorry to tell you, your Barclaycard hasn't.'

'It's in my wallet now,' I objected, flicking it open just to make sure.

'It's just bought a car in Singapore,' she said.

'You're joking.' I waited a second. 'No, you're not, are you?'

So I was the victim of another card fraud. It was the word 'another' that rankled. How many were there? Just to make sure, she said, she'd send my new card to my bank for collection from there. Just to make sure. And meanwhile, hell, I'd have to organise myself a Connect card and a guarantee card for my building-society account and – hell and hell and hell. And all I'd wanted was a simple ghetto blaster.

9

I never expected to spend my Friday lunchtime hurtling over to William Murdock and imploring my boss to protect me.

I don't think Mr Worrall expected to see me either, but I was admitted to his office straight away. Then he broke with all tradition and offered me a cup of the extremely fine tea he was drinking. I was even encouraged to sit down, and since his staff are usually expected to stand for audiences, in the manner of a junior rating before his captain, I took this as a mark of his considerable concern.

'Let me repeat to you, Miss Rivers, the facts as I understand them. We at William Murdock nominated you as our representative on the computer-assisted learning project. Because of procrastination by our masters in Margaret Street –' Mr Worrall always referred to Birmingham's education administrators as if he were the narrator of a C. P. Snow novel – 'the project did not actually commence until after the expected completion date. We should, in fact,' he said, allowing a thin smile to show he was making a pleasantry, 'have welcomed you back to what is now William Murdock Corporation at Easter, rather than bidding you farewell. *Au revoir*, I should say. And now –' he consulted his jottings – 'now George Muntz say they wish to reconsider their part in the project, and would like it to be relocated here.'

'Exactly.'

'And you were notified of this development only this morning, and by this memorandum?' He touched the piece of paper I'd thrust at him when I arrived, and then he held it up delicately, the better to sneer at the rather garish logo that decorated it – more of the new corporation's handiwork. 'May I ask if your colleagues on the project have had similar notification?'

'Two are on sick leave; the third was taking her morning off and I couldn't reach her by phone.'

'The union?'

I shook my head: I hadn't thought of that, and was surprised he should recommend what I'd have expected him to see as the enemy.

'All this is most irregular, Miss Rivers,' he tutted. His naval background had trained him very thoroughly in tutting. 'We had after all a gentlemen's agreement that the project would last an entire term. Have you discussed the memorandum with my opposite number at George Muntz? Mr Blake?'

'Mr Blake was unavailable for comment, as they say. He doesn't seem to be in college much at the moment,' I said, conscious I was saying something Worrall might find useful. 'He and the senior staff are working on a big project – the College without Walls, they call it.'

He looked at me shrewdly. 'I take it they haven't admitted you into their counsels?'

'Would you expect them to?'

'In the old days, yes, I think I would. Staff involvement was always valued. But since April all has changed, changed utterly, as I think the poet Yeats tells us. Now we've left the umbrella of Birmingham LEA, we're all to compete with each other. Money is the name of the game, Sophie.' He smiled. 'Tell me, have they introduced the new College Employers' Federation contract yet? The CEF contract?'

'There's a new contract, all right, but I've no idea which one.'

He gestured at the teapot. I poured for both of us.

'As you may know, the college principals have been invited to join an organisation apparently set up to enable us to run our colleges, our corporations, as tighter ships. Part of their strategy is to abandon the old contract that was negotiated between the LEAs and your union, the Silver Book contract – and let it be said that Birmingham's own contract was even more favourable to the lecturers.'

I nodded. 'And will William Murdock be adopting the new contract?'

He looked grim. 'We shall rue the day if it does, Sophie, but I may be forced into recommending something not dissimilar if all the other further-education establishments adopt it. Costs, money, funding – those are what are important now. Students are valued for their capacity to attract money. Their education *per se* matters less.' He sighed. 'So George Muntz are, I suspect, asserting their independence and forgetting their agreement as soon as it suits them.' He smiled and lapsed into silence.

I looked around me: his office needed decorating, and he had covered some of the more worn sections of wallpaper with naval prints. Tall ships, a not very good Turner, and Nelson, with those liquid and seductive eyes. No wonder Lady Hamilton fancied him. I wondered what he looked like without the white wig.

The silence was beginning to weigh heavy, and my lunch hour was oozing away. Perhaps I dared risk a prompt: 'Would it be possible to house the team here? As Mr Blake wants?'

He laughed, suddenly attractive. 'This morning's rain prevents me offering you hospitality: the top floors in both buildings are awash. Literally. The fire service did a fine job, but nonetheless I cannot envisage the rooms being in use again before September. We have a major rooming crisis anyway, with all the examinations coming up. Furthermore, your teaching timetable has been taken over in its entirety by a temporary member of staff, as I recall. On the strongest of educational grounds I would oppose a change of teacher at this stage.'

'I don't think your opposite number at George Muntz has considered that,' I said.

'I will suggest he considers it. In fact, I have an acquaintance on Muntz's governing body. I will contrive to raise the matter when I see him.' His face resumed its normal severity, as if managers were required to have frown lines to be effective. He must, I suppose, have been roughly the same age as Richard Fairfax. But Fairfax looked at least ten years older.

He stood and, ushering me to the door, asked me about my singing and my cycling. And then he mentioned, rather dryly, my uncanny propensity for discovering sudden death. News travels fast.

'I only found her,' I said. 'Someone else actually saw it happen. Suicide, it seems.'

'Ah,' he said, with apparent relief. And the interview was at an end.

I'd have liked to dash round the building and say hello to all my buddies, but I was supposed to be teaching back in Harborne in forty minutes. But I did think of someone I'd like to talk to, someone who might have some background knowledge of Melina's brand of Christianity: Philomena, one of our cleaning staff.

I could hear her voice in the porters' lodge: she was berating someone soundly. It was the head caretaker, as it transpired. But she left off to hug me. The head caretaker made good his escape.

'What's all this about a body at George Muntz?' She tapped the *Birmingham Post*. 'I'd have thought you'd have had enough of bodies.'

'Too right. And it seems I was one of the last people to see her alive. I feel bad about it, Philly: she wanted to talk to me and I didn't make time.'

'Not like you, that.' She looked at me shrewdly. 'Why not?'

'I was going out with Chris and—'

'Out? With Chris? That lovely young man! I'll have to tell Winston when I phone him. Says he can't afford to phone me on his student grant, of course, but I tell him, you doctors earn enough when you're qualified - a bit more debt doesn't matter now.'

I didn't imagine he'd dare argue.

'Not out like that - just out,' I said. 'But I feel bad about it. She was a nice girl. God-fearing.'

'Not many of those about,' she agreed. 'But it's not that that's worrying you, is it?'

I shook my head. I wished myself anywhere but here. Philly was a highly trained nurse with an OU qualification in computers. It would be as crass to ask her about obscurer forms of Christianity as it had been to question Aberlene.

'I don't know how her family would feel about my going round,' I said. 'Seems they belong to one of these churches that believes Saturday's the Sabbath. Would that make them a bit - fundamental?'

'Don't you talk to me about fundamentalism! Come here!' She pulled me to the door and gestured at some girls in the foyer. 'Look at them!'

They were dressed from top to toe in black: veiled, their faces covered so only their eyes showed, they'd not have been out of place in Saudi Arabia. But in Birmingham? And another thing – 'But Philly, they're Afro-Caribbean, not Arabs!'

'Right. But these young girls have got it into their heads they've got to be Muslim. So they do that to themselves. And goodness knows what else besides,' she added darkly. 'You ask me, I reckon religion does more harm than good, and thass a fac'.'

I grinned: I loved her excursions into patois. 'You're not a church-goer yourself?'

'Humanist, Sophie. I don't want no patriarch telling *me* what to do about sex and—'

I grabbed. 'That was one of Melina's problems.'

Philly looked at me sharply. 'Pregnant?'

'Lesbian.'

'Not if she was a fundamentalist, surely?'

'Can religion reorient someone's sexual inclinations?'

'Maybe not. But it can do a wonderful job repressing them. Lawks-a-mussy!' she exclaimed as the head caretaker reappeared. 'Look at dat ol' clock. Philly, she way behind.'

The 103 bus, which I caught at Five Ways, followed for a quite alarming proportion of its journey to Harborne a loathsome high-sided lorry carrying bones and other butcher's waste. It stank vilely, and unsavoury bits and pieces escaped from the inadequate tarpaulin to remind us of its load and of our own mortality. Certainly I was glad to return to the comparative safety of George Muntz and occupy myself with some teaching.

It was an A-level group, ready to take their exams in about five weeks. 'Ready' was the wrong word, perhaps. We started the afternoon with a quick revision of the apostrophe after one of the group had assured me that 'its' was the plural of 'it'. Not a grade-A candidate, perhaps.

At break I sought out Polly. Strange that it had taken Worrall to make me realise I needed union support. I could ask her about Sunshine while I was at it: it would be nice to know the identity of my roommate.

Her door was unlocked, so I tapped and popped into her office. It was empty; the computer was switched off, but still warm. On her desk, neatly organised with stacking filing trays, there was a convenient Post-It pad, so I wrote a line asking her to phone me – at home, if she couldn't find me in the building. I liked her room. It was newly painted, and someone had wax-polished the desk. The wall opposite her desk was covered with big railway posters and there were a couple of plants flourishing on her bookshelf. The chairs might be college issue, but the cushions were well-stuffed and covered in Indian embroidered elephants.

The only thing out of place was an open filing-cabinet drawer. Ever the Girl Guide, I kicked it shut as I left. I wouldn't want anyone to trip over it.

I'd have preferred Polly's support when I bearded Mr Blake, but on the whole I thought I'd go and see him while I felt angry enough. I had, after all, two legitimate complaints, and it would be courteous to let him know I'd already seen my old principal.

I had, of course, forgotten Mrs Cavendish.

If the carpenters and joiners worked overtime, by Monday she and those she guarded would be sheltered from the hoi polloi in the foyer by a solid-looking wood and glass barricade. No doubt you'd have to have the right voice or the right code number to get in. Meanwhile she sat impregnable at her desk, deeply engaged in a phone conversation. This time she covered her mouthpiece and mouthed extravagantly at me: 'Mr Blake is unavailable.'

I nodded, hardly surprised, and waited.

She glanced skywards in exasperation, and returned to the phone. 'Mr Curtis was quite definite about it. And common sense must tell you, you simply cannot afford to take sick leave of those proportions. No: your contract is quite clear.'

I pricked my ears.

'Oh, I'm sure you will, Mr Teague. Quite sure you will. And if you take my advice, you'll get that back of yours out of bed and back into the classroom on Monday.' She put down the phone firmly. 'You people don't seem to realise the world has changed,' she said, eyeing me with hostility. 'No more feather-bedding. The new contract will see to that.'

'What if people don't want to sign?'

'They'll sign quick enough if there's no food on the table.'

I winced: people had said things like that in Dickens's time, hadn't they? But there was no point in yelling at a messenger, so I merely pulled myself up to my full height and said firmly, 'I need to see the principal. On a matter of the greatest importance.'

'Mr Blake sees staff on Mondays,' she said, not bothering to open the desk diary.

The tape was rerunning, was it? I looked at her sardonically. 'I don't suppose he's even in the building, is he? Not at four on a Friday. He'll be off back to - Solihull, is it?'

'Knowle, actually.'

Knowle considers itself posher than Solihull.

I suppressed a snigger. 'First thing on Monday. And perhaps he'll want to know that I shall ask the union rep to come too.'

'The union has been derecognised,' she said.

'I beg your pardon?'

'Derecognised.'

'Since when?'

'Since eleven this morning. At the governors' meeting.'

'And is the union aware it has been - derecognised?'

'I should imagine so. Now, if that is all—' She turned back to her computer.

'No! I still don't have my appointment with Mr Blake. Monday, you'll recall.'

At last she opened the diary. 'Five thirty?'

'Nine,' I said, pointing to an empty slot.

She glowered but filled it in. Her pencil stopped. 'On what subject?'

'I beg your pardon?'

'On what subject do you wish to speak to Mr Blake?'

'On a subject that I will raise with him, Mrs Cavendish.'

'That's not good enough. The principal will want to know—'

'Oh, he'll know soon enough,' I said, turning on my heel.

My exit was blocked, not quite deliberately, by Curtis, cross-armed on what would soon be the threshold. He held my

eye for an unpleasant moment, then smiled, very slowly.
'Goodbye, Miss Rivers,' he said, standing aside to let me pass.

I had time to pop home and cook myself cheese on toast – after that lorryload from the abattoir, vegetarianism was clearly indicated – before heading back into the city for a choir rehearsal.

With my present run of luck, I suppose I wasn't surprised to find my toaster expiring with a pungent electrical fault. When I went to the building society for cash for that ghetto blaster, I'd have to get enough to buy a new toaster as well.

Friday is the choir's rehearsal night. I set off promptly, but suddenly realised the last thing I wanted to do was sing. Everyone would want to know the details – it's OK to take a macabre interest if the details come second-hand. But I didn't want to relive my inadequacy, my impotence. I didn't want to stand in a minute's silence for a death I – No! That way madness lay. I got off the bus in the High Street. The walk back wouldn't hurt me.

And then I saw another bus, one going towards Birmingham University and to the hospital where Dr Trevelyan was detained. On impulse, I ran for it.

The hospital occupies an enormous site, and it took me a few minutes to get my bearings. The area is so large that some of the corridors have to slope to accommodate the contours of the land, and it was up one of these I was directed to find the flower shop. Even flowers seemed, come to think of it, a pretty weak pretext for what I suspected was really a snoop. Back to the Psychiatric Unit. Stairs or lift? The stairs would give me more time to think.

As I approached the nurses' station, a young man pushed open the door to the day room, holding it for someone to follow him. Inside a woman was sobbing with the abandon of a child. Not Dr Trevelyan. She was hunched over her cigarette, rocking herself backwards and forwards. The fiercely cut hair was lank and greasy, and her face was bare of make-up. I didn't want to see any more. I dropped the roses and carnations on the nurses' desk and fled.

*

There is a theory that a bath and an early night will clear all ills. I helped myself to Irish whiskey, a dollop of lavender oil and *Pride and Prejudice* for my bath, and soaked until I'd finished both book and booze. But when I slept I saw blood and bone and heard the howling of a mad-eyed woman.

10

Only Chris would phone someone at eight on a Saturday morning. His voice had the ring of conscious virtue I associate with someone who's already completed a five-mile run and has showered and shaved. To compensate, I burrowed further under the duvet.

'What time do you want to start, then, Sophie?'

'Start?'

'Looking at cars. You were going to fix up some test-drives, remember?' If only his voice were not so disgustingly bright.

'Oh. Ah. Well, to be honest, I forgot.'

'Thought you would. Quite a week you've had, after all. But there's nothing to stop us turning up on the off chance. I'll pick you up in half an hour?'

'Chris, my sweet, if you dare arrive before nine I'll – Tell you what,' I continued, beginning at last to surface, 'why don't you stop off at Brown's for some bacon and eggs and we'll have a wicked breakfast? It's Saturday, after all. We can afford some cholesterol.'

'Anything else while I'm there? Or have you already shopped? Go on – dictate.'

I dictated. Chicken, mince, pâté. 'Why not get some bread from the deli? And some butter, come to think of it. We could have bacon butties. And what about croissants?'

'The woman tempted me,' he said.

I managed to crawl out of bed and into the shower. By the time he arrived, I'd washed my hair and was thoroughly decent in shirt and jeans. There'd even been time to put on some cosmetics: although Chris had seen my face in its natural state times without number, I still felt awkward about his watching the make-up process itself.

I shoved the *Guardian* to one side for him to dump the carrier bag on the kitchen table and wished I dared kiss him, he looked so pleased with himself when he opened the bag to reveal a tight little posy of roses. I grinned at him and shoved them in water. And then, because it was a nice sunny morning, I did reach up and kiss his cheek. He blushed, but managed to hug me in a reasonably fraternal sort of way.

A good start to the day. Especially with crisp smoked bacon between two pieces of bread cut to just the right thickness and buttered.

While he sprawled back dangerouly in the chair to read the *Guardian* and drink almost viscous tea from my Pooh Bear mug, I thought I might outline my revised itinerary for the day – taking in the building society on the High Street to get some cash and then Comet for my goodies. I didn't get much further than the word 'cash' before he returned to the vertical.

'Cash? You don't want to carry that sort of money around!'

'No option, Chris,' I said, getting up to fill the kettle. I wanted more tea, the sort you don't have to chisel from the mug.

'You're never over your credit limit!' He was clearly about to rebuke me for my improvidence, and I hated it when he got parental.

'No. But my card is.' I explained my card's overseas adventures. 'Hey, where are you off to?'

'To call a friend,' he said tersely, heading for the phone extension in the living room.

I made the tea, filled my mug straight away, and left the rest of the pot to brew for Chris. I turned to watch him, in silhouette against the living-room wall. His jeans fitted as if they'd been made for him. A nice, neat bum, and the shoulders appropriately broad, even if his tendency to stoop was increasing – I'd have to nag him about those Alexander Technique lessons.

I was reading the paper when he came back in – the early season's cricket reports. I looked up enquiringly, but not necessarily expecting a reply. Chris couldn't always reply to questions, and I never liked putting him under pressure. But this time he grinned. 'Just fixed up a mid-morning coffee meeting.'

'But I thought—' I said without thinking. He was doing me a favour, after all, and I shouldn't whinge if he had something more important to do.

'You too, Sophie. In fact, it isn't me he wants.'

'What rotten taste! Who is he, anyway?'

'Just a mate from the Fraud Squad.'

I was deadlocking the front door when the phone started to ring. I couldn't remember if I'd left the answering machine on, so I went back in and took the call: Simon. Could we have a drink some time?

I had an idea that it might not be the easiest of occasions, and in any case, I didn't know how long I intended to spend with Chris. Sometimes our days together drifted into evenings; sometimes they were terminated abruptly by the demands of the West Midlands Police. Whichever happened, in my book the needs of an old friend took priority over those of someone not much more than an acquaintance, albeit one I'd felt quite attracted to. So I temporised: if I had a chance I'd phone him back later.

Parking in Harborne was never entertaining, especially on a Saturday, so I wasn't surprised when Chris parked in his slot at Rose Road Police Station. We walked briskly up to the High Street, to one of the many building-society branches which now clogged up what was once a thriving shopping area. I always hated it when travel agents and building societies outstripped ordinary shops.

My purse replete, I expected us to collect the car and head off to Comet. But instead, we went into the police station and up to Chris's room.

It was already occupied when we went in. If Chris looked like a teacher, this man might have been a rather seedy pop musician. He was wearing scruffy jeans and the unlaced German paratroopers' boots much in vogue among the kids at college. His T-shirt advertised some band I wasn't familiar with. He even sported a ponytail and some rather inadequate blond designer stubble, although he was probably older than I and possibly older than Chris: forty-one or -two, perhaps.

Chris shook his hand, smiling as though they were friends, and slapped his shoulder. 'DI Dave Clarke,' he said. 'Sophie Rivers.'

DI Dave Clarke smiled not at Chris but at me. We shook hands. He had a good handshake and an open smile disclosing crooked teeth which, if they'd been seen to, would have made him remarkably pleasant to look at.

'So,' he said, 'tell me.' He settled himself on the corner of Chris's desk, one leg on the desktop, the other just touching the floor, so from the visitor's chair I had an unrivalled view of the bulge of his genitals.

'The credit-card business,' said Chris dryly.

I took a deep breath, shifted the chair slightly, and told him.

'Why will you people never learn?' Dave demanded rhetorically when I'd finished.

'Learn what?' I asked, always eager to enrich my knowledge.

'Never to let your credit card out of your sight,' he said, at last hitching himself off the desk and into a more conventional position on a chair. He reached out a familiar notebook and made rapid jottings. I wondered why he'd waited till I'd finished my narrative, but decided not to ask. The answer might have had to do with giving me his full attention, in view of the way he leaned towards me, treating me to little gusts of a rather nice body spray.

'Why?' I asked eventually.

He looked up, startled. Perhaps he'd forgotten his last pronouncement. Then he smiled.

'It would take me a couple of hours to tell you all the ways people can commit fraud with other people's credit cards,' he said. 'In fact, that sounds like a good idea. Why don't we fix up for you to come round to my base and see what the team are doing? I'll clear it with my boss.'

He sounded so enthusiastic that I was almost convinced his invitation was disinterested. But Chris's expression suggested otherwise.

'Tell you what, come along now and I'll take a statement,' Clarke continued. 'No problem.'

'Come off it, Dave,' Chris said. 'You're not at the

statement stage yet, surely to God. Jesus, Sophie, these people just love their paperwork. The rest of us disappear under it; Fraud bloody wallow in it.'

'Proper documentation,' said Clarke huffily. 'When you face trials lasting four or five years, you have to get the documentation right. Meticulous attention to detail, that's what we call it.'

'Why,' I interposed gently, 'don't we take a rain-check on the statement? I'm allergic to the things. Especially on Saturday mornings. And in any case, Barclaycard said they were taking it up with you people. I'd guess I'll be a very small footnote in your paperwork.'

'Not in mine,' he said.

Hell, what sort of man was this, to try to snaffle me from under Chris's nose?

'Rain-check all the same,' I said, reaching for my bag and catching Chris's eye. We were, after all, supposed to be discussing ghetto blasters and toasters. Not to mention cars. 'You won't be wanting me for the inquest, will you, Chris? Monday?'

'I don't know. This suicide-note business ... But I intend to ask for an adjournment.'

Clarke showed no sign of leaving; in fact, he looked pointedly around the office. 'There was a rumour you make good coffee, Chris.'

We all looked around the room. No sign of his percolator; not even a cup.

'Shit! The bastards! They'd have the shoes off your feet in this place!' Chris picked up his phone and started to talk.

But I missed what he was saying. I was staring at the carpet, at his elegant shoes, at Clarke's scruffy boots, at my own neat flatties. And I saw a pair of black shoes on the stairs that led past the drama and music studios to the roof from which Melina had fallen. I didn't want to interrupt Chris but I needed to ask someone why a girl preparing to kill herself might want to remove her shoes first.

Chris, when at long last he'd shed Clarke, wasn't able to explain the shoes either. To do him justice, he didn't yell at me for forgetting them earlier, or for being unable to describe them except in imprecise terms.

'You're sure they were there? Absolutely?'

I nodded. 'I nearly fell over them. In fact, I arranged them neatly side by side. That was before I ... And I can't remember seeing them since.'

'Don't suppose you can,' he said, reaching for a file and running his index finger down a page. 'No, the soco team didn't report shoes. And you know how meticulous they are – fine-tooth comb isn't in it. And –' he flicked through the file – 'Melina wasn't wearing shoes, was she? When you – when we retrieved her body.' He closed the file and leaned on his forearms, looking suddenly tired. 'How are you on artist's impressions of shoes, Sophie?'

I shook my head. 'Maybe if I saw a similar pair ... It's important, isn't it?'

He spread his hands. 'We could show them to her parents, establish she had something like them. And then find out what's happened to the originals. That'd be interesting in itself. And I think we should get an automatic adjournment. To hunt for the person or persons unknown who unlawfully killed her.'

'Her parents might know where she usually shopped,' I said.

The file again. Then he dialled a number. He let it ring and ring, but there was no reply.

'Shopping,' he said. 'Saturday, after all. Life must go on even when you've lost your only daughter.'

'Church, more like,' I said. 'Some fundamental churches follow the Jewish Sabbath tradition. Several of my black students at William Murdock couldn't go on theatre trips on Friday evenings, because of the Friday-dusk-to-Saturday-dusk dogma. And some of them would spend literally all day in church on Saturday.'

'All that God-bothering!' said Chris. 'Still, I'm sure He can cope. Question is, how do we sort out this shoe business?'

'We leg it round town,' I said. 'Any chain store that sells shoes.'

'Specialist shoe shops?'

'Mid-priced ones, perhaps. Melina didn't strike me as specially interested in clothes. Or is that just my way of saying I can't remember a single thing she wore?'

'Marks and Sparks bra and panties,' Chris read from the file. 'BHS slip. Boots tights. Blouse from Littlewood's. All bottom of the range. Skirt – they couldn't find a label. Well done, Dr Watson.'

I smiled: he looked happier again.

We were on our fifth shop.

'Poor old Prince Charming,' Chris said, fingering yet another pair of black slip-ons.

'Worse for him: at least we're poking round clean shoes. He was kneeling over sweaty feet.'

'With his glass slipper. Don't even dare tell me it was a mistranslation and they meant rabbit fur. Leave me with my fantasies.'

'You're the man who knew what a snib was,' I said. 'You're the one they invented Trivial Pursuit for. Hang on!'

Over by the cash desk was a deep cylindrical basket of oddments – left ones only – in a variety of colours one might have considered unsaleable, apart from that black one near the bottom. I started to burrow frantically. A black shoe. Flat, with a little gold button on a mock flap.

Mine were, however, not the only hands in the basket. A middle-aged woman was digging too. I stuck my bag between my feet so I could use both hands.

I reached it first. Size 6. Miles too big for me even to pretend if it came to an argument. But there needn't be an argument, despite the other woman's longing looks. She must have been an 8 or a 9. I looked round and brandished it at Chris. It was plain sailing after that. Within five minutes he had acquired his evidence.

He clearly wanted to hug someone, he was so pleased, and I saw no objection, even if I made him wait until we'd left the shop. All too soon, however, the stoop of his shoulders reappeared, and a little furrow dug in between his eyebrows.

'Sophie—'

'I know. You've got to go and sort out the shoe business. Melina's parents.'

He nodded sadly.

'There's always tomorrow, Chris.'

'I don't like to let you down. It was my suggestion, after all.'

'Chris, you put up with it when I have to wade through piles of marking. You're doing something more important than marking.' I smiled bracingly. Feeling like a mother trying to give a child a little treat even if it couldn't have a big one, I added, 'I suppose you couldn't drop me in Selly Oak? I can live without a car, but life's too silent without a radio.'

He nodded. Right there, right in the middle of New Street, I hugged him. I'd never loved anyone so much that I resented every minute life tore me from him, and I couldn't imagine which hurt Chris more, being with me platonically or not being with me at all. And if I was tempted to go to bed with Chris just to make him happy – and in my present state of celibacy I'd have no objections to a nice, friendly fuck – I knew I cared for him too much to offer it. He wanted more than a leg-over. Wanted? *Needed*.

'Maybe a quick sandwich too?' I prompted.

'Better not. But I'll drop you off at Comet with pleasure. Hell, I'll hang on for you there – you won't be more than a couple of minutes, will you?'

Nor would we have been, except for the massive traffic jam that was currently garrotting Selly Oak. Just where the arterial A38 is at its most congested, where it crosses the Outer Ring Road, they built an enormous Sainsbury's. To try to ease the subsequent chaos, they then made it and its car park into a giant triangular island at the centre of a primitive one-way system. Comet and some other superstores were on the other side of the three lanes of stationary metal from Sainsbury's. We crept round two sides of the triangle, and now had to inch into the far lane to get into Comet's car park. I knew Chris ought to drop me and fight his way back to Rose Road. So did he.

I decided it for him. I let myself out. 'Cut through Sainsbury's car park,' I yelled as I shut the door. 'And phone me as soon as you can.'

This time they'd actually wrapped the bloody ghetto blaster before I reached for my purse and found someone had fingered it and I was completely penniless. Worse still, when I realised what had happened, there and then, right in front of all the people on the cash desk, I burst into tears.

*

'At least my bus pass lives in my pocket,' I told Simon, phoning him as I'd promised. 'But I was too late for the building society, of course.' Chummie had missed my chequebook, so I wasn't penniless, but I did rate pretty high on any scale of pissed-offness. Two hundred pounds, just like that.

'You've reported it?'

'Yes, to a sergeant at Rose Road so newly striped he didn't know my relationship with Chris. But, as he said, there wasn't much you could do against opportunist thieves, and the best thing I could do was remember not to carry such large sums of cash in future.'

'How about I do you a stir-fry?' asked Simon. 'And Sophie, I'll pay for a taxi or anything.'

Just then I didn't want to argue.

Simon's house was a stately Victorian semi in Moseley, a suburb which prides itself on being a village without the bourgeois element they condemn in Harborne. Certainly it is home to many of the artier of Birmingham's denizens, and the Midshires Symphony Orchestra coach makes a special stop there.

Simon shared his house with another bass player – a golf addict – and a rugby-playing trombonist. It couldn't be all that easy having gender problems in such hearty, indeed macho company. He also gave houseroom to a family of orphaned basses, which grew, it seemed, by the month if not the week. Some were so battered you couldn't imagine music ever being coaxed out of them; others had been oiled into a comfortable sheen. This week I found one in the downstairs loo – rescued, apparently, from a skip. I didn't tell him about my find in similar circumstances. Not immediately. There were other things to talk about first.

I poured myself a glass of red wine – Simon's father's a wine merchant – and sat at the kitchen table. It was covered not with vegetables and meat but with the innards of something electrical, a soldering iron and a variety of tools.

'Another car alarm?' I asked mildly. The wine was very strong, and I was already woozier than I liked; I'd had no lunch and there was no supper in immediate prospect. I set the wine firmly to one side and picked up a screwdriver.

'Microwave,' he said. 'The magnetron's packed up.'

He passed me what looked like an old-fashioned radio valve, surprisingly bulky and heavy for what you expect to find in miniaturised technology. 'That's the magnet there, see: that's what makes it so heavy. That's the business bit that does the cooking.'

'Isn't it a bit risky, trying to repair things like this for yourself?'

'What d'you mean, *trying*? I'm bloody good at it. Damn it, that's what my degree's in. Well, physics.'

I nodded. Music and maths were supposed to go well with each other. No reason why music and physics shouldn't.

'Anyway, why shouldn't people take risks?' His voice was challenging, almost truculent. 'That's what's life's about, surely? Taking risks.'

I couldn't argue with that.

'You're talking to a risk-junkie here,' I said, reaching for the wine and topping up both glasses. He looked at me uncertainly. 'But there are more serious risks than physical ones. Emotional ones. In fact,' I said, 'I'm going to risk something right now.'

The kitchen went so quiet you could hear the hum of his soldering iron.

'No. Look, Sophie, I'm really not – no, I don't want ...' He flushed. 'You see, I'm not—' He spilled some wine on the table and dabbed at it.

I passed him a tissue from my bag.

'I've cocked this up,' I said. 'I'm not here to invite myself into your bed. I'm here for a drink and stir-fry and maybe a bit of a natter.'

'Oh?'

'Well, that's what friends are for. And I hope we *are* friends. There's nothing I need more than friends,' I added, 'after George's death.'

'He was with the MSO, wasn't he? The principal bassoon?'

I nodded. The wine had made me emotional. Simon passed me some kitchen towel.

'Were you very close?' he asked.

'We loved each other,' I said simply. 'We weren't lovers; it was more like brother and sister. It's good to have someone you can share things with, without sex creeping in all the time.'

I was telling the truth, neither more nor less, but I was being disingenuous, signalling that I was prepared to let our little flirtation atrophy without hard feelings. Perhaps the signals were too crude. He didn't speak, just switched off the soldering iron and started to gather up his tools. He put the microwave, minus the magnetron, back next to the cooker, and poured himself more wine, ignoring my nearly empty glass.

'What shall we do about food, then?' he asked at last.

'I'm in your hands,' I said, spreading mine. 'No card, no cash, not to speak of. And no food. But I'll chop and peel anything you want chopping and peeling.' I could feel my smile was too bright.

'Adrian called just before you arrived,' he said. 'He wants to come round later.'

I prepared to be hurt and offended.

'But I said I'd promised you a meal tonight. So he won't be round till quite late. I thought – I wanted – I need—' He broke off, gesturing helplessly.

'You need a friend,' I said.

'I hoped – you see, I really like you. But then along comes Adrian . . .'

At one level I think I was angry: had I been used as a sort of stooge to prove that Simon was straight? Surely to goodness that sort of pretence wasn't necessary in the 1990s! But how could I rage at a young man who seemed confused and disoriented to the point of tears?

'Simon, love, we were friends in the first place. Let's go back to being friends.' I stood and held out my arms.

After a frighteningly long delay he came towards me and accepted my hug.

At last I pushed him away and poured some more wine. 'What about this 'ere food, then?'

He looked at the electrical mess on the table as if he'd not been responsible for putting it there, shoved the lot into his toolbox, and then reached for his jacket. 'Come on, we'll have a balti. And then I'll run you home and I'll see what I can do for your radio. Adrian'll just have to wait.'

11

Sunday morning was so fine and warm that I set my marking on hold and pottered around the garden. It was one of those days that made not having a car irritating. Not that I wanted to rush like a lemming to the coast; I merely wanted a large bag of potting compost and a load of bedding plants, and a bike was inadequate. If Chris phoned – as I rather expected him to – then I could no doubt inveigle him into doing the honours.

So when the phone rang, even though I found I'd left muddy footprints, I answered it in my sunniest voice. It wasn't Chris, however, but a voice I had difficulty placing. Richard Fairfax! Why should he want to speak to me? Come to think of it, how had he got hold of my number?

His voice rang with confidence; anyone would have thought he was one of my oldest friends. He wanted, he said, not to take up much of my time on this glorious morning, but merely to drop off some papers for tomorrow's meeting. And he'd be with me at about noon, if that would suit me.

Although politeness made me agree, I felt steadily more irritated as the morning progressed. I couldn't greet anyone in my gardening jeans, and my old Oxfam T-shirt was decidedly disreputable. Not to mention my nails, which seemed to attract dirt from within the leather gardening gloves which were supposed to protect them. So at eleven thirty I came in and scrubbed up; I even brushed my hair. Even as I peered at myself in the mirror, wondering if a spot of lipstick might be appropriate, I pulled myself up short. Why was I making such a fuss for someone I didn't like?

It was a waste to be inside; I took my coffee and *Observer* out to what if it were larger might be called a patio. There was just room for a couple of chairs, a table and some big pots I'd fill with petunias and fuchsias once I'd got hold of the potting compost and there was no threat of frost.

The problem with the patio was that it made far too intimate a setting for what should have been the briefest of meetings. Ensconced in the better chair, with a cup of milkless Earl Grey to hand, Fairfax settled back for what appeared to be a long and meaningless chat about the problems of lawn maintenance. I couldn't understand it: here was a man to whom time must be of the essence, oblivious to the barrow of weeds with the fork and leather gloves laid, now I came to think of it, ostentatiously across the top. The proposals he was to put before tomorrow's meeting must be self-explanatory – certainly he made no attempt to fish them out of the A4 envelope that lay on top of my *Observer*.

'It must,' he said suddenly, 'be hard to balance the demands of house and home against those of your job.'

'No more than for any single person,' I said. 'Though teaching must rate pretty high on a Richter scale of stress.'

'You said you were working on some project: is that stressful?'

'Not the computer work itself. What I have found hard is taking on classes this late in the year. They all resent having their proper lecturers whisked away. And who can blame them? Their exams start immediately after the half-term break.'

'You teachers and your holidays,' he said. 'Why on earth don't you work proper hours and weeks like the rest of the world?'

'If you're referring to this particular half-term,' I said, 'then the students need the time for last-minute private revision.'

'What if they encounter any problems? Shouldn't there be someone there to help?'

If there's one thing that really makes me angry, it's people complaining about teachers without ever having done the job. But I've learned from bitter experience that there's simply no point in engaging in arguments with people who want more than anything else to cling to the belief that teachers work short hours for a lot of money.

'Wouldn't a conscientious teacher *want* to be there to help?' Fairfax pursued.

'I sometimes wish we could take their exams for them,' I said. There must be some reason for this interrogation.

'And shouldn't you be there when the results come out?'

'I've never known a college where the staff don't organise a rota to be there at the crucial time.'

'That's not the same thing. How do you know when the crucial time is?'

'By experience.' I hoped my tone showed I'd had enough of this interrogation. To emphasise the point I reached for the envelope he'd brought.

'I'd have thought it was in the students' interests,' he pursued, 'not to close in the summer. You don't get firms closing down wholesale.'

'You do in France,' I said, despising myself for taking the bait. Then I opened the envelope and started to withdraw the papers.

'Tell me, do you think Muntz is an efficient college?'

'I think it's well on the way to being an unhappy one,' I said. 'Someone seems to have forgotten that lecturers are people too.' I told him about the invasion of my office and the probable termination of my project. 'Oh, and they've denied the staff the use of their common room and the students are so hostile to our invasion of the canteen that none of us use it. Some of the staff are on this new contract, the rest aren't, so you can imagine what that does for staff morale. They've just derecognised the union—'

'How do you know that?'

I looked at him, torn between an urge to grass on la Cavendish and a strong desire to demand what business it was of his. Certainly it was time to end the conversation: dealing with the occasional vile student had taught me the flick of the eyelid and quick movement to my feet that would tell him I had had enough. But before I could dismiss him verbally, the phone rang. I gestured him, none too courteously, through the French window before me into the living room. I stopped to answer the phone and asked the caller to hold while I escorted Fairfax through the hall.

'Unusual design this, having the party wall between the two halls rather than between the living rooms,' he said, smiling as pleasantly as if we'd discussed nothing more controversial than compost heaps.

I nodded. I didn't think a comment was necessary.
'Until tomorrow evening, then,' he said
'Yes,' I replied, and closed the front door on him.
'Jesus,' said Chris, when I picked up the phone, 'is that Sophie or an iceberg? Who've you been freezing off, eh?'
'Richard Fairfax. Bloody fascist,' I added. 'Spoiled my day.'
'Can I unspoil it? D'you fancy going out to lunch?'
'Sunday? Everywhere will be full of cheery families.'
'My garden won't.'
'You're on.'

It turned out to be a working lunch, in the calm of Chris's dining room. The death of Melina was high on the agenda. The parents recognised the shoes – in fact, the father had wept at the sight of them. And no one had managed to explain why she wasn't wearing them when – if – she jumped. Neither had anyone explained how she had managed to fall on the skip without injuring herself on the lumps of rubbish – not, said Chris, dropping his voice, that she hadn't suffered horrific injuries anyway.
'The paving she should have fallen on didn't produce the bloodstains you wanted? Hey, this is a wonderful avocado.'
'Thanks. No, nary a one. Not that this is a subject we should be talking about over lunch.' He got up and twitched the curtain slightly. 'Sorry: I'm getting over one of my heads. Can't stand too much light.'
'Bad?'
'Bad enough. I think it was meeting her parents. Laid me low all evening. Didn't really surface till about ten this morning. And then Ian phoned about your purse. Why didn't you tell me?'
I scraped out the avocado skin and licked my spoon as if it were a lolly. 'Common theft. As the lady said, life's a bitch and then you die.' I hadn't wanted to worry him.
'I don't like coincidences. How much did you lose?'
'What I got out of the building society: £200.'
'Cheque book?'
'Safe inside a zipped pocket. But it was a pain. And the *real* pain is that Simon's mended my radio, so I didn't need a new one.'

'But you'll get one anyway. It's important.'

I nodded. Chris and Aberlene together constituted an irresistible force.

'Simon and Adrian – the viola player – are now an item, by the way,' I said lightly. I didn't want to trivialise it into gossip, but Chris deserved to know, and I didn't want to make any heavy explanations. 'He told me all about it when we went for a balti down Moseley Road last night.'

Chris gathered the avocado dishes; I followed him to the kitchen. It might never have seen a saucepan raised in anger, but a wonderful smell was emanating from the oven. He bent to remove a casserole, one of those heavy le Creuset ones, and bore it to the table. I followed with smaller casseroles: crispy roast potatoes and tiny buttered carrots.

'Chicken,' he said.

'Great. Somehow I'm off red meat.' I explained very briefly about the truck I'd followed.

And then we looked up at each other and said it together; 'A tarpaulin! Melina might have fallen on a tarpaulin!'

'How bloody premeditated can you get?' Chris exclaimed, pushing his chicken away untouched and reaching for his phone.

'No, leave it till you've eaten. Please. Five minutes won't make any difference to the case, and it might to your stomach. Here.' I topped up his glass. 'Go on: one won't hurt you, and it comes with St Paul's recommendation. Let's think about why anyone should want to kill her.'

We ate in silence for a few minutes. What had she said about her previous job? Something to do with the Jewellery Quarter. Computers in the Jewellery Quarter. Servicing them for industrial firms; 'quite a few'...

'If you service a computer,' he asked at last, 'does that give you access to all the files?'

'If you were very bright, you could explore all sorts of unauthorised highways and byways. Are you wondering if she might have found something in a computer?'

'I don't know. Maybe. Something about one of her old clients – I'll have someone follow it up. There's even George Muntz, of course.'

'But she was so discreet about her other job, and so cowed

by Dr Trevelyan, I don't think she'd have blabbed to anyone about anything. Except that she wanted to talk to me urgently the night she was killed.'

'So what had she found and what did she intend to do with her information? Do you see her as the blackmailing type?'

I wanted to protest, sharply, that Melina struck me as being very moral, but morality is not the same as discretion. And she seemed to have obeyed authority, in the form of Trevelyan, without necessarily respecting it.

'I think she might have seen it as her duty to warn whoever was doing wrong that she would have to report it,' I said at last. 'But the problem is her wanting to talk to me first, as if she might have wanted reassurance that she was doing the right thing. Oh, Chris, I don't know. If only I hadn't been in such a hurry that evening—'

'So she could have said to X that if he or she didn't stop whatever it was, she'd go to someone in authority,' Chris overrode me. 'Who would that be, at Muntz? Blake? Curtis?'

'Blake's the boss, of course. But he's elusive, and in any case Curtis would probably be in charge of the day-to-day finances. I haven't quite worked out who does what yet – and just to confuse me further they keep on changing their job titles. *You* could ask.'

'I could indeed.'

'But then, what if one of them was involved?'

Chris laughed. 'Sophie, you are incorrigible! It's a good job you didn't work for the Inquisition – you'd have sniffed out heretics all over the place. Especially in high places.'

'Where better to sniff them out?'

Although Chris had phoned Ian to get people on to the tedious job of trying to locate the tarpaulin, he decided, as I knew he would, that he wanted to get back to Rose Road and the heart of the investigation. But he didn't take much persuading to go via the garden centre run by Birmingham University.

He was staggering to his car under an enormous bag of all-purpose compost, and I was at the till by the open door paying for trays of petunias, impatiens, trailing lobelia and sweet outdoor herbs, when I heard a familiar voice.

'I was saying to my wife here – this is Sophie from work,

June; Sophie, this is the wife – you always meet people when you go out. Mrs Cavendish yesterday in Rackhams, though she looked as if she hadn't expected to find the likes of me there, and then young Darren down by the crematorium when I was visiting my old mum, if you see what I mean, and now you.'

'Hi, Phil. Nice to meet—'

June juggled two trays of snapdragons and a pot of sweet peas and shook hands with me.

'Like I was saying, it's funny seeing these old tills. Expect everything to be properly computerised – bar-codes and that.' He shifted a tray of young lupins more comfortably on to the other hip.

We watched the man operating the till count and recount the petunias, and I was just about to trot out the Brian Hanrahan comment about counting them out and counting them in again, when something more important occurred to me. 'Have you managed to crack Dr Trevelyan's password yet, Phil?'

'Went back to paper files in the end. Seemed to be nasty little close-down instructions on the program.'

'What'll you do? Take the thing apart and run it in bits?'

He nodded. 'And as I was saying, you can't wait. You need paper and toner and that when you need them, not when Her Royal Highness comes back to work. *If*, I should say. Not to mention computers. Need to replace those that were nicked.'

'Do we get many nicked?'

'Bloody shoplifting, that's what it's like. No respect, these days. Buy them ten at a time; only seven or eight left at the end of the month. Blame me and the team, of course. Lack of security, they say. But half the locks haven't worked for months, and you're right, you can report till you're blue in the face but no one takes any notice.'

Did I dare risk it? 'Who checks them in, Phil? When the new ones arrive?'

He looked at me blankly.

'Is it your job of hers? Dr T's?'

'Funny you should say that,' said June the wife. 'Had a bit of a cross word at Christmas about that, you and the lady doctor.'

'I told you, lovey, she's not that sort of doctor.'

'What sort of cross word?' I prompted.

'Nothing much. Not that you'd call cross. And like June said, if someone wants you to do less work, you shouldn't really argue, should you?'

'*Less* work?' That didn't accord with what little I knew of Trevelyan.

'Well, you might say less – though of course she found me other little things to do. But when she came, she went through all our job descriptions, crossing bits off here and there, and putting other bits in.'

I was almost screaming as Chris came back towards the open door. I willed him to keep out of the way a bit longer.

'So how did she change yours? What did she take off you?' I added hurriedly, afraid he might embark on a list – he already had his fingers ready to tick off items.

'Well, as I said, it's funny you should ask that. Security, for a start. Used to be my job, that. And I did it a damn sight better than her. I used to ID them in one of those pens—'

'Ultraviolet,' said June, shuffling her burden.

'I told you, lovey, it's the light that's ultraviolet, that you read it by. And she took responsibility, she called it, for everything to do with ordering. Everything. She said it was because of this incorporation business.'

Another couple of people were now heading towards the cashdesk. I moved us slowly out into the sun as I repeated, '*Everything*? So she decided what was needed, ordered, handled the invoices, signed for delivery?'

He nodded.

Over his shoulder Chris was listening intently.

'Seems a lot of work to take on if you're running a college department,' I said. 'On top of her teaching.'

Phil snorted: 'Her? Teach? No, that was the first thing she got out of. Tried to get me to do some, part of my new job description, see. Told her where to put that, didn't I, lovey?'

'Quite right,' I said. 'But you've managed to dig out enough of the paper records to know where to order new stock – that's brilliant. I had this vision of us all writing on clay tablets or something.'

'Some of the suppliers were a bit funny about supplying stuff at short notice, mind.'

'But surely, an old and valued customer like Muntz? Big contracts – must be worth a bit, Phil.'

'You can say that again. But seems we hadn't ordered from some of them for quite a while.'

'Since Dr T arrived?' I asked.

'Come to think of it, yes. Must have found somewhere cheaper, I suppose. But I can't bloody find out, can I!'

'No need to swear, Philip.'

'Sorry, lovey. Tell you what, Soph, I might just take a sickie tomorrow and see what I can dig out of her computer. How about that?'

I smiled encouragingly and then brought Chris into the conversation. Phil looked from one to the other.

'But you're the policeman.'

'Sophie's friend, too. Don't worry, I haven't come to arrest her, just to carry her petunias.' He took them from me, gave them back while he shook hands with June, and then took them once more. 'What did Dr Trevelyan do before she came to George Muntz?' he asked casually.

'Like I told one of your lasses, she never said much about it, her previous place. Sophie here, she's always saying, "We do so-and-so at William Murdock".'

I shook my head. 'I'm sure I don't mean to compare—'

'Only natural. Like I was saying to my June here, it's only natural you should compare the way Sainsbury's does something with the way Safeway does it. Right? But not Dr T. Mind you, she never talked to us much. Hoi polloi, that's us. Anyway, like we said, got to get on, ere the setting sun. And I haven't even got any slug pellets yet. Come on, June, what are you thinking of, letting me forget those? Here, put this lot in the car, lovey ...'

Chris laid a hand lightly on my forearm and we tried to look casual as we strolled back to his car. We were talking about the merits of different types of fertiliser when we passed Phil, locking his Escort's tailgate before heading back for his pellets.

Chris zapped his Renault and it obligingly unlocked itself. 'Sometimes I wish people were like that,' he said.

'Eh?'

'Point something at them and they unlock themselves. Your

Dr T, now: the medics say she's fit enough to talk but, believe me, she's keeping well and truly mum.'

I slipped into the front passenger seat; the upholstery was hot.

'Do you think it matters where she worked before? You could easily find out from her personnel files. Unless they're covered by the Data Protection Act?'

'Bound to be paper files. I'm just interested.'

'Interested enough to find out if they had spates of computer theft too? And if the records of the suppliers have disappeared with her?'

Chris started the engine and pressed the window-opening buttons before turning to me. 'You know, Ms Rivers, you really do have the most disgustingly suspicious mind.'

'I do, don't I?' I agreed affably.

I put the petunias and lobelias in big earthenware pots. They'd grow up round fuchsias I'd had in my shed over the winter. There were a couple of prostrate fuchsias for hanging baskets – one for me, the other for Aggie – and I tucked in trailing carnations and the odd petunia and lobelia. None of these would stay out overnight for a couple of weeks yet, not until there was no risk of frost, but during the day they could bask on the patio.

I was just going to pour myself a beer to celebrate a job well done when the phone rang. Chris?

'I was saying to June, she'd want to come with me. And I know it's Sunday, I said, but there's nothing on the box, never is, of course.'

'To see Melina's parents?' I guessed.

'So I'll be with you in ten minutes or so. You know my old car – I'll just give a couple of bips on the horn, save me getting out.'

The most appropriate outfit I could think of was my funeral suit, although it seemed rather excessive for a May evening. I needn't have worried, however: Phil was wearing the male equivalent. He hardly spoke during the five minutes' drive.

GOD LOVES ROTTON PARK claimed a large notice, but He didn't seem especially keen on the bit we were heading for – a little clutch of fifties houses squashed in on what had evidently been the site of a pair of Edwardian semis like their neighbours either side.

Apart from spectacularly white net curtains, there was nothing to set Melina's parents' house apart from the others. And I still didn't know their surname. I could feel the blush rising even as Phil rang the bell. With the sound of footsteps getting louder, now was scarcely the time to ask.

The man who opened the door regarded us with the least emotion I'd ever seen. Perhaps it had all been washed out of him by his mourning. His black skin seemed grey in the evening light. His whole body drooped, though I guessed from the breadth of his shoulders and heavily muscled neck that he'd been a fine athlete. He made no response to Phil's outstretched hand.

Even Phil seemed disconcerted by the quality of his silence.

'We've come from the college,' I said. 'To—'

'"*Blessed are they who mourn*",' he said. '"*For they shall be comforted.*"'

'I – I wanted to apologise,' I said. There was no help in his face for me, so I continued: 'I was one of the last to see her alive. She wanted to speak to me, to tell me something, but I was in too much of a hurry. I—'

'"*A thousand ages in His sight Are but an evening passed.*"' He put out his hand for the envelope Phil was holding.

'I was wondering – please—'

He turned to go in.

'Please, I have to ask you. Do you know what she wanted to talk to me about? Did she mention anything to you?'

He shook his head, as if he could hear little of what I was saying and cared less.

'I feel so bad – all she wanted to do was talk.'

'"*Know thou that for all these things God will bring thee into judgement.*"' And he went in and shut the door.

Before we could reach the front gate, the door opened again. An Afro-Caribbean woman, dressed in a navy suit as severe as mine, came out on the step. She raised her hand and then let it drop. 'He is a good man,' she said quietly, 'but they have taken away his ewe lamb. Blessed be the name of the Lord.' She too went in and closed the door.

12

I'm never a hundred per cent keen on Monday mornings, and as I strolled through the Martineau Centre's car park I could think of a whole list of things I'd rather be doing than going into Muntz. For a start, I wasn't looking foward to dealing with Sunshine and my office space. Then there was the interview with the principal. I hoped that Polly, the representative of the now derecognised union, would accompany me. She hadn't phoned me over the weekend, and I'd still not managed to contact the other project team members, so I could see the possible weakness of my position. On the other hand, armed with a dollop of honest self-righteousness, I was ready to do battle.

But not yet, it seemed.

Geoge Muntz's car park was seething with activity; there were more staff and students than I'd ever seen. My first thought was that there must be some sort of fire drill, or even another sudden death. But then I saw Polly and other NATFHE officials standing on the steps to the main entrance.

I'd only been on strike a couple of times, and they were well in the past, but even I knew that these days you had to have ballots for strike action, and to give proper notice to the management of your intention. And I knew too that picketing was strictly controlled. Since most college lecturers are moderate souls, I couldn't see this as some sort of illicit industrial action. Or, more accurately, inaction.

I found a couple of women I knew by sight – it struck me how very few people I actually knew – and wandered over to them. Before I could say anything, however, a megaphone sputtered, and Polly called for our attention.

'For those of you who've just arrived, let's tell you what's happening. Some of you remember signing our new contract at Easter. April the first - remember? Well, now we know who they were making fools of. All the engineering staff have now been given two weeks' notice. That's it. Kaput.'

There was a roar of anger and disbelief. Polly let it ride for a second, then held up her hand for silence.

'We can't ask you to come out on strike. Not until we've gone through the proper channels. We've contacted Head Office and they're sending someone down now. Bu—'

At this point the elegant and apparently bored figure of Curtis appeared beside her. He spoke briefly to Polly, then turned on his heel.

'Did you hear that, ladies and gentlemen? The law says if we're only partially completing our work, the employers can stop our pay accordingly. And Mr Curtis has just told me that if any of us are late for class, this will be interpreted as partial performance and we will be sent home. My students are three weeks away from their exams; so are yours. So I suggest we go in now, and I'll set up a proper ballot. We must be absolutely solid in this, or we'll all go down together.'

'Bugger the students!' yelled a voice. 'What about our future? What about our jobs? We want action now!'

'Action now! Action now!' yelled more voices. The chant rose and swelled.

The megaphone again: 'There'll be a meeting at lunchtime. Please come! Twelve thirty?'

'Action now!' A man stepped forward, fist in the air. 'We can't let them get away with this!' Tall, a shock of red hair turning rusty, he was a Viking ready to lead us against the foe. We applauded him, and then watched as the fingers of his clenched right hand uncurled, twitched and started to claw at his chest. He staggered back, his face contorted.

'Jesus, they've bloody shot him!' said a voice across the shocked silence.

For a moment it was almost believable. But then - perhaps we all realised simultaneously - someone called for a doctor, for a first-aider, anyone: the Viking was stricken with a heart attack. That was the last I saw of him, as he went down, surrounded by his colleagues.

‘Get an ambulance! Get an ambulance!’ We could see someone pushing frantically at the college doors. Dear God, they couldn’t be locking us out, not now?

I turned the other way: I could use my home phone. As I cut through the car park I ran, almost literally, into a police car. The face at the driver’s window was hostile, but when I gestured the window came down.

‘Can you call an ambulance? There’s a guy with a heart attack over there.’

For a moment I was afraid they wouldn’t believe me.

The news came round on a memo that appeared in everyone’s pigeonhole. We were all to lose an hour’s pay for noncompliance with corporation regulations. Those whose timetables meant they didn’t have to be in till later should draw the attention of their head of department to this fact. There was no mention of Tom Hendry, the Viking.

As an oddball attached to no particular department, I thought I might remind the principal of my timetable’s peculiarities when I saw him. I stopped off at Polly’s office to find her in a flat spin. She was crouching by her filing cabinet riffling through the bottom drawer with one hand, holding the phone handset in the other and making occasional staccato responses. I sat on the nearest chair with its embroidered elephant cushion and waited.

At last she put down the phone, and, still crouching, turned to me. ‘Sorry I didn’t contact you on Friday,’ she began, ‘but I was off-site all day. Examiners’ training day in Leeds. My people come from Sheffield so I spent the weekend up there. And then I come back to this lot. Monday morning with a vengeance.’

‘This business with the engineers?’ I thought there was something else, too.

‘Stupid buggers! I did warn them. Our old contract gives us twelve months’ notice; this one two weeks’. I told them – and all they did was resign from the union. Idiots!’

‘So why are we supporting them?’ I asked, thinking I knew the answer.

She stood up slowly, rubbing her knees as if they were painful. ‘“When they came for the Jews ...” If they start with the engineers, and we don't do anything, they can move on to other nonunion staff and then on to the older ones and then those with bad health records, and then ...' She shrugged. 'Do you see?'

Of course I did. 'Have you heard about being derecognised yet?'

'Can't do it. Not legal. And I gather the governors' meeting wasn't quorate anyway. NATFHE'll get their solicitors on to that. But—' She stopped and bent to the drawer again.

'Problem?'

'Some of my files seem to be missing. Not just union stuff – some of my confidential staff development records. And I know I locked it. I always lock it.'

'There was a drawer open when I popped in on Friday,' I said.

'"Popped in"? I locked the door on Thursday night. I always set the catch thing—'

'The snib,' I said.

'– and then test the door. Just like my mum. Always turns back and gives the door a shove to make sure she's locked it.'

'And your computer was warm.' She might as well have all the bad news at once.

'My God!' She sat heavily on the other chair. 'What the hell's going on? Why me? Do you know if anyone else has had this sort of thing?'

'Me for a start.' I was eager to tell her about the incursions of Sunshine. 'I'll try to find out for you. Anyone else?'

'Not that I know of. But then, stuck in a room on my own and working very much apart from the rest of you, I hardly know anyone to talk to. Not properly. And with exams coming up, everyone's working flat out anyway.'

The phone rang. Polly snatched it and barked her number. Then she slung it down.

'I really hate that,' I said mildly, 'when you answer and there's no one there.'

'There was someone there all right. I could hear breathing. Tell me, Sophie,' she said, getting to her feet and wringing her fingers, 'am I getting paranoid?'

'Just because you're paranoid,' I said gloomily, 'doesn't mean they're not out to get you.'

*

Polly and I waited side by side outside the new door, waiting for someone to admit us to the administrative section of the college; only the initiated, which didn't include us, the 'blue-collar' workers, knew what code to press into the lock. At long last Mrs Cavendish's voice, disembodied, told us we could enter.

'Miss Rivers? I recollect you have an appointment. But Mrs Andrews – there's no sign of you in the diary.'

'I asked Ms Andrews to come with me. To be present when I speak to the principal.'

'You're very late.'

'My lateness is unavoidable. Is Mr Blake free?'

'Mr Blake will not see you if you bring Mrs Andrews. The union has been derecognised.'

'Ms Andrews is here as a friend.' As I spoke I wondered if we might become friends. I certainly liked what I'd seen of her: a woman a few years older than I with convictions and a personalised office. But somehow I felt so impermanent, so out of place, at this college, I couldn't imagine myself forming any lasting links.

'That's as may be. But Mr Blake will not see you together. Nor,' she added, leaning back and smiling, 'as it happens, will he see you anyway. He's having his injections for his Australia trip. I'll book you in for this time on Wednesday, shall I?'

'Wednesday! What I have to say is urgent!'

'Mrs Rivers, Mr Blake usually only sees staff on Mondays Don't you appreciate that you're very fortunate to be slotted in at all?'

I bowed grimly. 'Wednesday, then.'

I waited till we were outside the gulag before yelling. Then, feeling better, I turned to Polly. 'What's this about Australia?'

'Well might you ask.' She sighed heavily and ran her fingers through her hair, which responded by flopping beautifully into place. 'In certain states in Australia – not all of them, not yet – the college managements have gone macho: the sort of thing you see here. They've gone even further: unilaterally cutting holidays, introducing weekend working with inadequate time off in lieu. Blake, of course, can't wait to see how it's done. So the miserable bastard's taken the entire staff-development budget for the rest of the year – money that should be retraining lecturers this recession has left without work – to finance his little trip. I refused to sign the paperwork, of course – don't think I didn't try to stand firm. I had the budget on my desk at nine thirty and at ten in walks Curtis with the principal's trip. I refused. At ten thirty I'm told I'm suspended for gross insubordination and sent home. At one I'm told the principal has generously reconsidered my case and I'm reinstated, only to find, of course, that in my absence all his Australian paperwork has gone through.' She slapped the flat of her hand hard against the wall. Peggy looked up from her crochet and Hector stiffened.

'Don't worry, Hector,' said Polly, 'I'm not going to destroy the place. I shall leave that to the management.'

By now it was time I went to my office to find out what was going on there. I'd managed to postpone what I expected to be a confrontation between me and Sunshine until about eleven. I ran up the stairs and strode briskly along the corridor. I wanted to pretend to myself that it was the exercise that was making my heart pound and my palms sweat.

The office door was open, and someone was in there. But even as I prepared to challenge him, I realised the intruder was not Sunshine but one of the caretakers. He gave the desk one last polish with the tail of his cow-gown and stood back to admire his work. All evidence of Sunshine was gone, and my room had been cleaned. There was a distinct piney smell in the air. I sniffed suspiciously.

'Bit of my body spray, like,' he said. 'Don't like the smell of them fags meself, not since I give up, any road.'

'Thanks,' I said, wondering how soon I could tactfully open the window. 'What happened to, er ...?' I waved my hand airily. 'The guy that was here.'

'Gone back to his own room, far as I know. Not for long, though. One of them engineers. All for the chop, like.'

'What sort of engineering?'

'Dunno. Something to do with plastic. I've seen him with odd bits of plastic, like. You know, shapes.'

I didn't. But I smiled reassuringly.

'They reckon as he may be one as keeps his job for all he's

new. Funny handshake brigade – see what I mean?' He winked hugely and tapped a knowing forefinger against the side of his nose. 'Lots of them in this place, of course – tap and they come out of the woodwork. Ought to be brickwork, oughtn't it? Gerrit? Masons? Brickwork?'

To oblige him, I chuckled. Perhaps with a bit of encouragement he'd continue.

'There's tales I could tell you – make your hair curl, they would. Now, there's the paper, for starters, that is.'

'What about the paper?'

'Look, I'm all behind, like, as Tessie O'Shea might have said. But she'd be before your time, of course. Two-Ton Tessie, they used to call her. This room wasn't on me schedule. Got put on at the last minute, like.'

'That was very kind of someone.' I smiled, hoping I wouldn't have to ask directly.

'Don't mention it, miss. All in a day's work.'

'Well, I shall mention it – I'm very grateful. It all looks splendid. And I'd better thank your boss, too.'

'Don't want to worry – ah! 'Scuse me, miss. Makes me feel quite grand, being paged.'

He switched off his bleeper and hurried out.

I sat at my newly waxed desk and thought. But before I could come up with anything worth recording, I had to go off to my class. *We are the hollow men* ...

I must say, I was surprised to see a set of police horses in the car park. There must be some appropriate collective noun for horses which I, as an English teacher, ought to know. When I was a kid, we'd been taught out of a floppy blue-covered book called *First Aid in English*. A troop of monkeys. A pride of lions. A something – something really quite poetic – of goldfinches. And we'd sat there in rows, a something of parrots. Now I needed a something of police horses. While I waited for the meeting to start, I let the somethings roll round my brain. What about college managers, now? A discord? A sleaze? A corruption?

I also discovered I was very angry. Who on earth could have imagined that a confabulation of lecturers would need such confrontational policing? All we wanted to do was talk, to protest quietly and constructively. I didn't want to believe those stories about the rhythmic beatings on riot shields, the chanting of provocative obscenities, but I might have to.

And then the word went round that we were to go inside. The historians had legitimately booked the conference room for a meeting, and we were to infiltrate, one by one, not as a surging crowd.

There was, of course, standing room only. Polly had to perch on a chair to make herself heard. Her message was brief. First of all, the news about Tom Hendry was promising. He was conscious, and the cardiac people hoped he'd make a good recovery. Concerning the cause of his distress, until we had held a ballot there was nothing we could do. Then she introduced a regional official, Seb, a bulky man with an enthusiastic beard.

He took her place on the chair. 'It'll take seven or eight weeks to organise official – *legal* – strike action. And remember that strikes cost you money and save the employers' wages bills.'

'What about working to rule?'

There was a roar of agreement.

'I think under present legislation you'll find that costs you more than striking. There aren't any rule books any more. If you refuse to set and mark exams, for instance, you not only harm your students, you risk losing *all* your salary for the *whole* period you take action. The same for refusing to mark registers, answering phones, anything. Truth is,' he said, 'we're pretty well impotent. If the miners couldn't win, I don't see how we can.'

I could hardly believe my ears: this was a union official whose job it must be to raise our morale. I had a terrible frisson of fear that even our union had somehow been got at. But then I remembered all that eighties legislation.

'To be honest,' he continued, 'I hope this doesn't come to a strike. Most reasonable managers – and I have no reason to believe that Mr Blake isn't reasonable—'

'What about Curtis, though?' asked a voice close to me.

'– most reasonable managers prefer to settle sensibly, without so much as an industrial tribunal. There is some legal action you can take, however. The results are through for the national strike ballot. The May strike's on! One day, just one day of *national*, as opposed to local, action, should help. Meanwhile, you have to work normally. Sorry.'

There were jeers of disbelief.

'Didn't this morning's memo convince you? We're not in the era of beer and sandwiches now, you know. And yes, of course it's unfair, we all know that. But I presume we didn't vote for them,' he added, with heavy irony.

At length we all acquiesced. But it was an angry acquiescence.

I got back to the sanctuary of my room exhausted after my afternoon GCSE class. You'd have thought that with so little time before their exams the students would have wanted to work. I might have understood it if their minds were too absorbed by the prospect of chaos taking over their Alma Mater slap in the middle of their exams. But all they wanted to talk about was some football scandal, which, since it did not involve a West Bromwich Albion Player, left me cold. Irritated and frustrated, I snarled them into submission and made them buckle down.

I was just contemplating the possibility of risking the canteen to get a cup of tea – the strong, sweet, milky sort that would have been anathema to Ian Dale – when the phone rang. A cool official voice told me that my Barclaycard had just arrived at my local branch of Barclays, and they would like me to collect it at my earliest convenience.

I checked my watch: I just had time to get to the far end of Harborne before four thirty. I'd come back to Muntz afterwards; there was still work I wanted to do on this project, and, since there seemed to be no sign of my co-workers, I didn't want to get too far behind. I dived out of the back entrance and hurtled to the bus stop, where the driver waited, not quite patiently.

The traffic at the far end of Harborne High Street was already pretty solid. Although there was a perfectly good pelican crossing five yards down the road, I gave no second thought to dodging between stationary cars, particularly when the driver of one on the far side of the road waved me on. And then, a quick, hostile roar of the engine, and he was on me.

I slapped my hand on his bonnet and leaped sideways. I'd meant to use his car simply as a lever, but the noise was terrific. And then I landed, awkwardly. As I watched, my left knee went in one direction, the rest of the leg in the other. The pain was exquisite. But then the whole lot coalesced: the joint was putting itself miraculously if agonizingly back together. I managed to lurch on to the pavement, clutching a lamppost to stay upright. The car was nowhere to be seen.

A discussion went on over my bowed head: although half were quick to blame me, the rest of the crowd I'd attracted were convinced they'd seen the driver wave me on and grin as he shot forwards. But no one had his number; one man thought he might have been on trade plates.

At last I forced myself to move. Each step made the pain explode, but now I was here I might as well get my Barclaycard, and persuade the bank to phone for a taxi. So I hopped and wobbled my way up the bank steps. Although someone was just shutting the outer doors, she let me in.

They were kindness itself: their first-aider slapped on ice and then strapped me up. The manager insisted on running me home. The only thing that truly pissed me off was that they couldn't find whoever had phoned to tell me my card was ready.

They couldn't find my card, either. And this was hardly surprising – a quick call to Barclaycard confirmed what I might have suspected. The card hadn't been sent out yet.

13

I kept a pack of frozen peas specially to use as a compress, and many a time had reduced an ankle swollen after a jogging mishap to a perfectly usable joint the next morning. I even had some tubular elasticated bandage, so I could support the knee when I moved around. However, it looked so ridiculous with the shortish skirt I was wearing, I changed into a pair of summer-weight trousers. Jeans might be regarded as inappropriate for the trustees' meeting that evening. I dug in the cupboard under the stairs for a walking stick. Damn it all, all I needed was a patch on my eye and a parrot on my shoulder. I was just applying some make-up when the front doorbell rang. The leg was definitely improving – I didn't have to go down the stairs on my bottom.

'My dear Sophie! Are you all right?'

Richard Fairfax. I hadn't been aware that I was in any way dear to him. But he stared at me with such solicitude I realised I must have forgotten my blusher.

I had also forgotten to clear the assorted rubbish from my dining table. I gathered it up with an impartial sweep – I could see membership renewals, a final demand, the Midshires Symphony Orchestra's programme of summer concerts, a card from my father suggesting I might like a weekend with him when I was next in Spain, and some notes I thought I'd lost for the computer project.

Fairfax regarded the assortment thoughtfully. 'A young person's table. It's only later one learns to be methodical, to keep one's affairs in order.'

I looked at him sharply. He was paler than I.

'A little tired,' he said deprecatingly, as if that was the price to be paid by a captain of industry.

If, of course, that was what he was. He was clearly loaded, but had not found it necessary to explain how he passed his working days.

'Whisky?'

He shook his head. 'Are you sure you should be standing on that leg?'

From the sofa, my leg propped up, I gestured him to an armchair. But he fidgeted around the room. I wondered by what standards he was judging my pictures and the framed sampler Chris had given me for my most recent birthday. 'My feet will seek the paths of righteousness. Catherine Mary Roberts. Anno Domini 1837.'

'How did it happen?' He pointed to my leg and sat on a dining chair, pulling his briefcase alongside him.

I explained.

He was suitably outraged. 'Which hospital did they take you to?'

I laughed.

'You mean you've ignored—'

'If I'd taken it to Casualty, I'd still be there now. And I'd be taking someone else's place in the queue. It's not terminal, you know.'

'I'll take you in after the meeting. I assure you you won't have to queue.'

I had a sudden and unattractive vision of him marching up to the reception desk and waving his BUPA card. I shook my head emphatically.

He was about to speak when the doorbell rang again. He sat and watched while I struggled to my feet, and I pondered the difference between taking a grateful me dramatically to hospital and offering the unobtrusive courtesy of opening the front door for me.

By the time I'd greeted Aberlene, and waited with her while Adrian and Simon got out of Adrian's lush new Mondeo, then explained to all three what I'd been up to and ushered them into the living room, Fairfax was just putting away his mobile phone. When the bell rang for the third time, Aberlene pushed me gently on to a chair and headed off. Simon darted out too.

Aberlene returned with Frank and the two trustees who hadn't made it to the previous meeting, but no Simon.

I greeted the three men as graciously as I could from a sitting position: Adrian; Michael Hobbs, an overblown man whose thick moustache and thicker neck combined to make him look like a species of seal; and Philip Berkeley, grey and nondescript. Hobbs was company secretary to one of Birmingham's few remaining manufacturing firms; Berkeley something in insurance. I never quite gathered how they fitted into the musical frame as trustees, but being in industry these days was supposed to make you an expert in everything. Now I came to think of it, more than half the governors of George Muntz and the other newly incorporated colleges were required by statute to come from commerce and industry.

There was a drift to join me at the table.

'No! Don't sit down yet! Not till we can see where's best for Sophie,' Simon called from the door. He was carrying my dressing-table stool. 'There! Just the right height, I should think.'

Adrian looked pointedly from Simon to me. I smiled blithely and, supporting my calf with one hand and my thigh with the other, manoeuvred into place. Fairfax moved himself and his briefcase to the seat opposite.

The meeting began.

I'm afraid that money has never really interested me for its own sake, and I suppose that Chris and Aberlene were right to suggest I wasn't very good at spending it. And my leg was beginning to think longingly of more frozen peas and more aspirin, so I paid no more than polite attention to Fairfax's proposals. He'd been talking about the advantages of broker-led investments, or something similar, when Frank, who'd been covering his agenda with extravagant and possibly Freudian doodles, looked up.

'How about investing some of the society's assets in that Newtown project I've heard rumours of?' he asked.

Fairfax looked at him coldly. 'I never advise organisations such as this to invest in anything with which I am connected. Now, if the orchestra insist on their ethical investments – and may I remind you how quixotic this is – I would draw your attention to the following items in the proposals before you. Page seven, I believe, ladies and gentlemen ...'

Aberlene insisted on making the coffee, dismissing me to the sofa, but Simon wandered into the kitchen after her. There was a quick burst of music; I presumed he was checking his handiwork. Adrian talked to Fairfax about something but kept looking at me. Frank hovered, waiting for a chance to speak to Fairfax, but it seemed to me he was deliberately snubbed. Eventually they exchanged perhaps three sentences, their backs hunched away from the rest of us, and Frank left without waiting for the coffee. Berkeley and Hobbs inspected me and my home with some condescension, and left a couple of minutes later.

Adrian lounged over to my sofa and applied a charming smile, which I found difficult to reciprocate. I could find no immediate reason for not liking him; could I be plain, old-fashioned jealous? Time would tell, perhaps.

Fortunately Aberlene and Simon returned with the coffee, and we managed to turn my lack of CD equipment into a conversational asset. Fairfax unobtrusively chomped a couple of large tablets and became more animated than he'd been all evening, describing the delights of his system with almost voluptuous gestures. Simon joined in. Adrian, presumably as ignorant as I, lapsed into silence, and Aberlene glanced from her watch to the window. Was Tobias too circumspect to come to my front door to collect her? I asked the odd question, and wondered if I might take some more aspirin on a very empty stomach. If only everyone would just go home.

At last they did. Everyone except Fairfax. This time the wretched man did act the host, ushering the others out. And then he offered to help me to my feet.

'You have to eat,' he said 'Le Provençale, I thought.'

I was too taken aback to argue.

'I booked a table earlier. We shall be a little late, thanks to all that talking shop, but they'll hold it till we arrive. You have a coat?'

'Hanging in the hall,' I said meekly.

He parked just outside the restaurant, on a double yellow line. I expected him to settle me and then go and find somewhere more legal, but he seemed unconcerned. Somehow I didn't want to hear what he'd say if I reminded him, so I kept quiet and told myself that anyone who drove a car like his could pay the fine as easily as I paid my bus fare. And I didn't like the thought.

On certain days of the week, Le Provençale had a cheaper, set-meal option, as well as the usual *à la carte*. Among the *table d'hôte* items was a salad with hot smoked cheeses which really engaged my foodie's imagination. And the chicken with cream and tarragon sauce appealed too.

But it seemed Fairfax wanted to order for me: 'Smoked salmon, surely? And then duck?'

At last he acquiesced, but with startling ill grace. He wasn't crass enough to say anything, so I was left to work out how I'd offended him. Eating my own choice of food – would that be enough to upset him on principle? Had I somehow implied he couldn't afford the most expensive? I let him have his minor revenge with the wine; I'd have preferred their particularly flirty Gewürztraminer, but it seemed we were to have champagne. Vintage, too. Who was I to argue? I'd better have the lion's share, too, since he was driving.

The conversation was horribly dull. I refused to mention life at college, because I didn't want another anti-teacher diatribe. The only response would have been to walk out, and I was in no position to do that. So we talked about the food before us, and the decor, and the future of Harborne, and one or two sites he saw as ripe for development and which I hoped would remain valued landmarks. Then he turned, with somewhat more animation, to my accident. He wanted chapter and verse.

'Truly, Richard, I can't remember much. I know it was essentially my fault. I should have used the pelican crossing. But I'll swear the man grinned when he accelerated.'

'What did he look like?'

'I don't know – all I remember is the wretched man's grin. Like the Cheshire Cat!'

'But the car, surely you remember the car?'

I shook my head.

'Surely!' he insisted. 'What about the number?'

I shook my head again. He would have pressed further, had

not Geoff, the proprietor, who knew me of old, strolled over to offer me condolences and a sweet. His suggestion, an extravagantly calorific ice cream, was inspired. Not just for the flavour and texture, but for the extraordinary effect it had on Fairfax; his face lit up and he started to talk about his youth and a particular make of ice cream he used to eat on holiday in Devon. I'd never before seen him unbuttoned, as it were. He talked solidly for ten minutes about his boyhood.

'No, of course you haven't been boring me,' I said, truthfully, when he interrupted himself to apologise. At last I'd seen the vulnerable side of this public man. Presumably it was the poverty of his early days in the Hospital Street area of the city that had driven him on to make money later. OK, as psychology it was pretty pat, but it gave me something to go on.

While he'd been talking, his sweet had congealed on the plate, and he pushed it away. More tablets.

'A touch of indigestion,' he apologised, patting his ribs. 'I'm too old to eat big meals late at night.'

My recollection was that he'd done little more than pick at anything except the smoked salmon, and his original glass of champagne had bubbled itself flat. But I merely smiled acquiescence. Neither of us wanted coffee or brandy. Geoff helped ease me into the car, which still reposed on its yellow lines, unsullied by a parking penalty. To those who have, shall be given.

The trouble is, I never can sleep after champagne. And that night, the questions kept bubbling up in my mind. What was I doing eating out with Richard Fairfax? What was I thinking of when I agreed to accompany him to the next concert at the Music Centre? And – this was the question that niggled most deeply – why should *he* want to spend time with someone so obviously out of tune with his own opinions?

At about three in the morning I got up and burrowed in the bathroom cabinet. In the depths lurked a little bottle of extra strong painkillers they'd given me after my accident. By now enough of the champagne must have left my system for me to risk them. I took two, and slept at once.

14

If I'd been back at William Murdock, I wouldn't have hesitated for more than a minute about going in to work. I'd have taken a taxi and somehow persuaded the lifts to work. There'd have been plenty of friendly, willing hands ready to carry things I couldn't manage while I was leaning on a walking stick. But I was at George Muntz College, just a hundred and fifty yards from my house. And the excuses for not travelling even that far sprang out like green leaves.

Eventually, however, my sterner self pointed out that my leg was so indisputably less swollen and less painful that I could hardly justify a day off. Not with things as they were. I ought to be in the thick of it, supporting my colleagues. I ought to be working on the project – any excuse that I could do exactly the same thinking and development work at home was a sad reflection on my lack of commitment – and I ought to be poking my nose still further into the Melina affair. And I ought to ask Phil what he'd found on Dr Trevelyan's computer.

So I was just about to cross Balden Road when a car pulled up ten yards ahead of me and then reversed sharply and dramatically towards me. The driver was out of the car, arms akimbo, glaring at me before I could look right and left again.

Dr Burrows: my GP ever since I'd been in Harborne.

'Get back into the house. Go on! Back on your settee and leave the door open. I'll get my bag of tricks and follow you.' She flung open her boot. Presumably she didn't worry about parking parallel to the kerb.

I did as I was told. I'd removed my jeans and the tubi-grip

by the time she swept in, flourishing her case.

I couldn't see anything obvious, even though it was my knee and I knew most of its bumps and lumps with reasonable intimacy, but Dr Burrows shoved two cold fingers on a place that made me scream.

'Pop along after work. See the physio. We've got one of those now. And a part-time shrink. And a guy that does hypnotherapy and a spot of acupuncture on the side. All mod cons. Anyway –' she gave my patella a final prod – 'she'll sort you out. Give you some exercises. Support and light exercise, that's the thing. But keep the whole leg supported for a couple of days, or it'll ache like hell.' She seized her bag and exited to the hall. Then she popped her head back round the door. 'Had an anti-tet recently? There's a campaign – more money for me if I give you one.'

'Had one last year. By the way, d'you need any jabs for Australia?'

'They may be descendants of the riff-raff, dear, but they're quite civilised now. I understand they even have running water.'

'Nothing at all?'

'Yellow fever. That's if *you* come from a country where yellow fever is endemic. Haven't had too many outbreaks in Birmingham recently so you should be safe. Australia, eh? I thought you teachers were supposed to be hard up. I'll fix you an appointment for that leg – about four fifteen? Shouldn't miss any classes at this time of the year, eh?'

I set off across Balden Road again.

This time the car that stopped was entirely familiar, and Chris slowed it quietly and undramatically, pulling up about three inches from the kerb. If he stood arms akimbo, it was momentarily.

'OK,' I said. 'Coffee for two.'

While he made it, I made a couple of phone calls to explain why I'd be in late. When I called la Cavendish I didn't mention the knee. Just that I was helping the police with their inquiries. The expression on Chris's face when he returned suggested he might have overheard.

'What I can't believe,' he said, 'is that you can't remember anything. You, of all people. Go on, you should keep that leg supported. All the way along.'

I reclined on the sofa and pulled a face. 'It was my fault, Chris. Just carelessness. I suppose I don't like remembering being a fool. What's the matter? What nasty little thought is polluting your mind?'

He shrugged. He looked round for something I could use as a table, but failed. He compromised eventually by reaching for a dining chair and plonking my coffee mug on that, just out of reach. He noticed immediately and shifted it closer.

'Biscuit?' he said, heading for the kitchen.

'Not for me. I'm not going to be able to exercise off extra calories for a bit.' But I took one when he brought them.

'What make of car was it?' he asked casually.

'It must have been an old one,' I said, 'mustn't it? After all, most modern ones have lowish bonnets, and this was high enough for me to vault on. Probably still got my hand print on it.

'Would it show?'

'Probably. On dark-blue paint – Chris, what are you up to?'

He shook his head. 'So, was it particularly dirty?'

'Dusty. And the idiot had those go-faster stripes down the side. And Escort in large letters. As if he needed to announce the fact … Mark Two Escorts are pretty easy to identify. Easier than the bloke, Chris. Truly I don't remember anything about him, except he was one of those irritating types who need to hold their roof on. Drive with the left hand, beat devil's tattoos on the roof through the open driver's window,' I explained.

'So you saw his hands. What about his fingernails? Rings?'

I shook my head. 'I'm trying too hard now. Let it simmer a little longer. Why the interest, Chris?'

He looked embarrassed.

'There was a cycle accident I never told you about,' I said. 'I got knocked on to a load of refuse sacks. Full, smelly refuse sacks.'

'All the better for bouncing on.'

'Lots of bad drivers in Brum,' I said hopefully.

'Oh, the place is renowned for them,' he agreed. 'But I suspect that, despite your well-known charm and tact, you may have annoyed someone, Sophie.'

*

I certainly annoyed Mrs Cavendish. Not because I had missed any classes but because I inhabited the same planet. She summoned me to her desk as soon as I got in, and I stood before her, just as I'd once stood in front of my secondary-school head teacher accused of the awful crime of playing cricket with the lads. Girls were supposed to stick to rounders, you see. Now, as then, I found I could keep my temper by thinking about something else. And the cricket season was just beginning.

'The *police*, Miss Rivers? It seems to me that you spend an unreasonable amount of your time with the police.'

'How infinitely superior to spending it with criminals,' I said, dead-pan.

I'd meant simply to be madly insolent, but I was rewarded by the expression on her face.

'What are you implying?' she asked at last.

'No more, Mrs Cavendish, than *you* were implying.' I smiled with implausible sweetness. 'Now, how can I help you?'

'I wish to remind you that you are not allowed simply to appear at whatever time seems to suit you. You are extremely late.'

'I telephoned my principal to explain,' I said. Mr Worrall had been only vaguely sympathetic; he probably realised I was calling him to protect my back.

I think she missed the pronoun.

'I took no call from you. And Mr Blake is not in his office this morning.'

'Another conference? Tell me, Mrs Cavendish, with a convenient centre just next door, why do Muntz's staff keep waltzing off to the Mondiale to chat? Must be pretty expensive.'

'We are able to negotiate preferential rates.'

I was enjoying this. It was a long time since I'd been able to bait anyone into betraying far more than they wanted.

'Oh, is Muntz like that Welsh water company, buying shares in hotels? This must be a benefit of incorporation the FEFC hadn't anticipated.' Thank goodness for William Murdock's principal and his useful acronyms.

Mrs Cavendish went pale. What on earth had I hit on?

The phone saved her. While she picked it up, I looked

around me, apparently casual. I'd left my stick outside, unwilling to give her the satisfaction of seeing me limp. After these few minutes on my feet the throbbing was becoming more insistent, but I soon found an excellent analgesic: two or three files stamped PRIVATE AND CONFIDENTIAL. They all bore the new George Muntz logo. I couldn't, of course, pick them up and read through them, but I couldn't resist reading the neatly printed headings. 'College without Walls' – that was quite a thick one. Then there was 'Newtown Site'. The top two almost obscured the third, but I could still make out the word '*Provence*'. If Mrs Cavendish would turn only an inch further from me, I could shift them to one side. 'Provence'? Not the sort of thing I'd expect to see as a file heading in a traditional further-education college.

I glanced at her; dare I risk it? But her eyes were already on me.

'I assure you,' she was saying, 'that resting a throat with tonsillitis will only make it worse.'

At the other end of the line someone expostulated.

'There are several proprietary treatments, and failing that you should be able to obtain an antibiotic from your general practitioner.'

The distant voice interrupted her, but she soon overrode it. 'All the classrooms have overhead projectors: I suggest you occupy your lunchtime making appropriate transparencies.'

She put down the receiver and, putting her fingertips together in an unbelievably complacent gesture, smiled up at me. 'I don't believe I need detain you any longer, Miss Rivers: I understand you have a great deal of work to do on a project that is already behind schedule.'

She contrived to make it sound as if it was my fault that my colleagues had been absent and thus, in her book, slacking. This time I did not bite, but smiled in what I hoped was a disturbingly enigmatic way. 'Don't worry, Mrs Cavendish. I'm way ahead on most of my other work.'

I always liked neat Parthian shots. But I've often been forced to regret them.

Someone had been in my office. I was sure of it. I told myself it must have been the cleaners, that to suppose anything else was mere fantasy, and settled to the more pressing problem of how to arrange my office to accommodate the game leg. Using my inverted stick as a hook, I manoeuvred the waste bin alongside the desk, and was just arranging the phone book and Yellow Pages across the top, knowing they would fall in if I shifted them a fraction off line, when someone scratched at the door.

Before I could answer, Phil pushed his head round and raised his finger ostentatiously to his lips. Then he beckoned me into the corridor.

'Have you found anything?' I whispered.

'Like I was saying, just you follow me.'

I hopped back for my stick, and then followed him down the corridor. I'd have loved to use the lift, but Phil legged it briskly down the stairs, so I had perforce to follow. He led me out into the car park. It was becoming a pleasant day, with the clouds beginning to thin.

'Walls have ears,' he said tersely. Then, as if noticing my limp for the first time, he grabbed my elbow to help propel me towards a bench. This was another reminder of the differences between George Muntz and poor William Murdock: if we'd ever had any benches they'd long since been vandalised into extinction. George Muntz had the sort of teak benches with wide, slatted seats that I associated with National Trust gardens. Phil had chosen to grab my left arm, so he was no use at all as support and the pace he set made me fear for the other leg too. I arrived at the bench with more haste than dignity.

'You should keep that up,' he said. 'If you let it sag, it'll swell up worse.'

So I had to recline like an overdressed Cleopatra while Phil first paced before me like a humble suitor, then, gathering his courage, perched on what space was left by my legs. 'Like I was saying, can't be too careful. You never know, do you?'

'Know what?'

'I was telling you, you can't trust people. Not these days. Electronics,' he said darkly.

I nodded. Then shook my head for good measure. 'You found something, then?'

'Could be something, could be nothing. Got past the password, into the list of suppliers, anyway.'

'Anything interesting?'

'Well, like I said Sunday, ever since I've been here, and that wasn't yesterday, I don't mind telling you, we've been to the same firm for our computers. Them dear old BBCs, your Amstrads, everything. And now we don't. Since Christmas or thereabouts. And you'll recall I said I thought the name of the new suppliers would be on Her Nibs's files.'

I nodded.

'Well, it was. So now we know where we've been getting them since Christmas.'

'And where do we get them from now?'

'Firm I've never heard of. PRT Computers.'

'You wouldn't have their address?'

'Only for e-mail.' He passed me a slip of paper.

Resisting the urge to memorise the message and swallow the paper, I thrust it instead deep into my jeans' front pocket.

'Like I was saying, doesn't do to hang around,' he said, scrambling to his feet. He hovered awkwardly, ready, no doubt, to hoist me to the vertical. I preferred to do it under my own steam.

We walked less urgently back to the main entrance. The sun was now fully out, and was giving everything a summer's glow of wellbeing. The cars in the management spaces were sleek, newly cleaned and polished, and someone with a sense of humour had parked them with consecutive numbers side by side.

I stopped. 'Tell me, Phil, am I seeing things?'

He shook his head. 'What sort of things?'

'Things like four Saabs in a row.'

'They're company cars, Sophie. Now we're a corporation we have to have proper cars.'

I glanced at him; I couldn't tell from his tone whether he was being ironic.

'Quite an investment in corporate identity,' I said. These weren't bottom-of-the-range models, either.

'Chief Executive; Deputy Chief Executive; Assistant Principal, Support Services; Assistant Principal, Financial Services,' Phil read off the newly painted boards over each parking space.

'Are they really doing enough mileage to justify communal cars?'

'Bless you, they're not communal. They've got one each.'
'They take them home each night?'
'You wouldn't expect them to walk, now would you? Not to Knowle and Lichfield and Stratford.'
'No. But I'd expect them to use their own cars! Unless they plan to buy me a bike,' I added, to lighten Phil's frown.

Before I returned to my room, I called in to Polly's. The door was closed, but she opened it to my knock. The sunlight flooding into the room behind her made it impossible to see her face until we were both in the room. And then I was afraid I might know the answer to my question: 'Any news of Tom Hendry, Polly?'
She nodded. 'Another attack last night. He's still alive. May pull through. But it'll be a long job, and he was one of those who signed the new contract.'
'The one the Trevelyan woman signed?' To my shame I couldn't remember her first name. Or had I ever known it? 'The one with limited sick leave?'
'That's the one. A bugger, isn't it?' she said, slamming her fist hard on her filing cabinet.
'Have you heard anything about her? Is she still bad?'
'Ena?' She covered her mouth, guiltily. 'You know, I'd completely forgotten about her. I know there was a collection, and I've an idea she's still in the Queen Elizabeth. Jesus, fancy forgetting that!'
I pointed to the filing cabinet. 'You've had enough to worry about. There's no sign of the missing files, I suppose?'
'As it happens, yes. I found them in a pile at the top of the stairs. Weird. Very weird.'

Despite a lingering sense of unease, I worked hard for the rest of the day. I managed to din some ideas into my GCSE class, who were clearly as tired of me as I was of them, and then dug into the project, making the sort of progress that leaves you pleasantly tired. I was in fact enjoying myself so much I almost forgot my physio appointment. I looked at my watch: four already. There was no way I could walk into Harborne that briskly, not in my present condition. I blushed at the thought of catching a bus for only four stops, but headed for the 103 bus stop anyway. This time the driver waited for me with great courtesy, and waited for me to clutch the grab handles before pulling gently away.

'Over your accident, are you? Must have shaken you up a bit.'

I could hardly believe my luck. 'Did you see it, then?'

'Your fault, of course. Should have used the crossing. But I'd say he drove at you. Smiled while he was doing it, too.'

'Didn't stop afterwards.'

'Maybe he thought he'd hit you. Panicked, like.'

'That's no excuse. Damn it, I'm young and fit. What if he'd done it to someone with a dicky heart?'

'Don't suppose he would have. Picked you out on account of your skirt. I dare say he thought it was a bit of fun – until you started screaming blue murder.'

'I never!'

'Wouldn't have blamed you if you had. I got a knee does that. Bloody agony. Patella, they call it.'

'Hope he's got one too!' I said viciously. We both laughed. 'Didn't notice his number, did you?'

There was a little tailback by the island. I prayed it wouldn't clear just yet.

'Funnily enough – it made a word. SEA. That'd be a West Bromwich number. Can't remember what year, though. Here you are, darling; and remember, mind how you cross the road!'

I could have kissed him. I probably would have done, if he hadn't called me 'darling'.

Aggie, my next-door neighbour, was weeding her front garden when I got back. If I wasn't careful, she'd be round doing mine, despite her seventy-odd summers, so I was glad I could truthfully tell her that the physio had told me that mild exercise would help the knee.

She seemed a bit offhand. I racked my brain for something I might have done to offend her. I couldn't think of anything, but I was too fond of Aggie, and too aware of her constant kindness to me, to want any trouble between us. So I went in to make a cup of tea for us both. Standing in the sink was an enormous bouquet, its stems secure in a cellophane balloon of water. Aggie must have taken it in. I filled two mugs and carried one out to her. 'Thanks for taking in the flowers.'

She nodded. We sat on her front step drinking in silence and watching the rush-hour world go by.

'Never came back,' she said at last. 'That man. To do your gutters.'

'Gutters?'

'You hadn't mentioned them to me. He came round yesterday. Meant to tell you; my memory can't be what it was.'

'What time?'

'I was just getting in from our Jean's, must have been about this time. A bit earlier, now I come to think of it. Yes, her Craig gave me a lift, so it would have been earlier. And there was this car parked outside your house. Just pulling up, he was.'

'Any idea what sort of car?'

'Our Craig'd know. Can tell you anything about cars, our Craig.'

'And he asked about my *gutters*? Had he got ladders and everything?'

'No. Just an ordinary car. Blue. Said you wanted an estimate. Thought it was a bit funny, like, because you and me always share things like that.'

I nodded. 'I'd have talked it over with you first, of course I would. And, come to think of it, I suppose they might need doing. But not by him.'

She turned to look at me. 'Something's upset you, me love.'

'What did you say to him?'

'Told him to come back when you were here. Didn't let him in or nothing, not after what that nice young Chris said last year. He said if I'd been here they wouldn't have made that mess of your house. He said I was the best guard dog you could have. Tell you what,' she added, blinking away her emotion, 'I'll get on to our Craig for you about that car.'

15

The rhythmic clatter of an old cylinder lawn mower pushed by one of Aggie's grandchildren made relaxing muzak to accompany my supper with Chris. He'd brought in a pizza and a packet of prewashed salad, some early strawberries and low-fat cream, and a bottle of Australian Chardonnay. He'd then exhumed a sun lounger from the back of my garden shed and insisted I lounge, if not in the sun, at least in the peaceful shade of a pleasantly warm evening, while he did the honours with the food. He didn't have to ask where he'd find garlic, oil and vinegar.

While the pizza cooked, he came and sat on the patio for a companionable drink. We'd been talking for some minutes about the chances of West Bromwich Albion scrambling up into the First Division before I remembered Phil's scrap of paper.

'Are you seriously asking me to believe,' he said at last, 'that you've had this all day and haven't tried the number?'

'There are some things,' I said mildly, 'that are best left to professionals. I reckon there's a can of worms there, Chris, and I wasn't sure it was one I wanted to open.'

He looked at me sideways. 'Come off it. What's this sudden aversion to worms?'

'Well, to be honest, I'd forgotten about it till a few minutes ago. And my computer isn't yet hitched to the great information superhighway. But I reckon there is something going on. The firm's called PRT Computers. I couldn't find them in Kelly's directory, though I suppose they may be too new for that.'

'PRT? Never heard of them.'

'I did have a perverse hope that it was run by the not late

but unlamented Dr Trevelyan, but I find her first name's Ena.'

I was interrupted by the oven bleeper; it made such an unpleasant din even out here that Chris got up. He returned a few minutes later with the food.

'And whence, since I'm being nosy,' he continued as if he'd paused only for a breath, 'that huge wodge of flowers in the living room?'

'I seem to have acquired an admirer,' I said.

'Another one! You don't sound very keen.'

'I'm not. Were I that way inclined, there might be things to commend him, like a brand new BMW Seven Series - and excellent taste in food and wine. He took me to Le Provençal last night. And, as you can see, extravagant gestures when one has a grotty knee. But—'

'I didn't think you'd have objected to any of those.' Chris's voice was hard and tight.

'As I said, there is a but. I don't like him. Don't even fancy him,' I added with more honesty than tact. It was not unknown for me to make a cake of myself with rich men, however unlikeable. 'Besides, he's much too old for me. And there's something ...'

'What sort of something?'

'Something about him I find unpleasant.'

'You have an odd way of showing it.'

'So what should I have done with the flowers? Put them on the compost heap? And last night I needed to eat and he organised it without asking me.'

'Not like you to accept something you don't want.'

'I wasn't in a state to do much else last night. And the food was excellent. But I can't say the same of his company. We have precisely zilch in common. And there's something else ... I don't know. I'll have to creep up on it and surprise it - like the details of that Escort.' I smiled, to establish friendly relations again. 'Do you think, by the way, it could be a complete coincidence that Aggie intercepted a bloke in a blue car last night?'

'Where?'

I jerked my thumb in the general direction of the front garden. 'There. About four thirty, I'd guess. You can check with her yourself later. I wonder if it might have the same number as the car that drove at me?'

'Sophie, you haven't—'

'No. But a 103 bus driver has. Remembered the letters at the end because they spelled "sea".'

'That'll be West Bromwich. What about the year? The number?'

I shook my head. 'Your magic computer?' I prompted hopefully.

'Oh, it was probably stolen,' he said. But the smiling crows' feet round his eyes belied the dourness of his voice. He topped up our glasses, and we were into friendship mode again.

Whenever Chris visited Aggie, I knew he would be made to eat something. She saw it as her mission in life to put a bit of flesh on his bones. What I'd never had the heart to tell her was that the first extra ounce would condemn him to an extra half-hour's running to get rid of it, so he'd end up stringier than ever.

While he was round there I pottered in the kitchen, loading the dishwasher and tipping the remaining salad into a lunch box. He was back sooner than I expected, however.

'What the hell are you doing? You should be resting that leg!'

'Mustn't let it stiffen,' I said. 'The physio said so. All her high-tech stuff and those frozen peas have done it a power of good. I should be back on my cycle by the end of the week. What's the news?'

'By some strange coincidence, that grandson of hers reckons it was a blue Escort with go-faster stripes. But he didn't notice the registration number.'

'You look like an expectant father,' I said. 'You go and phone Ian or whoever, and see what your computer will throw out, and I'll make some tea. Earl Grey?'

The computer, Chris said as we took in the last of the evening air, had offered a car registered in the name of Mrs Sarah Lloyd, a lady from Bearwood who'd reported it stolen from Tesco's at Five Ways. She'd loaded it with the week's food, including fresh fish, before locking it and toddling off to Boots on the other side of Broad Street.

'When she got back, there it was - gone,' he concluded.

'No further forward then,' I said, fishing the lemon out of the Earl Grey.

'On the contrary, I'd say we were. I'd say that you are honoured with the attentions of a professional hit man.'

'Lucky me. But he couldn't have known I'd be crossing Harborne High Street at that particular moment. Not unless hit men have psychic powers.'

'Sometimes,' Chris said, stirring his lemon round and round, 'they have luck. He could have made that call simply to make sure you didn't go straight home, for instance.'

'Or to get me out of my room at Muntz,' I said slowly. 'This sounds daft but, Chris, I'm sure someone had been in there when I arrived this morning. I told myself it must have been the cleaners. But I just had a feeling.'

He looked at me hard, then reached for my empty teacup. He gathered both lemon slices, spun them, frisbee-like, on to the compost heap, then stood up and offered me his hand. 'If you're up to a little light exercise I suggest a gentle stroll to the Court Oak, taking in Muntz on the way. Because you've left something vitally important in your room there—'

'Some fresh fish, like Mrs Sarah Lloyd's?'

'Why not? And you simply have to retrieve it tonight.'

As it happened, no one questioned our right to be in the building at gone nine o'clock. There were still some evening classes running: we caught snatches of earnest if hesitant conversations in a variety of tongues. Chris signed in, although the book lay unguarded on the reception desk. I noticed he gave himself his full title.

My room was just as I'd left it. I felt very foolish, but Chris didn't seem to need an apology. Quietly and purposefully he removed each drawer, sorted through the papers and returned it. When he got to the one I keep tampons and spare tights in, he tried to cover his embarrassment with a laugh, but that didn't stop him opening the tampon box. I sat watching, resting my leg as before on the bin. Then he made a thorough check of my filing cabinet, made easier because there was hardly anything in there: most of my stuff was safe at William Murdock. Chris looked steadily more exasperated. He pulled aside the curtains, ran his fingers over the window frames. At this point the telephone book and Yellow Pages did their inevitable collapsing act, and I howled with pain, in an adult and responsible way kicking the bin as hard as I could with the other leg. It landed right under the desk. There was no way I could bend to retrieve it. Shamefaced at my tantrum, I pulled a suitably apologetic face, but Chris was already on his knees. He set the bin upright again and put the directories on my desk without a word of rebuke. In fact, he seemed distinctly pleased with himself.

'Come on, Sophie. Time for the pub.'

'Will you carry the fish, then?' I asked, remembering our excuse for being there.

'But of course. Pray allow me!'

At the Court Oak we found a quietish corner for our halves of mild.

'Well?' I permitted myself to ask, after he'd opened an uncharacteristic packet of crisps.

'What would you say if I told you I had found a neat little transmitter on the underside of your desktop?'

'I'd say, "Gosh!" Or something equally inadequate. What'd you say if I asked you what it looked like?'

'I'd tell you it's a neat little plastic box, somewhat smaller than a cigarette packet. And I think I ought to tell you it's still there. If I'd taken it away, whoever put it there would notice it had stopped transmitting.'

'Why me?'

'May not be just you. Maybe your boss just wants to keep his ear to the ground.'

I swirled the last drop of beer round the bottom of the glass. 'We used to joke about that sort of thing at William Murdock.'

'I was joking too, Sophie! Industrial relations can't be that bad, surely?'

'Want a bet? Damn it, Chris, the principal brought in a bloody riot squad to deal with a union meeting the other day. OK, I know such a gathering's probably illegal these days, but for Christ's sake ...'

'I think that could have been a bit of overreaction at our end too,' he said carefully. 'Look, I don't want to talk about life and its rich pattern as lived at George Muntz. I want to talk about *your* life. Your accident may have been just that, but neither of us believes that a so-called gutterer prowling round your house had good intentions. And that bug's certainly not accidental. What the hell do you know that you shouldn't?'

I spread my hands.

'Sophie, someone wants to shut you up. Let's just assume for a minute it's something to do with Melina. Is there anything she said to you that casts light on all this?'

I shook my head. 'If only I'd made time to speak to her that night—'

'Don't start that again.'

'All I ever talked to her about was computers. Did you get round to checking her last job?'

He nodded. 'Her old boss even gave us a list of the firms whose computers she worked on. All respectable firms.'

'Big industrial secrets, though. Espionage? No, not Melina,' I answered myself. 'Tell you what, though: if she was doing the same thing here, she might have found something she didn't like.'

'And from what the people at her church said, she was the sort of woman who might have felt obliged to tell someone. What's up?'

I grimaced. 'Do you remember Philomena?'

'The lovely black woman at William Murdock? Who could forget her!'

'I had a word with her. I thought she might be able to cast some light on the church's attitude to lesbianism - you remember that suicide note? But she's become a humanist and I thought we were going to get tied up with female circumcision and I couldn't bring the conversation round to it—'

Chris laughed. 'What a good job I've got a whole police force to help me! Tina and Ian have already talked very nicely to most of Melina's family and friends. Why didn't you tell me you'd been round, by the way?' He didn't wait for my answer. 'Their conclusion is that she wouldn't have professed open homosexual love like that. They could be wrong, but they all seemed pretty certain. She seemed to be getting on nicely with one of the lads at the church, too. I know about smoke screens and all that, but he couldn't believe she was anything other than heterosexual. And, before you ask, he's got a watertight alibi for the evening in question: he was teaching a Bible-study class to twenty-three truthful Christian witnesses.'

'OK. I sit corrected. No need for amateur dabblings. Sorry. I just wanted to see—'

'A family devastated by grief despite their belief in the hereafter?'

I nodded. 'I suppose you're no further forward with the case? I must say, I'd have liked to see you a bit higher in the profile.'

'*Crimewatch*?'

'Why not? If it'd help.' But perhaps things were in train that he couldn't tell me about, so I let him off the hook. 'OK. Back to our *moutons*. This bug. What are you going to do with it?'

He gestured at my glass and picked up his. 'Another half?'

So he still hadn't decided. While he waited to get served, a couple of my neighbours came and leaned over the table. We talked late frosts and petunias and Warwickshire cricket for a bit, and then they drew up chairs and drank with Chris and me. All very relaxed and convivial. Except for that furrow between Chris's eyebrows.

'What I'd like to do,' he said as we walked gently home, 'is leave the bug in place. But I'd like another one – one of ours – in place too, so we know what information you're giving them. And I'm not sure how you'll feel about this, Sophie, but I'd really like to get your house done as well.'

'You mean bug it?'

'Keep your hair on. Just check for bugs, at least at this stage. I'll get your phones looked at too. OK, I may be overreacting. Just as you may think I'm overreacting if I ask to come in and make sure you've got no visitors now. Uninvited ones,' he added.

'If they've penetrated that alarm and all the other defences you set up last year, they'll be uninvited,' I said flatly.

He looked under every bed, in every wardrobe, with great exaggerated movements which reduced us quickly to giggles. At last we collapsed into each other's arms, howling with laughter. I gave him what was meant to be a friendly hug. And then I knew I shouldn't have done. The effect it very obviously had on him gave me ideas about ending my celibacy, but Chris would have wanted more than just a leg-over. Quite a bit more. And it seemed to me that right then my life was already complicated enough.

16

Polly and I were sitting on the bench that Phil and I had used the previous day, sucking fruit juice from packets. I'd used the sun as an excuse for leaving my room, but I did rather wonder if her office had had the bug treatment too. I could hardly ask, however; Chris would not be amused if I let anyone know what was going on. He'd arranged to meet me for a quick lunch, and, when he called to collect me, would no doubt be attaching his own device somewhere convenient. About such things one did not blab. If I were to ask Polly about security, she was bright enough to wonder why I should be suspicious. Clearly I'd have to choose the moment with extreme care.

For the time being, anyway, we were talking about Ena Trevelyan. Polly had taken the trouble to visit her in hospital, taking some flowers to augment the meagre bunch which was all the collection paid for.

'Did you know her well?' I asked. I sucked my fruit juice.

She shrugged. 'She's a human being, isn't she? That's what we're put on this earth for, after all – to do unto others ... Anyway, it's on my way home. I didn't stay very long. Not that she wanted me to.'

'Not want a visitor bearing goodies!' I thought of Fairfax's flowers – I enjoyed them even if I didn't rate the donor. And I thought of the flowers I'd so unceremoniously dumped at the hospital. I didn't want to tell Polly about that. Perhaps I might try again, if only I could think of an excuse. In my present mood, though, it'd more likely be an excuse not to.

Polly shook her head. 'I don't think she really wanted me there in the first place. We had nothing to talk about, anyway.

She was really rude when I asked her to join NATHFE when she first came to Muntz. Told me in no uncertain terms what she thought of unions. So I thought she wouldn't want to know about our goings-on here, and hearing about Tom wouldn't do much to cheer her up. When you come down to it, there isn't much to talk about except work, is there?'

I took one last suck of juice: the slurp and gurgle made me cringe with embarrassment. I crumpled the packet and slung it into a waste bin.

'I forgot to ask about your leg,' Polly said at last. 'How is it?'

'Much better. More physio tonight, then they'll see. It's not going to get me the sack for extended sick leave, anyway. Not like Dr Trevelyan,' I added, not quite guilelessly.

'Not her either, not any more. You could have knocked me over with the proverbial feather,' Polly said. 'Fancy Blake taking the trouble to write to her! In hospital, too.'

'Fancy la Cavendish condescending to type the letter! I wonder what her cure for mental illness might be ... Overtime and antibiotics, I should think. In that order.'

Usually Security would phone to tell you your visitors had arrived and you had to go down and sign them in. On this occasion, however, Hector brought Chris up himself – whether out of deference to Chris's position or out of kindness to my knee I didn't know. I rather hoped it was the latter: that sort of gallantry seemed sadly lacking at Muntz. Certainly he smiled and asked how it was progressing.

'Oh, I shall soon be on the move again.'

'My dad's got a dodgy knee,' Hector said. 'Does all these exercises for his quadriceps, but as soon as he tries to kick a ball he's on the ground crying. Had this operation and all. Off his feet for weeks, and then physio. But he still can't kick a ball.'

'Doesn't play for the Albion, does he?'

'Chris, you *know* they're going to be in the First Division next year!'

Whoever was listening to my bug must have had an invigorating few minutes. We argued football and progressed to cricket. We were still bickering agreeably when my phone rang: Peggy for Hector. He showed no especial inclination to take the call, still less to return to his post.

'It's so fucking boring,' he said. I coughed loud and long – it might just be a Muntz bug and I didn't want him to get the sack. 'Never any action. Now the police – that'd be something else, man.'

'I'll talk to you about it another time,' said Chris, laughing, but holding open the door nonetheless. 'Nice young man,' he said when he had shut it. 'Very helpful. I'd like to see people like him in the force. It was thoughtful of him to bring me up here, wasn't it? You were right about Peggy, too – a most charming woman. An efficient place, this.'

While he prattled, he opened the tampons and tights drawer in my desk, slipped in a small grey plastic box, unwound a piece of wire from it, and winked. He closed the drawer again and straightened.

'Lunch?' I prompted.

'Do you ever think of anything except your stomach?' he asked. 'And yet no one would ever know it, to look at you.'

I crossed my eyes at him and ushered him out of the room. 'Shall I set the whatsit?' I asked, pointing to the centre of the door handle.

'The snib, Sophie. What a good idea.'

'What beats me,' Chris said, lying back and looking up at a hyperactive squirrel, 'is why any reputable organisation should buy computers from an e-mail number.'

We'd come to Warley Woods, just up Balden Road and across the main Hagley Road, to eat what might be glorified by the term 'picnic'. Actually it was some overfilled rolls prepared by Chris himself, and a selection of fruit, washed down with mineral water which we swigged from the bottles. Chris insisted the grass was dry enough to sit on, but I'd preferred a single slat bench, on the grounds that he wouldn't need a crane to get me up.

'There must be more than an e-mail number,' I said. 'You couldn't pay an e-mail number.'

'You could tell it your credit-card number.'

'But there must be proper paperwork. Somewhere.'

'Ian and that technician – Phil, is it? – have gone through all the computer section's accounts. Not a sign.'

'What about the main college system? They must keep copies.'

'Mr Curtis does not seem keen to release them.'

'Can't you do something to encourage him? Like torture him until he does?'

Chris laughed, and returned to the vertical to peel a banana.

'Surely,' I said, 'you can trace someone's address through e-mail?'

'Sophie! I thought you were computer literate! No, it's not that easy. All you get to is the bulletin board.'

'But you have to pay to use the bulletin board. And I don't suppose you pay in used fivers. Must be a traceable cheque or credit-card payment.'

'But when you buy a service like that, you tend to buy privacy. OK, there are ways of doing it quickly. Fraud Squad – they've got some useful contacts. You'd better be nice to Dave Clarke.'

'*You*'d better be nice to him!'

'No need. I've already been nice to his boss. But since this isn't obviously germane to any inquiry, it may not be top of anyone's in-tray. And they've got very full in-trays. Meanwhile, I'd love to know where all the paperwork is. It can't have disappeared off the face of the earth.'

I contemplated my apple. 'If Dr Trevelyan's as paranoid as Phil thinks she is, I bet it'd be at her house. But how you'd get into it—'

'Don't even think of it! Don't let even the remotest possibility of it cast a shadow over your mind. You are not, repeat not, going to do your burglary act. Not ever again. Ever. D'you hear me?'

His face was absolutely straight: not so much as a twitch of a crow's foot. And I don't like being bollocked. Not like that. What I'd have liked to do was leap to my feet and stalk away I'd have to find another way of making my point. Without speaking I tidied up the food wrappings and put my apple core alongside his banana skin in the sandwich box that had held the rolls. There was room for the mineral-water bottles, too.

'Better get back to work,' I said.

'That burglary last summer saved a life,' he said to the

grass he was shredding. 'Another would risk yours. Sophie, for God's sake—'

'I don't know where she lives,' I said. 'I couldn't find out from college even if I wanted to – Personnel are apparently reasonably professional and won't disclose information about the staff.'

'So you had thought about it!'

'I hadn't so much as looked her up in the phone book,' I said truthfully.

'Please God, let her be ex-directory,' he said. 'Funny, how we no longer talk about a telephone directory – it's even called the phone book! – but we still retain that expression. I wonder why.'

If he had gone down on his knees he could scarcely be begging more fervently for forgiveness. I stuck out my hand. 'Winch me up, Scottie.'

We were sitting in Chris's car, outside Muntz's front door.

'Were you serious last night? About bugs in my house?'

'Planting them or searching for them?'

'Both, I think. The latter, certainly.'

I was always impressed when people like Chris could slip 'the latter' and 'the former' into normal conversation. There was a time when I thought he was trying to impress me. Now I knew him better I realised it was a natural preference for correctness and had begun to use them myself.

'Does that mean you're willing?'

'Does what mean I'm willing?'

'That long silence.'

I looked at my watch: I had five minutes before my next class. 'OK. You can check.'

'It'll be one of my forensic-science colleagues.'

'OK.' I didn't have much choice, did I? 'Better go. Here comes Hector to yell at you for parking here.'

But Hector had come to open the car door for me and to assist me, if necessary, up the steps. As I stumped off, clutching his arm, I refused to look back.

Later I hobbled home, my limp aggravated by my bad temper. As I approached the house, I was intercepted by Aggie, waving frantically from her front window. There seemed to be more excitement than alarm in her face when she opened the door.

She greeted me in a conspiratorial whisper. 'I've got a young man of yours here! He wanted the key to go in and mend something, but that nice Chris – remember what he said—'

'I don't need a body guard with you here, Aggie,' I said, wishing she were of the generation that hugged routinely. 'But you're taking an awful risk, inviting him in.'

She smiled. 'Thought I'd set him a bit of test, me love. Told him about my fridge – asked him to have a look at it. He's in the kitchen now. And Chris is on the way.'

How would he appear? With an armed-response unit? Or merely as a chance visitor?

Aggie opened the kitchen door with a flourish. 'Here he is,' she declared, standing aside for me to inspect him.

'Simon!'

He stood up and grinned, waving a pair of mucky hands. Then he looked beyond me to Aggie. 'Sorry, there's not a lot I can do with this. I reckon you're losing coolant. You could have it topped up, of course, but with CFCs—'

'Them's the things as is causing this global warming,' she said. 'Don't want to ruin the world for me grandchildren.'

'Right.' He patted the fridge. 'Don't reckon this owes you much anyway.'

'Ah. Be one of those as Noah threw out when he sailed his boat up the cut,' she said, grinning. 'Might as well go off into Harborne and get meself a new one – if you're sure he's all right, Sophie.'

'He's all right,' I said. 'But I'm glad you didn't let him in. Nothing personal, Simon. But it looks as if this –' I patted my leg – 'wasn't accidental.'

Back in my house, I offered him tea, but he declined. Aggie had pressed several cups on him and all he wanted was my loo. I tried to call Chris and his rescue party but couldn't get through on his own number, and the Rose Road switchboard was busy too.

When Simon came down again, I was in the kitchen. With a flourish, he laid a small wire framelike construction on the table. 'There!'

I peered. 'Half a mousetrap?'

'Toaster element. I spotted an old toaster at a car-boot sale the other week and bought it on the off chance. Well, sometimes they work. Then I remembered yours had packed up, and thought we could cannibalise one to repair the other. You haven't thrown yours away?'

I dug it out of the cubbyhole.

'Proper little Aladdin's cave, that,' he said. 'What's in all those carrier bags?'

'That one's for the bottle bank, that one's for foil, that's waste paper for the Scouts, and there's the aluminium-can bag. Oh, and the Oxfam sack. I never seem to get there in opening hours.'

'Sophie, patron saint of recycling.'

'Saint Simon, more like - spare toasters indeed!' I stuck my tongue out at him.

The doorbell. Chris. He was talking to Aggie from my front step, and as I watched, two patrol cars and a couple of unmarked cars drove off. Perhaps it was a good thing for both of us that we couldn't speak freely, what with Simon in the kitchen and possible bugs anywhere. Chris's voice was only just under control when I introduced him to Simon. Given that their relationship could have been one of arrester and arrestee, they seemed to take to each other remarkably quickly. Simon permitted himself one test slice of toast, and then bowed himself out: the MSO were playing in Lichfield at eight.

If Simon hadn't wanted tea, I did, and I filled the kettle. Chris put out the mugs and sniffed the milk suspiciously. I decided not to notice.

'Why don't we take this into the garden?' he asked. 'Is this the key for the patio door?'

I nodded. The possibility of someone listening to us was unbearable. And I didn't want anyone eavesdropping on my phone calls, either. When the phone rang I picked it up as if I might burn myself.

It was Richard Fairfax. I mouthed his name to Chris, who was dawdling over unlocking the door. He drew a question mark in the air and raised his eyebrows.

'Sophie, my dear, I was wondering if you might be kind enough to do me the most enormous favour.'

That was Fairfax: no messing around with preliminary enquiries about my health.

'If I can,' I said, cautiously: three possible listeners after all.

'My damned secretary – can't think what she was playing at: usually a most efficient woman. She forgot to diarise it forward for me or I'd have given you more notice. There's a function at the Botanical Gardens tonight. A reception for a Russian trade delegation. I wondered if it might amuse you. The gardens are worth seeing, after all.'

The Botanical Gardens were worth seeing at any time; that was why I'd taken out membership.

'Can you give me a few minutes? I have visitors and I don't know their plans. I'll call you back.'

He couldn't disguise the surprise in his voice: presumably most people agreed to his proposals. But he gave me his number.

Chris stolled down to the compost heap. I joined him and reported.

I suppose I expected a derisory comment about going out with a man old enough to be my father and my favoured makes of car. But he gazed into the humus as if considering a much more impersonal proposition. I waited.

'I don't think you'll enjoy seeing Gavin and his colleague searching your home. And as far as Fairfax is concerned – well, you might have an interesting evening.'

I stared. He smiled back, blandly.

'Have you got something on Fairfax?'

'Whatever gave you that idea? Surely he must be a most moral and upright citizen to be chair of your board of governors?'

'Board – oh, you mean a trustee.'

'I mean the governors of your college. Well, your temporary habitat. Didn't you know? Surely you should know all your governors by sight and name. In the interests of self-preservation at least!' He broke off a young shoot of rhubarb, sliced the leaf and root on to the compost heap and started to chew; from the expression on his face it was less sweet than he'd expected.

'In that case, I don't think I want to spend an evening with him. It seems he's not been entirely honest, to say the least.'

'I'll bet he thought you were just too tactful to mention it. Go on, let your hair down. That silk thing'll be just the ticket. You know, the one you wore at the Mondiale. But leave your credit card at home. Dave Clarke was asking after you this afternoon, by the way.'

'Hmph,' I said. 'OK. I'll tell Fairfax I'll go. And maybe it'd be better if you moved your car in front of Aggie's and arranged for Gavin to come after I've left.'

'D'you think he'd be embarrassed by the reception committee? Or would you be?'

I shook my head slowly. 'I don't know. I'd just prefer him not to know.'

'And you'd rather we weren't here, should you invite him back for a nightcap.'

It was either bite or not bite. It would irritate him more if I didn't, so I simply remarked, as I headed back to the house: 'If I've got bugs infesting the place, I'm hardly likely to have my nightcap here. No, it'd be champagne in the Jacuzzi *chez lui*. I do hope he's got satin sheets.'

A walking stick is definitely a conversational asset, though I'd not recommend one if you are supposed to be juggling a bag, a glass of wine and a fork buffet. Fairfax seemed to have brought me along as a silent, decorative appendage to match the silent, decorative appendages of the other middle-aged men. As such I failed miserably, of course, but my temerity in joing in conversations seemed to raise other women's spirits too, and I found that I was really enjoying myself. We sank liverish quantities of champagne, were treated by the peacock to a display on the terrace and were roundly abused by the mynah birds.

In fact we were so busy gossiping that we missed the function-suite exit and made our way instead through the hothouses. A shoal of fish rose to the surface of the big round pond, as if expecting to be fed. And then, silent and almost colourless, with opaque eyes and a blind, rapacious mouth, another figure joined them. Perhaps it was its sheer size - it must have been two feet long - that made it so repulsive. Or perhaps it was a reminder of another, more sinister world better forgotten.

The carp mouthed us silently out of sight.

17

Chris had left a brief note on the stairs. There was some good news to start with: his colleagues had found a tarpaulin after a hunt through rubbish tips, and yes, there were appropriate bloodstains, so he could push forward his inquiries. The second paragraph tersely invited me for a lunchtime pint the following day, which I couldn't help feeling sounded fairly ominous. We would meet at my house first, twelvish. Apart from this there was no evidence that he and Gavin might have spent the evening tearing my house apart.

I'd said good night to Richard Fairfax on my front doorstep. The question of coffee or more had simply not arisen. After a token sip of champagne, he'd been silent for the latter part of the evening, and I'd seen him slide a couple of tablets into his mouth two or three times. It didn't need the arrival of the monstrous carp to make him go pale. During the short drive back from the Botanical Gardens we'd talked in an uncritical way of some of our fellow guests and of his desire to grow better azaleas.

I swear that when I arrived at George Muntz I had no intention of doing anything of which Chris would not approve. But by absolute coincidence my college photocopying card ran out. We have a plastic-pass system to enable us to take up to two hundred and fifty copies; then we have to get another from Personnel. It was no longer a simple matter of tapping on their door and being let in. I had to battle with the sort of security system I'd always associated with blocks of flats. Although I was swiftly admitted, the service when I got in was nowhere near as prompt. Someone had just brought in her new baby: no doubt she'd started her leave before I arrived. There was, of course, a great deal of cooing and chucking under chins, which the baby bore with fortitude despite the fact that all the department must have been round it - probably fifteen or sixteen women. I looked round the office and, seeing nothing more interesting to do, plonked down on the nearest vacant chair to wait. Quite by chance I found one by a computer, the monitor of which was still full of data.

Down the left hand side was a row of names. Adams, S.; Ashcroft, R. B.; Atkins, P. J.; Barratt, S. R.; Blake, D. M.; and so through the alphabet down to Forster, who to my regret was E. N., not E. M. Between the names and the figures was a column of abbreviations: L, .5, MS 5; MS 10; Ch. Exec. It did not take much effort to work out that I was looking at a list of staff, with their rank and, by the look of it, their annual salary. Blake, D. M., Ch. Exec., £85,750.

Blessing the introduction of beautifully silent laser printers into the college's administrative system, I decided to print from the screen. I had a fair idea of what I might do when I got my new photocopy card.

The evidence was inescapable. The little grey plastic box sat accusingly on my kitchen table. None of us said anything. Finally Gavin picked it up and carried it back into the living room. I watched him stick it back under the shelf on which my phone sits. We exchanged glances.

'Pub, I think,' I said at last. 'For that drink you mentioned, Chris.'

The two men escorted me in virtual silence, not straight to the pub, however, but to a bench in Queen's Park.

'I'm really sorry,' Gavin said at last, as if it was his fault.

Chris nodded. He was slumped forward, elbows on thighs, hands drooping loosely between his knees.

'Have you had any deliveries recently?' asked Gavin.

I shook my head.

'Had your gas fire or central heating serviced?' he pursued.

I shook my head again.

'What about those flowers?' Chris asked.

'Aggie took them in and put them in the sink. In any case, the only bug they'd conceal would be the six-legged variety.'

'Are you sure about that? That it was she who put them in the sink? Not someone purporting to come from a florist?' asked Gavin.

'Ask her yourself. But I'd bet my holiday that she did it herself. She guards my place like her own, bless her. You've seen her, Chris!' I said, trying to sound positive when the only conclusion I or any of us could draw was that someone I knew socially, a friend, perhaps, had planted it.

'You cold?' Gavin asked.

I regarded my shaking hands with distaste. 'Probably. Yes, time to go in for that pint, I'd say.'

Chris shook his head. 'I think you should consider a few possibilities, Sophie. And they're much the same as those you considered when we found the device in your office. If we remove it, whoever planted it will know.'

'There's always a possibility that there are other, smaller ones around too,' said Gavin.

'Shit. Didn't you check? Or are you *telling* me there are others? Don't pussyfoot around. I have a right to know the worst. I live there, after all.'

'Let's just say, don't talk in your sleep.'

'Jesus!' I said bitterly. I found I was ready to cry. So I braced my back, and said jauntily, 'Any ideas, gentlemen?'

Lunch was relatively silent; I was too preoccupied to talk. My half of mild seemed lukewarm, and the sandwich couldn't tempt me. On the other hand, Chris and Gavin ate and drank with every appearance of enjoyment. After ten minutes I could bear it no longer. 'What you really want me to do is live with the bugs. And have some of yours for good measure.'

Neither tried to deny it.

'I ought to abide by your judgement. You're the professionals.'

'True,' said Gavin. 'But it's your life they're interested in.'

George Muntz was a-buzz when I got back after lunch. Everyone was clutching an A4 sheet of paper. Peggy gestured me over.

'You'll find one of these in your pigeonhole, dear. But you'll have to fight your way through everyone else to get to it. So have a little read of mine.' She passed me a familiar photocopy of rows of figures.

'See what I mean?' Peggy asked, over my shoulder. 'And you see that there? That's supposed to be his expenses: £25,000. Hmm,' she said meaningfully, while I whistled. 'And see, here's that little toad Curtis. Too-poor-to-give-to-Oxfam Curtis. We thought he was doing well to get £40,000, and there he's got £65,000, *and* £15,000 expenses.'

I pointed to the second Curtis column: Dep. Ch. Exec.

'Quite!' Peggy said. 'Getting that sort of job. I told you he's not got a qualification to his name.'

'An unqualified success, you might say.' And then I was suddenly serious. 'Are you sure about that? Surely you must need all sorts of accountancy exams to get to his level?'

'Well, you only need an art diploma to run the place,' she said tartly. 'That and a measly BEd. No,' she continued, 'Ellen, she was the receptionist before me, always swore that Mr Curtis never got above Ordinary National Certificate. Her nephew or someone was at college at the same time.'

'But he claims to be – got any college notepaper there? Let's look at the letter heading. He claims to be CIPFA and FCA. Have you ever mentioned this theory to anyone?'

'Never thought it was any of my business, dear. And in any case, even if it was my business, who would I speak to? Mr Blake? He always looks so harassed these days. Sophie, what's the matter? What have I said?'

'Nothing. Peggy, you wouldn't know which college Ellen's nephew went to, would you?'

She shook her head. 'And she died a year last Christmas, poor soul. Cancer,' she mouthed, as if saying it out loud might spread the disease.

I nodded solemnly, then added, 'I know this may seem an odd thing to say, but if you've kept quiet this long, it seems to me the sensible thing to keep quiet a little longer.'

I didn't rub my hands with glee until I got back to my office, and then it was a very silent rub. My little ploy had worked. I wouldn't have needed to use such underhand tactics back at William Murdock – they had a policy of open files on such matters, so if anyone wanted to know how much anyone was getting it was simply a matter of asking. Not for the first time, the tatty, underfunded old place glittered like an oasis.

I actually enjoyed teaching for the rest of the afternoon. At last I'd seemed to have persuaded the students that they, not I, would be taking the exams, and a gratifying number had produced essays for me to mark. I celebrated with a quiet, uninterrupted evening's marking at home. Quiet, that is, apart from Beethoven and Brahms played very loudly on the radio, which I carried with me wherever I went.

If the listeners had bugged my bedroom, I hope they enjoyed the World Service which I left on all night to provide a lullaby. *Today* kept me company over breakfast.

Most of Friday was a perfectly ordinary day, which I found disconcerting in itself. I'd have expected some repercussions from my activities with the staff records, but the college had sunk back into its usual sullenness. I taught; I worked conscientiously on the project; and at last I had one idea. What about checking Curtis's qualifications myself? Well, not quite myself. I wouldn't risk another visit to Personnel, but I did have another resource.

I found all the small change I could and as soon as I could decently leave Muntz headed for a public call box. At William Murdock was a colleague in the admin. team called Luke Schneider, with an unparalleled ability to pull figures out of his hat. He also had a long memory and a keen sense of justice.

He greeted me as if pleased to hear from me, though since it was only ten minutes before his weekend was due to start I might have been mistaken. Certainly he didn't seem to object that my enquiries after his health and wellbeing were perfunctory at best, and that I brushed aside his reciprocal questions.

'Luke, I have the longest of longshots here, but I want your help.'

'OK, girl, fire away.'

'I want you to check someone's qualifications. About fifteen years ago, say, and probably on some local government ONC course. The sort that could lead on to accountancy qualifications. I'm just hoping he did his exams at Murdock, but the ONC's all I've got to go on.'

'Fifteen years! But that's paper records, Sophie. We've computerised back to '86 now – but fifteen years!' Then his voice changed. 'Is it important?'

'Might be. I can't even promise that you won't be wasting all that time anyway.'

'Not so much the time, more my dust allergy. Look, I won't promise, but if I can find anything I'll call you back. Home or Muntz?'

I was about to say home, but then I remembered.

'No! No, I'll phone you, Luke! Don't try to—' But my money had run out and I had to hope he'd heard.

It occurred to me that if I had to live my working and home life within constant earshot of others, the less time I spent in either location, the better. Friday night was rehearsal night, of course, and then there'd be the pub afterwards. As for the weekend - well, there was a handwritten note from Richard Fairfax on my mat when I got home. Apart from brief surprise that he hadn't got his secretary to type it, my main emotion was gratitude. He was offering me a day out on the river. Which river wasn't specified, but I'd bet my life it wasn't Birmingham's mucky old Rea.

18

There were two messages on my answering machine when I got back from choir practice. The first was from Simon: if we were having a recycling competition (were we?), then I ought to go with him to a car-boot sale he'd spotted. He'd collect me at ten on Sunday. The second was from Aberlene. She and Tobias were now known to be an item. They'd like to make a foursome with me and Chris (would they indeed?) for a meal. And since when had George Muntz College, Birmingham, had an outpost in Bradford?

It was too late to phone back and ask what on earth she meant. I'd hung on as late as I could at the Duke of Clarence, though Luigi and Maria had left it to the tender mercies of their macho son while they went to a family wedding back home and the temperature of the red wine would have made Luigi weep. Jess (Brum for Guiseppe) had also let the jukebox loose. It was only the thought of the eager listeners wasting hour upon hour waiting for me to say something significant that kept me out of my home.

Still assisted by the World Service I slept deeply, only to be woken by my alarm. Saturday, and I'd set the alarm? I slapped it irritably but then heard the paper arrive. And soon I realised it was a sunny day and I was supposed to be spending it with Richard Fairfax. I'd set the alarm because he hadn't mentioned what time he'd be collecting me. For once it had nothing to do with my irritating overpunctuality; I simply didn't choose to be caught dishevelled and off guard with sleep.

As it was, I was very dishevelled and completely off guard

after showering and washing my hair when the doorbell rang. Surely not Fairfax already? I was tempted to let it ring; but then, at this hour, it might simply be the postman. Decent in my dressing gown, but my hair dripping because I'd put down my towel somewhere, I hurtled down the stairs. Not Fairfax; not the postman: Dave Clarke, he of the jeans and genitals, stood there. He stepped uninvited into the hall.

'News for you, sweetheart,' he said. 'About your big fraud case.' His voice rang out as if he were giving advice to a striker at the Hawthorns.

'Come on in. Make yourself some coffee,' I said, pointing him in the direction of the mugs. 'I'll be down in a minute.'

I put on the sort of jeans that wouldn't disgrace me. My trainers were new anyway, though of course they should have been espadrilles. I had a terrible feeling that I probably ought to look cutely nautical, with a little anchor motif in a prominent place on a horizontally striped T-shirt, but my wardrobe was sadly lacking: I found I didn't have a navy-blue blazer, either. Actually, now I came to think of it, a neatly cut jacket wouldn't come amiss. I felt spring coming on, and with it a strong desire to buy clothes. Meanwhile, I towelled my hair a little drier, and prayed that Roy's cut would carry it through.

'Did anyone ever tell you how sexy you look with your hair all tousled?' Dave bellowed.

Clearly Chris hadn't told him about the bug; did this mean I shouldn't either?

'It's a nice morning,' I said. 'Why don't we take this out on the patio?'

'Good idea. Might as well take some toast too. Honey or marmalade?' he asked, opening and shutting cupboard doors. He reached for both.

'Would you like to join me for breakfast, Mr Clarke?' I asked sarcastically.

'Thought you'd never ask, sweetheart.'

I shut the patio door carefully behind us. Surely that would be insulation enough? But then, I might not hear the doorbell. Hang the doorbell!

'OK, shoot,' I said.

'The Mondiale, right? With that lucky bastard Chris? You sure picked one hell of a waiter to pass your Barclaycard to.

Photographic memory, he's got. One look at your number and it's there.' He patted his temple. 'So when he's bowed you nicely off the premises – and I bet you left him a fat tip – he slopes off and makes a phone call. There's a pay phone for staff use. And he tells his contact all about your card. So they go off and make another card with your number and name.'

'But they'd need more than that: what about my signature?'

'On the carbon, of course.'

'And all that gubbins on the magnetic strip on the back?'

'Oh, they'd use someone else's info for that. Your details on the front, but someone else's gold-account details on the back. I take it –' he paused delicately – 'that your credit limit wouldn't run to an Audi? A nice, new, shiny Audi, not a beat-up wreck from down the Soho Road?'

'You take it correctly.' I waited. Surely neither lust nor a simple desire to report on a job well done had brought him out before nine on a Saturday. 'It's very kind of you to come and tell me all this,' I said at last.

He leaned forward, pushing his plate and mug to the middle of the table. Suddenly he was transformed into the sort of professional Chris would have approved. When he looked at me his gaze was shrewd, appraising.

'You're a bright woman,' he said. 'I only fancy bright women, come to think of it. Anyway, I wanted to ask a favour. I had a drink with a bloke the other day. In your line of country. Colleges. He reckoned his gaffer was –' he gestured expansively – 'let's just call it being a bit creative in his accounting. Claiming money from somewhere for students he didn't have, that sort of thing. Where do colleges get their money from, now they've left the local education departments? The FEFC, right?'

'Yes. Further Education Funding Council. Colleges have become more like a business. The more bums on seats, the more money.'

'Well, these seem to be real seats, but rather small bums,' Dave said. 'This guy reckons his boss has enrolled all his staff's children on to courses. And the kids in the crèche too. And they get extra money for them because they can't read or write – something like that.'

I nodded. 'Special Needs students, they call them. Lots of

extra dosh, I should think. A friend of mine teaches at a place where they've got a load of blind students: she reckons the money they've brought in paid for...'

'Go on.'

'She was only joking, of course.'

'And she reckoned the money had been spent on something other than these blind people? Hmm. OK, Sophie, that's only hearsay anyway. But you've got a foot in two colleges, right? Let's just say, if you come across anything at George Muntz that you don't think they'd do at your old place, you'll phone me and we'll have that drink you promised me. And make sure you're wearing those jeans, eh? Didn't realise anyone so short could have such long legs.'

For anyone else I'd have brought fresh rolls and salad and drinks as my contribution. But not for Fairfax. I had a sense that he would want it to be his set piece – in reality, probably organised by his secretary – and that he'd think the less of me for my interference. And I also felt quite strongly that he wanted my company more than I wanted his, and that I was therefore absolved from making much effort.

When Fairfax presented himself at ten, I thought he was coming to call the day off. His face took me back to my mother's illness; it was grey and glossy with sweat. He wasn't the sort of person to appreciate a rash enquiry into his health, but my face must have shown my concern.

He managed a pallid smile. 'Damned shellfish,' he said. 'Only takes one to be off, they say.'

'But—'

'Complained, of course: getting the public-health people in. Not that they'll do anything except talk. That's all you get from these people.'

His bitterness was like Mum's too. Suddenly I heard her voice: 'You'll need a sweater. Can be cold on the water.' And yet the nearest she ever got to the water was the towpath of a cut.

If Mum had lived, she'd have been about his age. What was I doing with a man not much younger than my dad? Going out for a day on the river, that's all, Mum. And keeping my eyes and ears open for Chris. It wasn't because I was attracted to the man; this wasn't the sort of dislike that indicates, Mills and Boon-like, a deep fascination for a dominant, sexy male. This was complete incomprehension, not least of why he should want my company. The word 'using' crept unbidden into my mind. If I were using him, to get me out of my house for the day, how was he using me?

He hadn't got round to telling me where he was taking me, but we slipped out of the city as if we were heading to the M5. Worcester? No, we took the A456 and picked up the Halesowen bypass. This is a good, fast road, but I was surprised when he chose to take it at ninety. Even when obeying the speed limits in Hagley or Blakedown, he was still of the Boadicea school of motoring, intent on pushing his way through no matter what the hazard. I braked hard on the carpet, time and again, yards before he did it for real. My knee ached with the effort. He took the downhill dual carriageway to Kidderminster at a hundred and ten.

I have no idea how much Fairfax's boat must have cost, but it was the biggest in the marina at Stourport by several feet in every direction. Stourport is a long way from the sea but the term 'ocean-going' seemed appropriate. Did you really need radar and what appeared to be sophisticated electronics for a boat meant to chug up and down a peaceful river? Or would Fairfax pay as little attention to the speed limit on the river as to the one on the roads?

He certainly didn't approve of our fellow navigators. He found fault with the way a flimsy-looking little cruiser was taking the lock below Stourport. He didn't like the line people took round bends. If he saw one casting, he would castigate fishermen. Which made it all the odder that he should choose to stop for lunch at Hampstall, at a pub swarming with them.

It was warm enough to sit on the terrace facing the river. Half of bitter, a satisfying ploughman's: only the good companionship was lacking. Fairfax was less pale, but the hand lifting his glass of tonic to his lips for invalid-size sips shook from time to time. A rowdy gang of Black Country lads jostled round the other table, yelling what I presume was the jargon of fishing. The noise made him wince. He pushed away his specially prepared omelette half-eaten.

I excused myself and headed for the loo. I stared a long

time at my reflection in the mirror. There was nothing wrong with my make-up, or even my maltreated hair, which responded willingly to a quick brush. Yes, I was afraid, not just of his driving, but what now seemed a risk of his collapsing at the wheel at the sort of speeds he'd been using. And then I grinned at myself. After all, I could always offer to drive.

Fairfax was at the bar, arguing about something. Change? A man drove a car and a boat like his, and he argued about change?

But he smiled with an amazing sweetness when he turned and saw me, proffering a courtly arm. 'And now I'm entirely at your disposal, my dear. What shall it be? A little further on the river, or a short constitutional?'

Further down the river meant a longer journey back. I gestured to a path. We'd only gone ten yards down it when I realised it was familiar. I stopped short and looked around me.

'You know these parts?' he asked casually.

'Never. Or perhaps it's *déjà vu*. No, I'm sure I've been this way before. That pub, the talk of fish; now this path ... Where are we heading?'

He shrugged. Nowhere in particular.

The path was worn to mud, and slippery. I was afraid for my knee and for him. But now he seemed brighter, and was pointing out wild flowers by name, and Latin name at that. As the path opened on to a field, he gestured to a red cliff opposite. 'Old red sandstone. Devonian.'

The field itself was waterlogged, and it was silly to venture further. But at least I knew when I'd been there before – to visit my great-aunt, who owned one of the shambles of little wooden bungalows over to my left. A vicious old Brummie who couldn't speak a civil word to my father, a foreigner from Durham.

'You see that place over there?' Fairfax asked suddenly. 'The converted railway carriage? My mother owned that. She used to rent it out to characters like that yob –' he pointed to a man laden with rods – 'so she could afford to spend her two weeks in the summer here. All she ever hoped for. In the days before all this planning,' he added suddenly. 'Paper for this, sweeteners for that. And you end with this charming scene.'

I risked a glance: no, he wasn't being ironic. To me it was a straggling mishmash of styles and colours that would have given any right-minded planner heart failure. But I held my peace. And for some reason, I said nothing about my great-aunt, either.

The walk back drained his colour once again, and I thought it no more than civil to offer to make him a cup of tea in his own little galley. The quality of the fittings, the elegance of the furnishings, the dense carpets throughout the boat, all led me to expect good-quality tea. I found round tea bags and powdered milk. The cups were china, but the washing-up liquid so cheap and indeed nasty I hesitated to use it. The kitchen roll was so hard it absorbed virtually nothing when I tried to mop up my slops.

When Fairfax offered to let me steer, he pretended it would be a treat for me, and I accepted in the same spirit. And it *was* a treat. With another, fitter man, I might have suggested turning the vessel round and heading down the Severn, plunging to the open sea.

19

Fairfax rocked as he stepped ashore, and I had to take his elbow to steady him. It was the sort of impersonal gesture you'd make to someone old or infirm. I wondered if he'd resent it. I released my grip as soon as I thought it was safe – he made some comment about still having his sea legs, but didn't otherwise acknowledge what I'd done. And he set off at a spanking pace, as if to prove that any aberration was only temporary. Not that it took all that much effort to cover the twenty yards to his car. I wondered again about driving it. He was the sort of man to resent any implication that he wasn't up to driving, but apart from his unsteadiness he'd been chomping those tablets of his at a prodigious rate which suggested he was in too much pain to concentrate. If he intended to drive at his earlier pace, I'd rather walk. He might well respond to a kittenish request to try his big car, but in general I'm not a kittenish person. I could manage wistfulness, perhaps – the sort of covetousness a young man in my situation might show. And walking round to the driver's side might be a good way to start.

I peered inside.

The trouble was, I'd never driven anything as big as this. My most recent car, a Renault eventually consigned to that great car park in the sky, would probably have fitted into this thing's boot. Hell, even if I drove along at dictation speed it would be safer than letting him loose – and furthermore, think of the satisfaction I would be giving all those people whose Saturday afternoon would be made if they could overtake something like this...

Fairfax zapped it with his key, and the locks clicked politely.

'I have to ask,' I said at last, since he clearly expected me to retreat to my own side. 'Where's the handbrake?'

He gave a short laugh and opened the driver's door. He slid on to the driver's seat and patted what looked like a little drawer on the dash. 'And there's a foot control too. See?'

'Ah. So why isn't it in the usual place?'

'Too many other things there.'

'And what's that lot on the steering wheel?' I had never seen a steering wheel so encumbered.

'The controls for the radio and the CD player, of course. And for the phone. Why d'you ask? You're not thinking of buying one?' If he meant it as a joke, it came out more like a put-down.

'On my salary? No, I'm just interested in cars. And I'm going to have to get one.' The conversation with Aberlene, the promise to Chris to test-drive, seemed a long time ago. But I could talk to Fairfax about it. It might give us a point of contact.

'On the subject of salary, what's all this asinine business at your college? Some joker circulating details of the senior staff's pay?'

I walked slowly round to the passenger door and sat down, though my knee had suddenly started to hurt too much to do it gracefully. I shut the door firmly: it would have been petty to slam it.

'Well?' he prompted.

This was going to be an interesting conversation. He'd never declared his role at George Muntz – it was only thanks to Chris I knew about it – and it suddenly and unpleasantly occurred to me that while I was keeping my eyes open for Chris, Fairfax might be doing the same on his own account.

'Have you heard about that, then?' I exclaimed like a stage ingénue. 'It was all over the college, of course, but . . .' I let my voice trail. I wanted to imply that doings at a little place like ours would be of no interest to those in the real world.

'Of course it was all over the college. Whoever did it was completely irresponsible. Mishandling confidential information. The bastard should be sacked.'

'How come you got to hear about it?' I pursued.

'My dear child, of course I got to hear about it. Your principal telephoned me immediately. I was able to assure him that I would support him in whatever disciplinary action he wanted to take. Summary dismissal, I'd have thought, for gross insolence. He'd be well within his rights, I told him.'

I was glad my principal was safely at William Murdock: he certainly wouldn't approve of what I'd done, and I might get a wigging through which I'd have to stand, but that was all. As far as I knew there were only two ways I could get the sack: seducing a student or forging an official class register. 'Are you sure? About this sacking business?'

'Surely you read the contract before you signed it?' He started the engine and lifted that handbrake drawer.

'I haven't signed it – I haven't been asked to. I'm not employed by George Muntz, remember. I'm merely seconded there from William Murdock – on account,' I added dryly, 'of my computer expertise.'

He turned in his seat to stare at me.

'And,' I continued, ' I shall be glad to get back there. Whoever's in charge of George Muntz is doing a pretty poor job. If you've got anything to do with the place, you should tell him so.' This was scarcely the conversation I'd intended to have, and scarcely one calculated to stop him driving like Attila late for an invasion.

'Lack of discipline, you mean?'

'Quite the reverse.' It was clearly time someone blew the whistle on the place, and no one would have a better opportunity. If necessary I'd get back to Brum on the train. I launched into a repeat, with variations, of last Sunday morning's diatribe. 'Look, you have a talented group of people who've been doing very well for the place as far as I can see. Then someone gives senior staff the idea they're Managers with a capital M and lets them have all sorts of freedom they're not equipped for. Look at the salaries they've given themselves; look at their so-called expenses. Worse still, they've taken it upon themselves to bugger around with the rights of their colleagues. No, all I want to do is get back to William Murdock.'

'That tatty, out-at-elbows place!'

'"She was poor but she was honest!" OK, we don't have Muntz's facilities. But we're all in it together, rows of little Dutch boys with our thumbs in the dyke. And the boss's thumb's there alongside ours.' I rather surprised myself with my nostalgia for the place.

He was silent, concentrating apparently on the awkward, bumpy lane.

I'd meant to let him reveal that he was chair of Muntz's governors but he'd shown no sign of it, and I felt suddenly impatient. Resuming a more languid air, I turned to him. 'Tell me, what *is* your connection with Muntz?'

'I don't believe you don't know. I'm one of the governors.'

'The Chair. I think you should have told me, right at the start. I might have been terribly indiscreet.'

He laughed. 'How would you describe your last few minutes if not as indiscreet?'

'Ah, but I *meant* to say all those things. Because someone had to. And I repeat, you should have told me. Better still, actually, I should have seen your picture in the foyer so I could have recognised you. All the bigwigs should have them. They've just done it at William Murdock – it means everyone from the students to the porters, not to mention visitors, knows who's who.'

At last on the main road, he accelerated briskly. I sighed with envy. Or possibly fear.

'I do believe,' he said at last, 'that *you* wanted to drive this thing. Didn't you? Like you did the *Marilyn*.'

So the boat had a name, did it? I should have taken more notice.

'I'd love to,' I said, as if he'd just given me a formal invitiation.

He laughed again. 'Have you any idea how to drive something like this? A five-litre engine?'

'No. But as they say in another context, it'd be fun finding out.'

'I do believe you mean it. I really do believe it. Alas, my dear, you'll have to preserve your soul in patience: I'm very much afraid it's insured exclusively for Me.'

I could almost see the capital letter.

'And for my chauffeur, of course.'

I shrugged lightly.

'But a simple telephone call to my insurance broker—'

'Even your broker must have Saturday afternoon off,' I said, as the number rang and rang. 'And there are plenty of days beside today.'

'You're wrong. You mustn't think that way! The only way to live is as if this is your last day. But then, you must also act as if you're going to live for ever. That's the secret.'

There's a bit in the Bible where the Devil takes Jesus up on to a high mountain and shows him everything he can possess if only he accepts the Devil as boss. That's how it was beginning to feel, seeing all Richard Fairfax's kingdom. I'd been shown his car, his boat; now I was to see his house. I didn't want to see it; I wanted to go home and resume my normal life. I only agreed because he said he needed to pick up some more medication and I could quite see he needed it. He'd taken one phone call which seemed to upset him, from a man who didn't give his name. He just announced that the work was incomplete because William had turned up unexpectedly.

'Finish it as soon as he's gone,' Fairfax barked. And then had started to press his stomach as if to push away the pain.

'You really ought to take it easier if you've got an ulcer,' I said mildly.

'I do not have an ulcer.'

'But—'

'My dear young lady, I do not have an ulcer. Do you wish to see the X-rays? Stress, that's all that's the matter. And stress, in my position, comes with the territory.'

I couldn't argue.

Fairfax lived in the most exclusive part of Edgbaston, in a late Georgian house. Its gates opened as he approached, and shut themselves behind him. His garage doors were equally obliging. There was a trellis-covered walk to the side door.

Inside was a narrow hall – presumably one used by the servants years ago – with a Minton-tiled floor that put Aberlene's to shame. It led to a big, square entrance hall, also tiled, and graced by what appeared from where I stood to be a marble statue. But I wasn't to penetrate that far yet; I followed Fairfax into the kitchen. It was huge. This floor had Provençal tiles, and the sort of expensive wooden fitted units that look as if they grew there. Nothing plastic for Fairfax. Someone had laid a tray, covering the china with a lace cloth. Without asking, he made tea, but didn't object when I picked up the tray and followed him down the corridor to a room he called his snug. The snugness had nothing to do with an intimate size; this room was bigger than my living room, and there were clearly others too.

Neither was his dog a contributory factor. Fairfax spoke to it briefly; it stared at me, and resumed its position in front of the French window. Fairfax settled in a green leather chair at right angles to the one he gestured me to, and let his eyes close. I poured. He opened his eyes a moment to acknowledge the cup beside him, and then shut them again. I drank my tea; had another cup. His went cold. I removed it. He slept on. He looked too ill to disturb, and there were a couple of magazines on a side table, so I thought I'd let him rest for a few minutes. When I reached for the magazines, however, the dog growled. I'm not a dog lover at the best of times, and black creatures the size of small donkeys with an imposing set of teeth upset me. Was this a Doberman? I was afraid of their very reputation! I let the magazines lie where they were. The dog subsided.

I looked around for something else to occupy my mind. The pictures were rather poor but impressive, with heavy varnish. I suspected the books on the floor-to-ceiling shelves were the sort you get in some stately homes – spines only. There was a panel set in the bookcases that looked the right size for a TV screen. It was about time for the sports results, but Albion weren't playing so I resisted the urge to press a few buttons on the remote-control handset beside me.

By this time the need to fill my mind was getting more urgent – I had to think about something other than my bladder. On the floor by Fairfax's feet was a set of pocket files, the ordinary coloured card sort we had at college. They bore the new college logo – and the same names as those I'd seen on la Cavendish's desk. 'College without Walls', 'Newtown Site'. By some excruciating coincidence a third file was masked by the others, so I could still see only 'Provence'. I shifted slightly. No response from Rover. If I moved my toe another inch I could at least slide the top files an inch sideways. There. 'ntre, Provence'. A town? Or – another half-inch? This time Fairfax stirred. But at least I had 'ent Centre, Provence'. Perhaps another inch? It would be no bad thing for my bladder if Fairfax woke. I'd only got as far as 'ment Centre, Provence' when he opened his eyes.

He started to splutter an apology.

'No matter,' I said. 'I'm afraid, though, I have to go now. And your dog doesn't want me to.'

I didn't like Fairfax's smile. 'He wouldn't. But he's a friendly old chap when he gets to know you. Here.' He chirruped.

The dog stood immediately and padded over. He put his head in Fairfax's hand and his tail wagged blissfully as Fairfax scratched his ears.

'Say hello to Sophie,' Fairfax said.

The dog came and stood before me. He lifted a front paw the size of a cannon ball.

'Go on: shake it.'

Dog and I did as we were told.

'I really have to go now,' I said. I stood up.

The dog wagged his tail and shoved his head into my hand. I found myself stroking it. I moved towards the door, and he stopped wagging his tail. But as soon as he saw Fairfax was on his feet he lolloped back to him so they could both accompany me to the door.

'I'll have to use your loo first,' I said.

A downstairs cloakroom complete with shower. Some loo. But it was a good job I used it because Fairfax didn't offer to take me home, or even enquire how I proposed to get there without him. Normally this wouldn't have worried me, but my knee had seized up and was demanding its frozen peas. So I limped slowly to the nearest bus stop, which turned out to be half a mile away – they obviously didn't rely on public transport in this neck of leafy Edgbaston. At least I had plenty to think about while I walked and while I waited.

20

I suppose it was a sign of my times that when I saw police cars in Balden Road I associated them with some further tragedy, major or minor, in my life. I limped up from the bus stop as fast as I could, my eyes ready to shed tears of self-pity. But when I saw the policeman on duty outside Aggie's house, anger took over.

Several of the neighbours were straggling over the pavement. I ought to have shown a friendly and gossipy concern, but I slipped through and tried to catch the red-headed constable's eye. As luck would have it, he was a young man I'd not met when I was out socially with Chris, and I've met more cooperative Belisha beacons. But I heard a voice calling from inside, 'If that's young Sophie, wheel her in.'

Yes, I nodded, and prepared to step inside; but the constable stretched his arm out to stop me. It took me an irritating moment to realise he was unlikely to consider me young.

'Come on, Sophie!' Ian yelled. The constable bowed to greater authority.

Ian was standing in Aggie's kitchen looking disparagingly at the tea bags. Before I could speak, though, he said, 'She's OK. Stirred but not shaken, if you get my meaning. I'll take you over.'

'Over?'

'Selly Oak Hospital. I'll explain on the way.'

I didn't fancy the frisson that went through the neighbours as Ian and I emerged. Perhaps it had something to do with the fact that I stumbled down the step, and he caught my elbow to steady me.

'Leg still bad?' he asked. 'Chris told me what happened.'

'Bad business when you can't even jaywalk without getting run over,' I suggested.

'And you can't even spray your neighbours' roses without getting smashed on the head. That's right,' he added, opening the passenger door. 'She didn't approve of your greenfly so she decided to give them a dose of whatever she was using to attack hers. And these two guys come up to your front door, she asks if she can help, and they turn and push her over. Hard.'

'Who found her?' I fastened my seat belt and Ian started off.

'She found herself. In your front garden. And *crawled*, bless her, crawled back to her place and phoned Chris. Didn't want to bother the ambulance people, thought he wouldn't mind.'

'Did he?'

'He'd just got into the shower. But he turned out, of course. And then called an ambulance anyway. Thing is, she reckons she might have seen them before, earlier this afternoon. Which is why Chris asked me to hang on for you.'

I felt as if someone had hit my stomach. 'Visitors?' I asked with dull irony.

'Visitors. But your security system's pretty good, of course—'

'Ought to be: young Gavin fixed it.'

Ian sighed. I knew that sigh.

'Oh, Ian, give it a rest. Chris and I are friends, and he's as free as I am to fancy someone else.'

'But he doesn't.'

'Well, neither do I at the moment, as it happens. In any case,' I added maliciously, 'it isn't Gavin that's asked me out for a drink - and to see his office, Ian, so he must be serious! - but Dave Clarke.'

'You wouldn't go! He's had his hands in more knickers than ... no, Sophie, love, not Dave.' He looked sideways at me. 'OK, OK. But didn't I hear something about you and a musician?' He managed to curl his mouth round the word as if it were next thing to a blasphemy.

'Another friend, Ian. And he won't be after my knickers. Not that way inclined.'

'You don't half pick them. Honestly, Sophie, I sometimes

think you go out of your way to choose wrong 'uns.'

'Chris apart, of course. Tell you what, Ian, pull into Sainsbury's car park: I can get Aggie some flowers.'

Chris was sitting on the far side of Aggie's bed, holding a saucer while she drank from a cup. Her free hand, bandaged, was patting his other wrist. They looked relaxed together, as if he were a favourite grandson. He reached to tuck away a wisp of her hair. She noticed me first.

'You shouldn't have,' she crowed, her eyes gleaming at the sight of the flowers. 'They'll have cost you a week's pocket money.'

'And the gravy,' I said cheerfully, wondering if I dared embarrass her by kissing her. I compromised by taking the hand that had held the teacup. She gripped it and shook it a little from side the side.

Ian took the flowers and went to charm a couple of vases from a nurse who looked ready to weep with weariness.

I perched on the bed, still holding Aggie's hand. 'Couldn't they have got you into a private ward?' I asked, and was suddenly appalled to find myself using Fairfax's tone.

'I'd fixed it,' said Chris.

'And I unfixed it,' said Aggie, with a cackle. 'Might as well see a bit of life while I'm stuck here.'

'But you promise me you'll go and stay with your granddaughter when they let you out?' Chris said urgently.

'I reckon as I ought to stay and guard Sophie's house,' she said. 'I've done a good job so far. Mind you, I liked that young Simon better than this afternoon's lot. You know what, he smiled when he done it. While he was clouting me, there was this ugly grin on his face. I'll give him smile when I see him.'

'Didn't notice his car, did you, Aggie?' Ian said, rearranging a rose to his satisfaction.

'No. Be nicked anyway, wouldn't it? Young Chris tells me they often nick a car to do a job. Stands to reason – wouldn't do it in their own, would they? Now, you see that girl over there? They reckon,' she said, dropping her voice to a carrying whisper, 'that she's been on TV in that Bill thing.'

When her granddaughter arrived, we left them to it. This

time I did kiss her, and gripped her hand again. Chris got the full works, both arms round his neck, while she winked hugely – and, I think, painfully.

'Not often I get the chance to cuddle a handsome young man,' she said. And she gave Ian a sound bussing too.

Once outside, Ian made himself embarrassingly scarce, leaving Chris and me together.

'You look dreadful,' I said.

'Tired.'

'Anything in particular?'

'The usual. Pressure. I keep missing my Alexander lessons. And now bloody Trevelyan's done a runner. Signed herself out of hospital. No idea where she's gone. Not home, not without us knowing.' He rubbed his hands wearily over his face. He needed a good hug, but wouldn't want one.

'Tell you what, why don't I drive? I've been itching to get behind the wheel of a decent car all day. I'll go via Sainsbury's if it's all the same to you – I've forgotten to shop this week – and I'll fix you a meal while you have a snooze on my sofa.'

He smiled and held out the keys.

The Sunday-morning car-boot sale was in one of the Harborne car parks, organised, I now saw, by Roy, in another existence my hairdresser. He was looking harassed and didn't notice me. Neither did Phil, Muntz's technician, burrowing through some rusty garden tools. Simon was in his element, citing all the times he'd seen on the *Antiques Road Show* car-boot items worth thousands. I was not to show excitement, no more than casual interest. The racks of women's dresses, the piles of books – they were being sold by dealers, and I should avoid them. He would let me prowl on my own: he didn't think I'd be interested in electronics. What I was interested in was what ordinary people like me should want to get rid of. There was a microwave cooker in the tail of someone's Peugeot. That might interest me. Another man was selling a heterogeneous collection of CDs: had he bought the Bee Gees at the same time as Yuri Bashmet playing the Brahms Viola Sonatas? Come to think of it, he didn't look the type to have bought either. I didn't say anything, just handed over the cash for a whole pile of promising-looking material to form the basis of my new collection – it really was time to get a proper sound system. That would please Aberlene and Chris – and, yes, George.

'You OK?' Simon asked, returning to my side. 'Hey, where d'you get those?'

I gestured.

To my amazement he wrote down the man's car number. 'You never know,' he said enigmatically. 'People pinch the weirdest things. A mate of mine lost all his CDs the other week – and his video, his computer and his best clothes. Maybe your Chris or one of his minions might be interested. Anything else you want?'

'There was a microwave over there.'

But it had been sold already.

We had a last stroll round together. By a boot overflowing with home-made raffia work I just managed to avoid Sunshine, who looked as pleased to see me as I was to see him. Instead I had a natter with a couple of people from William Murdock – it was reassuring to learn I hadn't been forgotten.

Simon found nothing to take his fancy, and was due on the MSO's coach at one – the orchestra was playing in Worcester in the evening. So I had a solitary lunch. Then the weather, which had been grey and overcast all morning, started to brighten. I would leave visiting Aggie till later and spend a little time seeing how my knee enjoyed cycling.

It would have made sense to buzz off somewhere pleasant, but on a whim I fished out my *A to Z* and headed towards one of Brum's less salubrious parts. 'Newtown Site': I thought I'd have a look for it. If Muntz was moving, maybe the staff ought to know.

I'd given up and was painfully picking my way through mean streets of derelict factories when I saw the Muntz logo. It was stencilled on a letter box beside the front door of a dilapidated warehouse, which now, judging by the droppings at my feet, housed half the area's pigeon population. Where there had been windows, there was now corrugated iron. Grass grew from what guttering was left. To the left of the building was a huge gate covered in BNP slogans. Someone had obligingly kicked in a few panels, so I could see through to what resembled a bomb site. And this was to be an outpost of Muntz's empire? Another outpost – hadn't Aberlene mentioned one somewhere else pretty unlikely?

I stood back for another look. There were some hand-painted signs: TRADE ONLY. NO PUBLIC ALLOWED. BILL POSTERS WILL BE PROSECUTED. Not much help there. Without looking inside, I could have no idea how much work it would take to convert it into buildings suitable for students. I was tempted to try and prise away a piece of corrugated iron, to explore this *Marie Celeste* of a place. And then I thought sensibly of rats and rotting floorboards and vulnerable knees, and resolved to leave it. At least, I amended, getting stiffly on my bike, until I could find a like-minded person to explore it with me.

21

I was reclining on the sofa, the picture of decadence, a glass of wine in the hand that wasn't steadying the review section. The only thing that spoiled the image was the bag of frozen peas attempting to return my knee to something approaching normality. There was another thing, actually: I was bored.

Six o'clock on a Sunday evening is not a good time to be bored.

I heaved myself over to the kitchen clipboard, found a pile of bills awaiting my attention, and wrote a number of cheques, including a large one for my phone bill. Full of self-righteousness, I wanted to cheer myself with an evening of phone calls to distant friends.

But what could I say to them with those ears alert?

I decided my knee was well enough to go for a walk to the post the long way, and set off along Court Oak Road away from the city. But I was mistaken. Eventually I compromised; I'd post the letters since that was what I was supposed to be doing, then cut back through the rear of the college grounds. It would save only a couple of hundred yards, but even that was worth it.

I followed the path round the back of the building, where the computer technicians' lab and Dr Trevelyan's room lay. Even there, where hardly anyone ventured, the grass was neatly clipped, and someone had dug over the flowerbeds under each window, raking them into a fine tilth. If only they put as much effort into making the staff happy as into maintaining the grounds, the college would indeed be a fine place. Only one bed was disturbed, with a couple of little craters a foot or so apart. Paradoxically the general neatness made me depressed again –

when could I attend to my own little patch? Not this evening, certainly, I reflected as I crossed Balden Road, dodging the sad little corpse of a grey squirrel newly squashed and awaiting the attention of the Harborne Fox Posse. Frozen peas and the sofa for me again. Thank goodness for thick Sunday papers!

I'd been reduced to the business section when the phone rang.

I hobbled briskly over. For a moment there was silence. Then a man's voice, not one I recognised: 'Hello, Sophie. When you going to give it me, then? This nice long suck?'

I said nothing. To be honest I could think of nothing to say. I always told people on those self-protection courses at William Murdock to make the caller suffer – blow a whistle down the phone or, failing something as efficient as that, make as loud a noise as possible. Hurt the bugger's ears, that was it.

Then I said, so foolishly I hang my head to think of it; 'Why me?'

All those ears listening to me making a cake of myself!

'Come on, Soph – all those ads –'

'Shut it!' At least I think that was what another man's voice said. But I couldn't be sure, because the line went dead.

I tried to make sense of it. Did heavy breathers hunt in pairs? And why should one stop the other?

The phone rang again. This time, when I snatched the receiver, I was ready. I sang, very loudly, as if I were raising the roof in the 'Hallelujah Chorus'.

'Goodness me,' said a quiet voice at the other end. 'What on earth did I do to deserve that?'

'I've had an obscene phone call, Chris,' I said dully. 'Didn't you—?' But I remembered in time about the other bug, and swallowed the rest of the question.

He waited a moment, as if thinking. 'I'll be round in ten minutes,' he said.

I'd abandoned the peas and resorted to the tubi-grip by the time his car arrived. He didn't even get as far as the front door before I was out there, locking up and hurtling towards him. 'I want them out!' I yelled. 'Now! His too! I can't live my life with those bloody bugs! I can't even cry in peace!'

'OK, OK. Tomorrow, I promise. Moving his may provoke something interesting, of course,' he said more reflectively.

'How interesting?' I asked, opening his passenger door and

fastening my belt. 'And where are we going, anyway?'

'I did think of the Court Oak – no? Somewhere further away?'

I nodded emphatically.

'What's happened, Sophie?' he asked quietly, as he started the engine. 'Something's really rattled you.'

'It's so stupid: just a nasty phone call, that's all. You know, the lewd-suggestion sort. But there were two of them on the other end – I'm sure there were. What's up? What's so funny?' My voice was sharper than I intended.

'Just that we'll be able to check from the listening device. These things have their uses, after all.'

He'd found a canal-side pub out on the far side of Bromsgrove before he told me why he'd phoned earlier. At first I didn't take it in properly: somehow the weekend had managed to cloud what had once seemed a major issue – who was supplying George Muntz's computers. Yes, Dave Clarke and his contacts had come up with something. PRT Computers did indeed have an address. One in Birmingham. And a lot closer to home than I'd imagined.

'I'm surprised we didn't twig earlier,' he said, swirling the bitter in the bottom of his glass. 'But the initials PRT – you said Dr Trevelyan was called Ena.'

'She is.'

'Wrong. *Row*ena. Paulina Rowena Trevelyan.'

'What a mouthful! No wonder she abbreviated it! So where is this little firm of hers?'

He looked embarrassed.

'Don't worry, Chris, it was just a matter of interest. I'm not burgling anyone till my leg gets better.'

'You don't need to burgle,' he said, the crows' feet round his eyes in hyperactive mode. 'It can all be done by warrant. The trouble is making charges.'

'Particularly when your perpetrator is a few lines short of a program and being dosed to the eyeballs?'

'What a fine mixture of metaphors,' he said. 'Time you went back to teaching Eng. Lit. at William Murdock to re-sharpen your critical faculties. Anyway, she's still missing. No sign of her anywhere.'

I ignored him. 'And what corroborative evidence do you

have? I'd hate it to be a one-woman job,' I added, suddenly urgent. 'I want you to nail a couple of people at Muntz – at least two.'

He looked at me over his glass.

'Oh, just because I don't like them,' I conceded. 'And I don't want it to be Phil, because I like him. There's logic for you. Tell you what, next time I want some exercise, why don't we come out here? What could be nicer than a level walk along the cut and a good meal to come back to?'

'Next weekend, if your knee's up to it,' he said. 'It's a date. I may need to cheer you up – did you hear the news?'

'The news?'

'Poor old Albion lost 2–1. Looks as if you're stuck with Second Division football for next season. Thought that would make your weekend.'

SOPHIE FUCKS GOOD. And there was my home number, accurate to the last digit.

My first reaction was rational, I suppose. I locked the lavatory from the outside, scrawled a CLOSED notice on a sheet of computer paper and Blu-Tacked it to the door, and called the caretaker.

'Yes, Miss Rivers. I'll see as it comes off as soon as I've got a man free.'

'*Now*, please. And I'm timing you.'

Now I had time to think about it, I wasn't simply angry. Where had a student got my number? At William Murdock, when I'd known a student for some time I might tell them to call me if they were beset by problems that weren't controlled by college hours. But I'd not cared enough to give it to any Muntz student. Since I was ex-directory, I was worried.

I was staring out at the rain wondering what to do next when the phone rang. A man.

'Sophie Rivers? You got ten minutes? 'Cause I need a bit of hand-relief—'

I slammed down the phone.

I don't know how long I stared at it. Then I reached for it again and dialled the switchboard.

'I've just had a nuisance call,' I said.

'A what?'

'An obscene call. Here, in college. I want you to intercept any incoming calls for me – ask who the caller is. I know it's a pain, but—'

'We can't do that without permission. Ever so busy we are, not that you lot give a damn. I'd need Mr Curtis's authority to do that.'

I wanted to yell at her, but forced my voice down to a more normal register. 'Could you get it, then? It's important. You can see that.'

'Our instructions are not to put calls through to Mr Curtis today. He's got important meetings.' And she cut the line.

By the time I'd visited every women's loo I wanted to scream. Each had my name and number, but the type of sex I offered varied. I ran back to Polly's office: I had to tell someone.

Polly was sitting at her desk, staring unmoving at her computer screen. She was so still, so pale, I thought she was ill. But at last she raised her hand and pointed at the screen. An e-mail message. Anonymous. Tom Hendry died yesterday.

'When I taught basic communication skills,' she said, her voice so quiet I could hardly hear what she said, 'I used to get the kids to do an exercise about giving information. I used to crack that old joke about announcing a death. The sergeant major says, "All those with mothers step forward. What the 'ell are you doing stepping forward, Private Jones?" '

I pulled her head to my chest and held her. She started to cry. I waited.

'We'd had this row,' she said at last, her face and voice blurred with tears. 'About the union. It was too bloody supine, he said. And I said we had to stick within the law. And then – and I couldn't even – not when he was lying there – couldn't—'

'Apologise? He wouldn't have heard, Polly. But when he was in hospital, didn't you make up then?'

She laughed, a savage, painful laugh. 'Hospital! I couldn't see him there. And I can't even go to his funeral. Can't say goodbye.' She pushed away, but let me take her hand.

'Let's get you home,' I said.

'Home? Home! So my husband can see me like this? I've not kept this secret for eleven years for it to come out now, Sophie.'

*

I was back in my office when there was a tap at the door. Hector came in, closing the door carefully. He looked hard at me. 'You heard about it then, Sophie? That shit about you.'

'Seen it, Hector. Every single women's loo. Haven't checked out the gents' yet.'

'Don't even think about it. It's real bad, man. And permanent. They won't get that off in a hurry. Jesus, Sophie – it's as bad as I've seen, man.'

I nodded. Now I came to think of it, it oughtn't to be cleaned off until it had been photographed. Evidence.

'You better see the boss, man. This is harassment, you know. Someone got it in for you. Say, is it really your number?'

If he had to ask, he didn't know. Did he?

'Jesus, man, it is? You better get on to Telecom, man. Change that number now.'

I nodded.

'And tell that inspector friend of yours. Some of them things, they're sick, man. Real sick.'

This was important enough for me to demand a meeting with the principal, Curtis and any others in the hierarchy who might be interested. 'Might', come to think of it, was the wrong word: 'ought' was better. Too bad if they thought they had something else to worry about. And that included Mrs Cavendish too.

I penetrated the security systems and strode up to her desk. I suppose I was too busy presenting an assertive front – and, to be honest, trying not to cry – to think about anyone else, including her. But in mid-sentence I noticed her face. If I'd made her inexplicably pale in previous encounters, today, without any provocation from me, she was grey. That didn't arrest my flow, however.

'And I propose to see him now. Not next Friday at ten. Now.' I swept past her and threw open the principal's door.

His room was empty.

Curtis's next. That too was empty, but the bin by his shredder was extremely full. Unfortunately he'd finished the job.

Out to la Cavendish again. She was busy screwing tissues into unattractive balls.

'Well? Where will I find someone with a modicum of authority?'

She reacted as if I were six feet tall: 'Truly, I don't know. I'm so sorry, Miss Rivers. This is a terrible thing, and someone should do something. But I don't know where they are, I really don't.'

I sat on the edge of her desk and leaned forward with as much menace as I could muster. 'Write this down, Mrs Cavendish. Ms – no, not Miss, Ms – Ms Rivers's name, telephone number and vicious sexual allegations are on the wall of every lavatory in this building. She demands an immediate investigation into the serious and reprehensible lapse of college security which has enabled someone to misuse confidential personal information.' I paused for breath. Now I came to think about it I wasn't so keen on the style, but perhaps officialese might work better for Blake and Curtis. I continued, 'She also requires immediate action to remove the offending graffiti from every site, no matter what the expense, as soon as paint samples and photographs for analysis have been taken. Failure to remove it immediately will result in legal action for the most serious sexual harassment.' I looked down. Her hand was shaking so much her shorthand might be indecipherable. 'OK. Now get it on to computer. Four copies, please, when you're ready.'

'Four?'

'One for Mr Blake, one for Mr Curtis, one for the chair of governors and one for me.'

The memo crept quietly from the laser printer. I signed each copy as it appeared.

'Thanks.' I managed a smile. Then I remembered my manners: 'Are you all right, Mrs Cavendish?'

She shook her head. 'Like I said, Miss Rivers, I really don't know where he is. Mr Blake. There's no sign of him. His car's in the car park, but he's not in college. And his wife said he came in last night to do some work and that was the last she saw of him.'

'Does he often do that – sleep here?' I tried not to sound too incredulous, but I always associated such long hours with us lower orders.

'He has a room. From when this used to be a residential teachers' college. It's locked. I've tried the private number in there. No reply.' More tissues disintegrated in her hand; she stared at me when I passed her a bin, and then dropped them in it.

'Have you thought of calling the police?' I asked.

She looked at me aghast.

'If there's no sign—' I began.

'What's *she* doing here?'

I turned: it was Curtis, as red as Mrs Cavendish was pale.

'Poor Miss Rivers has been the victim of a most unpleasant prank—'

'*Prank*? Harassment!'

'Hm?' He picked up a couple of files and affected to read them, flicking back a lock of blond hair as if he were a matinee idol. It irritated me that such good looks should accompany a personality I'd so far found nothing in to like.

Mrs Cavendish pushed one of my memos at him. He took it idly and read it.

'Well?' I prompted him at last.

'The best thing that you can do is clear your room and return to your old college – Cadbury.'

'William Murdock,' I said automatically.

'Wherever. The caretaker'll give you a couple of boxes for your stuff. Sooner the better, Iris.'

I think even Mrs Cavendish was shocked. She watched his departing back, and turned to me, shaking her head.

'He can be quite ruthless at times. He was quite unkind when Dr Trevelyan was taken ill. He told dear Mr Blake they were to make sure she kept her mouth ...'

'Go on.'

'No, perhaps I've got it wrong. I heard someone saying that to him.' She flushed. 'Mr Blake'll do something, I'm sure he will. I'll tell him the instant we find him. But – I hope you don't mind me saying this, Miss Rivers – maybe he's right. Maybe it would be better to take a day off.'

I left before I laughed out loud.

I did leave the building, but didn't go home. Soon I'd have to phone Chris, but I needed a few moments on my own. I'd take a breather in the park – the rain was steady enough to put off most people. I followed the path, dodging dog shit, and made my way to the scented garden. Something smelled sickly sweet in the rain and I turned away, almost nauseated. Finding a phone that hadn't been vandalised, I read the graffiti about other women who didn't have even my limited powers to get rid of it, and phoned Chris.

'It's too much of a coincidence,' I said, drying my feet in the warmth of his car heater. He'd picked me up and driven into a side road. 'This guy Hendry dies, so they vandalise the college to give everyone something else to talk about. Could that be it?'

'Could be. If Hendry's sufficiently important as a catalyst to rock the college. But it seems a mighty big sledgehammer to crack a nut. No, if you asked me, I'd say that you were the target. Sorry. And I don't think it's personal. I still think that Chummie thinks you know something. Do you?'

I watched the windscreen wipers – backwards, forwards, backwards, forwards. 'No. I've seen bits and pieces of things that worry me. Someone dropped an odd hint – about paper ... but they're more Dave Clarke's area than yours.'

'Have you told him?'

'Haven't got my chastity belt locked yet!'

Chris laughed dutifully. 'Shall I get him over to my office? Or take you over to his?'

I shrugged. 'Whichever. Why not just phone him?'

'What's on your mind, Sophie?'

I shook my head 'You know, I think you ought to search Muntz.'

'You can't just go busting in on a place uninvited. There has to be some very good reason.'

'Like a crime.'

'A crime?'

'How about the principal's disappeared?'

'Has he? Is he a missing person?'

'I've only met him twice so I suppose I don't miss him. But he has gone AWOL. Tell you what, why don't you come and have a look at my graffiti and see what else you find? Just as a friend, you understand.'

'OK, Sophie. Just as a friend.'

22

My long-awaited meeting with Mr Blake was undoubtedly memorable. It took place in Dr Trevelyan's office. Mr Blake was sitting in front of a state-of-the-art computer, wearing a viritual-reality headset and overalls from which emerged clusters of wires, apparently connected to the rear of the headset via a tube an inch and a half or so in diameter. The tube looked like a narrower version of the stuff they line central-heating flues or extractor-fan ducts with.

Mr Blake was dead.

On automatic pilot, perhaps, Chris felt for a pulse. He shook his head and fished his phone from his pocket. He should, I suppose, have told me to leave, and I suppose I should have left without being told. But I wasn't in the mood for passivity. I didn't touch anything, of course, and I even restrained myself from wandering around the room lest I damage any footprints Chris's team might be able to lift from the carpet. But I didn't switch off my eyes or ears. I didn't even hold my nose.

I turned to Chris. He was busy logging the time in his notebook. Then, like me, he used his eyes. I followed them around the room. Packs of software on shelves. A phone. A waste-paper basket. A couple of boxes of laser-quality paper. The desk itself was bare – Phil or someone must have tidied Dr Trevelyan's desk for her. No one had been in her room – officially – since her hospitalisation. So why should Mr Blake have chosen to use it? He'd certainly made himself at home. His suit was hung neatly over the back of the chair, his folded shirt partly covering white cotton vest and pants. I could see the Marks and Spencer label in the vest.

Chris noticed me at last. He smiled, almost apologetically.

'All right, I'll go quietly,' I said. 'But first, tell me – what can you smell?'

'Smell? Of course it stinks in here: the man's bodily functions packed up when he died.'

'And? Anything else?'

He shook his head. 'Only your perfume. Different from usual. Sweeter. Very nice, actually.'

'Time I went away, then. So you can smell what I can smell.'

'Tell me.'

'Not sure, but – No, I don't know.'

He nodded doubtfully. 'Anything unusual will be mentioned in the pathologist's report.' He started to look round the room again.

'Is there anything useful I can do, like tell Hector not to let anyone out of the building?'

'Are you having me on?'

'Not entirely. Thought you might want him to collect IDs or something before they leave, just so as you know who's in the building.'

'Who *was* in the building last night – that's more to the point. He's cold, Sophie. And in any case, I don't want you wandering round this place on your own. Stay with me till Ian and co. arrive. They shouldn't be long. And while we wait, for God's sake try and work out why someone should want you out of the building by the time Blake's body's found.'

'What d'you mean?'

'All that graffiti about you, all that harassment. Don't you see that it all ties up? I've said it before, and I'll say it again. Someone thinks you know something. And I'm beginning to think you ought, just for once, to be sensible.'

'The students have their exams in less than a month. They were messed about having me wished on them for their last term. I can't mess them about any more.'

'Arguing again, are you?' Ian asked, making me jump. 'Team's on its way, Gaffer. Anything I can do?'

'I think you're supposed to mind me,' I said tartly, 'until you can find someone more lowly to do it. But I'd have thought you could be doing something more useful.'

'Can tell she's a teacher, can't you?' Ian said.

'Look, you'll be in the way here,' said Chris. 'But I can't let you roam round waiting for someone to do to you what they did to Melina.'

'Or what they did to this guy? Don't you think he's been done in too?'

'Let's see what our expert has to say.' Chris smiled at a figure out of my vision. The police surgeon was a young and very attractive woman. 'Dr Patel may conclude it's a natural death.'

'Must have been a pretty exciting video game,' Ian said. 'What you going to do, Gaffer?'

'Just preserve the scene until we've got something else to go on. Can't waste good taxpayers' money.'

'But—'

'Look, Sophie, I reckon there's something fishy. You know I do. But we live in the real world. We need evidence. OK, Dr Patel?' Chris smiled and gestured. 'He's all yours.'

They summoned a youngish PC to escort me to my office.

'Funny thing, Ms Rivers,' he said, pausing on the stairs, 'but this place is so quiet. At the place where I taught there were always students on the move, whatever time of day it was. This place is like a ghost college.'

'Study leave, I suppose. Where did you teach?'

He opened the door to my office for me, checked there were no unwelcome visitors, and smiled. But before he could reply, his radio crackled and he sped off.

He was right, of course. Compared to the noisy chaos of William Murdock, for instance, the corridors were unnaturally quiet. They always were. I was never jostled on my way to classes, never jammed into a corner of a lift. There was always space.

I sat down at my desk. I didn't want to think about Blake anyway, and perhaps someone at William Murdock would be able to help me. I might as well start at the top. I reached for the phone and dialled.

I didn't recognise the voice on the switchboard but whoever it belonged to put me straight through to Mr Worrall.

'Sophie! What a pleasure!' I couldn't help feeling that he

was over-enthusiastic. 'Perhaps you could explain why every time I've tried to speak to my colleagues at George Muntz this morning they've reacted as if I've been speaking Chinese?'

'I believe –' how much could I tell him? – 'that Mr Blake is, er, indisposed.'

'Indisposed! He spends enough time looking after himself – squash, badminton, golf. Very fine player, as a matter of fact. Perhaps,' he added with commendable waspishness, 'George Muntz takes less of his energy than William Murdock does of mine. Now, Sophie, how may I help you?'

Even as I opened my mouth to reply, I remembered those hidden ears. Someone thought I knew something. Would an innocent question confirm their suspicions?

'I wanted to ask about that new contract,' I lied, blithely. 'A lot of people here seem to have signed and I wondered what the advantages were.' Perhaps I could drag the conversation round to student numbers.

'To the employer there is every advantage. You give up your holidays for a maximum of thirty-five days to be taken when I tell you. And you work a minimum of thirty-seven hours a week.'

I couldn't suppress a whistle. I hoped it hurt someone's ears.

'Seems a drastic change. Why on earth should people want to?'

'The employer usually offers a little financial sweetener to those who accept. And denies an annual pay award to those who don't. And, of course, it is to the benefit of the college. If you can persuade everyone to work longer hours, it means fewer staff, and thus a better staff–student ratio.'

'Better!'

'From the point of view of our new masters, it's better. We're being funded on the basis of an 8 per cent growth in our numbers. If we don't reach our target numbers, our funds will no longer match our outgoings, most of which, of course, are on staff salaries. *Quod erat demonstrandum.*'

'What happens if a college doesn't have enough students?' This was what I wanted to know.

'It has to find them pretty damn quick.'

'How could it do that? Press gangs apart, that is?' I had a nasty feeling I might have gone too far.

'That would be up to the college,' he said repressively. Of course he'd be circumspect: he was in charge of a rival institution. 'But any college failing to recruit would go to the wall, Sophie.'

Would it, indeed?

'You must excuse me: I have a governors' meeting in two minutes. I take it you'll be winging your way to my office to sign on the dotted line?' And then he added, as if for the benefit of those suspicious ears; 'And next time we speak, perhaps you will be kind enough to tell me why you really phoned.'

Because I want to come home! I thought. Because I hate this place where when I want a cup of coffee all I have is the memo forbidding it. Perhaps orange juice out of a cardboard packet would help, but I was shaking so much I couldn't fit the straw into the little hole. I started to laugh.

By the time I'd wrenched free the under-desk bug and dug out the one Chris had planted, and hurled them both from the window, I found I wasn't laughing but trying not to weep. I might have been laughing again when I let Chris into the room and pointed at the open window.

'At least it'll have given someone earache,' I said, trying to smile.

How I came to be sitting down with his arm round me and his damned smelling salts making my eyes pour with tears, I'm not sure. But for the moment I wasn't moving. What I wanted more than anything in the world was warm, human comfort. I put my head against his neck and shoulder. The smell was warm and clean, a man very much alive. I could feel the pulse speeding in his neck. I would have to move my head only an inch or so to kiss him. If I kissed him, it would be for the wrong reason; if I had sex with him, it would be for the wrong reason. But just at that moment that was the only thing I wanted to do.

I don't know how long we stayed like that. Occasionally his fingers would stroke my hair, and he would move his head to touch kisses on to my neck. And then I knew that he wanted me at least as much as I wanted him.

'Come on,' he said.

'But Blake—'

'They can manage without me for a bit. Everyone knows what they've got to do. You're not staying here any longer.' He tried to make his voice authoritative, but his eyes betrayed him.

Even as he tucked me into his car and I looked at the fine hairs on his hands, I had to stop myself touching him. I had to stop myself pulling his face down to mine so I could kiss him. It would be a dreadful mistake. I couldn't be his woman. There was nothing logical about the way I felt – in many ways we'd have made a most suitable partnership. But not now.

His conscience got back into gear as soon as he let us into his house. 'I'd better let them know where I am,' he said, as if surprised to find himself there.

I went into the kitchen to wake up his percolator, and dug out the whiskey. Jameson's was a habit he'd caught from me. A tot each, that should help. I held my glass in my hands as if it would warm them as much as it warmed my stomach. Chris came in and took his glass without comment.

'I said I'd got a migraine coming on, and had had to come back here to take some medication.'

He was so pale it could have been true.

The sitting-room phone rang. He strode off to answer it. I finished my whiskey, considered another glass, but decided against it. The coffee was ready, so I poured myself a mug; Chris regarded sugar as something entirely alien to tea and coffee, so there was none in the basin, and I had to ferret in his store cupboard to find a packet. The milk was virtually fat-free, of course. Right then I'd have loved the comforting richness of cream.

When he came back, I poured his coffee and pushed the sugar at him. He winced.

'I'll have to get back – shit!'

His radio this time. Automatically he turned from me to talk. I took bread and low-fat spread from the fridge, and looked for something to make into sandwiches. Plenty in the salad drawer, of course. And what I was sure would be low-fat cheese.

He slumped at the table and stared at the whiskey.

'Medicinal,' I said. 'Here. And you need to eat.'

He shook his head.

'Chris, you're much more used to it than I, but I bet you don't like finding corpses either. What's the surgeon think it was, anyway? Heart attack?'

'Almost certainly. But she said she couldn't be sure until after the autopsy - something inconsistent, she said. Didn't understand her jargon, I'm afraid. Wonder what was on the computer to give him the heart attack.'

'Cybersex?'

'I beg your pardon?' He didn't know whether to laugh or look shocked.

'Well, there's cyberspace and—'

'But cybersex? Where d'you get the sex from?'

'The smell of semen.'

'What are you on about?'

'That's what I could smell - I'm sure it was! I'll bet the old stoat was watching Internet porn. There's a brisk exchange of it these days. And of course he'd be safe in Dr Trevelyan's room. Might have given him an extra little frisson, wanking himself off thinking she's safe in the loony bin.'

'You do have the most elegant turn of phrase,' he said. 'I'll get them to check the computer, anyway.'

'Tell you what, Chris: get them to get a real expert to take it apart. Don't let anyone just switch it on and try and get into his program.'

'Why on earth—?'

'In case someone's loaded a program that deletes everything it doesn't want intruders to see. Can happen. Honest, Gaffer. Please.'

He raised a cynical eyebrow, but spoke into his radio. And wouldn't, interestingly enough, accept any protests.

I looked at his clock, a handsome Victorian specimen I'd often thought would look better in my kitchen than in his. 'I've got my GCSE class in half an hour. An exam class.'

He didn't protest. Just reached for his sandwich and picked it up as if to eat it while he drove. Then he caught my eye and took a bite. His mouth so full it was hard for me to hear, he said; 'But you're moving in here until you can find somewhere else to stay - right?'

'All right,' I said. And ate the last of the cheese.

*

Some malign fate must have had it in for my GCSE students. Having shed my ministering PC at the door, I'd done no more than take the register, calm and normal as if I were used to having my (erroneous) preference for oral sex plastered in front of anyone wanting a pee. The students themselves looked ill at ease, as if I might be about to interrogate them. Or as if they were ashamed that someone could have been so vicious, even to one of the enemy.

The fire alarm rang.

I think they were actually as irritated as I was when they realised they were to lose their class. They left their belongings, as requested, and trooped out in front of me. We processed down the main stairs and joined the throng in the car park. And not such a large throng either. Perhaps there were others elsewhere. I registered the group again to make sure none was trapped in a potential inferno, and wondered how I could manage to go walkabout. The arrival of the fire appliances, two ordinary ones and a Simon Snorkel, provided a diversion. I set off purposefully, as if wanting to speak to someone in an adjoining group. Then I went to the next, and the next. Finally I dodged behind the main buildings, into the areas of kitchen bins and other tat.

God knows what I thought I was looking for. A fire, maybe. No joy on that front, anyway. Not so much as a smouldering rag.

I worked my way round. Over to my right lay the yard where Melina had landed. Another skip waited there.

By now I was by the computer suite, and another couple of yards would take me level with Dr Trevelyan's room. I looked at the window. The blinds were still down, either out of respect or to conceal the activities of the police. There was police plastic tape festooned everywhere, and when I stared too long a WPC moved purposefully towards me. But I'd had time to see that all the flowerbeds were equally flat.

Back to the path. Chris had better know. Fast.

My quickest route was past the skip, the last thing I wanted to be anywhere near. I told myself I didn't have to look, that I wouldn't find anything if I did, that surely to God there'd be no more bodies. So I looked. And – if only my GCSE students had been there so I could have explained the meaning of 'bathos' – there was nothing there except a load of old wire and some electrical bits and pieces: valves, cable, the innards of what might have been a video. Simon would have had a field day. In fact, I might just phone him, to tell him what riches some Philistine was about to dispose of.

I strolled casually back to the car park and my group.

Everyone was restless by now. Usually there'd have been an announcement, probably that it was a false alarm, and that we were to return. Certainly there was no flurry with hoses, though the fire fighters were still standing by their appliances. There was a zooful of pandas by the main entrance, and a couple of patrol cars, their drivers sharing a quick fag with Hector. I detached them – Hector tried very obviously not to overhear – and explained what I'd seen. The younger had to stop himself saluting me, and scuttled off.

My class and I were just trying to arrange an *ad hoc* class at a time to suit us all when at last Curtis appeared with a loud-hailer. Acting Principal Curtis, with, no doubt, an emolument suited to such a position, probably with effect from the moment the poor guy died. I would judge his speech accordingly.

'Ladies and gentlemen, we have had a report that a bomb has been planted in the building. The police are taking it seriously. You are asked to remain where you are. More announcements will be made in due course.'

It did not score highly.

So, there we were, in the fitful sun of a May afternoon, with absolutely nothing to do. It was then I had my good idea. With permission from Curtis – no, he didn't remember my name – and from a harassed WPC, I gathered together my group, herded them across the road, and spent the rest of the afternoon helping them revise in the privacy of my back garden. They had to drink their tea and coffee in relays because I didn't have enough mugs, and they finished my biscuits, but altogether it was the most positive, if not ultimately successful, teaching session I'd had at George Muntz.

And the good thing was, it took my mind almost entirely off the problem of sex with Chris.

23

When the students left, the house was very quiet. There were a couple of messages on my answering machine, so I broke the silence by playing them. Nothing obscene this time. Aberlene reminding me about fixing up supper with her and Tobias; Richard Fairfax trusting that I had suffered no ill effects after my weekend jaunt and hoping I might join him for a drink on Tuesday evening. Nothing to inflame the listeners' ears. Suddenly I felt very cold; I shut and locked the patio doors. By now those listeners would know I'd discovered the bugs at work. Chris's colleagues would already be planning their next move; I had a nasty suspicion that A. N. Other would also be busy.

When Chris phoned, I was at the dining table working away with pencil and pad.

'I'll pick you up soon,' he said.

Nothing more. Well, not a lot of point, really.

I didn't bother with supper, expecting that Chris and I would eat together. I just packed an overnight bag. I found some condoms left over from a previous relationship. They were perilously close to their end date, but I could no doubt trust Chris to be meticulous in such circumstances. The more I thought about it, the more I was afraid our bedding would have disastrous consequences for Chris. It's one thing to love someone from afar, another to have sex with her and then have to return to the *status quo*. I flung down the condoms on the bed, and myself after them. 'Shit and shit and shit!' Let the listeners make of that what they might.

I was back at the table when Chris arrived two hours later.

He marched straight past me when I opened the door. By the time I'd locked it again, he was standing at the table, studying my notes.

'Well?'

'Bastards!' He threw the pad down so it slid across the table and down to the floor. 'Bastards!'

I touched his arm and put my finger to my lips. He stalked round the table, snatched up the pad and headed for the front door. Picking up my bag, I followed more circumspectly, and set the alarm. I deadlocked the front door behind us.

He didn't say anything as he drove through Edgbaston. He didn't drive as well as usual, and once or twice I found myself squeaking as we approached a crossing too fast. He parked badly but it was his drive so I didn't say anything. I merely reached for my things, struggled out – bracing my knees had brought the throbbing back – and watched while he locked up and set the alarm. He looked grey, with great blotches under his eyes. And he kept brushing the right side of his face as if to clear his sight.

He walked up the path like an old man: clearly it was touch and go whether he could get in before his migraine overtook him completely. I knew his drill, knew where to find the tablets, where he kept an ice pack in his freezer. I even found his wristbands, those that stimulate the acupressure points, and managed to slip them over his clenched fists. What I couldn't deal with was the sight of Chris's tears, so I drew his curtains and tiptoed from his bedroom.

There I was, at a loose end I was only half grateful for. I decided against music or TV – Chris's bedroom was directly above his living room, and I wanted to do nothing to disturb him. I read through his newspapers: the *Guardian* and the *Birmingham Post*. News-shocked at last, I decided to make some tea and sat in his kitchen watching the kettle boil. When the phone rang I pounced.

It was someone from Action Aid asking him to sell raffle tickets. I wrote down their number, but didn't, for a moment, put back the handset. There was someone I ought to phone about Muntz, wasn't there? Someone unlikely. Aberlene!

I got through on the fourth ring, but only to her answering

machine. It's often like that, communicating with musicians, who live in a different section of the day from those of us with nine-to-five jobs. George and I used to joke that his answering machine and mine had more conversations than we did.

Apologising for the delay in returning her call, I told her about my bugs. I gave her Chris's numbers, both his home and Rose Road, and asked her to phone one of us urgently about Muntz's Bradford connection. And then I remembered that she'd got a week's leave to prepare for her Wigmore Hall recital, and might well be staying with her parents in Henley for a bit of peace. But she'd no doubt call her machine from time to time, so I wished her luck anyway, and rang off.

It was about six when at last I heard Chris using the bathroom. I slung on my dressing gown and padded from the spare room to offer help. Now he'd be ready for my ministrations – vomiting was a signal that his migraine was more or less over.

He managed a pallid smile.

I smiled back. 'China tea?'

'How did you guess?'

'And some dry toast for breakfast? When you've showered?'

'Wonderful.'

Since it was a very long time since that lunchtime sandwich I was ready for rather more. There didn't seem to be much in his fridge or store cupboard – another sign he'd been working overlong hours. But even as I set out plates and cutlery I remembered I'd better dress first.

Thoroughly decent in jeans and sweatshirt, I returned to my search for food. His muesli looked uncompromisingly healthy, and would be more so if I laced it with fat-free milk. On the other hand, the toast smelled good, so I settled for some expensive-looking marmalade, the sort that comes in small jars with large price tags.

'Sit,' I said, as Chris appeared. 'No excuses. No eating on the hoof.'

'OK.'

I looked at him sharply: such docility was unnatural. 'Are you sure you're all right? Can't you take a sickie?'

He grimaced. 'Got to be all right, haven't I?'

I poured him a mug of tea and passed it to him without speaking.

'Until this lot's sorted out, I've just got to be.'

There was plenty of time for him to stop off at Rose Road before taking me in to work; I followed him in, responding to friendly faces. He snatched a fax from his desk.

'Bugger!' He thrust the offending paper at me, so I could read it myself.

Much of it was incomprehensible, the jargon of the medical world, but I managed to work out one thing. 'So there's no evidence of foul play?'

'Why should a man die at a computer? And see, no evidence of a heart attack.' He pointed at some more polysyllabic phrases.

'Am I being stupid? How can someone simply die without rhyme or reason?'

'They don't. Here's the rest of the fax. Something about a red patch on his scalp – see? And changes in the brain tissue. They're asking someone else to have a look. But those upstairs won't like this. I can't justify a full-scale murder inquiry if there's no hard evidence. All this business of cost centres and budgets: damn it all, Sophie, stopping crime isn't a business. I'm not selling so many pounds of apples here! It's human lives we're talking about.'

I nodded. He'd heard much the same speech from me about education many times since they started the cuts.

'There's got to be something, hasn't there?' he said. 'This report confirms Blake's sexual activity, so when the forensic-science team start on that computer we should be able to find out what was so exciting. But not exciting enough to give him heart failure. I'm sorry: I'm going round in circles.'

'You're not. I tried to work things out myself yesterday.'

'All those notes of yours – I meant to—'

'They don't make sense to me yet. But if you looked at them – you and Ian, the more heads the better – maybe you could see what I can't.' I hoped, of course, he'd reciprocate, but I could never tell with Chris.

He responded with an old-fashioned look. 'What is it they say in your neck of the woods? I'm not as green as I am cabbage-looking? OK, Sophie, we'll talk later, the three of us. I'm seeing the pathologist first.'

And the body. I wouldn't mention that. 'Maybe four? How about inviting Dave Clarke along? Surely you and Ian together could protect me from his ravening hands? It's just that there are things going on that I think may be more in his line of business than in yours.'

He looked doubtful, then brightened. 'Why not? Them upstairs would like it if we could tap into another cost centre. We'll recruit him to the incident-room team. Hint he'll see more of you if he comes.'

I stuck out my tongue.

We were just about to set off for Muntz when his phone rang; he'd be able to sell his idea to them upstairs earlier than he'd expected. I'd have happily walked in to college - I had plenty of time and it was a cool, clear morning - but Chris summoned Ian to offer me a lift and I didn't want to waste any of his limited energy by arguing.

'Looks bloody awful, doesn't he?' Ian said, as he let me into his car.

'I'm not surprised. He didn't finish his migraine till about six this morning. I wanted him to take a sickie, but he wouldn't hear of it.'

'Do as I say never works as well as do as I do,' Ian observed, checking his mirror and pulling out. And stalling; obviously he'd just realised the implication of what I'd said.

'I got scared last night,' I said as coolly as I could. What I wanted to do was laugh at the expression on the poor man's face. There was nothing he'd like better than to see Chris marry me, but in his book marriage preceded bedding, not vice versa. 'I'm very concerned for him,' I added.

'Blame Sheehy,' he said.

'He's still worrying about what'll happen to him?'

'Wouldn't you be?'

I nodded. 'And if I were a fixture at Muntz I'd be worrying harder.'

On impulse I decided to walk round the college buildings before I went in, following the route of the previous day. No one had got round to taping off the border where I was sure a ladder had rested. I wanted to phone Chris and remark on the fact, but I couldn't, not until I'd checked I was bug-free. And I hadn't phoned Simon to tell him about the electronics graveyard in the skip. I had another peer inside. If I was going to lure him over, I'd better have some idea of what there was. He wouldn't want retired soldering irons, or an enormous convector heater just like one my gran used to have. Nor valves, surely. Except that wasn't a valve. It was like the bit that was wrong on his microwave. The magnetron, that was it.

'Watch yourself, love!'

How I'd missed the approach of a skip truck, God alone knew. I moved smartly. And then thought again. I ran round to the cab. The knee gave just as I got level with his door, so I had to lean heavily for a moment. The driver scrambled down.

'You OK, chick?' He peered earnestly at me. He was about thirty, blue-eyed and fresh-faced.

'Just my knee.' I rubbed it resentfully. How could I manage the rest of my life if it was going to do this every time I asked it for a bit of effort?

'Got one of them, have you? Spot of the Gazzas? Ligament trouble?'

I shook my head. 'Not exactly. But I can quite understand why he cried.'

'Cried meself, love, when I did mine. Finished me footballing days, I can tell you.'

We grinned at each other. I started to limp away. Then I turned back to him.

'You couldn't do me the most enormous favour, could you?' I invented a little to make my request more plausible. 'Only my microwave's in the same state as my knee, and I can see a magnetron in there might just do.'

He walked back with me, his hand cupped ready to support my elbow should I need help.

'There – can you see? Only I'm too short to reach in there.'

'Bet you have problems with chest freezers, too,' he said. I didn't think a sexist pun was intended, so I grinned obligingly. 'Hang on, that'll be all dirty. Got some rags in the cab.' He jogged back unevenly, and then returned, flourishing what had once been a tea towel celebrating Australia's wildlife. He looked at his own hands, still clean before what would no doubt be a filthy day, and grimaced. 'This muck's giving me dermatitis too,' he said. 'But there aren't that many jobs for ex-footballers with delicate hands. Not round here.' He arranged the cloth in a rough mitt and leaned over into the skip. 'There!'

I took both cloth and magnetron from him, and finished wrapping it before I shoved it into my bag. No point in advertising my acquisition.

'Thank you.' And then I added, 'Not many people would have been this kind.'

He considered the matter quite seriously for a moment. 'I s'pose not. There's a lot in this world as would as soon spit in your eye as look at you. Best be on me way now, though, love.'

I waited while he reversed his truck quickly and accurately, and winched up the skip. And then I waved him out of sight. Even if he was only a chance visitor, it was nice to meet someone at Muntz who seemed to be on the side of the angels.

24

Tuesday morning's e-mail told me that my printing awaited collection. This was a posh way of saying that I should fetch from the print room a photocopied set of hand-outs on *Hamlet* for my A-level students. Back at William Murdock any printing arrived in your pigeonhole, so I rather resented having to go to the bowels of the college, especially as I wasn't happy about prowling round on my own, however much I might have hated having a police escort. Since my route took me down the main staircase, there were a number of people around, but the emptiness that had so impressed the constable was again noticeable. I caught a glimpse of Sunshine, but it was clear that neither of us wanted to engage in conversation. He headed off towards the engineering wing, which made his previous choice of my room for a new pad even more puzzling.

The print room had no obvious system for retrieving your material. As you entered, on your right there was a long table covered with piles of paper. You searched through this until you found yours. If you were less fortunate, your stuff might be on the floor underneath. More important – that is, management – printing was on another long table to the left. There was a ledger for you to sign when at last you found what you wanted. If you wished to complain that the set-up was tediously inefficient, you risked incurring the wrath of Mr Heaven, whose domain this was. His acolytes were a pair of lads from Cradley Heath built like pit-bull terriers.

I nearly fell over Polly, scavenging under the management table.

'Hi! Everything OK?' I asked quietly.

Flushed from the effort, she pulled out a pile of photocopies about fifteen inches thick. 'Been waiting for these since last half-term!' she gasped.

I held out my hands. 'Don't try and lift them all at once. Let me help. There! Hey, did you mean that – about waiting all those weeks?'

She passed me the rest and got up, dusting her knees. 'Yes.'

'Why not complain?'

'And know that the next batch I sent down would mysteriously disappear? And the next come back printed mirror-image? I'm a tough old bird, Sophie, but there are some things even I'd hesitate to risk. Thanks,' she said, taking the pile from me. 'Why not join me for an orange juice at break?'

'Great!' I smiled her on her way. That was the first time anyone here had ever made any real overture. All the more unfortunate, then, that I should be forced to snub her. But I was sure she'd forgive me when eventually I could explain.

There was something Chris had to know. As I agonised about phones, it came to me that the simplest thing to do was get my bike and simply deliver my message in person. I'd got to the far end of Wentworth Road when a familiar car appeared. I flagged him down.

'What's all this?' Chris gestured to my bike.

'Needs must when the devil drives and you haven't a safe phone. I'm due in class in forty minutes, so I can't hang about.'

Neither could he. The drivers stuck behind us both were getting vociferous.

'OK. Back to my office!'

I grinned and headed off down the hill, dodging round a very sick car on a tow truck. Chris would have to take a more circuitous route, but probably arrive before me, if I knew that glint in his eye. To my great satisfaction, however, I'd already chained up my cycle and was removing the saddle when he pulled up alongside me.

'Don't trust anyone, do you?' he observed.

'Do you? Got your percolator back yet, by the way?'

'It returned yesterday evening. Dirty. Even now it waits your pleasure.' To my surprise he gave a courtly bow.

To encourage him in his frivolity, I responded in kind. Curtsying was never meant to be easy, but I'm sure that my short skirt made it trickier. The knee locked as I tried to return to the vertical, and he had to give me his hand.

'Shoot,' he said, two minutes later, as he filled the percolator – decaff, I noticed – and switched on.

I dumped myself on his visitor's chair and my bag on his desk. 'I found something you ought to read.' I burrowed in my bag for the memo I'd removed from the print room.

He fished for those wretched spectacles, shoved them on and started to read.

> **George Muntz College of Further Education**
> FROM: Mr D. M. Blake, Chief Executive and Principal
> TO: All teaching personnel
> RE: COLLEGE REORGANISATION
> With effect from 1 June, all teaching posts will be reviewed and new job descriptions drawn up. Staff will be required to apply for each post as it arises. The posts will be subject to the George Muntz Contract, copies of which are available from the Cheif Executives Personnal Assistant.

He whistled. 'Impressive interpersonal skills. And spelling.' Then he added, 'So we now have approximately a hundred and fifty lecturers who are suspects for what may or may not be an unlawful killing. When was this released? Why haven't I seen it till now?' His voice was becoming distinctly official. I suppose it went with those specs.

'Perhaps you weren't shown it till now because I didn;t liberate it till about ten minutes ago.' I told him the circumstances. 'Who says crime doesn't pay?'

'At least you didn't do a repeat of last summer's breaking and entering,' he said gloomily. 'It took a lot of explaining away, that did.' But he poured me a coffee and passed me the sugar amicably enough.

'Me? Break and enter? Chief inspector, sir, I found the sheet of paper attached to my own photocopying. I must have picked it up by mistake when I put my pile of papers down to help Polly to her feet,' I said in a robot voice, staring at the far wall. 'And what you said about unlawful killing – any news yet?'

'They've got this expert neurosurgeon working on it. I'm seeing him later. He said he thought there were signs of a very high fever—'

'Meningitis or something?' I was prepared to be disappointed.

He shook his head. 'No. There's that business about no sign of infection in the blood. No antibodies or whatever. Why didn't you do a medical degree so you could translate all this guff?'

'Because you'd have nailed me as a suspect years ago. And you must know some long words. Getting a PhD in astrophysics argues more than your average vocabulary. But in any case –' I started to read over his shoulder – 'I wouldn't call those long words. What's this? "From the consistency of blancmange to the consistency of an omelette"? Jesus! "In a cone roughly four centimetres at the base on the outside of the skull." What in hell's caused that?'

He shrugged. 'Christ alone knows. But I guess the forensic-science team will come up with some suggestions. Got time for another coffee?'

'Haven't finished this yet. And I'm due in class in eleven minutes flat.'

'Leave your bike here. I'm running you up.' He grabbed his keys and ushered me out. 'And you can tell me all about that mysterious business of the earth having been disturbed and laid flat again. I should have picked it up last night, of course. But I want to see the place – that's why I was on my way to Muntz.'

'And you can tell me what you're doing about Melina. She's just as important as Blake, you know!'

'All I can say – and it's the honest truth, not a cliché for the media – is that we're pursuing our inquiries. But, for your ears only, we're not getting anywhere fast.' He struck a filing cabinet with the flat of his hand. 'Can't people see there's a connection between resources and results?'

It's unusual for me to be on the receiving end of a meeting's vote of thanks, but I accepted it modestly enough. And I did deserve it. I'd done more on our project than the rest of the team put together, and they knew it. Not that we were anything like finished yet. We drew up a new schedule and re-allocated work, to reflect my extra efforts. And then we adjourned to the Court Oak to celebrate. It felt good, for a change, to be sitting among friendly people who didn't want anything from me.

Chris had received the news of my evening's planned drink with Fairfax with predictable lack of enthusiasm, but since he was expected to wet some baby's head with hard-drinking colleagues, he could scarcely object. I wondered if I could wish myself on any of the people with me in the pub, or even on Polly. I still had to explain to her why I hadn't turned up at breaktime. At least I had no classes to worry about in the afternoon, only the minutes to write up, so I had another half. I'd see her later.

I don't think I'd ever seen so many policemen and women in Birmingham, apart from at the odd demo, that is. They swarmed over George Muntz, filling all those empty corridors and stairwells. If Chris had underreacted before, he was certainly making up for it now. I'd have loved simply to sneak off home, but on the principle that if anything was going on I wanted to know about it, I'd joined the little queue waiting to be admitted and then was asked by a squeaky-voiced youth to go to my office and stay there till summoned.

On the grounds that no one could get at me with so many large blue people around, I did as I was told, collecting a photocopied note from my door as I entered. This was not a Muntz memo, but one from Chris.

> I have to ask you to remain here until you have spoken to one of my colleagues. There is evidence that a serious crime has been committed, and naturally we want to exclude everyone we can from our enquiries. We will be speaking to everyone this afternoon. If you *have* to leave early – to collect children from school, for instance – please contact me on extension 2721 (the principal's secretary's extension) before you go.
>
> Thank you for your co-operation.

It was signed simply Chris Groom, with no reference to his rank. I awarded him a high grade for communication skills.

There is nothing like having to stay in a place to make you want to get up and go somewhere else. The place I most wanted to go to was Polly's room, to apologise for missing that orange juice. At least I could phone her. But other people had the same idea, if for another reason – her phone was consistently busy. I settled to a tedious half-hour writing up the minutes of the meeting, and waited for my summons. I knew Chris wouldn't make any obvious distinction between me and my colleagues, just in case anyone was still unaware of our relationship.

What relationship? That was another problem. I couldn't rely on Chris having migraines *ad nauseam* to keep me out of his bed. I had no objection – except for his sake – to being in his bed. And then it struck me, as I watched a BBC outside-broadcasting van pull off the main road, no doubt to report on the Muntz story, that I was doing to Chris precisely what I most disliked him doing to me: treating him as someone incapable of making his own decisions. Clearly Chris and I should sit down like the adults we were and talk through the whole business. And we should talk about the other things too.

At last I managed to get through to Polly, who sounded more than harassed. It seemed that not every copy of the principal's memo had been there when the police went to collect them, and Chris wanted to know how many had found their way into circulation. He saw Polly, as union rep, as a likely disseminator of information, and it sounded as if he'd given her a rough time.

'But I think I managed to convince him,' she said breathlessly. 'Sophie, that scenario is just unreal. Can you imagine what it would do to the place if we were forced on to the contract? All those part-time teachers made redundant, probably a lot of full-time ones as well. But the stupid thing is that they couldn't afford the redundancies bill. Not by my figures.'

'Surely Curtis would have worked that out?'

'My – my husband worked them out. He – he was an accountant, you see.'

I couldn't understand the hesitations; I knew about her and Tom Hendry, after all. I changed the subject, albeit rather crudely, and asked about a temporary refuge, should I need one.

There was a pause; I had clearly put my foot into something. At last she spoke, her voice constrained. 'I'm afraid – Sophie, you wouldn't know this, no reason why you should, after all – that my husband's got this ... He's paralysed, you see. One minute he's fit and healthy, the next he's got this wasting disease. The nerves and muscles. We have volunteers in to help him with ... with everything, really. His brain – that's still as clear as a bell, that's why I got him to do the figures for me – he's got this wonderful computer he can operate by blowing into a tube. That's why ... that's why I could never, ever, tell him about me and Tom, you see.'

I could think of nothing to say that would begin to be adequate.

'It's all right. I can survive. Really. That's one reason why I do all this union stuff, I suppose – to keep my mind off things at home. And it's not your fault I didn't think to tell you. Everyone here knows, see. Some people even remember him the way he was.'

'I'm so sorry. I really am. If there's ever anything – you know—'

'Thanks. Look, I'd better—'

'Hang on just a sec. Was there anything special – you know, this morning?'

'Just wanted to know if there'd been any progress with Melina. And then all this blows up. It just shows, of course, doesn't it? The fuzz take hardly any notice when Melina's killed, but when Blake dies there's all this song and dance. Even in death we're not equal.'

I could think of nothing to say because she so clearly voiced my own suspicions, but she'd already put the phone down. And then there was a knock on the door and Ian was summoning me downstairs. I set the snib carefully and followed him.

The police had taken over a couple of classrooms, running telephone extensions presumably from the admin. gulag. Outside each room was a chair for us to wait our turn for inquisition. As I took my place, giving my name and address to a middle-aged woman who looked as if she were making her shopping list, I was irresistibly reminded of queuing for head inspections at school. On whose head would they find the lice?

Chris himself ushered out the economic-history lecturer, grinning broadly and shaking his hand. I raised an eyebrow as I followed him back in and sat down.

'This guy Muntz, Sophie, what d'you know about him?' He sat too, peering at me over his glasses.

I gazed at him, nonplussed.

'Come on, George Muntz: surely you've looked him up?'

'I suppose he must be one of Brum's famous industrial sons.'

'Right. Famous for?'

I shook my head.

'You'll like this, Sophie. That guy Jim reckons he's famous for two things: owning the land on which Dorridge Station stands so one London train a day has to stop there even to this day; and replacing the copper bottoms of ships with a metal of his own invention. I wonder what he'd think of your old contract and this new one?'

I waited; it was good to see him as relaxed as this. He took his glasses off and rubbed his face, but the gesture suggested a fresh start rather than fatigue or stress.

'These holes,' he said suddenly. 'You're sure about them?'

'I told you this morning,' I said.

'Great. Because it looks as if the SOCOS have found a couple of flakes of paint missing from the windowsill of the window you identified. Dr Trevelyan's window.'

'So someone could have put something with two feet this far apart –' I moved my hands fifteen inches – 'on the ground and rested whatever it was on the sill. I suppose your missing paint flakes aren't a similar distance apart?'

'Spot on, my dear Watson. I suppose you didn't actually see anyone with a ladder?' His voice was serious again.

I shook my head. 'But why on earth would anyone want to look through Dr T's window?'

'To spy on Mr Blake? Or photograph him to blackmail him?'

'Or to watch him die?' Our eyes met. 'Or to kill him?' we said together.

25

Chris agreed that I might as well accept Fairfax's invitation for a drink that evening. He himself would be far too busy to think about me. The whole team would be at work, and some of them, he said, would be looking quite hard for Dr Trevelyan. If she was that good with computers she might well have expertise in electronics. Meanwhile, he'd probably be happier to have me tucked out of the way somewhere unlikely; Fairfax's house might not have had a moat and drawbridge, but it certainly had the twentieth-century equivalent.

In the event, Fairfax sent his car for me; as he held open a rear door for me, his chauffeur said he was delayed in a meeting. I did wonder how Fairfax himself would get home – I didn't quite see him fumbling for change on a bus – but it transpired we were to pick him up from the Mondiale. Instead of going into the city centre via one of the roads through Harborne, which I'd have thought the natural route, the chauffeur – a middle-aged man who reluctantly admitted his name was Alan – took us back up to the main Hagley Road. It was, as usual, stressfully busy, but I suppose I'd never been as safe in a vehicle as I was now. We certainly cut an impressive swathe through the traffic, and emerged from the Five Ways underpass quite regally, I thought, before pulling up on the Mondiale's forecourt. I wondered how the Mondiale would fare now Blake would no longer be holding every conceivable meeting there, though of course it was quite possible that Curtis would maintain the tradition. Would he become principal? Surely even Muntz would have to advertise the post? And even Muntz's governors might feel it incumbent on them to appoint a principal – or, rather, a chief executive – with a modicum of teaching experience.

Fairfax emerged briskly from the Mondiale, kissed my hand and, rather to my surprise, took his place in the back with me. Despite the yellow grey of his skin, he talked perkily of the improvement in the weather. It occurred to me that I hadn't even noticed the weather, but now I came to think about it, it was very warm. He asked about my knee, I about his stomach, but he waved my question aside as an irrelevance. Meanwhile the car purred its way the short journey into expense-account Edgbaston.

This time we used the front door. The bloody dog started baying as soon as Fairfax put his key into the lock. Involuntarily I put my hand on his arm.

'You really are frightened,' he said, to the accompaniment of great booms from the far side of the door. 'There's only one thing to do with fear, my dear: confront it. If Pilot senses you're afraid—'

Pilot! I didn't see Fairfax as the sort of man to read *Jane Eyre*. Or had he a memory of it from his schooldays? Perhaps he even saw himself as a Rochester figure. I'd have to ask him if he had a horse called Mesrour – or even a mad wife in the attic. And then I realised that he shared his name with the Thornfield housekeeper, the loquacious one who so irritated Jane. Perhaps, after all, he had a sense of humour.

He stepped inside and was clearly expecting me to follow. Pilot's barks dropped to a low, sustained growl, which Fairfax did nothing to abate. When I stepped forward, I could see the huge muscles and teeth preparing for action. I couldn't run away, because he'd follow; I couldn't go forward. And Fairfax maintained his implacable silence.

A grandfather clock inside struck eight. Fairfax and the dog waited. At last I found what might pass for a voice. 'Say hello, Pilot,' I said. 'Say hello.' And stuck out my hand.

I braced myself for the pain of his teeth sinking into it. Surely Fairfax wouldn't let him do any worse? But instead, my hand took the weight of his paw, and he sat, presumably waiting to have his head patted. I obliged, and when his silly litle tail started walloping the hall floor I found a little more enthusiasm.

'We'll go into the snug,' said Fairfax.

We followed.

'No, don't sit yet. He still sees you as a guest. You have to be more than that – to dominate him.'

Pilot watched with narrowed eyes as I followed Fairfax around the room. We stopped by what turned out to be a drinks cabinet disguised as a set of encyclopedias. I was disappointed – I'd expected better taste.

'Help yourself,' he said.

From the tone of his voice I knew there'd be a catch. There was. Pilot didn't like to see me touching his master's property. He snarled. So did I – I was sick of the pair of them. 'Sit down and shut up.'

He must have recognised the first verb at least, and obeyed.

'Good boy.'

'And good girl,' Fairfax echoed. 'Whisky? There's malt. Or some wine?' He opened a little fridge.

'I'd rather have red, please.' I was setting myself the tests now. Could I order Fairfax about, and how would I fare in the room with the dog?

Fairfax acknowledged the challenge with the nearest thing he'd so far managed to a smile, and I continued to wander round the room. When I thought I'd proved my point, I sat down and patted my lap. Pilot looked interested and padded over, sinking at my feet with his head on my knee. At this point Fairfax came in, and laughed out loud. He proffered an Australian Cabernet Sauvignon. 'To your taste? Yes, I thought you'd be a New World woman.' He drew the cork and poured. He made no pretence of drinking it himself, sipping mineral water. 'You did well, my dear. I wouldn't have let him hurt you, but you did well. You should face up to your fears, you know, all of them. Confront them.' He sat down opposite me. Pilot shifted so he could transfer his head to Fairfax's lap.

The wine was excellent, a wonderful bouquet and fruity on the tongue. I relaxed, as much as I ever did in Fairfax's company, and looked at him as he played with Pilot's ears. For all tonight's *bonhomie*, he was a very sick man, I was sure of it: his breathing seemed to be something of an effort.

'You really ought to break out of this rut,' he said, as if

concluding a conversation, not initiating it. 'It's clear you're bored. Everything about you says you're bored. Your job doesn't challenge you; you have the personal life of a gerbil. When are you going to get on with living? You only get one life, you know.'

I couldn't help laughing, though perhaps it was more with embarrassment than with amusement. And there was some irritation there too. 'What is this? Some conspiracy? You're the third person this month to say the same thing. But I don't see myself as a gerbil!'

'You spend your waking life doing pointless work. Then you curl up in a corner of your cage and go to sleep. I'm an expert on gerbils. My children inflicted generations of them on me. They used to live in aquariums, and die inconveniently. An exercise in pointlessness.' His face fell into bitter lines. Then he smiled again. 'They used periodically to escape. We'd find them cowering in corners. They didn't want to be caught, of course, but when they ran away they'd always go to another corner. I sense you like your corners too, Sophie.' He reached across and topped up my glass.

I could think of nothing to say, and to my chagrin found myself flushing. I told myself that it was with annoyance, but perhaps it was because I recognised a truth only a friend should have been privileged to tell me. And of course they had, Aberlene and Chris.

'Risks, that's what you should be taking at your age. Risks.' His eyes glowed and his face softened. 'A respectable job, respectable home in a respectable suburb. I bet even your friends are respectable. Nice women like Aberlene.'

I swallowed the impulse to tell him to mind his own business.

'Don't look so sulky. It's an old man's privilege to advise the young.'

I didn't interrupt to contradict him. In years he might be less than sixty; tonight he looked old.

'My advice,' he continued, 'would be to walk out of Harborne tomorrow and put yourself on a plane, go somewhere with some challenge. A one-way ticket, mind. And when you've worked your way back here, find a job that'll make you tingle with excitement. Drive a real car – none of this piddling around on a cycle.'

'Don't you mean pedalling?'

We started to laugh.

'Find yourself a decent man. No, you don't have to marry him, or have children. But someone ought to be out dancing with you, wining you, dining you. And don't tell me that anyone in your life at the moment fills the bill because I can tell you now it's quite evident no one does. You're bored. Agh!' He pressed his hand against his stomach. No more Old Father Time dispensing wisdom, just a sick man crying for help.

I was on my feet. 'What can I get you?'

'Cloakroom. In the cupboard. In a bubble pack.'

Pilot attempted a snarl.

'Stay!' I snapped, and was too anxious about Fairfax to look back.

I stood in the luxurious loo, holding the packet of tablets. They were horribly familiar; the medics had put Mum on them about two months before she succumbed to her cancer. She had fought and fought, but her constant message had been the opposite of Fairfax's. I shook myself. This was no time to think about philosophies. When my mother had demanded her tablets it meant she was in unbearable pain, and every second I dawdled meant more pain for Fairfax.

The relief was almost immediate, it seemed, but he sat with his eyes shut, fondling the dog's ears, for ten minutes.

'Shouldn't you have some food?' I asked gently at last.

'There are times,' he said without opening his eyes, 'when I want a rice pudding.'

'Rice pudding?'

'A very comforting food. Not the bland and watery variety. Thick and creamy and cooked for hours alongside the Sunday roast. My mother-in-law was a Tartar, but her rice puddings – indeed, her sago puddings – were heavenly. My wife tried to make them, but never managed it. It was a matter of honour for her not to ask her mother, and I truly believe the old bat would have died sooner than tell her. In the meantime, you'll find some water biscuits and cheese on the kitchen table. You might care to feed Pilot. Insist that he sits before you open the tin, and be prepared to hit him if he tries to eat before his bowl is on the floor.'

I stood, and clicked my fingers to the dog. 'Food?'

He got up, stretched briskly and followed me. He did sit when told, but inched closer in a rather endearing bottom shuffle. But he flinched when I caught his eye, and waited, head down, till I'd scraped the last of the meat into a red plastic bowl and put it gingerly in front of him. 'OK, get on with it.'

I picked up the tray already set with cheese and biscuits and two plates, and left the dog to it.

Alan, the chauffeur, appeared as soon as Fairfax opened the front door, and ushered me as before into the back. Had Fairfax not sagged so visibly as soon as he thought I was no longer watching him, I would have laughed all the way home at the ridiculous spectacle of me being whisked home in such state. This time we did take the suburban route, past the Botanical Gardens and then along Augustus Road. At this point I realised what I might have realised before, had the wine been less strong; another car, a Cavalier, was uncomfortably close to our tail. Some boy racer out to out-drag a flash car; no doubt Alan could shake him off if he wanted to. However, apart from increasingly irritated checks in his mirrors, he did nothing. Perhaps he was relying on the sheer power of the car to shake off the pursuer if he became too impertinent. At last he shot across the lights with some determination.

'We're being followed, aren't we?' I asked.

'Someone playing silly beggars,' he said repressively.

'Could we go straight to the police station then? I don't – Christ!'

Just before our left turn into Gillhurst Road, the tail pulled out alongside us. Simultaneously, a van shot out and pulled up nose to nose with us. Why the hell didn't Alan use his superior weight to shunt his way out? Why didn't he use the central locking to protect us?

The two drivers were out of their vehicles, one on either side of the car. The rear doors, or course. Simultaneously, they started to open them. I grabbed Alan's headrest and rolled up and over the front seats. I didn't have time to turn round to open the passenger door – I dived across his lap, ending up on my forearms on the tarmac. If I hurt him as I kicked free, I didn't care overmuch. The attackers must have taken a moment to register what I was up to; in any case, the door itself held up the man on the driver's side. I had a second – no more – to think. The Walkway!

I slid between the van and the Cavalier, and darted across the road. Just off a narrow gulley lay an access point to a disused railway, now set aside for walkers. I slithered down the cindered path, slaloming round barriers designed to stop anyone doing just that. Right, through the tunnel under the road. It's always damp under there, and I dared not lose my shoes – silly lightweight flatties. Up to my right, I could hear cursing and crashing. Perhaps they were trying to save time by forcing a way where there wasn't one. Encouraged, I slowed enough to sling my bag across my chest, and then picked up speed. If I encountered a walker, I'd ask for help. Otherwise I'd run to the end – only a mile – and pray I had enough wind to take me straight up Rose Road and the sanctuary of the police station.

Not a walker, not a cyclist in sight. I kept on, trying despite the deepening gloom to watch where my feet should go, desperate not to twist that knee again. Branches had been allowed to droop and a hawthorn slashed at my face, but I couldn't tell whether the wetness was blood or sweat. I was tempted briefly by the track through the bird sanctuary – there might still be someone in the allotments at the far end to unlock the gate. But there might not, and I'd have to battle up a steep slope through unforgiving undergrowth to get back to the main path.

Now I could see the end of the walkway, with the shallow steps back to suburban normality. Yes. But a whim drove me another twenty yards, on to the newly repaired bridge. Which way?

Dropping to my knees, I raised my head just enough to peer over the bridge's parapet. One decision made for me. No wonder I hadn't been bothered by my pursuers – a reception committee of a van and a Cavalier was waiting on the road below. I'd have to double back somehow. A vicious throb from my knee as I dropped back told me I couldn't go far, not in near darkness. The committee wouldn't wait all that long and any second the others would catch up. I'd have to risk a scramble. And then I realised the rubble on the bridge stretched on, and I could pick out fence posts. They'd extended the path into the pretty new development of tiny houses at the bottom of Park Hill Road.

It was only a matter of yards up that hill to safety. There was a gulley they might not know about, one which cut through to Rose Road. It would be amusing to lead any pursuers straight into the arms of the police. If my knee would manage. Up that hill. Then my lungs gave out. Bloody asthma!

By the Fire Station. Strong people there. Uniforms.

No! I'd make it to the police station.

And at last I pushed open the blessed front door, only to collapse in an asthmatic heap on the reception counter. I didn't even have enough breath to dig my Ventolin spray out of my bag; all I could do was gesture feebly. The woman on duty must have called for help – there'd be people trained in first aid in a police station, after all – and I suddenly heard words like 'ambulance' and 'hospital'. I managed to drag in enough oxygen to let me tip up the bag and scrabble.

There! Two miraculous drags and I was alive again.

I agreed with someone's suggestion that I could use a cup of coffee, and then put my brain back into gear.

'I suppose it's not possible to contact DCI Groom, is it?' I asked. For in the heap of detritus I'd shaken from my bag lay something that suddenly seemed very important.

26

'DCI Groom's not on duty,' said the receptionist, in a voice that said I had a cheek to ask.

'I know. I'm sorry.' He was out at a head-wetting, wasn't he, and probably Ian with him. 'Is there anyone on the team dealing with the George Muntz business I could talk to?'

There was a muttered colloquy.

'Because,' I pursued, 'I didn't get this way having a quiet evening jog.' I spread my hands, sticky with gravel rash I'd only just noticed. 'I need to report an attempted attack, and I think I'd like some protection.' I tried not to look over my shoulder as the door whooshed open. Reason told me that no one would try to pick me off under the very eyes of the police, but I found that although my mouth was making reasonable, indeed responsible, noises, the rest of me was shaking in a huge, silent scream.

One of the WPCs muttered urgently: 'She's the gaffer's woman. Better get Tom to sort her out.'

Wrong. I wasn't anyone's woman, and I didn't need sorting out. But I would be glad to get out of the reception area, where the latest whoosh of the door had admitted a stinking wino whose lice I could see from here.

I followed the WPC through the airlock to an interview room. Tom proved to be a man in his thirties with pale orange hair, a *retroussé* nose and white eyelashes. He had one of the thickest Geordie accents I'd come across outside the northeast, and was drinking tea from a Newcastle United mug. At first his expression was one of ineffable cynicism, but as my story unfolded he grew more alert.

When I paused at the point where I had dived out of the car, he raised his pencil. 'I want the gaffer in on this,' he said.

'He's on the booze tonight,' I said lightly.

'Didn't anyone ever tell you, man,' he asked, 'that we're trained to hold our beer? And knowing Chris, I'll bet he's on nothing stronger than slim-line tonic. He only left here half an hour ago, mind. Believes in his work, does Chris. Specially if it's murder. Tell you what, d'you want to get those hands seen to while I raise him? I'll get one of the lasses to sort you out, pet. And we can always start on a statement and get you looking at some faces while the memory's still warm.'

I was in their incident room scrutinising photographs when Ian surged in.

'Sophie! What the hell are you doing? They said there'd been a development, but they never said it was you who was involved. Silly buggers! The gaffer'll have your sodding hide for this, Tom.'

Orange Hair looked as serious as it's possible to look when all your features turn naturally upwards.

'Always give the full story, lad, remember that. Part of your story should have included the name Sophie.'

The men grinned, enjoying, no doubt, the thought of their serious boss soft in the head with love. I smiled gently, because my face needed some expression, but inwardly I was resolving to tell no one except Chris about the magnetron in my bag.

'I don't recognise anyone in here,' I said, patting the photos. 'And I'd say that neither of tonight's attackers was the man that drove at me on the High Street. Which reminds me, your canteen couldn't run to a tea towel and some ice, could it?' I could feel the heat from my knee. I'd stripped off my ruined tights when a WPC had dressed my hands, and could simply bundle ice cubes into the towel and swathe it round my leg. Not elegant but effective.

Tom padded off; Ian stared at me. 'What I can't work out, Sophie, is why you ran all the way up here and made yourself bad. Gave them quite a scare with your asthma. Why didn't you knock at someone's door and raise merry hell? Much more sensible.'

'I know that now. I wasn't expecting the asthma – must

have picked up some pollen to set it off. But how d'you select a household to disturb? Be tough if you chose one where they were deaf or something. Chummie getting closer all the time and you trying to yell through the letter box!'

Ian laughed but without amusement. 'There's something else, isn't there?'

'Lots of things. The first is that I'm bloody scared. Someone else's car – and I wasn't safe in that. And their nerve – a couple of hundred yards from here, and police cars constantly turning up the hill! Ian, I can't get it out of my head that the chauffeur may have been involved. Surely he could have put up more fight?'

'And if he was involved, would that mean your gentleman friend was involved?'

'Surely he's too ill?'

Before Ian could answer – and goodness knows what sensible observation he could have made – the first WPC returned, and made a point of drawing him to one side before whispering to him. They both looked at me.

'Back in five minues, Sophie – OK?'

It had to be, didn't it? I shifted my knee and thought patient thoughts.

After rather more than five minutes, Ian returned. He sat down heavily, as if trying to balance his thoughts.

'I reckon your chauffeur may be in the clear. He was out front shitting bricks – sorry, Sophie – saying his passenger had gone missing. Quite upset, he was. Seems he drove round looking for you. I almost had him in tears when I said I'd have to talk to Fairfax too.'

'Good. I'd like him to fry a bit. What about Fairfax?'

'We shall have a conversation tomorrow, don't you worry. But this chauffeur character reckons the old guy's as sick as you think he is. He begged me not to disturb him. Quite convincing. What do you think?'

Ian had so rarely asked my opinion that I was silenced. At last I managed a weak shrug of acquiescence. 'I'm in your hands. You're a pretty good judge of character.'

He hesitated.

'What would Chris do?' And suddenly I found myself yawning till the tears came. 'I think he'd say leave it.'

Ian nodded. 'I've phoned Val and she's airing the spare bed. I know you don't like her cooking, Sophie, and I dare say she wouldn't like yours, but it's a safe haven. Chris'll no doubt want to work out something more permanent tomorrow.' He looked at me meaningfully.

I chose to ignore his insinuation. 'Tina as minder?'

'Tina's too grand for that now she's a DS. Not that we couldn't ask, of course. Owes me the odd favour. But I'll warn you, she's still into chicken and chips - and reggae.'

Tina had moved in to guard me some fifteen months earlier when someone had designs on my life; I don't know which of us had irritated the other more. She had since fallen in love with a friend of mine, which was a bit of a problem because he was gay.

'Has she got over Courtney?' I asked, smiling my thanks to Tom, who'd returned with a red plastic bucket full of ice, apparently from the inside of a freezer, and a striped tea towel.

'Still hoping, still visiting him in Durham nick when she gets free time. And busy decorating a flat for him for when he comes out in June. I don't know, Sophie, these kids. Mind you, you didn't set her a good example - which you should have done, being a teacher.'

'I told her he was gay. What else could I do? She's in for a lot of heartache if she doesn't accept that.'

We nodded solemnly; and I realised I didn't like Ian's assumption that I at least was old enough to know better.

For form's sake, and to divert the conversation, I flicked through the photos again. Where on earth was Chris?

'Come on, love, you look as if you've done enough for one day,' Ian said at last, taking the file from me. 'We'll stop off at your place and get your things, and then I'm taking you home.'

I was forced into it: 'What about Chris?'

Ian laughed. 'You won't want to see him. I've never seen a man get pissed as quickly as he did tonight.'

Val, Ian's wife, pressed another Weetabix on me, but I was firm: I had to get back home, if that was where Chris had said he'd meet me. I also wanted to be there before him, so that I could get into some clean clothes. Washing my hair and showering were on the agenda too, provided I could fit rubber gloves over the bulky dressings on my hands. On further consideration, however, it might be a good idea to soak them off and put on fresh ones, and I was engaged in this when Ian called upstairs to say Chris had arrived. My hair, alas, still hung wet about my ears.

'Give me a couple more minutes! Brew up some coffee while you wait,' I called over the banister.

The slam of my front door suggested either that he'd taken umbrage or that he'd sent Ian off. I finished my hair, wincing as I shifted my grip on the brush or dryer, and then slapped on some make-up. I had a feeling I might need a false front as the day progressed.

At least I looked better than he did – he gave the impression that he'd prefer quieter Alka-Seltzer. I slotted a couple of slices of wholemeal bread into the refurbished toaster and slapped both butter and low-fat spread on to a tray on the table. When he merely looked martyred, I dug out a pot of apricot jam and plonked that down too.

'Sophie—'

'I'll talk when you've eaten,' I said. And, since the toast smelled good, popped in another couple of rounds for myself. 'I think we'll eat on the patio.'

He took the tray while I unlocked. It was cool, but looked as if it might warm up later.

'About last night,' he began.

'Titus Andronicus, were you? Never mind, this coffee'll sort you.'

'I'm sorry, I should have—'

I didn't want apologies. I fetched my handbag and, dropping it on the table, ferreted inside.

'There!'

'What the hell?' He looked at the object more closely, but glanced up at me before touching it.

I shook my head. 'I wouldn't. It might be perfectly innocent, of course, in which case it'll be covered in prints, but let's not risk it. Be more interesting, I suppose, if it's been wiped clean.'

'But what is it?'

'The business part of a microwave – at least I think so. I found it in a skip at work. I rescued it to see if it would help Simon – you can see what a good job he did with my toaster. But . . .'

'Come on, spit it out!'

'Do you remember,' I said slowly, 'that old story about a woman shoving her poodle into a microwave to dry its darling fur – and cooking it? We have this guy whose brain ends up more like an omelette than a blancmange. There couldn't possibly be a connection, could there?'

'Jesus! How revolting!'

'Is there someone in the forensic-science lab who wouldn't laugh at the idea? Because I'd like to ask Simon if it's possible. I wanted to last night, but I thought I'd better get your permission.'

'You *are* taking this seriously!'

'I am.'

He pushed away his coffee, rubbing his hands over his face. 'How good's this chap?'

'He'll fix anything electrical. He fixed my radio. And the toaster. He'd be discreet, too. He'd tell us if the theory's viable. Better than making laughing stocks of ourselves?'

'Phone him and tell him we're on our way. Bloody bugs!'

Adrian, wearing a towelling bathrobe and quite clearly nothing else, opened Simon's front door. I could have done without him; I was going to be in the awkward position of swearing Simon to secrecy even from his lover. Even more unpleasant for him, perhaps, especially in view of Adrian's flounce when we asked to speak in private, and the prima-donna slam of the door when he'd shown us into the living room and gone off in search of Simon.

Chris raised his eyes heavenwards. 'I thought viola players were supposed to be the serious, reliable types of the orchestra.'

'There's a whole set of jokes about them on the Internet!' Then I heard Simon's voice in the hall outside.

He hadn't shaved but had pulled on jeans and an Oxfam T-shirt, a shade of green that didn't suit him but with gaudy parrots, which did. He flicked his eyebrows when Chris repeated the need for absolute confidentiality, and wouldn't sit down. But as Chris outlined the problem he stopped fiddling with an out-of-control spider plant and gave us more and more of his attention. Without speaking, he dug in a cupboard for some paper, and sat down at the table. Then he pushed away again, and hunted irritably before pouncing on a calculator.

'There!' he said at last, pushing the paper towards us.

Chris and I stood shoulder to shoulder and read.

I suppose with Chris's background it meant more to him than to me. I got as far as F = 2,450 MHz before my interest wavered. But Chris dabbed his forefinger on one of the further equations. 'Yes! And it would be conical, wouldn't it?'

'But how would you deliver it?' asked Simon.

'Would some ducting do? Because the headset cables were in ducting?'

'Ideal.'

'That's what I thought. So if you assume a heat rise of, say, 20°C, then –' His voice dropped, he took Simon's pencil and started some equations of his own. 'There! Less than ten seconds to kill a man.'

'But from outside a window?' I chimed in.

'Remote control. Like on your telly,' said Simon. 'You'd need thoughtful preparation beforehand, but you wouldn't be long doing it. And a couple of minutes afterwards to remove the evidence.'

'With the victim sitting there plugged into his machine. Hey, Chris, was the computer still running?'

'Fancy your not noticing! Yes, the screen was blank, but the computer was still switched on.'

'Some sort of shutdown programme,' said Simon. 'What was this person watching, anyway?'

'I wish I could tell you,' Chris said, sounding genuinely regretful, 'but it's still confidential. Out of my hands, now, actually – it's been taken over by another team. I'll let you know when I'm allowed to.'

The men smiled at each other.

'It's a bit unusual, isn't it, someone in your position knowing this stuff?' Simon said.

'I could say the same of you. Playing a big wooden fiddle and this sort of knowledge ...' Chris shook his head. 'My background's no use at all to my job, but at least it got me accelerated promotion. I can't see it whizzing you up to the front desk of the basses.'

Simon bowed his head ironically at Chris's use of the appropriate term. 'Nor on to the coach for Cardiff. I'm sorry, but now you'll have to excuse me.'

Chris was in the driver's seat of his Peugeot, staring at Simon's calculations.

'I'm not going to wait any longer,' I said. 'What's this about the computer? What the hell was Blake watching?'

He looked at me repressively and then laughed. 'OK. So long as you promise—'

I crossed my heart exaggeratedly and pressed a finger to my lips.

'Commercial Vice are involved. Very high-class, very professional virtual-reality porn. The electrodes would be attached to, er, the parts you wanted stimulated.'

'So much for Mr Blake's being a pillar of the Methodist Church. So where would he have got the stuff?'

Chris rubbed his forehead. 'There's no sort of identifying material, no warnings about copyright, no salacious trailers, nothing. Just straight in – as it were.' He blushed, then started to laugh, but more, it seemed, with embarrassment.

'Are you implying that it could be home-grown? Made at Muntz? I mean, doesn't that sort of thing require an enormous amount of expertise – and resources, come to think of it?'

He nodded. 'I'm going to have to ask some interesting questions. Me and some Commercial Vice people. Any ideas?'

'Tricky, since he made most of the engineers redundant last week. I suppose you could pursue a couple of lines – those who were disgruntled and those who were favoured enough to stay.'

'Sophie, love, we shall be pursuing *every* line.'

27

'Better get you back to work,' Chris said at last, starting the car.

'Work? Hell! I never phoned in or anything!'

He passed me his mobile phone and pulled into the traffic. 'Never thought I'd see the day when you forgot to go to work,' he said mildly, when I'd left a message with a secretary I didn't know to say I was on my way.

'Me and Mrs Cavendish both. Christ, she must be dying if she's taken time off!'

'I'm not sure you ought to mention the D-word in the context of George Muntz. And I may well have been joking – are you sure you ought to be going back?'

'A-level class this afternoon. Only a couple of weeks to D-day. But I'm not convinced I want to sit in my office waiting for someone to come and get me. Chris, I just want to go and lose myself in Rackhams or somewhere and get some clothes and make-up and then go and have my hair done – like normal women do!'

'You look all right as you are to me.'

'*Oh, reason not the need!*' I said, rather more passionately than he seemed to think necessary.

He looked at me sideways, but probably did not dare speak, even to identify the quotation.

We were halfway along Edgbaston Park Road before I condescended to speak to him again. 'You're not going to like this,' I began, 'but I want to find something out.'

'How?'

'I don't quite know how to go about it.'

'Try legally.'

'Do you want to pull this lot together or not?'

He checked his rear-view mirror and pulled sharply across the road into a shallow lay-by nibbled into the grounds of some of the university halls of residence. Without speaking, he got out. I followed. He turned long enough to zap his alarm, but then set off briskly towards the ornamental lake. I followed at my own pace, which, after the previous night, was slow. I rather thought that what would clear the air better than most things would be a nice friendly bonk, but still hesitated to suggest it. He looked so painfully vulnerable - something about the set of his neck, perhaps. At last he turned, dug his hands in his trouser pockets, and waited.

As I got level with him, I shoved my arm through the crook of his. 'You do jump to conclusions, Chris.'

'Usually the right ones.'

'OK. Try this for size. I think there's something fishy about that little outpost of the Muntz empire out in Newtown. I'd like to know what it's got planning permission for. I'd also like some idea of just how much would have to be spent before it became viable - as anything. I'm sure one of your people could easily find the former - is it the Land Registry where you can look things up? And I dare say it might be possible to get official access to the premises, but I'd guess that would take some time. All I wanted you to do was drive past and smell gas.'

'Smell gas?'

'So you can reasonably break in to check your suspicions,' I said, smiling limpidly.

'The old Ways and Means Act?' He stopped and rubbed his feet against the grass, wiping some goose droppings off his shoes. I couldn't blame him. He always had the most elegant shoes, which he kept immaculate. But I didn't like the expression on his face. 'OK,' he said at last. 'I'll find out who can do what there, check for planning applications—'

'Including any that have been turned down!'

He nodded. 'But you are not, repeat not, to go diving into a dangerous derelict building. And neither am I. Sophie, don't you realise the days of bending the rules are over? I have to play things by the book. I have to *try* to find the keyholder and get permission. And – and I don't – please, please understand – I—'

If ever a man needed a hug, it was Chris. I gave him one. After a moment he returned it. When we separated I reached up and kissed him lightly on the lips. But I didn't make the promise he was hoping for.

As Chris pulled into his slot in the police-station car park, another car drove in alongside him: Dave Clarke. He grinned and gave me an overintimate wave of the fingers, then got out and opened my door for me.

'How about some of that excellent coffee of yours, Chris?'

This time Dave sat on a chair like everyone else, and made no attempt to flirt. Chris filled him in on the affairs at Muntz, and then I chimed in.

'I think the college finances may be in a mess. You see, colleges need lots of students to survive these days, and Muntz – as one of your lads, that ex-teacher, pointed out – is singularly lacking in that respect. There's a project called 'College without Walls', I've seen the file – no, only the outside. And I had a phone call from Aberlene saying there was a Muntz outpost in Bradford, of all places, and there's that warehouse I was telling you about in Newtown, Chris.'

He picked up the phone. 'Thanks for reminding me. I'll get someone on to that now. Now what's this about Bradford?'

'I tried to phone her, left a message on her machine, but she hasn't called me back. Bradford already have a college – I had an interview there once. I can't see why Muntz should want to muscle in on their territory. I don't suppose you've got any contacts up there?' I paused while Chris spoke into the phone. 'There was also a file about Provence.'

'I think I ought to go out and investigate that myself,' said Dave. 'When you've got a couple of weeks free, Sophie.'

I didn't need to make much effort to ignore him. I had a genuine idea to divert me. 'Hey, I'll tell you who might know – my boss at William Murdock. James Worrall.'

'That stuffed shirt,' said Chris. 'Ex-navy.'

'That's right. But he's been very helpful to me recently, when Muntz tried to pull the plug on our project. Insisted we kept it going.'

'At Muntz or at William Murdock?' Chris asked delicately.

'Bastard!'

'Ah, at Muntz.' He laughed. 'Have you spoken to him about this?'

'On a bugged phone?'

Dave Clarke whistled. 'Bugs? What the hell do you know, Sophie?'

'I wish I knew. But tell you what, that morning you came leaping into my house yelling about fraud - I bet they heard that.'

Chris looked up sharply. Had someone suppressed that bit of information?

'When we had that lovely breakfast date?' Dave smiled lecherously.

I raised a cooling eyebrow; he had the grace to look a touch ashamed. 'It was the day Fairfax took me on the river, the day Aggie was duffed up, two days before all that graffiti and Blake's death. The long arm of coincidence, maybe. But it's worth thinking about.'

'Money makes people do weird things,' said Dave. 'There was this guy we took to court in Leicester—'

The phone rang; Chris pounced. Then he got up wearily and gathered up his jacket. 'Got to go and tell them upstairs why I've been spending our precious budget. I may be gone, to coin a phrase, some time. Sophie, I—'

Dave and I stood up too.

'Dave - any chance of a lift back to college?' I preferred to ask in front of Chris. 'I had a bit of a fall last night and I'm—'

'Afraid for her life,' said Chris grimly. 'You'd better feed her too, Dave. And watch it - she's got hollow legs, that woman.'

'And very lovely they are too,' Dave added, as if on cue.

Once in his car, however, he made no attempt to flirt. 'Tell me about this warehouse place.'

'I could show it you - it's not all that far from Lloyd House. Get us into the city and I'll give you directions from there.'

'Only if you let me buy you some lunch.'

'Of course. But it may have to be another day; I'm teaching this afternoon.'

‘And you think this is important enough to miss lunch for?’ His profile was serious and alert.

‘Yes,’ I said baldly.

Nothing about the premises had changed, except the number of cars outside. Dave had to snake round several unsavoury streets before he could find a slot, in which he made rather a pig’s ear of parking.

‘OK,’ he said, hitching round to face me and laying his arm across the back of my seat, ‘what next?’

‘Follow me,’ I said.

We stared at the locked gates, the corrugated iron over the windows, the locked front door. He peered through the gaps in the gates, and then at the Muntz logo. The sun warmed the pigeon droppings. I swear it was he who said it: ‘You know, I’m sure I can smell gas. Hey, what’s so funny about that?’

I cackled, but forbore to tell him.

It was easy enough to slip through one of the loose panels in the gates. Dave took my arm to steady me as I followed him. The willowherb promised to be magnificent later in the year, but there was nothing else exciting. Stacks of very rusty drums near the building, some cables the size of hawsers over to our left, and beyond the building itself, as we picked our way over what might once have been a tarmac road, a huge expanse of very little indeed except tussocks of grass and odd piles of old bricks.

‘Funny,’ said Dave, as we headed back to the road. ‘I can still smell gas. I really think, as a responsible citizen, I ought to find the source. What do you think?’

I nodded, but then blurted, ‘Chris won’t like it! He’s trying to get access officially.’

‘That could take hours. Look, Sophie, Chris won’t know. And you won’t be doing anything to upset him, either. You, sweetheart, are going to sit here in the sun – sorry about the pong, but there you are – and give a little whistle if anyone comes. Oke? Come on, kid, with that knee you could be a real liability.’

I grimaced, but sat on a drum. ‘Any particular choice of tune?’

‘Tone deaf, sweetheart, that’s me.’ And with that he dragged a couple of drums to a flattish spot by a window, stacked one on the other, and swung himself up on them. It took him seconds to pull the corrugated iron away.

I expected a long and boring wait, and was mentally planning what I'd do with a site like this, when a door a few feet from me opened slowly but noisily outwards. Dave! He gestured with his head, and I got off the drum and joined him. As soon as I was safely in, he closed the door behind me.

'Never seen anything like this, sweetheart.' He dropped his voice as if in church. 'No, there's no one here, but college this isn't. Look!'

I had never seen cobwebs like these, skeining from floor to ceiling. Swarf glistened in great tubs beside milling and grinding machines. Half-finished work awaited the end of a long-gone lunch break. Like children we stared and, in silence, tiptoed onwards over dusty floors. Other people had been here recently enough to have left tracks, but already the dust was smudging them. In one corner was an office; the typewriter still had a sheet of paper in it. The boss's tray stood on a cupboard, green and silver-spotted cups stacked on saucers that must have matched, though from where we stood we could see only grime.

'It's magic,' Dave breathed at last. 'Fucking magic!'

I nodded but did not speak.

Silently we explored: storerooms; the time clock; the lavatories, even.

'So it wasn't gas, but them.' Dave pointed at encrusted urinals, and laughed. The sound echoed uneasily, and with one accord we turned away.

We were in the main workshop area when we heard it. The scrape and slam of our escape door. And then a cough, and a slowish shuffle of footsteps towards us. I pressed my hand across my mouth to hold back my scream. Dave, under blurs of dust, was greenish pale. He, like me, was scanning for escape routes. But we'd left footprints in all that dust, of course, and further prints would betray us wherever we tried to hide. Dave took my arm, gripping firmly just above the wrist.

Though I was sure I could hear nothing else except the beating of my heart and the whooshing of blood in my ears, it occurred to me that those footsteps had stopped. Well, they would. Someone out there was as scared as we were. There was no click from a safety catch being released – but then, he might be carrying a knife, not a gun. Then the steps started to recede – he was backing off! At last we heard the door slam, and then a dreadful scream.

Dave moved before I did, pushing me aside as he pelted out.

'Take care, you silly sod,' I hissed, but nonetheless I followed him.

I pushed open the door to find a pool of blood. Dave was half crouched over a frighteningly still shape. I knelt.

'Don't touch him, you silly bitch! Get the fuck out of here. Here, take my keys. Get my first-aid kit. Get!' He was already talking into his mobile phone as I stood up.

As I hurtled through the streets, I tried to make sense of it. The blood. A bottle. The figure, male, any age between thirty and sixty, emaciated. Was the bottle broken? Did that explain the blood?

I snatched up the first-aid box and started back. But my chest was tight from all that dust, and I had to slow down and fish out my inhaler. So the ambulance and a panda car were already there when I pushed back through the gap in the gates. They set up a drip – he must be alive, then – and were ready to lift him on to a stretcher. The WPC seemed to know Dave, but I wasn't sure whether in the circumstances that was a good thing. And I wasn't sure how welcome any contributions from me might be. I watched while he shepherded her inside, and then decided to tag along. The more feet messing up evidence that Chris wouldn't like, the better. Dave seemed to have much the same idea. He was veritably dancing with enthusiasm where my tracks were clearest, and encouraged my carefully feigned cries of shock and amazement.

I pieced together the official story; we had come to look at the place – well, that was undeniable – and had seen this man with a bottle breaking in. Dave had naturally followed, but the man had turned and bolted back past him. He'd then collapsed, haemorrhaging.

'I thought he'd cut himself on that bottle.'

'Yeah, so did I at first. But then Sophie here – she was only going to touch him, Sue, with no gloves or anything. So I sent her off for my first-aid kit, only to realise he was coughing up his lungs. Christ, never seen anything like it. The rest you know. But look at this, Sue.'

'You know what it reminds me of?' Sue said slowly. 'That place in the Jewellery Quarter. That factory they've set up as the Discovery Centre. I took my parents round when they came last time. The curator said everyone - bosses and workers - just walked out one day; they even left their tea and jars of jam. They're still there. And now this place.' She stopped and looked around her. 'Someone's got to know about this, Dave. This is treasure trove. This is real history.'

'You'd never guess she's got a bloody degree in the subject, would you?' said Dave, with a mixture of affection and asperity.

'Talking about degrees,' I said, 'my class starts in twenty minutes' time. And I'm going to need someone's wheels to get me there.'

'What d'you teach?' asked Sue, as we all walked back.

'English. Really I work at William Murdock—'

'My kid brother's going there,' she said. 'To do his A-levels. Science.'

We talked about the place while she drove us to where Dave's car was parked. Despite the alarm, someone had taken a coin to the paintwork on the driver's side, and ripped off the wing mirrors for good measure.

28

I taught the class without incident and was safely at home when Chris arrived. The kitchen was smelling warmly aromatic. He sniffed, suspiciously.

'Rice pudding,' I said. 'And sago, too.'

'In May?'

'For Richard Fairfax. He's very ill, Chris.'

He looked sceptical.

'Where would you like your tea? On the patio?' I reminded him.

Sighing, he took the hint and the tea tray. We sat side by side, the silence between us growing till I decided to end it.

'In fact,' I said, pressing a lemon ring against the side of the cup, 'I'd bet he's got cancer. Stomach cancer, to be precise. He's taking the same sort of tablets as my mother took when she was dying. Morphine-based. It may even have spread: his breathing's getting laboured. His housekeeper leaves him cheese and biscuits on a tray and he craves milk puddings. Sugar leaves them too bland, so I've used golden syrup to sweeten them. I've cheated a bit – I started them in the microwave while I warmed the oven. I hope they'll be all right.'

'And how do you propose to take Mr Fairfax his puddings? Even his car doesn't seem to be immune to – to the interest of other motorists.'

'Taxi. Nice and anonymous.'

'And nice and visible. And not trained in protective driving.'

'How about you, then? He lives not very far from you, as it

happens. It would only take you an extra couple of minutes.' What perhaps I ought to have done was confide in Chris the other reason for my going, but I wasn't happy with my duplicity. Visiting a dying man merely to read his files seemed in poor taste, but there had to be something important about the Newtown site. I had a terrible fear that Fairfax and Muntz were not about to donate an important piece of industrial and social history to the citizens of Birmingham: their altruism was much too limited for that. And you don't try to kill someone who might be about to find out that sort of secret. I wished I had the resources Chris – or the opposition! – could summon at will: a miniature camera would make this evening's work far simpler. 'You could even collect me afterwards,' I added, conscious of another silence.

For answer he turned to me, cupped my face in his hands and kissed me extravagantly. Soon he was out of his chair, kneeling so his body pressed against mine. And then two things happened: the kitchen buzzer buzzed and my chair collapsed. It was some moments before he joined in my laughter.

His face was stern as he pulled me to my feet. 'Are you sure the events of this lunchtime occurred in the order Dave Clarke says they did?'

I blinked at his change of mood. I didn't answer immediately, largely, I suppose, because my conscience was far from squeaky-clean, which made me unreasonably angry. In fact, I decided not to reply at all, but to sweep, as best I could, into the kitchen. The milk puddings lay golden on the table by the time he joined me. I didn't acknowledge him, but reached for a basket which I padded with newspaper to hold the casserole dishes secure. I covered the lot with a red check tea towel. It occurred to me that should I be able to purloin Fairfax's files, then they'd fit nicely into the same basket and arouse no suspicion. Until he realised they'd gone, of course. And then he'd think the puddings had been nothing more that a ruse. Yet I was genuinely sorry for a poor bastard dying a vile death when I myself was fit and healthy.

I slung on a lightweight jacket and picked up the basket and my handbag.

'You look like Little Red Riding Hood,' he said sadly.

For the first time I looked him honestly in the eye. 'Chris, you did double-check his chauffeur, didn't you? He's completely in the clear? You see, what I'm afraid is that it won't be Granny but the Wolf I find there.'

'What'll you do if he isn't in? And I must say, turning up without warning on the doorstep of someone as busy as Fairfax seems to be a pretty long shot,' said Chris, pulling neatly into the drive up to the Fairfax mansion and applying the handbrake.

'You know something: I'd be happier if he weren't in,' I said truthfully. 'I should leave them in the porch, go home with you and leave a message on his answering machine.' And await developments.

'I'll wait for you here,' he said.

'And if I don't come straight back I'll phone you and expect either you or Ian,' I confirmed dutifully.

There were a couple of cars in the drive, big Rovers. Good. Plan C: ring the door, hand over goodies, leave – no spying possible. Nonetheless, as I rang the doorbell, my heart was beating unpleasantly hard.

I heard Pilot long before Fairfax's step, and I suspect that when the door opened I smiled first at the dog, who to my relief promptly offered his paw. Fairfax seemed completely bewildered, but then smiled with what appeared to be real pleasure.

'The meeting is just ending,' he said to me – and to the meeting, perhaps, for, as I entered the snug, Philip Berkeley and Frank, the solicitor whose surname escaped me, got to their feet. Meanwhile Pilot kept nudging my hand with his head, a quite blatant request to have his ears scratched. I obliged.

'You know Berkeley and Laker, don't you?' Fairfax asked, but not as if it concerned him. As perhaps it didn't – he was greenish grey about the mouth. 'And Michael Hobbs?'

I nodded.

'Not as well as I'd like,' Hobbs said. 'But I'm sure we could work out a price.'

Before I could respond – and my tongue leaps into action of its own accord in such circumstances – Fairfax snapped,

'Perhaps I haven't made it clear, Hobbs, that Miss Rivers is a friend and colleague I value very highly, very highly indeed.'

Pilot's amiable panting chilled into a much less homely rumble. I wondered what would happen if Fairfax or I told him to kill.

I fussed his ears and sat down while Fairfax showed the men out. What the hell was going on? Valued I might be, but Fairfax had closed his files and shuffled them into a heap on the occasional table next to his favourite chair. I could hear sharp words being exchanged in the hall, but the door was too heavy for me to eavesdrop. When I stopped fondling Pilot, he started to sniff at my basket, which I'd put down at my feet.

'Not for you,' I laughed, reaching for his collar to pull him away.

He turned on me, snarling.

In a moment, he reeled across the room, whimpering. Fairfax, the business directory in his hand, stood over him.

'Sophie: come here.'

I obeyed. He passed me the directory.

'But—'

'Hit him. And yell at him.'

I managed the yelling. Pilot cowered. Fairfax took my wrist, and forced my hand first towards my chest, and then into a hard backhanded slash. I was as powerless as the dog.

He took my elbow and compelled me graciously to my seat. 'The Australian red, wasn't it?'

'I only came to deliver these,' I said, lifting the basket to my lap.

He took it from me and lifted the tea towel. The sago's golden skin had split in a couple of places, but not much had slopped. The rice pudding was intact.

'What can I say? My dear, I'm very touched.' He kissed my hand and held it a moment to his cheek.

It had been foolish to drink even one glass of that heady Australian wine on an empty stomach. I covered my glass to stop him pouring more. He, of course, was entirely sober, having had nothing but those big stomach tablets and mineral water.

He'd been talking, I think, about his sponsorship of several concerts in next season's MSO calendar, and about the tax advantages. I'm good at nodding sagely even when entirely out of my depth – and, indeed, half asleep. But there are times when the mouth takes over of its own accord.

'Tell me, Richard.' It still felt strange to be using his first name. 'All this money you're busy doling out to the MSO – and don't think I'm not really grateful on their behalf, because I know they need it – tell me how you make all this lovely dosh.'

He laughed. 'Property development, my dear.'

'But I'd have thought that was dodgy in a recession like this. Look at all the money the Church of England's lost.'

He laughed again. 'But the Church doesn't have the benefit of my knowledge, my experience, Sophie. One man's loss is another man's gain – though no doubt you'd prefer me to use the word "person". And I've had one or two little gains. But I get the feeling you're not interested in money.'

'Not *per se*. But for what it'll do.'

'What would you do if you suddenly found you had – let's say £10 million?'

I stared at him. '£10 million? Would that be enough?'

'My dear Sophie, how much would you want?'

'Enough to make an impact. Enough to fund something that would change people's lives – travelling clinics in Africa, maybe a women's hospital in—'

'My dear child, it's supposed to be *your* life that's changed! Remember my advice the other day?'

I nodded. I'd let slip a splendid opportunity, and I needed another. I might have to make it.

'Are you going to take it?' he prompted.

'Not until after my students have taken their exams. And there's all this business at Muntz to be resolved. Poor Melina —'

'Melina?'

'The computer technician.'

'But that was clearly suicide.'

'It doesn't seem at all clear now. And Blake's death too, of course. I suspect until they've got to the bottom of it, the police wouldn't like us to go bombing off on unscheduled trips round the world. Any of us.'

'And you especially. That policeman of yours—' He grabbed his stomach. 'Dear God!'

I went for his tablets.

When his colour returned, I said, 'You'd be better in bed, if you ask me.'

'That sounds terribly medicinal. Perhaps you're right, my dear. But on one – no, two conditions. One, you fetch me a bowl of that ambrosial concoction of yours; two, you accept a little gift from me.' He didn't wait for an answer, but gathered his files up and carried them to the far wall. Tweaking a Flemish interior, he revealed a wall safe. He zapped it with his key fob and that was that.

Pilot led me to Fairfax's bedroom, which glowed warmly in the late-evening sun. The Impressionists on the wall didn't look like Athena prints. Fairfax reclined on a day bed at the foot of his bed, the gorgeous brocade of his dressing gown making him look paler and frailer than ever. He accepted the tray graciously, then produced a small, flattish package, beautifully wrapped. I opened the package in front of him. A bra and pants set in apricot silk. I stared at him.

'What would make me very happy,' he said, 'would be for you to try them on – my bathroom is over there. No! I shan't ask to see them, don't think that! And in any case ...' He let his voice drop and his hand suggested a regretful farewell.

I suppose in real time it didn't take me long to make my decision. He was sick, too sick for sex. Maybe too sick even for fantasies. I could stomp out in outrage, or I could laugh at him, or I could simply take his request at face value. Without speaking, I headed for the bathroom, which was overwarm and rich with mahogany and brass. There was no sign of any peepholes or spy cameras. There were alarm bells by the lavatory and over the bath, little trickles of plaster showing how recently they'd been fitted. In a moment I undressed. The undies fitted.

'If you don't come out now, I shall demand to see them on,' he called.

I slung my clothes back on and, more shyly than I liked, re-emerged.

His eyes worked up and down my body. 'Yes. But maybe

you should go now. Or perhaps I might forget myself.' He pressed a phone into my hands. 'Make your travel arrangements, my dear.'

We spoke of azaleas for five minutes before his doorbell rang.

29

'I blew it, Chris. I'm sorry.' I forgot the elementary rule for dealing with Chris: never let him know all I was up to. Part of my mind was still circling the business of Fairfax and the lingerie, the rest was trying to blot it out.

Chris was at his kitchen sink, draining pasta. Some of it escaped from the colander.

'Look, if you fish it out of the sink and scald it, no one'll be any the wiser.' Not the most intelligent observation, since there were only two of us there anyway.

He stared appraisingly at the amount left in the colander, grimaced, and scooped ineffectually with a spoon.

'Here!' I fished with my fingertips, thus, of course, making the procedure even more distasteful. 'Damn it, Chris, your sink's the cleanest in the Western world. My hands were clean. That sauce is rich enough to disguise any faults.' I lifted the lid and gave it an extra stir. Magic. Tomatoes – sun dried, of course – wine, olive oil: Chris's cooking had come on a great deal since I'd taken him in hand.

'What was that about blowing it?'

'Look, of course I was being a nice little angel of mercy. But I wanted to get a look at his Muntz-related files. And I wanted to ask about his money making. And I thought I might just mention Melina to see what his reaction was. He thinks it was suicide. I didn't get round to asking any other questions. But I'll tell you this for nothing: the man has power and enjoys it. Thank God he's not a teacher or a copper. Think of all the harm he could do.'

I poured another glass of mineral water. My head was

starting a slow, throbbing ache, so I fished in my bag for a couple of aspirins before sinking down at the table.

'But why you, Sophie, for God's sake? Why not leave it to us professionals?'

'Because I'm involved, remember, and also – though I hate to admit it – because I'd rather you than Dave got the credit for sorting it out.'

He plonked the heavy casserole down beside me, and some of the sauce splashed up – viciously staining, of course. He'd grabbed a J-cloth before I knew it, and there he was, dabbing at the shoulder, and then at the patch below the top button.

'I'm sorry, I'm sorry—' he began.

But then the button was undone, and the next, and he was kissing my breasts, tipping me backwards and sideways and grabbing at my zip. And then he pushed himself from me, the effort visible in his face. He turned away quickly, gripping the back of a chair. 'I'm sorry, I – I'm losing control.'

I put my hands on his shoulders, rested my face against his back. 'Chris, don't you think that's the best thing you could possibly do? Come on, love.' I moved round so I could lead him upstairs or wherever.

His knuckles whitened.

'Come on, love.' I reached up and kissed him.

At first he was wooden under my lips, but at last I could feel him relax. Hand in hand like children we went upstairs.

I'd rather expected he'd be overcome by passion again, but he sat solemnly beside me and, without speaking, started to undress, hanging his trousers over the back of a chair. So I grabbed him and rolled him backwards, kissing him everywhere I could find and willing him to respond. There were lots of little delays: my skirt button flying off; the bedside drawer sticking as he groped for condoms; the wretched foil refusing to tear; one of his pubic hairs getting stuck on the adhesive of a dressing on my hand. And then my undies. I'd forgotten the bra had a strange front fastening. This couldn't have been the destiny Fairfax had intended for his gift. I wanted to laugh, but couldn't risk upsetting Chris. In any case I could hardly explain the joke. I wanted, after all, to boost his ego, not destroy it.

I don't know that at any point he let himself go. And when

it was time for him to enter me, he drew back, gazing at me with an expression that frightened me in its intensity. Then he came almost at once. I held him there, comforting him, stroking the sweat from his face, wishing what I'd done would help him feel happier.

At last I had to move. He watched me as I padded off to the loo. Another way of cheering him up occurred to me, and I retrieved a couple of glasses and a bottle of Penfold's red from the cupboard under the stairs. Pity I had to go back for a corkscrew.

The condom had discreetly disappeared when I got back.

'You could have had my dressing gown,' he said, sounding almost aggrieved.

'What for?'

He looked embarrassed.

'Chris, love, why should I want to cover myself up? After what we've just been enjoying?' I kissed the nearest bit I could find – his left shoulder – and slipped in beside him in bed.

'All the same.' He carefully kept the sheet in place.

I poured and, reaching across him, set the bottle on the bedside table on his side. My breasts touched him as they passed. The nipples promptly stood to attention. He took no notice. It wasn't the rejection that worried me so much as the expression on his face. If this was merely postcoital *tristesse*, he had it in a big way. But I was sickeningly sure it was something worse.

'Chris? Chris, love?'

'Hmm?'

'Problem?' I took his hand, shaking it gently from side to side. The gesture was meant to be ambiguous – either friendly or amorous, whichever way he needed to see it. I hoped at very least he would turn his hand over to clasp mine. But he didn't. He turned his face from me.

This was something I hadn't been prepared for, and I simply didn't know what to do. Sex with my long-term partner Kenji had always been brilliant, even when the relationship itself was dwindling into a battle between my marking and his research, and a couple of more casual affairs hadn't entailed anything like this. I shook his hand again.

No response.

'Chris? What's wrong?'

He muttered something.

'Guilt? Why guilt?'

Again no response.

'Chris, we're adults. Unattached. Came here of our own free will, both of us. Where's the guilt in that?'

For answer he shook his head; and all I could do was speculate on what his upbringing had done to him. Surely the modern Catholic view of sex wouldn't be screwing him up like this?

What I wanted to do was fire him up again so he could simply smother guilt with lust; what I did was simply rest my spare hand on his shoulder, the nearest I could manage to a cuddle without appearing seductive. We lay like that long enough for our skin to chill and for the room to drift into darkness. Still he said nothing.

Eventually, of course, my stomach got the better of me.

'Ready to eat?'

'Good idea.' He reached for his pants.

I reached for my bra, which had, coincidentally, tangled with his socks.

At last he started to thaw. 'Very nice,' he said, his fingers exploring the silk. 'I'd no idea you were a sexy-underwear woman.'

'I'm a Marks and Sparks white cotton-rich person,' I said without thinking.

He looked alarmed. 'You mean you wanted – I mean, did you plan . . .'

He wouldn't have wanted to be seduced, would he? He'd be the sort of man who preferred all the effort to come from him. He misunderstood my hesitation. 'Or was this effort for . . .' I don't think he trusted himself to continue.

The truth might be safest. He might just believe it.

'Chris, listen to me. The reason I went to Fairfax's tonight was, you'll recall, two-fold. I truly did want to give him the puddings. All the meals I've seen him at –' and that was hardly the most sensitive thing to say – 'I've never seen him eat. You can see how thin he is, what a dreadful colour he's going. So maybe the puds will help. The other reason I went, one which I knew you wouldn't approve, was to get my mitts on those files. Which, by the way, are so important that even when he's almost too ill to stand, he locks them in a wall safe so I can't. And then he gives me these, asks me to try them on—'

'Jesus Christ, woman!'

'In the privacy of a locked bathroom. Then I call you and while I wait we talk gardens. That's the truth, the whole truth and nothing but the truth.'

He took a couple of steps away from me. I couldn't see his face, but I could almost feel the tension in his body. And I knew from his voice there was something terribly wrong.

'And where are your own bra and pants?'

'My God, I've only gone and left them there! Never mind, I'm sure his housekeeper—'

I didn't finish. Chris's hands were on my shoulders and he was shaking me, shaking me so hard my teeth hurt and my ears rang. At last, with extreme deliberation, he released his hands.

'You'll have to tell me what's the matter!'

'There are some men,' he said, his voice tight with anger, 'who get their kicks by smelling women's underwear. There's a whole brisk trade in it. And that's what he'll be doing.'

'Don't be ridiculous!' Tenderness had failed, so I'd trust honest anger. 'He's not some sleazy erotica merchant making money from my pants! One rotten pair of Marks and Sparks cotton-rich? You're off your head! Or are you worried about something else? Do you think he's lying there now, wanking himself off with his nose in my bra? Because I'm telling you, Chris, Richard Fairfax is too ill for any of that. The man's dying – can't you get that into your thick policeman's skull? And if he is, what of it? We've just had the real, proper thing – and you'd deny a dying man a bit of pleasure!'

Maybe yelling is a good prelude to sex. This time at least it seemed to work.

Afterwards we lay for a long time in each other's arms, tender fingers dabbing away the remains of tears on both our faces. I kept a hand across his mouth in case he should try to apologise yet again.

At last, pulling on his dressing gown, I slipped downstairs to reheat our pasta. I stacked one tray on the other, put the plates of pasta side by side. We'd have to share the bowl of salad. He was still in bed when I got up, spread luxuriously across both pillows, the sheet fully back. The condom still lay at the side of the bed, half concealed in a tissue.

I'd have liked to pop choice morsels into his mouth as he lay there, or to lick his fingers as he fed me. But spoons and forks were the order of the day, and when we had finished we did not make love again.

30

Chris's office, eightish in the morning. His calendar told us it was Thursday, but I felt so punch-drunk after the week's events, I wouldn't have taken any bets on it. His percolator was burping, perhaps with pleasure at the sight and smell of fresh croissants from Safeway. We'd been home long enough for me to change from top to toe, and to put a new tape in the answering machine. We would play the messages on the old one in safety.

Most were routine or social: Aberlene reminding me about a meal – but she made no mention of Chris or Tobias; the dentist's receptionist telling me I was due for a check-up; two to sell me double-glazing – Chris jotted down the numbers. And one from Luke, the admin. marvel of William Murdock. Why hadn't I responded to his messages at Muntz? If I didn't call him by teatime on Wednesday, there was no point for a couple of days since he was off to Exeter for a conference on information technology for college administrators. But he had some interesting news concerning our friend.

'Sophie? Sophie? What's the matter?'

I felt very sick. I walked to the window and peered down at the safe streets. Turning back to Chris, I caught the concern on his face. 'Someone's left a message at work. If he's been circumspect, it might be OK. But if he hasn't – how d'you get an outside line?'

He passed me the phone without comment, pressed a button and held the handset for me. William Murdock: fingers crossed that the switchboard would be awake this early. And that a familiar voice would answer.

Yes and no. 'Hello? This is Sophie Rivers – from the fifteenth floor,' I tried.

'How can I help you?' came a voice with no matching friendliness.

'I need to contact Luke Schneider at home. It's really urgent. And I don't have his number.'

'The Personnel section opens at nine. If you contact them, they will phone Luke and ask him to phone you back.'

'It's too urgent to wait till then.'

'You know the rules, Ms – er. They're there for the staff's protection.'

I nodded, I'd been staff representative at the meeting where that decision had been made. 'Thanks, anyway.' I put down the phone and looked at Chris, his face now professional again. 'There's a man somewhere between here and Exeter who's just blabbed something I suspect someone else will be interested in, and I can't tell him to watch his back.'

'Sit down and tell me.'

'There's no time! Chris, don't you have some sort of computer he'd be on?'

'Only if he has a criminal record.'

I gestured: impossible.

'The phone book?' he said mockingly.

I shook my head. 'His name and ethnicity offended some of the Muslim mafia. First of all they tipped his daughter into the Chamberlain Square fountain, then they started posting him excrement. He moved and he's ex-directory.'

'You wouldn't have his address anywhere? An old diary?'

'We don't have that sort of relationship. He spends all his spare time, and I mean all of it since Naomi went off to uni, looking after his mother. Alzheimer's. And he doesn't want her to go into a home. Chris, what shall we—?'

'What's this all about?' came Dave Clarke's voice. He swanned in and sat down. 'Hi, sweetheart.'

'There's a rumour,' said Chris, fully the DCI again, 'that one of the college staff – Curtis, the assistant principal in charge of financial services, to give him his title – may be claiming to have accountancy qualifications he doesn't in fact possess.'

'If it's public money he's dealing with, he'd be CIPFA –

Chartered Institute of Public Finance Accounts,' Dave said. 'Maybe FCA, too.'

'That's what it's got on the letter heading,' said Chris, producing a sheet of college paper from a file but not otherwise acknowledging Dave.

'But Peggy—' I began.

'The receptionist,' Chris glossed.

'She says her predecessor, now dead, reckons a relative knew he got no further than an ONC. So I asked one of my William Murdock contacts, Luke Schneider, to check if there was anything in our files. You see, William Murdock was *the* centre for local-government students in the bonny far-off days of day release for all. They came from all over the Midlands. And though he's shed most of his accent, I reckon Curtis is a Brummie. OK, it's just a shot in the dark. But that was a message from my colleague Luke on the tape, saying he'd left messages at work. So I may have hit something.'

'Which you haven't received?' asked Dave.

'No. But with Mrs Cavendish away, the system's probably breaking down completely.'

Chris's laugh was perfunctory. 'You're afraid that whoever's been trying to shut you up may try and shut up this Luke character too?'

I nodded. 'Chris, I—'

'Calm down. The West Midlands Police Service has one or two resources left.'

'Even if we do have to charge them to the appropriate cost centre,' added Dave, getting up and helping us all to coffee.

'I'll go and get Tom on to this lot. You never know, he may have a conviction for something. Otherwise it's working through the electoral roll for some poor sod. And the conference – Exeter, did you say?' He was on his feet already, eager for some action, I suppose, since he could just as easily have reached for the phone.

'I'm afraid he'll have driven down. He's got this penchant for bright yellow cars – dead easy to follow.'

'New ones? Not many manufacturers make yellow ones.'

'Fiat do. Or Peugeot? Didn't they do a special edition in yellow?' I'd been rather tempted myself.

'OK. I'll get them moving.' He ducked out of the room.

Dave leaned confidentially towards me. 'Tell me, sweetheart, did he buy the story as we told it?'

'Possibly.'

'The guy died, by the way. TB,' he said flatly.

'But this is twentieth-century Britain! I know one of my students had it once, but he brought it with him from India. I always thought it was a Third World disease.'

'Some of these winos live a lot worse than folk in India. Think of the climate. And then the dosshouses. And getting them to take their medication. New York, now, it's reaching epidemic proportions, and London – it's getting bad down there. Antibiotic-resistant strains and all.' He stopped abruptly. 'My last girlfriend was big in environmental health, see.'

'What's the news about that building?' I thought that a safer topic than girlfriends.

'What indeed?' Chris was back. He stayed where he was, by the door.

'It's George Muntz's all right. But to be honest I'd like to get a preservation order slapped on it. You got to come and see it, Chris. Now you know who owns it you could get proper access and all.'

'What an excellent idea!'

'But why the hell should they want it?' I asked. 'It'd take millions to make it usable. And they're up to something in Provence. I only saw a corner of the file, but it said 'ment Centre, Provence', clear as you like.'

'Management, probably.' Both men laughed dourly.

'And there's the Bradford connection, too,' I said. 'Any news on that? I've not heard from Aberlene.'

'I'm seeing your James Worrall at two,' said Chris. 'He concedes that it's not impossible that he can offer one or two suggestions that might prove of some tenuous assistance.'

'He's not as bad as that,' I said and laughed. 'Not quite. What about Luke?'

'According to the conference organiser, he's not due in Exeter for another hour. No RTAs involving a yellow car on the M5 yet. I've alerted patrols.'

'You take Sophie very seriously, our Chris,' Dave said, looking at Chris and then back to me.

'Yes. I do,' he said.

There was a little silence.

'Did you tell Dave about those rumours about paper at Muntz, Chris?' I asked, to break it.

Dave's eyes gleamed. 'There's a college up north,' he said, 'where they always bought paper from the same man. Not the same *firm*; the same *man*. Whichever firm he was at got the contract. And it was worth a bit. Everything. Exam paper, memos, letter heading—'

'Muntz have just got a beautiful new logo. It's on absolutely everything except the loo paper. Whoever got that contract must be happy.'

'Are you trying to imply something, sweetheart?'

'Just making polite conversation. No, I'm not. Someone there mentioned paper, I'm sure. What was in it for your northern college?'

'Funny you should ask. This salesman had a nice little place in the Dordogne. Seems he felt he'd like to lend it to certain senior staff every holiday. He got to see other people's tenders and always managed - by coincidence, of course - to undercut them. When we've sorted out all the missing documentation, I wouldn't be surprised to find the same scam going on here.'

'But surely that's fraud?'

The two men laughed.

'Happens, sweetheart. And it keeps me off the streets.'

'So: we have a building that doesn't make sense,' I began. 'An outpost in a city that doesn't make sense; a technician who's worried about his computer supplies - including paper! - and a loony lecturer. Chris, is she still missing?'

He nodded. 'Despite all our best efforts.'

'What else? A dead technician; a dead principal.'

'And computer porn, sweetheart. And someone who - and this shows rotten taste - doesn't like you. What the hell do you know?' Dave wasn't cuddly, sexy Dave any more. He sat at Chris's desk and leaned on his forearms. 'Come on, get your bloody act together.'

I glanced at Chris; he was leaning against his door, arms folded. I could detect no signs of irony.

'Sweetheart, we haven't got all day. Your bloody interference may have sent an innocent man to his death. So just interfere a little bit more. Come on. Give.'

I felt very close to losing my temper. 'What are you implying, Dave?'

'I'm not bloody implying, I'm saying it, for crying out loud! You know something. We want to know it.'

I wouldn't look to Chris for help. I gathered myself up with dignity. 'Read my statements. Listen to what I'm saying.'

'You're not saying it clear enough.' He slammed his open hand on the desktop.

'Clear*ly*.' I took a breath – he wasn't going to intimidate me. 'Let's get this straight. The only connection I have with any of this is the fact that I didn't listen to a girl who was frightened someone would kill her. And then she died. I'm an outsider.' I felt like one now, too, confronted by two men I'd thought I'd known, one of whom I'd slept with, as tenderly as I knew how.

Chris must have picked up a note in my voice I hoped no one would hear. 'OK, Dave, why don't you have a shufti at Sophie's notes? She passed the time one evening trying to make connections – didn't you?' His smile sprang for just one moment from formal to tender and back again. But Dave would have seen that moment.

'I just listed people I'd been talking to, and summarised the conversations as best I could. There's Phil, the technician, who seems as loquaciously honest as the proverbial day. But he was able to hack into Dr Trevelyan's system, and – I know this sounds weird, Chris, and maybe you've put something in your coffee – I saw him at a car-boot sale near a microwave. In all fairness I also saw an engineer whom I have unlovingly christened Sunshine in the same place. And not long before, Sunshine attempted to take up residence in my room and to investigate *my* files. I would love it to be Sunshine who dunnit.'

This time the silence was uneasy.

'I think you can rule him out,' said Dave at last.

'Why?'

'Can't explain – not until the job's over, at least.'

'Do you seriously mean to tell me – to let me infer, rather – that one of your officers was investigating me?' That sounded unforgivably pompous. '*Moi? Moi?*' I got deeper into Miss Piggy's voice. Then I found my own. 'Fucking hell! Which of you two do I kill for this?'

'Neither. Another area of investigation altogether. Look, Sophie,' Dave said, 'there's so much shit flying round at your place, you can't expect us not to have picked up the odd rumour – and to have acted.'

'Would this rumour have anything to do with the pornography? OK, I know when to keep quiet.'

'Except, if you'll forgive me saying so, Sophie, you don't,' said Dave, hard again.

'It was you who came into my place yelling "fraud"!'

'How was I to know the sodding place was bugged?'

'Children, children!' Chris had donned his glasses and was looking over them. He held up his left hand, pulling the spread fingers down with his right as he mentioned names. 'Dr Trevelyan. We know she's up to something. Petty fraud. Bound to get picked up sooner or later. But she didn't strike me as the sort of woman to get involved with pornography. Mr Curtis. You don't like him, and I'd guess the feeling was mutual, but you've nothing currently on him, except he claims qualifications he may not have. An altogether easier way of discovering the truth would have been to ask me. As soon as nine strikes, Tom will get on to the accountancy organisations Curtis claims membership of. OK? Mr Blake. Because of his sexual proclivities he is unable to make a statement.'

'How come you were at the dratted place anyway, sweetheart?'

'I was part of a team working on computer programs to develop literacy skills. Idiomatic English made easy for people whose first language isn't English.'

'A geek!'

'Far from it! I know a bit about programming, but it's the English-teaching bit that I'm best at. In all honesty, I reckon Worrall hatched the plot to get me off Murdock's turf for a bit.'

'Does everyone realise that? *Everyone*?' Chris repeated. 'Because you always seem to know what I'm talking about these days. Sometimes more, come to think of it – you were dead keen for them not to switch on the computer Blake was using.'

'Only because I'd been reading about it in a mag at the doctor's. And teachers specialise in bluffing,' I added.

'Not hacking?' Dave put in.

'I've never hacked in my life. The only time I ever saw it done was actually at Lloyd House,' I said, with a grin at Chris, 'with an audience of senior police.'

The atmosphere had eased at last. Dave and Chris stretched, and I looked at my watch. Nearly nine.

'Is it worth trying William Murdock – the personnel people – again? You never know, Chris, they might respond to the blandishments of you or Dave and tell you his car number and everything. Oh yes, it'll be on file – for our car-parking records.' I dialled the number, got through to Rosie, a fellow cricket lover, and posed the problem. She demurred, as of course she should, then came up with a bright idea.

'Tell you what,' she said. 'Why don't I phone the police and ask to speak to this Chris and then I'll know he's real, won't I?'

'You're a genius. It's Detective Chief Inspector Groom. Got that? Great.'

'Except the switchboard's always so busy it'll take her ten minutes to get through,' said Chris. 'In any case—'

There was a sharp tap at the door. Tom poked an anxious Geordie head round the door. 'Chris, man, there's something you might want to know. I've had a call from the Transport Police. Some guy beaten up just outside Bristol Temple Meads. Managed to pull the communication cord.'

'Name of Schneider?'

Tom nodded, big-eyed.

We were scuttling down the corridor when Chris asked, 'Why should the Transport folk call us?'

'Because I thought, if there were no accidents on the motorway, there was always the train, sir. So I got on the blower to them. Ian always said to get all the information, Gaffer,' he said, almost in extenuation.

'Where are we going, anyway?' I said, breathless from the rush.

We all stopped, abruptly.

'Back to my office, I suppose,' said Chris, turning and leading the way. 'The Avon lads can ask him what we need to know. It's just – you know – after all this inactivity a bit of action would be nice.'

'You're right,' Dave said glumly. 'There are times when war, war, war is better than jaw, jaw, jaw.'

31

Chris took me back to his office, leaving me there probably against every rule in the book, while he and Dave adjourned to the incident room. Since he made no prohibitions at all, I felt myself honour bound to do nothing to upset his moral code. I read the *Guardian* twice and even tried the crossword. I hadn't any marking, of course, or any of the books I'd long been intending to read, and was, in a word, bored.

One thing I could usefully do was make that dental appointment, and I couldn't see Chris begrudging me one phone call. The phone book sat neatly on top of the Yellow Pages by the phone, and I hunted for the Cavendish Road Dental Practice. What I always forget is that the Birmingham directory has business numbers at the front, and my search through the main residential pages brought me no joy at all. In fact, there were hardly any Cavendishes, and one, I. M. Cavendish, made me forget about my teeth. She hadn't been at work when I phoned in yesterday. Chris and I had joked about it; at least I had, and Chris had been rather dampening. I turned to the business section, got myself an outside line, and fixed my appointment for mid-July – the start of the college holiday for those of us not on the new Muntz contract.

My hands found their way back to Cavendish, I. M., and dialled. No reply. But then, she'd be back at Muntz, wouldn't she? Not a woman to take sick leave lightly, Mrs C. I dialled Muntz and asked to speak to her.

'I'm afraid Mrs Cavendish is unavailable.'

'Do you mean she's in college but is too busy to speak to me, or that she's not in college? It's Sophie Rivers here,

Stella, one of the computer-project people.'

'Oh, I thought I knew your voice! It's ever so strange, she's not in, and I don't know when she last had *one* day off, let alone *two*. And I don't think she even phoned in today. At least I didn't take the call. Hang on a sec. Sylv, did you take a call from Mrs C this morning?'

I heard a decided negative.

'No, Sylv didn't either. Strange, isn't it?'

'Hmm,' I said enthusiastically. 'Must have gone to a sale or something.'

'Well, she's got the money, of course, since her father died.'

'Oh, I'm sorry – were they close?'

'Never mentioned him until she came in with this lovely pair of shoes, Italian, the softest leather. £159 she said. Lovely.'

'Wish I could spend that on shoes.' Well, actually, I could. Maybe I *should*. 'Look, Stella, is Mr Curtis around? Because maybe I'd better talk to him direct.'

'No. Hey, Sophie, you don't think they've done a bunk together! Thick as thieves, they are.'

'Wouldn't she be a bit old for him?' A very ageist thing to say, but needs must.

'Well, I wouldn't look at either of them. *He*'s nice looking, of course, and now he's got that posh car, but he's not really my type. I like warm brown eyes and nice tight little bums.'

'As opposed to nice tight little fists?'

She crowed with laughter, hurting my ear. 'Look, Sophie, Sylv's pulling faces 'cos she's having to take all the calls. Talk to you again – OK?'

'Cheers!' Yes, I rather thought we might be talking again. But I didn't tell her why.

Meanwhile I was left with the problem of what to do next. Mrs I. M. Cavendish knew more about the goings-on at Muntz than anyone, I reckoned, and I cursed myself for not having talked to her properly on Monday morning when she'd seemed altogether more kindly disposed towards me.

Not really expecting a reply, I dialled her home number again. I let it ring and ring, before replacing the handset.

No one had ever spelled it out, but I suspected that

unaccompanied members of the public were not encouraged to stroll around inside a police station, particularly one as full of important information as this must be.

I opened the door and looked out on an empty corridor. No, though I knew where to go, I couldn't do it, lest it should rebound on him in some way. Back inside. How about an internal phone call? There was a directory thumbtacked to the wall beside the phone. I'd try Ian's number.

I was just going to put the phone down in despair when Ian answered, breathless, apologising for forgetting to reroute it.

'It's OK, Ian - only me. Look, Chris has left me in his office, and I've just thought of something he might want to know. You couldn't help, could you?'

'In what way help?' Ian's voice was instantly suspicious.

'Either escort me to see him, or tell him I want to talk to him, or simply give him a message. You can choose! And when you've chosen, you can buy me a cuppa in the canteen - I'm getting claustrophobia up here.'

'OK. Save my legs if it's message first, then I come and get you.'

'Tell him that neither Curtis nor Mrs Cavendish, Blake's secretary, is in college, and I can't raise Mrs Cavendish on the phone at home.'

He agreed, albeit reluctantly, and promised to come and raise my siege.

'As and when we want to talk to Curtis, we'll talk to him,' said Chris in a fierce undertone. 'Sophie, I really do not have to account to you for my movements.'

I pushed away from the canteen table, leaning back in my seat. I suppose the gesture I made was pacifying, but inside I was seething. 'OK. What about Mrs C? Are you going to look for her?'

'Sophie, this is police business.'

'It's been made my business too, and you know it has.' My seethe was showing. 'Chris, she knows more about what's been going on at Muntz than anyone. The number of times I've caught her off guard and didn't think about it till now! She's like a spider pulling together all the threads of a web. And without her loyalty to Mr Blake, she might sing.'

'Interesting mixture of metaphors,' he observed. This was a peace offering.

I refused to be drawn. 'And you never know, someone, knowing she could sing, might have decided to silence her.'

'Do you have any evidence at all for that?' He could sound so very paternal at times.

I caught his eye and held it. 'No. And I've been wrong before. But—'

'But?'

'If I were you I'd want to see she was all right.'

He straightened up, looking away as if the floor might provide some answers. 'I've hardly any officers left. Look, I'll talk to Ian.'

'And tell him I want to go with him,' I yelled at his departing back.

'These hunches of yours, where d'you reckon they come from?' asked Ian, opening the passenger door for me. He was driving his own car, a Rover a couple of years old.

'No idea. And don't think for one minute I believe you or Chris gives them any credence.'

'No?' He started the engine and eased out of his space.

I waited until he'd found a gap in the traffic and pulled into the main road before replying. 'No, of course you don't. Otherwise you wouldn't be going without backup and I wouldn't be sitting here beside you.'

'You'll do,' he said, and we settled down to talk about bedding plants and hanging baskets.

Mrs Cavendish lived in a pleasant road in Warley, in a semi notable even among other respectable semis for its air of well-being. It must have been a bit younger than mine, perhaps 1935, and was joined to its neighbour in the conventional way, by the living-room wall. The neat front lawn was surrounded by pansies and primulas, still flourishing. The drive had been recently swept. The double-glazed front door was locked. I'd have given up at that point, but Ian headed off down the side of the house, on the path between the house and the detached garage. Two more points of entry for him to check – the door to the kitchen, and a French window. He mimed flipping a coin, and tried the French window first. It was locked. This made him quite casual about the kitchen door, so that when it opened he nearly fell on the floor. Recovering, he raised an eyebrow at me, and spoke into his radio. Then he started calling: 'Police! Is there anyone there?'

There was no reply.

'You stay here, Sophie.'

'Not on your bloody life,' I said, following him into the kitchen and looking round.

It was perhaps a little too plastic but it was as immaculate as my friend George's. The whole house was. Unlike his, however, this held no neat shelves of books, records, tapes and CDs. There were no books anywhere, in fact.

Her bedroom was pleasantly chintzy, everything matching but not offensively. The guest bedroom was more austere, and the boxroom full of neatly labelled boxes. The bathroom was a bit on the frilly side for my taste, but Ian saw no harm in it, probably because it was almost identical to his Val's.

The front room was definitely too floral, and smelled of something a bit sickly, but the back one, with the French window, was cosy and welcoming. Needless to say, there was not even a freebie newspaper out of place. We stood and stated at each other, mirror images of puzzlement. We went back into the kitchen. Ian opened the fridge door with a pencil. It was clean and relatively full of food. The opened milk bottle wore a blue and red plastic lid.

'I don't know, young Sophie, I really don't.'

I shook my head; neither did I. But there was something, wasn't there, something out of place. I covered my face with my hands and smelled Chris's soap. That therapeutic bonk hadn't done him any good, had it? He was more abrupt than ever this morning.

'One more look round,' said Ian. 'Just in case.'

It was in the living room we found it. An apple, not fully eaten, brown, on the mantelpiece.

Goodness knows why I dropped my voice. 'There!'

'Eh?'

'Get on to Chris. Tell him she's been taken, but at least whoever's done it left his calling card. That bloody apple. She'd never leave anything like that there, she's far too well-ordered. And look at those tooth marks. They'll match with someone's teeth, even if there's no DNA in the saliva. You get whoever it is, Ian, and by Christ that'll jail him.'

'An apple!'

'Yes! There was a terrorist waiting to ambush someone. When the target appeared he threw down his apple. After the murder, some bright young bobby picked up the apple, and it became the clinching evidence. It was on TV.'

'Ah, a film.'

'No! A documentary. Ian, please! Oh!' At last I noticed the expression on his face. 'You've been winding me up!'

He grinned tolerantly and spoke into his radio.

'I suppose you'd prefer me outside in your car by the time people arrive?'

'Not a lot of point, love. Forensic'll need to eliminate your shoe prints and – no, you didn't touch anything, did you?'

'Would I dare?'

'You know,' he said, consideringly, 'I don't reckon there's much you wouldn't dare. But you do know the difference between right and wrong. That's something.'

32

I stood by Ian's car, looking wistfully at the team now gathering to give Mrs Cavendish's house the going-over of its beautifully maintained life. Not that I'd have wanted to pick over her clothes or check her waste bin, but they at least were doing something useful and constructive whereas I was neither use nor ornament, just someone it would take valuable resources to protect. There was the problem of where to put me, too: somewhere I'd be safe, not a liability. After some discussion over my head – I might have been a stray cat – it was agreed that Ian should take me to his home, from where Chris would collect me later. I acquiesced – to argue would have wasted their valuable time – but made one stipulation: I could go home and get some books and other necessaries first. Chris nodded curtly, and had turned away before I was in Ian's car.

Ian took a circuitous route, but no one appeared to follow us. Then, as we headed down the home straight of Balden Road, a car I recognised came up towards us. The driver pulled over to our side of the road, coming to rest outside my house.

'Richard Fairfax's,' I said briefly in response to Ian's whistle.

'Nice car, anyway,' he said, parking nose to nose with the BMW.

We got out and greeted Alan, the chauffeur, with no particular cordiality. I felt he should have done more to protect me – tried, at least. Perhaps Ian distrusted anyone in a car that size, or perhaps he knew *he*'d have done better. But Alan looked so distraught I soon thawed. 'Are you all right?'

'*I* am, miss. But not Mr Fairfax. There's a message on your machine, but you didn't answer so I thought I'd come myself. He doesn't know. So if you were to phone as if I hadn't asked you to . . . ?'

'It's his stomach?'

'The cancer's spread. Secondaries all over the place. He phoned the hospice this morning.'

We stood there in the bright sun, cold from his words. I looked from Alan to Ian, grim-faced and perhaps already working out what I should be allowed to do without an outburst from Chris.

'Come in, both of you. Ian, can you fix us all some tea while I phone? Alan, just keep an eye on both those cars, will you? I know I'm getting paranoid, but—'

'I'm sorry,' he muttered, taking up his station by the window. 'I bottled out, didn't I? But that car's his pride and joy, miss, and with him so ill I couldn't have faced him if it had been all smashed up. Mind you, I think he'd rather it had been the car than you. When you took him those puddings, with your hands all covered with plasters . . . He was took bad soon after you went last night, miss.'

I nodded, biting my lip. To be having sex while he was dying . . .

I dialled the number. A woman answered it, the housekeeper, her voice strangely familiar. She put me straight through to Fairfax. Richard.

'Ah, my dear. A little local difficulty here. I wonder, could you do an old man another favour? I need someone to drive me to an appointment this morning, and I'm afraid Alan is unavailable. I've fixed the insurance.'

I nodded to Alan across the room. I'd keep his secret. 'Of course, Richard. I've got someone here at the moment. I'll get him to give me a lift.'

In the end, I got Ian to drive me, while Alan set off briskly via a more direct route.

'Chris won't like your doing this,' he said, checking I'd locked my front door. 'But I think you're right. When I spoke to Fairfax yesterday morning – just a little follow-up visit after Tuesday evening, you understand – he hadn't any fight in him.'

'Fight?'

He unlocked the passenger door thoughtfully. 'I don't know how you'd describe him. Resigned? You'll see soon enough.'

'He is up to something?'

'I didn't say that. Chris would like to nail him for something, because—'

'Because Chris is jealous. But does he have a criminal record? I know he's got those bloody files, but he's the Chair of the governors and would have to—'

'Let's wait and see. I'd rather it was Curtis. Still not talking, you know – roll on the Criminal Justice Act, say I. OK, I know what you're going to say. I don't think even Chris really agrees with it, either. Anyway, he's got this solicitor character sitting there with him—'

'Not one Frank Laker?'

'The same. Know him?'

'Not well. Hardly at all. But—'

'Ah, there's always buts ...'

'Is there a but about Fairfax?'

'Never give up, do you? Proper little terrier you are. Tell you what, Sophie, I can't ever believe a man gets that rich without, let's say, bending the odd rule. Some people think that doesn't matter. I happen to think it does – and remember what they taught in chapel about rich men and eyes of needles. And –' he took his eyes from the road to glance at me – 'I'd reckon it would matter to you, too. Smethwick Baptist, were you, or Oldbury Congregational?'

'Put it this way, Ian, I shan't mourn him as a friend. Just as a man who's had a nasty death rather before his time.'

'Oh, they can work wonders with drugs these days,' he said brusquely.

Fairfax's front door opened.

'Mrs Cavendish!' I squeaked. 'No, you're—'

'Iris's twin,' she said. 'Violet. On account of our eyes. Come along in, dear. He'll be glad to see you.'

I got no further than the mat. If only I could have consulted Ian, but he'd parked discreetly down the road. I had rather expected he'd tail me – and possibly make adverse comments on my driving. 'Your sister,' I began, hoarse with embarrassment.

'D'you want to talk to her? She's in the back somewhere.'

'She went out leaving her kitchen door unlocked,' I said.

'No, that'd be Alan. I always told him it'd get him the sack one day, being careless like that.'

'And he left his apple on her mantelpiece.'

'Stupid man – but it isn't that he got the sack for!' She turned on me. 'That was you! You got him the sack!'

I shook my head, stupid in the onslaught.

'If it hadn't been for you it would have been redundancy, wouldn't it, but no, you have to—'

'That will do, Violet!' said Fairfax, coming into the hall, his hand on Pilot's head. 'Sophie, my dear, if you could just feed Pilot, we could be on our way.'

I wouldn't argue. 'Come on, then,' I said, snapping my fingers.

Mrs Cavendish was in the kitchen, unloading the dish-washer. She'd been crying. 'Sophie!'

'Hi!' I said mildly, and found Pilot's tin and bowl.

'You must understand—'

'I think we should talk later, Mrs Cavendish. I don't think Mr Fairfax ought to be kept waiting.'

I took his overnight bag, but wouldn't humiliate him by offering my arm. The car was outside the garage, but locked, and he handed me the keys with something of a flourish. I zapped, and the central locking responded. I stowed his case behind the driver's seat, then accompanied him to his side of the car, opening the door, and finally letting him grip my hand as he sank awkwardly on to the passenger seat. But he eased his legs across the sill himself. Then he waited for me to pull down his seat belt, and I leaned across to fasten it for him.

It was time to drive the car. I set the seat, the mirrors, the position of the gear lever. 'I've never driven an automatic before,' I said.

He nodded but did not speak.

When we got to the hospice, he didn't want me to stay, that was clear. I was almost an irrelevance in his fight against the pain. I was out of the room when he called me back. There was a set of keys in his hand. 'You will have these when I die.

This is the one to the safe. You will find the code on your answering machine.'

And so I was dispatched from the bright, airy room, past other people's flowers and wheelchairs, past other people's tears, back to the monster car. What I wanted to do was head out of the city for a motorway; what I had to do was get out of the car park without hitting anything and go back to Fairfax's house. Perhaps it would be sensible to invite Chris to join me. I cut the engine and reached for the phone.

'There must be some questions you can answer, Mrs Cavendish,' said Chris reasonably, taking the cup of tea she offered and sitting down. 'I accept that you won't want to implicate Mr Fairfax in any way, but a crime has been committed - a number of crimes - and I need to bring people to justice.'

'Think of poor Melina!' I urged. 'Poor kid! Being thrown from the roof and left to die before being thrown in a rubbish skip. Who did that? Mr Fairfax?'

'That was nothing to do with him!' she said. 'Nothing. Nor Mr Blake. He was furious.'

'Because it drew attention to the college?' Chris asked, his voice more gentle this time.

She nodded.

'Do you have any idea who did kill her?' he asked.

Her head shot up with amazing venom. 'Dr Trevelyan, of course. She wouldn't want anyone talking about that computer business of hers. Melina had found out about her ordering from her own firm, having fewer delivered than were on the invoice and then claiming they'd been stolen. The stupid woman! It was obvious she'd be found out eventually, obvious.'

Pilot growled.

'Shh,' I said, clicking my fingers to him and welcoming him with a rub between his ears. 'Sit.'

The sun had pushed round into the room; I wondered if it was warming Fairfax yet.

Chris leaned forward and poured more tea for himself. He gestured with the pot but she shook her head. So did I.

'Why did Mr Blake give her extended sick leave?' I asked, forgetting I was supposed to be no more than an observer.

She dropped her voice to a confidential whisper. 'I think it was because of – you know. I think she'd found out about that – that *stuff* he liked to watch.'

'Blackmail? You're saying she blackmailed him?' Chris asked.

She nodded. 'After all, she was in charge of all the college computers: she was a computer expert. She came with the very highest references.'

'And we've checked her qualifications,' put in Ian, 'just in case. Best student of the year, everything.'

'But if she was so good, why on earth teach in a place like George Muntz? Surely she'd have been at a university or in industry? More money!' I was doing it again, but Chris said nothing.

'Because of her health record,' Mrs Cavendish said, shuffling forwards in her enthusiasm and carefully smoothing her skirt. 'She was only on a short-term contract with us, in case she did it again – had another breakdown. There was one in her sixth form, one at university, then, when she got a job in the City, they came in one day and found her tearing up ten-pound notes. Her own. She did her PhD to help her convalesce. I did warn Mr Blake, don't think I didn't warn him! I told him, she's trouble, I said. But he wouldn't listen, and now look what's happened to the poor dear man!'

'But she couldn't have killed him, could she?' I exclaimed.

'We still haven't found her,' said Chris in an undertone.

'They say if you kill once,' Mrs Cavendish said, 'you find it easier to kill a second time.'

Chris and I blinked at her tone.

'You haven't seen her round the building, have you? Recently?' Chris asked.

'I promised that young man from the north that I would telephone him, should I encounter her again.'

'So you haven't?'

She shook her head.

Chris stood up suddenly, towering over her. 'So why did you miss work yesterday, Mrs Cavendish?'

She looked taken aback. I certainly was. This was a side of Chris I'd not seen before. I probably wouldn't see it again: I'd never be admitted to a formal interview room.

'Mrs Cavendish?' His voice was harsh.

Her eyes filled with tears. 'Because of Richard, of course. Richard. Your only brother, dying – wouldn't you? And now he doesn't want us with him . . .'

Pilot yelped; I soothed the ear I'd pulled.

'Violet keeps house for him. She never married.'

'Alan is . . .?' I asked quietly.

'Her friend. And now he's sacked. Because of you, Sophie!'

'OK, Mrs Cavendish,' said Chris, tapping his notebook. 'Now, is there anything else you can tell us? About Mr Blake, perhaps?'

She shook her head and started to weep quietly. 'Will it have to come out? About him and – you know. Because he's got such a sweet wife...'

Ian nodded. 'Very nice. A real lady.'

What had she done to impress him? Offered him excellent sherry? I wished they'd told me about her. But then, what could I have done?

'I don't think many people will be interested in his private life,' Ian said soothingly. And probably mendaciously – what would the gutter press make of it? COLLEGE HEAD DIES IN PORN SCANDAL. Forget all George Muntz's excellent staff and students.

'I've done it again! I've forgotten to call Muntz!'

'Well, you needn't bother,' said Mrs Cavendish, tart and upright. 'Not if you're in that union. National Day of Action, they call it. Inaction more like.'

I started to laugh. 'You know what I've done, Chris – I've only missed a day on strike!'

Ian joined in, but dourly. 'And you'd have been on the picket line, no doubt.'

I laughed again – but then saw in my mind's eye those who would be, and one who would never strike again.

Chris dispatched Ian to talk to James Worrall, Mrs Cavendish to Rose Road in the company of a WPC, and stopped off with me at the Botanical Gardens. The nearest pub was only a couple of hundred yards down the road, but it got noisy at lunchtime, and Chris was clearly in the mood for quiet. We bought sandwiches and fruit juice and wandered down to the terrace to eat, only to be joined with indecent haste by a peacock who insisted it was starving. Its bright little head followed each bite. I dropped a few morsels. I was grateful to it for providing something for us to laugh at: it would have been a very silent meal otherwise.

'Time for a stroll?' I asked at last.

He shook his head, but got up and followed me anyway. Other couples were on the long slope of the lawn, close, even feeding titbits to each other. Chris maintained a five-inch gap, as if afraid of touching me again. I needed to be touched or, better still, cuddled: he hadn't exactly had sex alone, and I wanted to feel valued, cherished. And I had taken a man to die. The silence had to be broken soon.

It was. By his phone. It was Tom, full of himself. Luke had been declared fit to leave hospital. Could Tom go down and fetch him, have a bit of a chat, like?

'Blow the expense – off you go! And phone me as soon as you know what he wanted to tell Sophie.'

I pressed up to his left shoulder so I could hear properly. He grinned and tilted the phone slightly. Then, holding it in his right hand, he suddenly made room for me, tucking my head on his shoulder.

'I know that already, man. Gaffer. And I've told Dave. But it's a bit late, man, because we can't find Curtis at the moment.'

'Shit! Tell them to keep looking – harder. What's your news, anyway? Out with it!'

'It seems Curtis got his ONC, like the lady said, but he did go on to get an HNC. So I thought I'd check a bit more at other places, and I find he's got some Open University qualifications. But it seems they're not in figures, like, but in electronics.'

'Jesus Christ! OK, Tom, off you go to Bristol. Take your time, and remember there's a speed limit.' He switched off and replaced the phone in his inside pocket.

I suppose I might have expected a hug, maybe even a celebratory kiss. What I got was Chris pushing his hair back with both hands. 'Christ! I start off with no suspects and end up with two buggers who could have done it. Three, if you count

Phil. Shit, I'd better get back and start looking for Curtis. Why the fuck didn't I bring him in earlier?'

It was more tactful to say nothing. I could only think of 'I told you so' anyway, and that wouldn't help our relationship. 'Let's think about Dr Trevelyan. If you'd signed yourself out of hospital, and you got home to find it guarded by the fuzz, what'd you do?'

Chris considered. 'Go and talk to someone who owed me – like Blake.'

From the terrace came a dreadful scream. It took us a second to realise it was the peacock giving voice. But neither of us laughed.

'And what might Blake do? Give her some money to make herself scarce?' I asked.

'Or – depends how scared he was – get rid of her. Or if he was too much of a gentleman, he might still know a man who could. Sophie? What's up? Sophie!'

'What do people smell like when they're dead?' I asked, my voice carefully neutral.

'How dead?'

'Three or four days. Maybe longer. Because maybe it wasn't gas, maybe it wasn't pigeon shit we smelled at the Muntz outpost.'

And I stopped then because Chris already had me by the wrist and was running fast up the hill.

33

'You are not coming in. I don't want to go in myself. I've seen a body after a week's warm weather and I wish I hadn't. I don't want you to.' Chris gripped me by the shoulders, but this time he wasn't shaking me. 'Sophie, this sort of thing is part of my job – comes with the territory. I can get counselling if I need it; and I may well. Please, please, don't do this to yourself. It won't make it any easier for me.'

We were in Newtown, in the yard of the Muntz annexe, the sun warm in a clear blue sky. The smell was more noticeable, and there was a steady buzz of bluebottles.

'But—'

'You see that little window up there, no more than a skylight? You see that black blind across it? Ask yourself why there's a blind there.'

'I suppose –'

'I don't think it's a blind. I think it's a solid mass of flies. No, a live, seething mass of flies. Now will you promise me you'll not try to come in?' His voice was harsh; when he stopped speaking, he started to shudder.

'On one condition. That you wait for backup. Just in case, Chris. Please.' I reached to grip his hands.

He released a hand to touch my hair.

He didn't have long to wait anyway. We could hear cars turning into the street outside, and Chris pushed back through the hole in the gate to greet his team.

It was hard to sit in Ian and Val's front room and watch everything on the regional news. I could see the strain on Chris's face as he spoke to the press, understand something of all the frantic activity as the cameras panned rather pointlessly across a little knot of bystanders, a WPC spruce in shirtsleeves and a great deal of police tape. There was also a shot of a closed van driving ominously away.

And there was I, in a close, overfurnished room in Quinton, drinking instant coffee from a china cup and saucer with a pink rose decoration inside as well as out. Other people's lives: how did Ian, so fastidious about his sherry and his tea, cope with Val's coffee? And how did she, forty-something but neat in the clothes she wore to work as a school secretary, cope with a man who would come home after an afternoon that culminated in the company of a corpse?

'Would you like another cup, dear?'

I jumped.

'Another cup?'

'No, thanks. Look, Val, I don't know quite how to say this, but I'd rather be a friend than a visitor. You don't have to wait on me just because of Ian's job. Let me come and help with the supper. Please.'

'It's only chops, I'm afraid,' she said, 'and Ian says you're a good cook.'

'I could peel the spuds?'

In fact they were tiny new potatoes, hardly needing a scrub, and she steamed broccoli over the carrots. There was mint growing on the windowsill for mint sauce, which she made with cider vinegar. She cooked the chops to perfection - crisp outside and pinkish within.

And Ian's stayed on the table, covered by a plate.

'You'd think he was married to the police!' she said at last. 'I'm so sorry.'

It wasn't, was it, just another spoiled meal. It was the fact that Ian had talked of my exotic supermarket trolley, and she'd made the effort to impress me, and he'd let her down by not being there.

'I think Chris is too,' I said, and found myself ready to weep.

I didn't go with Val to her keep-fit class, but sat instead at her kitchen table, staring at yet another sheet of paper. This time I didn't try to make sense of the murders. I simply wrote down some of the things that had happened to me. The Barclaycard fraud; the theft of my money: they could be dismissed as part of one of the more badly stitched corners of life's rich tapestry. The silly jaywalking accident. That had to be a coincidence – no one could have guaranteed my presence at that particular time and place – but it was not so silly if it was the same smiling man who'd attacked Aggie for defending my house. Blake had tried to get the project moved back to William Murdock. There was Sunshine – but I could discount him, of course. There was all that graffiti and the obscene call. And then I rubbed that bit out. It was the obscene call and then the graffiti. Someone had called me at home on the Sunday before the graffiti appeared at college on the Monday. Someone had tried to shut him up. Someone had given something away.

If only I knew what.

Mrs C's horrified response had surely been genuine. Curtis's had, too: why don't you get out of here? Was that all that someone wanted? Me to be out of the action? And surely the fact that I had the phone call on the Sunday evening suggested that the graffiti wasn't the work of a malevolent student. Someone had been busy over the weekend.

The accident could have been more serious. It could equally well have been less serious – it was only my dodgy knee that had made it bad. The graffiti was deeply unpleasant but not physically threatening. The attack on Aggie that Saturday afternoon could have been infinitely worse. That Saturday afternoon – the phrase stuck. The afternoon I'd been safe with Fairfax. The afternoon when he'd had a phone call saying that William had interrupted a job. I'm no crossword expert but even I could now see that William and Old Bill were not so far apart.

So did it all point where I thought? To the Chair of governors who happened to have property interests? Did he want the Muntz land? Enough to persuade them to take on new premises? No: although George Muntz was a corporation, all its property actually belonged to the Further Education Funding Council. All its existing property. What if it bought something else, with monies acquired by savings on the engineers' salaries?

Why had normal decent teachers got entangled with wrongdoing – the pornography, the dubious property deal? Overpromoted, perhaps, yet they were people who'd once been as concerned about their students as I or any other teacher.

On impulse I reached for the phone. Dave was at Rose Road, but he'd welcome a break, he said, and he'd be right over. I found myself burrowing for my make-up and smoothing my hair. Then I did up the top two buttons on my shirt and put away the perfume unopened.

I needn't have worried. He was interested only in the Muntz business.

'I'll tell you this for nothing,' he said, slumping at the table, 'I've never seen figures in such a mess. The auditors'll have a field day next April.'

So whoever wanted to commit fraud would have until April to do it?'

'Yes. But they'd have to have skipped to bloody Patagonia by then. Jesus, sweetheart, they've lost paper records, wiped computer ones. Total shambles.'

'Anything to do with the fact that Curtis wasn't qualified?'

'Everything. How did he get the job, for Christ's sake?'

'Placed there? Muntz doesn't seem to have any qualms about appointing people without advertising and interviewing.'

'Placed?'

'By Blake and the Chair of governors? There are some interesting files in his safe.'

'Let's get at them, sweetheart!'

I shook my head. 'Fairfax is going to put the code on my answering machine and give me the key. But I shan't get the key until he's dead.'

'Come on, sweetheart, we can get a warrant, get in there somehow.'

'A warrant against a dying man? Let it wait till morning, Dave. He's dying. You're knackered. Let it wait.'

He nodded reluctantly. To give him something to do, I said; 'You know, I'd love to see if any of Luke's messages reached my desk. Fancy running me down to Muntz to have a look? Maybe a pint afterwards?'

He shrugged but agreed.

*

It was rather nice parking in a management space at Muntz. There was still a police presence, of course, but no one stopped me walking in, though perhaps I had Dave to thank for that. In fact we were halfway up the stairs when someone called him back. I told him my room number and pressed on. His knees would move more briskly than mine.

As soon as I opened my door, I knew something was wrong. I tried to back out fast and slam the door behind me. Not a chance. Whoever it was behind that door was too slow to get a proper grip, but he kicked at me, and grabbed my hair as I went down. I managed one good scream before he clamped his hand over my mouth. One of the heavies or Curtis? I assumed it was the latter. And made sure he couldn't shift his grip on my hair by throwing myself one way, then another. He got behind me and started to drag me backwards.

'Sophie, what the hell?' That was Dave. Better late than never, I suppose.

But now of course it didn't matter whether I screamed or not, so, his one hand still in my hair, my attacker could move the other. Next thing I felt was something cold and sharp on my neck.

I could see the whites of Dave's eyes. Maybe he could see mine.

'Hang on there,' he said, inadequately.

'I want a helicopter. Money. Now. Tell him, Sophie.' Yes: it was Curtis.

'Seems like a good idea, Dave. Please.' I tried not to scream as the point jabbed a little.

'Do it. And stay here while you do it.'

'Please, please, Dave. Use your radio so he knows for sure.' I was finding it hard to be brave.

Dave spoke hurriedly, incoherently. I couldn't catch the reply.

'Now turn round and walk down those stairs. Get!'

Dave tried to walk backwards, watching me till the last, perhaps.

'I said, turn round and walk. Do it!'

'Dave, tell Chris—' I yelled. But it was a good job Curtis jerked me into silence because I didn't know what message Dave should give.

And now we started to move, backwards. Along a corridor. Round a couple of bends. Difficult to say where I was. Then up some stairs. Stairs? The roof. That's where he was taking me. Melina had slipped off her shoes to leave a clue. Should I take mine off too? No, I might need to kick. And I didn't want sore feet – though that might be the least of my troubles. Perhaps there'd be time to do something when he stopped to unlock the door to the roof.

But someone must have left it open, for suddenly we were breathing fresh air.

He was panting. Was it from the effort? No, I'd co-operated. His hand was shaking too: the knife jagged against my skin. Must be fear. Perhaps if I could talk, it would keep him in one place, keep him still. Give them time ...

'Why – why are you doing this?' I began. I ought to call him by name, make him realise I was human. But I couldn't call him Curtis. And I couldn't remember another name. 'Please?'

'I said they should have got rid of you. But no, not them. Keep her quiet, they said. Get her out of the place. That's all!'

If he was telling me all this, it wasn't transport he wanted. At least not till he'd disposed of me.

Better try again. 'Did you – was it you who ...' The words wouldn't come. 'Was it you who killed Melina?'

'Who? Oh, that technician.'

I took that as a negative. It fitted in with what Mrs C had said.

'But it must have been you that dealt with Blake? The electronics? How did you do it?'

He laughed. For a moment I thought I might be winning. Then I decided I didn't like the tone after all. 'Neat, wasn't it? A lot of thought, mind, then just a dab of a zapper.'

I thought of the squashed squirrel.

'How did you do it?'

'It'd take too long to tell you. Get moving!' We started a sideways progress.

'Why kill Blake? Why did you want to kill Blake? Because they told you?' Dared I risk it? 'Did Fairfax tell you to?'

We must be quite close to the parapet by now. Why were there no sirens? Why weren't they coming? Chris, please!

'Chris says it was a brilliant piece of work,' I said. 'You ought to be working for NASA or something. I mean, all your qualifications—'

That was a mistake. The knife jabbed. I could feel a trickle of blood, nothing much. Not yet.

'Curtis?'

We both jumped. Loud-hailers have that effect.

'Des? This is Dave Clarke.'

Dave! But he was about as subtle as a bulldozer. I didn't want him negotiating for my life.

'Des?' Was that Curtis's first name? 'We're over here.'

'Here' wasn't on the roof. Nowhere I could see, anyway. He dragged me backwards again, yards this time. Then he heaved me upright.

'On the parapet. Right on top. Now,' he said, pushing me.

People lose control, don't they, when they're afraid. They pee or mess themselves. I started to retch. Val's beautiful lamp chops. And I had long enough to know I was going to drown in my own vomit because he wouldn't let me tip my head forward.

'Des, let her go, she's ill. Can't you see she's ill?'

Then there was so much noise I couldn't hear anything else they said. They must have alerted all the emergency vehicles in Birmingham. I couldn't hear Curtis's response either.

I could hear another voice, though, close at hand. Another person who didn't know how to address Curtis. A mild little voice with a Brummie accent.

'I mean, this is a bit much. Come on, a bit of fair play, mate.'

'Just fuck off out of here!'

But Phil's intervention had diverted him enough to let him slacken his grip on my hair, and I slumped forward, choking so fiercely I lost sense of what was going on. The lamb chops went over the parapet. I was still on the safe side of it. I retched again.

'Look, chum, you got to face it – you been caught out good and proper. That Trevelyan lady, she's left enough on her hard disk to—'

'You talk – over she goes. Right?'

I was halfway over. My feet! I still had shoes. I kicked

back, up, as hard as I could. I made contact, but the effort drove me further forwards, my arms flailing over nothing but that drop. I was going over.

Suddenly I was on my knees, wondering why I was still alive. And then I didn't bother wondering any more, because I passed out.

I came to, still on the roof, surrounded by very tall people in black overalls and woolly hats. No smelling salts, so no Chris. But Dave was there, kneeling beside me, looking as green as I felt. I'd been sick again. I touched my neck, and my fingers came back dry. A siren retreated into the distance - several sirens.

'Is that your lot taking Curtis somewhere?' I asked.

'Yes. And a few of us making sure he stays in the car.'

I nodded. I found I could sit up and take interest. 'How did you get up here?'

'Fire escape. While he was looking the other way.'

'You were very quiet.'

'Trained to be.'

'Phil? Isn't that Phil?' I could make him out the far side of some very white shirtsleeves.

'The bugger damn nearly blew it for us,' said Dave.

I felt a bit more enthusiastic. 'Hell, he stopped him—'

'If he'd told us what he was on to a bit earlier—'

'What was he on to? Hell, this is ridiculous. Phil?'

He sidled over, looking sheepish.

'Thanks, Phil,' I said. 'I owe you.'

'Like he was saying, perhaps I should have let on earlier.'

'Bloody right,' Dave muttered.

Phil ignored him. 'But you never know. And like they say, there's more than one way of skinning a cat. Now, you know Dr T didn't want us to know who we were getting our stuff from. Right? Well, I reckoned there might be other stuff on her hard disk, too. Even stuff she'd wiped. Now, I've got this mate who knows about hard disks. Bit of a whizz, you might say. And so I asked him to get back the material she'd denied me access to. I just put another hard disk in her computer. Didn't think it'd matter since no one knew there was anything on it.'

Dave opened his mouth, presumably to boast about police computer expertise, and shut it as I clipped his shin.

'Any road, she must have got hold of his accounts –' he jerked his head in the direction they'd taken Curtis – 'and copied them on to her machine. And I'll bet he thought he'd wiped them. But my guess is she was bright enough to do what my mate did: retrieve them, then wipe them. And then transfer the files to her disks. And "lose" them again. Clever woman, though, like I say, it didn't do her much good.'

The conversation dwindled. The various men and women started to go their various ways. Someone slung some sand on the remains of my supper. I felt cold and alone and sick. Perkiness was my usual response to situations like that, so I'd better try perkiness.

'I suppose it's a bit late for that drink, Dave, but I've got some whiskey that might settle my stomach. Tell you what, could you all look the other way while I take these disgusting laddered tights off?'

'I think you ought to make a statement—' Dave began.

'You and your bloody statements, Dave. Not until I've had at least a finger of Jameson's! And got some different clothes on. OK?'

In the end, it was Dave who took me to the hospice. I'd phoned on impulse at about eleven thirty, and spoken to a kind-voiced woman who said she'd just been going to call me.

'Can it be as quick as that?' I whispered.

'Yes, if you've saved a supply of tablets and left a note propped against your water jug forbidding resuscitation.'

'My God!'

'He's still alive, Sophie, if you want to come and say goodbye.'

'His family . . .'

'No. He doesn't want family. Just you.'

I had to go. I stayed there all night, a counsellor ready to help me when I needed it. I think he died at five thirty-seven, but I waited on a while. At last, I spoke to him: 'I don't know why you did all this. I think you killed – or had killed – at least two people, one of whom was a sick young woman. I wonder why you spared me?' There was much more to ask, of course. But my voice sounded too loud.

I laid his hands together, closed his eyes and wandered into the dawn-cold garden. A young man joined me. I don't know who he was. None of the staff wore white coats of uniforms. He steered me back into an office for tea, and waited for me to talk. When I didn't, he reached into a filing-cabinet drawer and passed me an A4 envelope. Keys to the safe, and a set with a BMW fob. A set of papers, some witnessed at the bottom. There was a note that Mr Fairfax must have dictated for the writing did not match his signature, still strong, almost fierce. It was a codicil to his will. I found I was responsible for Pilot, but only until I could find him a good home. He'd been overhasty in his treatment of Alan – would I ensure his solicitor made amends? He wasn't going to leave me his house; what he ought to have done was burn mine down so I'd have to cut free. What I was to have was his car. The insurance certificate and deed of gift were attached. And the sago pudding was more successful than the rice, which for my future information needed more salt.

I took a taxi home, wrote down the number he'd left on the answering machine, and set the alarm for nine. Justice could wait a few more hours.

Chris could hardly exclude me from the unlocking of Ali Baba's cave. I was there in Fairfax's snug with Dave, Ian and a number of people from the team. I set the number and turned the key. Inside were the files: 'Management Centre, Provence', 'College without Walls', 'Newtown Site' and a number of others with different logos. I distributed them as if they were exercises for homework, and then stood staring at the empty safe until moved quietly aside by a young woman in glasses, who peered at the lock mechanism and a couple of bits of gubbins inside and announced it was fortunate we'd not tried to force the safe because the whole lot would have gone up in flames if we had.

'Here we are!' Ian yelled. 'They were only setting up a bloody holiday home down near Nîmes.'

'What about this business of the College without Walls, Ian? Did Worrall say anything yesterday afternoon?' Chris asked, grinning.

‘A lot. But that might be franchising,’ he said. ‘Seems they might be franchising courses. You work out how much it would cost you to do it in your college, and then license someone else on other premises to do it cheaper. Only you get the profit, see.’

‘Especially,’ I said, ‘if you get nonunion labour to do it on the cheap. Does it say how much they were proposing to pay the lecturers?’

‘Does £5 sound right?’

‘It sounds bloody awful.’ I couldn’t stick it any longer. I fed and fussed Pilot, and found my way into the cast-iron conservatory. It was so humid I needed air, and figured it wouldn’t come amiss for poor Pilot to relieve himself. He dashed out with vigour, lolloping and somersaulting like a pup. Then he froze, his face ugly with purpose, and hurtled for the orchard at the far end. There was a scream. I remembered who was supposed to be in charge. ‘Pilot! Pilot! Heel! Heel!’

He slithered to a shuddering halt, snarling.

‘Stay! Stay! And you there,’ I yelled at a figure trying to keep Pilot at bay with a garden fork, ‘stay exactly where you are or I shall let him go. Chris! Dave! Come here!’

Pilot didn’t like them any more than he liked the man in the orchard, but so long as I held him with one hand and patted him with the other, he consented to stay with me. I recognised the man when they brought him back to the house, even though he wasn’t smiling. Gardener and odd-job man, he said he was. Some very odd jobs indeed.

‘He’ll squeal,’ Ian said. ‘Give us other names.’

There was a lot of booze still to be drunk in the incident room, and they’d be glad to see the back of me so they could rib Chris about going down on his knees to shake paws with a dog. There might be other things they could rib him about, such as sharing his girlfriend with an old man who turned out to be Mr Big. It wasn’t the existing Muntz land he’d wanted, but the derelict Newtown site, to get access to the land at the back. There were plans in his safe for a hypermarket. Whether he had further plans for the Harborne site wasn’t clear, but it certainly seemed to be he who was steering Muntz into bankruptcy. Clearly he had Curtis by the throat.

'Has Curtis said much yet, Ian?' I asked, gathering my bag.

'Enough. Incriminating his solicitor as much as anyone. You mix with an interesting class of person, young Sophie.'

'But they're all respectable businessmen!' I said, wide-eyed with innocence.

'Less of your cheek, my girl. You're sure you won't have a drink? I've got some Tio Pepe here.'

'Quite sure.'

'And you're sure you'll be all right on your own tonight?' Ian pressed. He looked at me kindly.

'Alone? With that fucking great hound in the house! Best chastity belt I've ever seen, sweetheart,' Dave said, emerging from nowhere and putting an ostentatious arm round my shoulders.

'D'you think he was running all that porn? Fairfax, I mean,' I asked, ignoring him.

'A bit of private enterprise from Curtis, that. He had a college with facilities, a lot of money he could spend on specialist software and hardware, and some staff who'd do anything they were told to stay in a job,' Dave said. 'That's all he's talking about - the porn. Oh, and Blake getting his come-uppance.'

'Sorry?'

'For overreaching himself? He'd certainly done something to annoy Fairfax - protested about his treatment of Trevelyan, for one thing.'

I found a chair. 'OK, why did Fairfax want Trevelyan treated badly? Spell it out.'

Dave grabbed a chair too, but he straddled his. 'That little scam of hers was an irritant, and it drew unwelcome attention to the college, reduced the time available before people started inspecting the books. Blake couldn't do much about it, of course, because *she* knew about *his* merry pastime. Fairfax decided the easiest thing was to shut them both up. Now, Curtis may have taken this a little too literally. "Shutting them up" can mean bribing just as much as it can mean killing.'

'Curtis likes running over squirrels,' I said.

'I'm sorry?'

'I think he'd have preferred the nastier alternative.'

'You wouldn't be biased?' Chris asked quietly, drifting over with what I was sure was a deceptively casual air.

Equally casually, Ian drifted away, more or less dragging Dave.

'Even if he claims he was acting under orders, that would scarcely exonerate him,' I said.

'Messy bloody business all round,' Chris said. 'Trevelyan runs a silly little scam. Melina finds out and confronts her; Tevelyan kills her and goes mad – or feigns madness: we shall never know. And then she too is killed. What people do for money!' He looked hard at me, but then asked; 'Any idea what'll happen to Muntz now?'

'I should have thought the FEFC would do something. There are a lot of jobs involved, and they own the Harborne site, too. They'll probably send in some inspectors to run the place, get someone to prepare a report, and hope it can be revived. Either that or merged with another college. It'd be nice if William Murdock would take it over – I could carry on walking to work!'

Chris laughed politely.

I got up to leave, and then found I couldn't avoid it any longer. 'Do you think the whole of Fairfax's empire is built on blood?' I asked, looking him straight in the eye.

'Absolutely. And Sophie – no, tomorrow will do.'

I hated it when he looked sorry for me, hated it. 'What else? Come on, spit it out.'

'I phoned to tell young Simon he was right about the microwave, about the magnetron, that is. The pathologist ran some tests using Simon's figures and they worked out hunky-dory.'

'I won't ask what they tested his theory on.'

'No. Don't. Anyway, he said he'd had a call from someone here. Not me. About some CDs you bought. Simon suspected they might be dodgy, so he contacted us and passed on the car's registration number. Remember? I'm afraid you bought a whole lot of stolen property, Sophie. It'll have to go back to the owners.'

I shrugged. 'Win some, lose some. Look, you need to get pissed and I'd better go and feed Pilot. See you, one and all!'

It didn't take me long to drive back home.

34

I looked at my watch. Nearly lunchtime. I had to get back for my afternoon class, not that I'd expect too many students this close to the exams – especially not after all the trauma of the last few days.

I leaned against the only wall in the bus shelter with any glass left and let my eyelids droop. I'd already had a long day, after all. I'd been up at four, picked up the M5 at Junction 3 and been down in Devon with my cousin Andy in time for breakfast. Pilot had romped in the meadow of the home farm, and then had resumed his place in the back of the BMW. I'd left him at the kennels Andy always used, with instructions to let no one have him till I'd met them and checked their home. Then I'd driven home again, coming off at Junction 2 this time, and picking up the A4123. Auden wrote a poem about it once. I spent perhaps half an hour at Rydale's. They didn't want to do it at first, but I was adamant: they were to service the car, bring it to perfection, and sell it for the highest price they could get – at auction, if necessary. I gave them Aberlene's number, thinking they and the MSO Friendly Society Fund could get some mutually useful publicity. The money might even save that little boy's life, though for the life of me this morning I couldn't remember his name. A saleswoman tried to interest me in a Three Series, but so soon after the Seven Series anything would have seemed puny. Maybe, however, one day I would take Chris up on the offer he'd made weeks ago to squire me round all the local garages for test-drives. Or perhaps I should get a new bike. I patted the blood-red car one last time, tossed them the keys and crossed the road.

The 126 bus seemed to take for ever to come.